THE ENTERTAINMENT BOMB

New Futurist Books

The Entertainment Bomb

by

Colin Bennett

New Futurist Books
London

First published in 1996
by New Futurist Books Ltd.
72 New Bond Street, London W1Y 9DD

Printed in Great Britain by Redwood Books Ltd.
Typeset by Jillian Pierre

British Library Cataloguing in Publication Data.
A catalogue record for this book is available
from the British Library.

ISBN 1-899690-01-8

For Robert Arnold

Preface

From Dr. Hieronymus Fields'

STARPOWER

Entertainment Maps - A New Journey of Spirit

Ideally, within a map of Entertainment State, within the conventional lattice of heights and land-strata, the foliage tints, and compass points, will be the dwellings and birthplaces of Entertainment Stars, geographically located and highlighted. In our ideal Complete Entertainment Cosmos, previous outmoded analogical geographical features will be replaced by an emerging structure of the places of concerts and personal appearances; the origins, associations, and creation of plays, shows, concerts, films, opera and ballet; all these being essentially expressions of the personalities and work of great Stars. Already, in many of the popular tabloids, the reference point for a wide variety of common events is not a known spot of old, such as a mountain, a church, or a road, but to a previous dwelling of Eric or Ernie, the proximity of the mansion of a film or pop-star, or the place of work, rehearsal, or place of inspirational image of some famous personality in Entertainment.

Entertainment State will be a place of great activity, a society of continuous elemental creation. With fresh reviews, new work, and limitless new creation and recreation of performances, the maps will be constantly updated, and thus the character and face of the land will be ever-renewed by fresh spirit, recharged by the new sources of delight and inspiration.

All cultures are built of a landscape of questions. Thus in our ideal Entertainment State will the whole framework of human enquiry be gradually changed. By comparison, older industrial questions of why, where, or what, will be cancelled out because they are become confusing and meaningless. Older analogue exactness such as the distance between a traffic victim and a hospital will no longer matter. This typically obsolescent industrial question will pale before the new Entertainment State question of where exactly is the nearest Entertainment Shrine to relate the suffering, the loss, the victory or joy, the triumph or disaster.

As in all true magics, Quantity and old Ordnance Survey Distance hardly matter as compared to Spirit. If the only thing that can be found just over the hill for victim, lover, or dreamer, is the sister of Charlie Drake's hatter, then that is really just as good as finding out that Madonna herself used a local pub telephone on a tour some four years previous. Star influence is not subject to the vicious weather and decay of industrial Time.

Thus the older maps are eventually to be replaced, because as Entertainment-systems they have failed to keep up their advertising schedules. They have been outperformed. As I have already pointed out, it is becoming standard practice to discreetly mention the proximity of any Star's mansion or Royal estate, if any particular event happens to occur outside the entrance-lodges and guard-gates of such high Star-Folk. Entertainment State merely takes this practice to its logical conclusion. These places (particularly Royal places, for the Royals are the pinnacle of Entertainment Excellence), these places are to we Entertainment Citizens, true Holy Places, magical spatial points, Entertainment Shrines; they give comfort and a new and evolving expiation of a kind which older industrial geographical points and analogue-mythologies as mechanical explanations can no longer offer.

These new proposed Entertainment Maps for our future Entertainment Society thus re-establish a network of contemporary modern sympathies which maps pregnant with rational assumptions have long since tried to demolish. We thus have the exciting prospect of an entirely new social and political transcendent landscape. In this new Entertainment Country, beatified Stars will replace Patron Saints, and mere travel will become a de-triangulated voyage between complex emotions, between any point of Entertainment association or affection, such as a particular song, show, play, dance, poem, film, or book. The equations of universal Entertainment structure therefore will represent highly individualised spheres of influence rather than geometrical points merely sculpting anonymous spaces. The dusty dashboard-managed miles of Paragraph Person in Sierra, Ford, or Cortina, will become transcendental travels in Entertainment Time through what I have called domains.

These domains are the often overlapping fields of influence of the Star Priests. The Ideal Entertainment Traveller still sees of course the infinite beauty of Loch Lomond, the Lake District, or Stonehenge, but is at the same time supremely aware of another landscape of spiritual light passing through these glorious natural manifestations. Our Traveller is aware of even the site of a past house of Arthur Askey, Gracie Fields, or George Formby, Harry Tate, Sharon and Tracy, or even long ago, Marie Lloyd, Dan Leno, or even Mrs. Siddons. No matter who lives there now, no matter if the house has been completely demolished, such a place is still a sacred site of First-Class Entertainment Magi. Their spirit has gone into the earth, and cannot be diluted or destroyed, falsified, or corrupted.

In love or pain, in joy and sadness, in loss and achievement, a Traveller along the Entertainment Leys joining these domains, these zones and points of sympathy, will therefore never ever be alone. Rod Stewart's cousin might be near, or Elton John's grandfather might have died just up the road. Be it suffering or transcendent joy, an Entertainment Traveller is held in an intercontinental web of healing glory which doesn't cost a penny, and has absolutely no concern for your previous moral life. Entertainment Priests are not deeply troubled men in nightshirts, most of whom have so many psychological problems before breakfast their personal depression nearly kills them promoting the comedown, the comeback, the punishment, the price to be paid at the toll gates of both sides of the schism. If the new Entertainment Priests are not fun, there is an absolute lock on their spiritual progress. They have to be Entertainers first and foremost, and they are to cast out of the temple the depressing landscape of fear and guilt and horror of the Old Analogue Age, which was the pre-Entertainment Time. As Entertainment Citizens we will come to see that this past was a bleak opencast industrial geography, a landscape in which everything was poisoned, gassed, and strangled. It was a psychopath's world of tortured animals and old iron of industrial and scientific determinism. Now, like a billion-ton ice-pack, this spiritual hell is beginning a perceptible shift of paradigm into a landscape of the purest Entertainment Legend.

Let us rejoice!

What we of Entertainment State must construct is no less than a complete and coherent theology whose elements are practical and clear. Much that is of important historical significance could emerge through a contrast, say, between the time-schemes of Brief Encounter and Casablanca. Much that is of great beauty could emerge from a study of Charlie Chaplin, Jimmy Edwards, The Singing Postman, Betty Boo, Tiny Tim, or The Big Bopper. Away with these wonders tied to some academic analysis, read to four high-domed beard-and-glasses at a subsidised film club on a rainy Friday! We must liberate such things and form them into a practical theology, a set of values to be integrated into a daily devotional commitment for a whole new society!

The Electronic Village has always looked for a religion.

It has now found one.

Praise the Star!

Chapter 1

1

Dawn In The Laboratory

The violence of the sudden snowstorm broke the stagnant lock of an almost fetid January. The mass of ice scouring the parched mouth of Shakespeare's city was a violent inspiration to weather-beaten souls. The high cliff-face moods of old unredeemed Nature had returned, thought lost forever in stillness of tepid light and an ominous dust.

High over Whitehall, through gaps in the uneven blizzard, a full disc of moon poured white-flecked silver upon the flat top of the soaring glass rectangle which was Tower House. Under its mass of reflections, broad base-lintels sunk into the southern bank of the wide river showed the massive spore of unmistakeable State intention. Below the pulsing red and green aircraft navigation lights of the rectangle, the circle of city was a broiling desert of cloud-white, broken only by curling tracer of phosphorescence from the last high tide of the day.

On the roof of Tower House, under a growth of aerials whose sharp outlines were now softened by snow, filters in a windowless concrete cube registered high-to-medium pollution levels. Pen recorders told of momentary bursts of airborne low-level radiation. The sources of the radiation will remain a mystery, just as will the sources of finance for the instrumentation. To the west, Heathrow Airport Traffic Control registered three illegal flight tracks of different height, direction, and speed; none responded to standard interrogation calls. Operators noted the average number of recorded civilian anomalies for the evening.

40,000 feet above the roof, two momentary spots appeared on the tracking radar of a patrolling RAF *Nimrod,* ready to pass over the Channel for a fifteen-hour North Sea patrol. Radar Operator Class One, Sergeant Mack, only half-believed the computed 5000 m.p.h tracks. Later at the debriefing, he will only half-tell of these things, the average number of military anomalies for the evening.

The steel door of the instrument shack opened, and the bulky figure of a man moved carefully to the roof-edge of Tower House, his carpet-slippers leaving a trail of wide prints in the grey slush. He gazed astonished at the whirling galaxy of moonlit snow settling upon the seething tide beneath him. His thoughts banishing such an elementary feeling to him as chill, he put his hands on the iced metal of the roof rail and looked at the great river as if it held the drowning hordes of some vast shipwreck.

Below the curious Yeti-like footprints of the man at the rail, on Floor 6 of Tower House, British Telecommunications Investigations Branch engineers watched with professional fascination as a computerised oscilloscope captured and showed an unauthorised stream of digits momentarily interrogating the security address-codes of extremely sensitive computer systems of the Ministry of Defence. Flash, and the mysterious questioner was gone like a canny pike into dimensions of noise from where she or he will no doubt venture out yet again upon another midnight.

If the man had known of such events, he would probably have claimed that there were many other such digits, tracks, blips, shapes, and speeds of the impossible out there in the night; to him, such things were the sea-serpent stories of the electronic watch, the pointer-readings and antennae registering the ice-pack splitting at the seething edge of a Europe once more alive with dream. These eerie screen-displays, these ghosts in whatever detecting technology, were the beat of new drums to greet whatever the fantastic shadows of a new day. To the man at the rail, the fossil-paradigms were dying, and new animals broken from the tether were leaving tracks as they prowled and hunted in the sky and the snow.

This bleak roof high above a winter London was the his favourite place of meditation. Struggling against creaking spun-steel hawsers, the aerials swayed and shook, towering high over him; he saw them as ever-chained gibbering spirits, their ruthless objectivities maddened by indestructible rituals still present as friction, heat loss, bad propagation, transmission losses, and the ravages of the sins of their makers. Through the snow and the night went transmissions so mythological, that to the man, the roof-top was a Hobbit wood, or Grimm mountain; its never-ending stream of changing frequencies and codes were speeding Furies, shrieking in the elemental air as they spurred their horses on through the raging tempest. The mind sitting on top of the massive body whose hands still gripped the rail, knew little of animals, trees, or rivers. It saw the physical creations of Man as mountains, seas, and forests in themselves, great articulated skeletons of ideas, whose blending and activity knew no death, only endless transformations of intellectual landscape.

2

'*Poetry in motion...*' deep baritone bunker-echoes resounded as the massive form re-entered the instrument shack, slamming the steel door shut. After a careful steps on a ladder, the man descended into a damp and wire-lanterned warmth, and sang again to the open doors of a lift, whose deep-pile floor looked as though it didn't meet the stained concrete of the upper levels very often. The lift shot down extraordinarily fast, as if anxious for more welcoming levels below this place of seeping mortar and chilled fortress-iron.

His drenched carpet-slippers now flopped along the light grey serviceable lino of a bland and square corridor of equally utilitarian lighting and colour. Emptying coins into a very large palm from a frayed leather pouch which looked as if it might easily have belonged to any one of Chaucer's less well-off pilgrims, Dr. Hieronymus Fields brought himself to a swaying stop before the pulsing glow of a food and soft-drinks machine. Gazing into the interior as an explorer might stare with wonder into a newly discovered tomb, he burst into song. '*Oh my darling, please surrender...with your love so warm and tender...*'

A recently recruited young security guard, on hearing Presley lyrics along deserted corridors at dawn, was calmed by the words of an older colleague, who assured him that this was one of the great sights of the job: the renowned Dr. Fields taking a short break at first light after working in his 'laboratory'. To show his command and professionalism, the older guard spoke to Dr. Fields in a language ever-formed by practicalities.

"Repsbeen, sir!"

In canteen-pidgin, *repsbeen* had joined *chows-up, come-and-get-it,* and the increasingly popular *on-the-table!* Without the 'rep' reinstalling the pantomime-food of wall-machines, half the Western World would probably die, thought the older guard, fall apart on spindly legs, incapable of eating food which had nothing to do with theatre.

Dr. Fields replied in a Dylan Thomas bass which almost made the younger guard put his hands over his ears.

"Thank you. There's a good selection tonight."

Crick, crack, whap! The wall-god disgorged *Twatties, Wonklet-Bars, Cony-Crackers,* and *Gang-Nuts;* these were followed by a suspicious-looking *Pisky-Patsy,* and to Field's delight, a steaming *Bumper Jumbo Wombat Sausage,* which had, according to the claim on the label, been subject to 'Virtual Deep-Fry Auto-Micro'. He squinted at the smaller print with the dedication of a train spotter. Send off three of the *Wombat* labels, and an initiate got a free *AWACS-dish Frisbee,* a set of nontoxic *GAZZA IN ACTION* transfers, and a voucher for two free cans of non-diet *Umbongo* at any High Street Happy Jack Bap House. Pleased with these offers, he promptly tipped his treasures into what looked like a

3

trader's money-pouch around his extensive waist.

The younger turned to the elder.

"He's going to die."

"Not without a fight. All right, sir?"

"Splendid. Thank you. Good morning to you, gentlemen."

With his waist-bag full of congealing wonders, Fields vanished as quickly as he had appeared, carrying a large styrofoam full of a dark elixir which sent forth an odourless vapour which settled momentarily on the thin yellow gloss of the reinforced-concrete ceiling. This beverage had been christened *ersatz* by his staff, apparently after a wartime German civilian drink made of wallpaper paste, bone-glue, and boiled leather. Only this wall-machine could make it and sell it, and only he could drink it, or so the story went.

'Dream lover, where are you-oo-ooh...' the ancient lyrics from a world before what many of his colleagues called The Fall, echoed in a low-lit almost-deserted wide acreage of computer-screens, some fully lit, even in these early morning hours. This was Fields' country, and he was working late. Not that he had ever been known to do anything else in his thirty years employment with the rather shy organisation he worked for. Although now of a rank which entitled him to what Tower-House wags called a limo and a dacha, he hardly lived or slept anywhere else but within a curtained niche in the Main Computer Hall, that is whenever he slept at all, which, according to Tower House legend, was miraculously rare.

Drawing aside the faded psychedelic patterns of torn and unwashed curtains, the massive form now entered its personal abode, called by colleagues his Dansette Den. A double camp-bed occupied most of the space of what could only be called a curtained alcove. Reinforced with welded angle-iron, this unusual item was the source of many rude and blushing legends. A large old valve radio rested precariously on a small shelf above the bed, just by a poster of Jane Mansfield. Flyblown sticky-tape held on the wall tattered magazine cutouts of Marlon Brando and William Wordsworth. A kidney-shaped table of pink glass sported a chipped statuette of Marilyn Monroe in the famous pose of holding down her blown dress.

He flicked a switch. *'It's now or never...so hold me tight...'* rose from a priceless red-plastic 45 rpm *Dansette* record-player to a ceiling from which hung straw-wrapped wine-bottles and an ancient 'mobile' made of blinking cardboard owls. Old *Mirabelle, Face,* and *G-Spot* magazines were scattered amidst stale cans of *Diet Macaroon;* browning apple-cores and crushed *Pig n' Chicken* cartons lay upon open volumes of Newton's *Principia*, and Coleridge's *Biographia Literaria*. Above a

4

yellow formica kitchen table by a small sink, framed faces of Conway Twitty, Alan Turing, and the historian Josephus, no less, gazed down upon photographs of Robert Oppenheimer, Winston Churchill, and Frank Sinatra. By an elephant-foot umbrella-stand rested a full-size cardboard cutout of a moustached and bow-tied Colonel Saunders, who looked almost proud at finding himself in such company.

Fields laid his 25-stone down on the bed, and poured the ersatz into a scratched picnic-beaker which sported transfers of the faces of the young Tony Curtis and Albert Einstein, no less. Snapping thick fingers, and singing along with the bumpy revolutions of the ancient record, he unwrapped his *Wombat* sausage, and bit into it with relish. Taking another deep draught of the jet-black *ersatz*, he stared with great satisfaction into the far distance of the neon-lit Main Computer Hall, where a few clusters of sheep-eyes peered at console screens like all-night luck-junkies in a fruit-machine arcade. Somehow, he thought, in computer rooms and laboratories, it was always three o'clock in the morning. That hour he supposed, was when the tricky Spirit of the Correlation stalked along the battlements, speaking its dread words to an awestruck and chosen few.

As the ever-blinking owls moved in a slight draft, he looked in vain amongst piles of festering *Harry Mecca's Bacon Parlour* wrappers, perhaps for some lost remnant of a thousand and one nights of philosophy. The warm air floated crumpled notes and scribbled queries across the floor; the scraps danced past a nibbled ham bone which was almost hoisted by a quite stiff discarded sock. More scraps of thoughts settled on a large volume of Pope's verse-translation of the *Odyssey,* which was book-marked with parts of a much-decayed *Spud-You-Take* onion-fritter. A fallen slice of time-coloured cheesecake lay on the pocket of his Old Etonian cricket blazer, making a suitable talisman for the Fields *mysterium.*

In this Dansette Den, as it was called, Fields was happy. His one fear was the dread footfall of the ever-complaining Senior Cleaning Supervisor, the fearsome Nellie Goby, who on occasion was wont to seize a broom and chase the loudly complaining 'err Professa' from his steaming Faustian splendour to a hot tub somewhere in the nether regions of Tower House.

For many years, apart from professional visits abroad, Fields had hardly seen the outside of the building in which he worked. On a high summer's day he would wander across Glasshouse Street to the *Vendetta* sandwich bar, to take intriguing glances at the pretty girls in their flimsy dresses for a minute or two, before returning to his 'test tubes' as he jokingly called his work. Come Christmas, he would have a glass of port wine with the cleaners and staff, and apart from quite a few mysterious visits abroad, that was practically the extent of his social world.

It was not easy to describe what Fields did in this world, what his position was, who gave him orders, and who paid him. Officially he was listed as a Lecturer for the University of London Medical Department, seconded to the Home Office as a 'medical and psychiatric consultant'. Few could decode this to mean that Fields was the Deputy Director of the Psychological Warfare Department of the British Security Services, of which Tower House was the Headquarters. Fields' staff of thirty-two men and twenty-five women, with their lavish planning, communications, and computer facilities, were paid for by a hardly detectable pinhead of a pattern within a mighty blizzard of Treasury accountancy-noise. The few very clever chappies who happened to come across this pinhead in their too-clever-by-a-half line of enquiry or duty, tended to look at their lovely house and glowing family over the breakfast table, and think it might just be even more clever not to reveal their interesting discovery. Perhaps such stout fellows had made even more significant finds than this, and had decided that the night-side of a modern industrialised democratic nation was such an astonishing animal that it was best left to roam in the bush alone, quite invisible and undisturbed, a ghost whose occasional thumps in the night were best well ignored.

The forty-five-year-old Fields himself was both a fully qualified medical psychiatrist and academic psychologist. Since he was also a decent mathematician, and had a degree in Computer Science, he had emerged in his middle life as a much in demand specialist in media and advertising within the Security Services. Such agencies were very definitely just as much into such things as they were into what enquiring journalists called the 'sharp end'. Giving excellent in-house lectures, which included the celebrated 'Basic Psychology of Persuasive Image-Structures', Fields had been an influential behind-the-scenes adviser to both the BBC and the IBA, particularly with regard to management structure, policy-formation and appointment boards, and also a something called Emergency Liaison. No-one employed in the murky business of his Department was very worried about the more doubtful side of their activities. Provided the 'sharp end' was confined to floors on which the main lifts did not stop, it was universally assumed by Fields and most of his colleagues that ever since some *mensche* had taken up a piece of tree-branch and marched towards a cave-mouth with the intention of getting a little more respect that day, societies had developed methods of controlling behaviour both simple and complex, both humanitarian and cruel.

Fields knew of course that bunker-culture as represented by Tower House fostered such moral and political oversimplifications. But that apart, he found that working within secret organisations maintained in him a sense of mission, an old-fashioned romantic bubbling test-tube thrill of old, probably, he often thought, last experienced at Los Alamos, or by Crick and Watson. But science was no longer the open culture of the dream of Sir Arthur Eddington, or even H.G. Wells. From the mushroom-cloud year onwards, 'secret colleges' had been the form of the developing main body of science. These closed societies involved all kinds of disciplines, cross-referencing Intelligence, Industry, and Media. In industrial societies with the burden of ever-evolving technologies, such secret colleges were a newly evolved part of a hidden constitution. Most professional scientists accepted this condition without asking disturbing questions. Within this largely covert blending, money was available for projects which would never have received sanction within the 'official reality system' (for such was the term). Such projects now even involved research into UFOs, the paranormal, metal bending, telepathy, and even remote telepathic viewing. The utter failure of some of these projects caused much laughter within Fields' team, although it must be said that the complete success of some others wiped away the smiles almost as quickly as they appeared. Another occasion of laughter came about when the Americans constructed two soap-opera series based on Fields' research concerning emotionally-calming image-sequences. Both pilot series became international successes.

In his opinion, that none of these operations and a thousand other operations more important and fundamental had anything to do with the normal and publicly sanctioned process of social democracy was self-evident to anyone who had the wit to walk up and scrape the paint off any twentieth-century product. Professionally dedicated as he was to the art of trickery itself, he conceived that he worked within the massive body of a fraud so big, the bones of deception were buried in all the systems of human surveillance and endeavour, weaving the fact and fiction of a techno-industrial culture into a quite seamless robe. As he often told his trainees, without illegalities, you couldn't make a damn thing for the late twentieth century, still less feed it. In his view, there was no way a developing materials technology alone could take place within the confines of good sense or even good intentions. Whatever was being built had to shake off all its legal and liberal rights restrictions, as lately the number of Trials and Enquiries concerning the manufacture and export of defence equipment alone, gave witness.

But when stout hearts stood up to these ideas, he had to admit that it was anything but a healthy state of affairs, this schizophrenic splitting of ideas and resources from a common body, this feeling that trickery was needed in order to create anything at all. Fear-ridden institutions such as the one he worked for, naturally formed closed self-protective elites, some of whom who knew no moral (and often hardly any financial) limits. Many of the men and women who worked in such places no longer lived next door to ordinary folk, and were not subject to the normal wear and tear of the ordinary world. Even the very best of minds were often changed for the worse by working within top-secret castle walls; specialisation within specialisation was often practised without the kind of enforced socialising that conventional university departments offered. Apart from one or two rare characters like himself, there was also no utterly refreshing plain daftness and laughter in lecture-hall and corridor; no contact with the anarchic young; and certainly no admitting of mistakes, waste, or contradictions. But as far as he was concerned, within common universities on the other hand, there was no longer in professional science a real sense of cultural unity, just a disoriented fragmentation of an obscure sense of liberal purpose. This was scrabble-game gadget-oriented science, a game played for the lack of anything else better to do.

As he often said, with the death of Communism, the world scene was changing as rapidly as a fast-food advertisement. He himself guessed long ago that like the paramilitary, all in Tower House were bottling themselves up, that the strands of social relations would wear thin, and that the danger was that secret colleges would die off like dried branches, offshoots of a natural selection of a series of sterile intellectual directions. One Doubting Thomas even recently suggested to him that within the enclosed world of the bunker-project, illusions multiplied like mushrooms in old fortress damp, and these secret colleges were the rickety stage-fronts which inevitably preceded the onset of the kind of complex decay which preceded the loss of any empire, scientific or otherwise.

But meantime, in this high-rise bunker, quite sealed from what less charitable denizens of Tower House called a barbarous Age of Pigmy-Clerks, here in a monastery of protected and preserved secrets, Fields intrigued his juniors, irritated his superiors, communed with the Ancients, and planned a world Raid of Raids, the construction of a self-created artificial *mysterium* of wonders, whose finespun world-semblance would be superior to what he considered to be the faulty bedrock of God, no less. Here he planned the greatest heresy of all. The construction of a new and better world.

Surprisingly for a senior British Security Service operative, just perceptible in Fields' accent was a very faint guttural strain, for he was hardly British. His mother, Leah, was half-German, a noted psychiatrist, who had been a close relative of Freud. His father, a high-ranking civilian technical administrator with the old War Office, was a half-Polish half-

8

Russian Count, with a strain of old Magyar blood; the War had changed much, including names. Isaac Dobzhansky always wept when he heard his stout young Hieronymus play excellent violin.

Fascinated and frequently baffled colleagues would often listen to Fields with heads slightly to one side as he claimed that he did not accept any simple and obvious distinction between Life and Death. With such a mixed background, he often described himself as bursting into fragments over Europe, some pieces of him disappearing into hamlet and forest perhaps never to be recalled. One particular delta mouth opened in North Germany, where a large part of him was distributed amongst families of endlessly disputing priests of various opposed faiths. He said he often keenly felt these ancient presences as if they were still sermonising and disputing by his side. From these ranks of ever-debating theologians it had always seemed to him that he had been bequeathed a kind of universal machine rather than a particular personality, or particular body of knowledge. He often astounded listeners by claiming that his present self had been reconstituted precisely for an historical moment in which his entire purpose and destiny was to reactivate an inherited philosophical *machina*. The purpose of this engine was to create what he called a Theology of Advertisements. This New Theology was to create that body of belief which he called Entertainment State, the idea of which he had outlined in his newly published book, *StarPower*.

With the first light of a cold dawn now emerging, Fields bit deep into his now rapidly cooling *Wombat* sausage, and gazed at the oozing stump as if the dangerous and spectacular impurities therein were the very satisfying expression of his thoughts in *StarPower*. Written in his private *persona* as London University Reader in Psychology, the book had been published several months previous, and had received worldwide interest and attention.

He had first been struck by the idea of an Entertainment State when as a boy in his early teens, he had been taken by a devout uncle to a Cathedral service. To him then, the world of bishops in their ceremonial robes seemed almost identical to the world of Elizabeth Taylor, his first dream love. The young Fields, probably in jest, asked his parents where was the big Christmas-cracker or cornflakes packet the hats, costumes, and gilded staves had come from. His queries to this end were not well received by anxious parents, both already worried enough about their son's astounding girth. However, such was their relief when their fortunately heterosexual offspring married Alice, an equally stout daughter of Golders Green, who looked exactly like Elizabeth Taylor, but who happened to be a deaf mute. Fields worshipped his wife as if she were an actual chip from the super-block of his teenage visions.

9

When the ever-smiling but ever-silent Alice died of cancer in 1968, he locked himself away with his *Dansette,* his dreams and his job, and never looked the outside world in the face again. An impossible love had betrayed him, and in his dreams he was often going back to the ancestral seminaries, ghettoes, and even the doll-making gabled houses of North Germany to ask where Alice had gone, and if the ancient toy-craftsmen there could make her live again and even speak.

He threw the *Wombat* stump across the Den, and did not wince as he saw it land on a valuable first edition of Hegel's *Philosophy of Religion.* Brushing the greasy remnant aside, the beautifully flowing, archaic German of the Age of Goethe caught him, and he was lost to the world.

Theological disputes were always a background of mental traffic within him; he would sometimes awake in the midst of night to animated cartoons of such debates. The scenes had one theme: the care of souls. He often thought of the soul. To him, it was that legendary immortal part of *homo sapiens,* which had eventually become a totally ludicrous piece of a piece of fictitious absurdity. The soul was now an obscure, stupid, ridiculous bit of spittle of an idea, the last remnant particle of metaphysics, stamped on, disregarded, laughed at, dismissed. No, he could not imagine anything more utterly cast out in the cartoon-dark of the dying century than the beautifully daft idea of an immortal soul. Yes, the soul was a thing cast out to Stygian night only to be disinterred on occasion as a pickled curiosity in a jar, a joke at the centre of a joke universe, a piece of theological Piltdown. He often relished the idea of the soul as such a joke, or perhaps a toy; he saw the soul indeed as sometimes he saw himself: a mere scrap of bright paint, with a pair of wooden wheels, and a hook for a piece of string, a half-forgotten bit of an almost completely lost tinsel afternoon of humanity's childhood. But perhaps, he thought, looking up from the Hegel, such a thing as a soul was even more fragmentary than the toy, more completely lost than the afternoon, more damned indeed than the Century. Yet even its fragile name was still enough to strike the deepest shiver, sound a long-lost and utterly buried bell.

But often he liked to suppose that the idea of soul was still preserved somewhere, lying quiet under the dreaming ice of an ideological eternity, awaiting the call of a new seasons of Advertisements. Not fallen, corrupted, or contaminated, just back into management store, an idea perhaps grateful for a rest. The soul as such became to him just one more modern Almost Inconceivable, like an elf, a fairy, or indeed effective resistance to the modern State. The soul he saw as being laughed out of court, counter-colonised by facts, reduced to a cartoon, pickled, frozen, and stored in the corner of the conscious eye; he saw it as slow-framed down to a flickering nothing, become a flutter of gossamer and tap of elfin toes down the scale of being to conceptual degrees Absolute at the bottom of some octave of appearances. The soul, like political resistance, he saw as being a mere part of the endless restocking of the glaciers of abandoned belief. He imagined such things as kept carefully at the side of other shipwrecked mammoths of consciousness, leaving only bits of seaboot and spar, a whitened shank or two, or a few patches of salt-rotted mainsail pushing up through the eternal snow for the still warm-blooded ones to ponder on in the rare and wondrous climate of a non-electronic evening.

The care of souls. Thoughts amongst the mental cartoons, now about to vanish with the coming of morning. Before him was another twentieth-century industrial day of false tasks, and artificial purposes, this being the universal technological lot, from Prague to Zululand, from Bogner to Bali. Before him was another fifteen hours of the management of the myriad fallen horizons of the Enlightenment. To him, the Western World's project-time was born on a lake of burning sulphur, and so loaded with deception, hypocrisy, and corruption, even the mighty computers frequently hung their heads in part-animal shame and withdrew their labour.

In the comfortably warm atmosphere, he smiled at his shiver. Philby's Revenge. That was what they all called it in Tower House. Some said it was worse than the revenge of Montezuma. Some said that it was because a major body of belief was being drained from the institution he worked for, leaving its living constituent parts with an occasional but definite feeling of chill. Others said that the waves of the onset of fever were only just beginning to make their way up to a conscious surface. Fields remembered having read somewhere of the sweating and shaking before the departure of a spirit. Tower House had woken up one morning to find big bad Communism had gone, and now it seemed to the big man emptying the dregs of his beaker, that laboratories, those tree-root castles of the fairy lore of his intellectual youth, were also now destined for historical sleep.

The *Dansette* screeched on. *'You ain't nothing but a hound dog...'* In the far distance of the Main Computer Hall, a team of shirt-sleeved workers appeared for early-hours duty. A slim girl carrying a lunch-box snapped her fingers to the music and waved to him, and he waved back with his beaker. The great machine of Tower House was about to start another long and secret day.

It had often occurred to him that Tower House was not protecting people, nations, or patriotic interests, but was really protecting the

11

laboratories. From weaponry to the most advanced computer planning, from chemical engineering to social analysis, such places of specialised endeavour had become the churches of bunker-culture. But laboratories, like psychiatry and social studies, did not have a good press. Like German doctors, laboratories formed part of a unique twentieth-century demonology. Most fearful contemporary fables wove in and out of these increasingly inaccessible walled places, whose impressive security arrangements had increased of late in inverse proportion to their positive social contribution. From Dr. Faustus to Dr. Frankenstein, from Mesmer and Galvani, to Chalk River, Los Alamos, and Silicon Valley, all the fabulous structures of the modern world at some time or other threaded through the laboratories and their masters. All the early mysteries of speculative intellectual innocence were here: the intrigues of awe-inspiring wiring tangles and massive switch-gear and voltage-leaps and glows in tubes and bubbling jars; here were the first marks on the Curie's hands, and the screams of countless tortured animals for a few rigged paragraphs of medical statistics. He saw the laboratories of the world as battery-fed animals succoured by the corporations, and always involved in some form or other of what many in Tower House called ratio-death. This was the manufacturing-cost of each manufactured fact, or what some of his more subtle colleagues called the rate of exchange of impossibilities. To less subtle colleagues in Tower House, Science and Security both had become two great bulls in the diminishing china-shop of an increasingly desperate planet.

To Fields, the first sign of real trouble was not the almost defunct space-race, the disaster of the Strategic Defence Initiative, or the inevitable failure of nuclear power, but the Banks shutting down the great Mirror Fusion project in the States. It was now a great modern *henge* for tourists. At some time future, he imagined, the operations manuals would be lost, become drifting pages picked up to stuff the cracked windows of a new generation of sharecroppers no-one ever thought to see again. He supposed that early cobwebs would glisten upon the helmets of the drowsy gate-guards, heads would fall to laps, eyes close. Like the stone circles, the laboratories would become places where electricity and money, belief and theory, vision and labour, all finally flickered out with the unpaid power bills, and the technical handbooks became the only temporary fuel source. Low buildings, ruined guard-towers, a few broken chimneys by the deserted railhead and power station would be all that would be left. Skull-and-crossbone signs would hang over the perimeter wire, where not even cursed weeds would grow. The laboratories would finally begin to look like other places of the century's devastated heart, whose names were legion. Places where nobody went any more, particularly at night, and the dust was to settle and the weeds cover all, until some dread knocking on the door yet to come.

He gazed into the dregs of his *ersatz*, whose blotchy patterns became the haunting of the years. He looked to a blank wall, as if some long-lost impulse had made his eyes expect an old leaded and mullioned window, bellows by a red-hot kiln, and rows of crudely-blown chemical glassware. He looked down at his odd socks. The gap in the psychedelic curtains widened slightly in the draft, and the owls blinked, mirroring his thoughts. How could he get out? The curtain-gap became a time-tunnel leading him to focus in the now screen-flickering distance of the far room beyond, onto the slightly curved shoulders of the case of what he knew to be a computer only two years old. Just two years, and it was already accelerating down a tunnel to meet flintlock pistols and powdered wigs. Advertising time couldn't run that fast for long.

Time. It was eating him alive. He was popular. More girls arrived to wave. His blood raced. His solitary bed beckoned. But he was too fat, and a great cliff-face etched by solitude and contemplation didn't suggest easy small-talk. Carrying a tray of papers to the shredder near the lift doors, a particularly attractive female face and form appeared like a radiant smiling vision. My God, that Sarah Finch had a body that would have panicked the Trooping of the Colour. But turning back into his den, he guessed that for himself, as for science, it was getting late. In a moment of dawn desperation, he felt a stab of panic. The clocks of the world were striking all at once, and Tower House became to him a group-mind finding the tunnel blocked, the routes become maze after deceptive maze.

Calm down. Stay still. Think. Enter the weaving of many dreams working on a single problem. The break-out. Soon, he must run for the wire. He must develop the thought-equivalent to silk maps in shoe-heels and tiny compasses concealed in rings. Very private conversations. Secret colleges. Hints and a few glimpses. Find the way. Don't tell. Just whisper.

Whisper what? That it might be possible to escape. Fields stood up quickly. He put a hunter's twitching nose through the curtains of his den.

7.30 am, and the first breakfasts were being served in the Staff Canteen of Tower House.

13

II

Events at the Olde Brewery House

In the twenty minutes it took Fields to wash, shave, and take the lift to the fifth-floor canteen, all signs of raging winter outside Tower House had almost totally disappeared, and a high sun was warming the glistening city. The country was getting quite used to such unusual weather changes. Their cause was attributed to many things. Chatting now to a group of close colleagues tucking with great relish into politically incorrect British heart-attack breakfasts, Fields said there was what he called a grey-scale choice of causes, from the almost-acceptable *advertisement* of global warming, to the almost-not-acceptable *advertisement* of the activities of UFOs. Quite hypnotising a somewhat popeyed circle, he declared that there was no such thing as fantasy. There was a scale of illusions, declared he, which could be more or less solid according to the way they were *sold.*

The Tower House Canteen, like the British Security Service itself, had never been known for enthusiasms, still less inspirations of any kind. That it was still early on a cold morning presented another difficulty for any would-be raiser of the spirits. But Fields, who had acquired legendary status in Tower House long before he wrote *StarPower,* had now developed into quite a welcome performer, even at this hour. To minds facing a relentless and paranoid fifteen-hour shift playing a game whose moves were often quite beyond any conscious category of right or wrong, he often provided a refreshing start to the day.

As Fields talked on before more dropped jaws, and not a few raspberries, the sun they could all see through the bullet-proof special glass (which did not have any acoustic resonance), was also warming the *Olde Brewery House* just beyond the main street of a perfect village enclave between Oxford and Woodstock. Some older locals said that the newly-built *Olde Brewery House* was so sinister in its tooth-paste-smile perfection that it looked almost like a TV advertisement. Around its exquisitely planned patterns, perfect children played on the perfect lawns of its gingerbread pose. Perfect cars posed on tinted gravel drives kept raked and free from all leaf-fall by local worthies. Some of these same worthies said that the last stage-sets of old England were here, propped up by thin stanchions against a twenty-four-hour cycle which could bring about more changes than the surrounding hills and rivers had known in a thousand years. The nice couple a hundred yards down the road who had converted the old coaching inn into perfect colour-supplement, could disappear overnight and be replaced in the morning by stout men in suits and ties who took down curtains, and padlocked all the doors. They then usually took a short walk to the local estate agent, who, it was rumoured, always had the correct paperwork prepared as if by magic.

But it did not look as if any such uncertainties surrounded the six-year-old twins, Joyce and Peter, the children of the recently divorced Dr. Leonard Holt. The pair played happily in the heated swimming pool of the newly erected extension of the *Olde Brewery House*. Now the weather had turned, the twins were looking forward to a drive later into town for a new video game, and probably some ice-cream, after they had brought their father a birthday present.

As Fields, waving a complete sausage on a fork, made a point about something called advertising mystique, Joyce and Peter heard a splash. What was that? Daddy had thrown a strange ball into the pool. What was that? Where was he? Hiding, no doubt. Joyce, followed by a fascinated Peter, jumped into the pool and gleefully picked up the strange object.

It was Daddy's head.

III

Entertainment Zionism

As neighbours ran towards the hysterical screams of the children, shards of toast and *Umbongo* spray flew from Fields' lips as he continued to give forth to a circle of a dozen or more fascinated faces, whose brains held more secrets than Europe now had independent factions. Despite some jocular remarks, he could not have had a much more attentive audience. Each member was a professional in various forms of concentration, for some operations required an almost alchemical patience. This ability was described by the train-spotters (for such was the term) as being able to wait long enough to catch a statue scratching its nose. Others, equally as unbelievable as human types, listened intently to Fields. These were quite different bundles of nerve-endings to the train-spotters. They consisted of a few actual James Bond types, thought by all (including their enemies), not to exist, which was the way they (and their enemies) liked it. Rumour had it that they made the famous films look quite pale as they passed through airports, hotels, and bedrooms in a saga of death, violence, and certainly gross deception on far shores, and often very much nearer.

When *StarPower* was first published, many of those who thought the book was going to be about some aspect of science, psychology, or advertising (Fields' favourite subject), were thunderstruck. The theme was what he saw as the neglected political and *religious* possibilities of the whole range of the world of arts, media, and entertainment - from films to theatre and video, from television to dance and rock and pop. The book's argument was that conventional, or what Fields called 'objective' political systems had all failed, precisely because organising human societies and their myriad complex needs and functions into any kind of meccano-set principle produced only slaughter and misery. Semi-rationalised ideas about what had eventually proved to be little-understood and irrelevant class or economic functions, always resulted in what he called an 'Auschwitz of Degrees'.

As he explained to a fascinated 60-year-old Annie Grower, these 'Degrees' were the levels of gross oversimplification which any mechanical system had to make with regard to human beings. The blue-rinsed Annie, on the verge of retirement, still had that coolness of nerve

16

which had once saved the entire Royal Family from instant incineration. Three decades previous, when she finally lowered her ex-Lease-Lend *Colt .45*, three men were dead, and a women had a broken neck. With the same twinkle in her eye as she had on that occasion, she now turned a keen ear to Fields as he lowered his voice out of earshot of his superiors two tables away. After forty years in places like Tower House, Annie thought the gesture was rather touching.

"Human legs, Annie, are always too short, toes never fit, and people are thankfully almost always totally preoccupied with either subversion, defiance, or escape."

"What from?"

"Plans."

"I know what you mean."

Annie glanced in envy at the massive fry-up the big man in front of her was consuming as he hissed conspiratorially at her.

"In my opinion Annie, all the Great Sages ever want is more shoulders applied to some gods-forsaken wheel or other."

"What do people really want?

"Rest."

"Now that's interesting,"

"All the great sages of history have made the same mistake. They think people want work, tasks, directions. What people really want is Entertainment."

Annie put down her single digestive biscuit in surprise.

"My God, haven't they got enough?"

"I fear not."

The smiling hippo features stared up at her, flanked by poised knife and fork.

"Not enough at all."

"I can't wait."

As a second plate of sausages and bacon vanished in seconds flat, she gazed in amusement at the very face which had stared up at her from cover of *Time* magazine as she had made her way to work that morning; although whether she could now call it work she did not know, since it bore no resemblance to her previous occupations in Tower House.

The Eastern sectors had lost at least their tactical military complexion, and a Northern Ireland at a possibly permanent peace was, in her opinion, sliding back into the history from whence it came. Over the past five years Annie had dropped her specialisation of detecting sympathetic Russian academic contacts (who were now all sympathetic), and had taken intensive retraining courses in analysis of worldwide computerised banking and investment systems. She had done much-praised work in the relation of these networks to the laundering of drug money, the amounts of which quite often exceeded the gross national product of entire third-world countries.

Annie liked Fields. Though only forty-five, he nevertheless represented to her a way back to a time when young gentlewomen (then there were no other) of the Security Services had to wear trousers in order to preserve modesty whilst on top of the ladders of the tall library stacks.

By her side, listening with similar enthusiasm, was the equally cool 27-year-old ambitious Cyril Barsby, a specialist in nuclear espionage, who on one occasion had saved almost the entire south of England from devastating consequences in a terrorist incident which, like Annie's previous adventure, history would perhaps never record. That such superbly practical minds listened closely to Fields, despite his often amusing appearance and eccentric views, was a sign of the very deep respect in which he was held. This morning, fore and aft of the trio, were yet another sixty of such intensely rational creatures. Occasionally, more by chance than anything else, the general public whose presumed servants these almost-good folk were, caught sight of tiny fragments of their manifold intrigues, seeing them momentarily, as with a pencil-torch in a bat-cave.

Aerials always turning, Barsby had duly consumed *StarPower*, ever eager as he was to impress those with influence.

"You propose a new kind of society, Dr. Fields?"

"Why not? Somebody should."

Barsby, in character, went on to quote extensively the text of *StarPower*. Fields, aware of Barsby's well-known ability to ingratiate himself, thought he would go far.

"A new form of human organisation whose complete sets of legal, moral, and social reference levels would be based entirely on what Dr. Fields calls ..."

For a moment, as a mildly amused Annie caught his eye, Fields thought that Barsby the computer was going to forget his lines. Both were wrong.

"...a technologically sustained Total Entertainment Experience?"

The celebrated author tried not to sound condescending.

"I think that's what I called it."

"Sounds useful."

"Useful sir, useful?"

Fields gazed in alarm at the row of pens in the top pocket of Barsby's sports-jacket.

"I mean there are a lot of separate new energies flying about which as yet have no what shall I say: *fulcrum?*"

Fields admired his focus, if he didn't like his trainers, and the fact that he could not quote Caesar from the original.

"Unification, Barsby, unification."

"Would you say that social and political unification in outdated and discredited forms is perhaps no longer possible?"

"I would indeed."

Annie had a genuinely puzzled brow.

"I don't understand some of *StarPower*."

Barsby practically leaped forward at this chance to impress. Fields lay back. He loved to hear himself explained.

"As I see it, the glue which would hold together the machinery of Dr. Fields' proposed new Leviathan would be the performance mystique of the great Stars of the world, with their various Acts and Shows, which would collectively constitute a new and original State *corpus*."

"Entertainment is a waste of time."

"But there is all that power and energy running about quite loose, unable to lock onto a single unifying formula of nationalism, religion, or political philosophy."

"Thank God for that. I still think Entertainment is a waste of time."

"But surely, Annie, Dr. Fields would not possibly waste his talents on such a thing, if it were?"

Fields put down his knife and fork, which was always a sure sign of trouble.

"Barsby?"

"Yes, Dr. Fields?"

"Entertainment *is* a waste of time."

Barsby, inwardly crestfallen, rallied with a smile, and crouched, waiting for the slightest change of wind.

"But you call it trash, don't you?"

"Yes. But what I mean by trash is something which has no industrial analogue."

"Entertainment is fuzzy?"

"What? Oh nice one, Barsby. I like it. Fuzzy, indeed!"

Fields rolled the intriguing computer-phrase in his head as if he were sampling a good wine.

"Entertainment is a fuzzy set. Barsby, you have made my day."

Annie's voice sounded as if she were trying to stifle laughter.

"What is *fuzzy?*"

Fields, smiling, nodded to Barsby to take up his cue. Pleased at this, Barsby regained his textbook confidence. But many painful self-improvement hours under the reading-lamp had made him a bit of a sergeant-major.

"I think it means that Authority becomes neither violent nor nonviolent. It hides, becomes a cool medium; its restyled persuasive powers will be embedded in the engineering and technological systems which will form the broad support and development base for a massive emerging Entertainment culture. On thing is sure. Entertainment is important. Without it, the entire human race would go mad within a matter of hours."

Fields touched his arm. This made Barsby's day.

"I couldn't have put it better myself, Barsby. Brutalising is not cool."

Annie looked uncertain at one, then the other.

"Not immoral?"

Any version of the word *moral* was known to be one of the few things which produced visible nervousness in Fields. Barsby sprang to his defence.

"He just said it. Brutalizing is uncool."

"Just uncool? Not wrong?"

Barsby looked baffled. Fields put up a combined defence.

"Put it this way Annie. Cruelty could be designed-out. Its advertising is deficient."

"Advertising, Fields? Does the truth advertise?"

"Of course."

"I don't believe you."

"Tell her, Barsby, tell her."

As he spoke, Barsby looked as if he had won the school prize.

"As *StarPower* says, like the wing of the chaffinch, both the truth and authority have to undergo natural selection. The new means of persuasion Annie, are to be as smoothly and stylistically designed as a 48-track digital tape studio, quiet as a Rolls, appealing as a glamorous face. From hot systems of social control, destructive of the environment, wasteful of sensitive and limited power systems, the progress is towards elegant and entertaining designer-systems of pressure and influence. These will be fun to experience, and they will tend to short-circuit completely any troublesome value-judgment questions, still less any intellectual doubts. After all, only a complete churl would ever complain about a Donald Duck film."

This last image pleased Barsby immensely. He adjusted his tie, fiddled with his pens as he spoke, and glanced around quickly to see if the right people had possibly noticed the good company he was in. But Annie was not impressed.

"Intellectual doubts, Barsby? I've never had any of those, I'm sure."

Annie, looked at the pair now eagerly swapping antennae-touches, and thought that if this was the new world, she was glad that her bungalow in the South of France was very near. She dabbed her lips and got up from the table.

"I wish you joy of your Entertainment lobotomy, gentlemen."

"Annie has doubts, Barsby. What are we to do?"

"A pity."

Annie turned on him.

"Pity? That's the first time in this conversation that a moral concept has been used."

As Fields blushed, Barsby stuttered, and Annie prepared for one of her famous sulks, a pair of fighter-pilot eyes glistened, and shot an almost visible ray of powerful concentration towards the trio. Sir Harry Marshall, Fields' boss, dining with a few of Them Upstairs at the 'better' table few yards away, was his ever-alert self. Making a mental note to tell Fields for the tenth time that week to smarten himself up, he had caught a few phrases of the conversation, and wished he were there to talk to them. Anything would have been better than having to listen to polite evasive chat about golf and cricket from men who were deep into investigating gunpowder, treason, and plot.

With jutting chin, and fine blond hair, the very English Harry Marshall was a powerful holograph of national and personal camouflage. A pulse of many secrets was in the brain, from the mystique of the hard-nosed street-fighter's eye for the right deal, and the hard sell, to the darker dealings of the Organisation. The always slightly clenched fists alone suggested that by comparison with old Etonian Fields, ex-door-to-door salesman Harry Marshall had come a long way, and probably harder than he ever told. Other Department Heads of a more refined nature than he, and whose deeper relaxation was far too well-protected, had, fallen flat on their faces, and men and women from the Organisation had died by the secret score as a result. Marshall's knighthood had come with the saving of many agent's lives due to a previous ruthless efficiency in organising job-lots of plastic picnic- furniture, fluffy teddy-bears with Chinese eyes, and 'Onyx' ashtrays, 'Free With Every Wash n'Lube Job'.

Fields and Marshall worked very well together. But when one of their inevitably successful joint ploys came about, Marshall often felt that his propaganda specialist was less interested in achieving pure Intelligence objectives than in following up and proving some theory of his own. Since purely practically, the cerebral Bunter couldn't organise a toothbrush, it often seemed to Marshall that Fields was using the Organisation purely as his own tool, often with a humorous contempt, and just as frequently with a quite chilling effortless superiority; this caused more middle-class brows to flutter at the egg-stained waistcoat, slipper of cooked ham on collarless shirt, the chanting of Presley lyrics, and the ever-present smell of Saveloy baps with fried peppers fresh from the Black Taxi hut behind Tower House.

Meanwhile, Barsby was still trying to convince a doubting Annie, now obviously anxious to be away.

"You see what Dr. Fields means is that implicit political coercion now has its headquarters and operations deep in the quiet anonymous software systems of the planet."

"Is that what he means?"

"Authority, like any mafiosi, always wants to go legitimate. Legitimacy is the perfect cover."

"Is that what legitimacy is?"

Barsby was a marvellous chameleon, thought Fields, diving into yet another plateful, served automatically by experienced (and most thoroughly debriefed) waitresses. He could hear not only his own phrases, but a little of his own voice coming from the adaptive computer which was the mind of Barsby. The boy would go far. Fields closed his eyes as he almost heard himself speaking.

"Hot authority has to go. A Fieldsian world-model would produce the pure cerebral balm of helping, guiding, being sincere in offering advice, gradually controlling, comforting."

Fields pivoted a large slice of bacon on a fork to make his point.

"And entertaining, Barsby, entertaining. Don't forget that."

But Annie was not amused.

"Codswallop."

The pair looked rather embarrassed as she walked away. But on reaching her office, her first thought was not computerised bank account code-cracking, but the thought that Fields was rocking a hell of a lot of boats. It also occurred to her that in a modern democratic State, Fields was very lucky still to be alive.

Hoping that after such an inspiring breakfast, the more goggle-eyed diners would now see their plots, intrigues, and codes in a new light, Fields returned to the Main Computer Hall to prepare for his day's work. Finishing the last of yet another *Wombat* sausage, and coughing *Pisky-Pasty* crumbs over the control consoles (a source of much staff complaint), Fields checked his E-mail. He was pleased. More reviews of *StarPower*. He rubbed his hands in particular delight over a slashing attack from the formidable Müller, of Nuremberg University, an old neo-Nazi academic enemy. Fields giggled his famous giggle and finished off another *ersatz*, which had a taste he imagined the ancient Müller having last experienced in 1945 as a terrified ten-year-old in an air-raid shelter with a *panzerfaust* on one shoulder, and a big fascist chip on the other.

To get rid of Müller's gaseous presence, Fields put on a very precious Pat Boone quarter-inch tape on his *Grundig*, which was even older than the *Dansette*. *'On a day like today...'* Fields smiled to the bunkered walls and breathed in deeply the filtered air of which he alone was appreciative. *'...we'll pass the time away, writing love letters in the sand...'* A pleased sigh. Yes, that was a lot better. Nothing like a bit of rock n' roll to get rid of Nazis.

After doing a few twirls to the music outside his alcove, much to the amusement of the young folk of the newly-arrived morning-shift, he re-entered his cave, and turned off the distorted two-watts of the ancient tape-recorder. He lay down on his camp-bed to compose himself before an exhausting day began of endless conferences and planning sessions. He tried to concentrate his mind on current key issues, but the memories of the past two months drifted before his almost closed eyes, leaving him quite wide awake.

Things were changing rapidly in his professional world. The Intelligence creature itself now grazed with many other systems-animals, most of whom no longer had much to do with any direct military dimension. Fields was now called upon to attend conferences which were organised by agencies which interfaced banks, corporations, and other Intelligence organisations, both public and private. As high-technology was now universally international, the old idea of finite sets of national secrets had almost gone, replaced by the antennae of international circles of technocratic elites. Their aim was no longer physical war against each other, but survival amidst ever-increasing populations whose literacy-levels and intelligence quotients were developing in inverse proportion to their social and cultural expectations. As he lay on his bed, Fields could almost hear this new animal breathing; he could feel for its heart like a surgeon, and he knew its moods as well as a farmer knew how to interpret the change of light over the woods beyond the corn field.

Hong-Kong, midsummer, last year. Anglo-American conference concerning the re-imaging of combined Far East Intelligence fronts whose covers had been blown by extremely sophisticated drug-smuggling operations. He remembered Special Forces faces in bulky, almost rectangular suits against equally slab-like buildings. Food good, but at night, when the virtual fire of city lights faded quickly to the east, a disturbing reminder of pre-wall Berlin. Sleep impossible; the Americans paranoid, the Japanese extremely difficult, and the Hong-Kong Chinese corrupt almost to the point of inverse puritanism. He spoke to an old friend, John Lawrence, a good-humoured crew-cut National Security Agency official, in a lounge bar which could have been straight out of a mid-sixties film. The *Tora! Tora!* Bar came complete with straw-wrapped bottles, spray-haired girls with tangerine lipstick playing bongoes, and in all likelihood, he thought, even a *Walther* or two lurking in shoulder holsters.

He was amusing Lawrence by reading out aloud from one of the many hilarious books on what was blushingly termed the 'New Cosmology.' The National Security Administration official, with his worked-wrecked face, looked as if he more than welcomed the light relief always provided by Fields.

"Listen to this, Lawrence. This bloke leaves the creation of space itself to 21 words in parenthesis: 'Remember, the universe did not expand into existing space after the big bang: its expansion created space-time as it went.' *As it went;* you got that, Lawrence?"

"It sounds like the instructions on the back of a can of fly-spray to me."

"No damn good, Lawrence, is it? I tell you these are the last days of the last engines. It is all over. Science is just desperately trying to re-advertise itself, that's all. Wrecked joke machines of science-culture are rusting and breaking down and exploding and irradiating the whole planet."

"Unfortunately, they're the only things we've got."

"What are?"

"Reactors, accelerators, radio telescopes, computers."

"Do you think that they are any different as pure Entertainment to the beautiful jokes of the long neck of the giraffe, the armoured weight of the rhino, the great hops of the kangaroo, or the summer afternoon's dance of some mouthless insect?"

"Is dentistry a joke?"

"Dentistry was a long time ago, Lawrence. So were anaesthetics and piped water for the peasants. After those things, I've yet to see anything but big sticks to bang heads with."

The ex-Marine Colonel chuckled, and gazed across the harbour as a four-masted cutter Joseph Conrad would have recognised, glided alongside a sleek jet-hydrofoil. It was a sight to inspire, but Lawrence was exhausted. They were all tired out here in Asia. It didn't look like Africa, but it rubbed out Westerners even more efficiently.

"What about organ transplants?"

"Would you have an organ transplant, Lawrence?"

Lawrence gulped as a *cheong-san* split almost to the thigh passed close by. The Chinese girl wearing it was alluring as the hydrofoil, now running fast past the cutter to the open sea.

"Not yet."

"Exactly. Now listen to me. For objectivity, read performance."

"Say again?"

"I tell you that the entire twentieth-century constellation of scientific explanatory apparatus is nothing more than a series of rundown systems-jokes."

"Fields, you are always very entertaining."

"Good. Because Entertainment is the only human institution in which the idea of linearity, the Ark of the Scientific Covenant, means nothing. Do you realise what we have on our hands now as a possibility? Pure Entertainment has no physical industrial product but a state of mind."

The ships and the woman were gone now as Fields' urgent voice came to Lawrence from a far distance.

"Entertainment?"

"We could have a world in which the entire product would be performance. Not coherent policy, singular concrete direction, logical aims, dangled carrots and rewards, inputs and outputs, but performance. Do you realise that if we effect these changes, there would be a truly magical transition, because nothing serious such as an industrial product, would be able to stand against it?"

"Magical? I'll buy you a drink on that, Fields."

"It would be the ultimate weapon."

"An entertainment bomb?"

"You have it, Lawrence, you have it. Have another shot of *Red-Eye* on me."

As a slightly baffled Lawrence left for the airport, Fields remembered thinking that if anyone had bugged the conversation, and thought it code, they would have an interesting time interpreting. He would have loved to have heard a Japanese translation. He would also have liked to have heard Lawrence's cracks about Entertainment at the NSA Headquarters at Fort Meade. But he could smile, secretly. Just as he intended, the jokes were spreading like a pollen. Soon he guessed they would form the nucleus of an intention, a kind of half-form, like Heathcliff, Hamlet's father, the Economy, or even the Easter Bunny.

Autumn in Italy. Weekend in Milan, beginning of last November. An polluted atmosphere, but somehow he breathed here more easily than Britain. Play of light and shade on unfamiliar architectures affecting his sense of time and history in this city, older than any in North Europe. He was here to attend a restricted conference on state-of-the-art chips at the hotel *Principe Di Savoia*. He looked through his hotel window at incessant rain over what was still somehow a World War 2 city, complete with some bomb-damage, surprisingly still around. Though he was born many years after the War, somehow all the big European cities were still wartime places to Fields, as if something in them and also in himself from that era wasn't yet finished.

Whenever he was abroad, he would leave acres of plate-glass and chrome, and search amidst weeds and bracken for small sections of pocked and blackened masonry. These he would find, together with a burnt-out gap between skyscrapers, and by bridges and roads, an overgrown crater or two. Whenever he found a deeply embedded tank-track, or a cartridge-case under an upturned slab, he would stay for a moment, and wonder which bit of him was buried there. At such times, he thought he was merely a lone ideological strand lurking in the ruins like a lost ghost. In all European cities to Fields, it was always the same. He had come home. But home had gone. Here was just the blackened ditch where he had died, the section of pitted road where he had fought and killed; over there, by an alley, he had escaped, running breathless for his very life.

Escape. The gap in his curtains became the road to freedom. The idea would not him leave night and day. It possessed him in the night like the face of an old love which would not go away.

The first Milan lecture had been delivered by a tiny 16-year-old Japanese girl, Dana Chong. She talked about what she called Negative Arms Sales. This was a euphemism for the factory-doping of off-the-shelf chips. This meant that genetically-bred hidden Artificial Intelligence systems implanted within chips could be programmed not only to shut down defence electronics, but to actually guide in incoming threats to where they could do most damage. With such virus-mines in place, within hours, these cash-and-carry chips could make a belligerent country blind and helpless before a shot was fired. Such chips were now being sold to banking systems, with all that entailed. Fields had been invited to suggest suitable investment fronts and models of corporate identities through which to move such doped chips and their associated management systems.

As the memory came back, Fields couldn't help a smile. Somehow, chips always managed to produce a genuine whiff of pure sulphur. The tiny plastic blocks with their rows of little metal legs represented national debts galore. Though their operational principles had long been an open book, their manufacture was only thoroughly understood by a few hundred bonded craftsmen of a corporate elite. From Entertainment to Science, from war and peace in air, sea, and land, chips now held the planetary culture together, controlling everything from tills to satellites, from wristwatches to nuclear power stations.

And yet chips had something very old about them: something of the ancient guilds and crafts atmosphere. There were as many tricks involved in their manufacture and the design of their functions as there were in building cathedrals. The lines trailing out from the technology smacked of elite intrigues within power-labyrinths, and even ancient esoteric practices. Chips also spoke of industrial sabotage, of mysterious disappearances, and even deaths. Byzantine plots were involved in chip-based modern information technology, whose growth was exponential. Information was the heart of almost all power in the modern world, and these tiny blocks as a core-reference had replaced the castle, the cathedral, the court, and even the filing cabinet. Their power had also almost completely demolished old national structures of identity, most of which were beginning to look rather like a school play after a scenery disaster.

Putting these daydreams aside, he leaned over to his small corner-sink, filled a pan with water, and lit his primus for a last coffee before work. These days his mind was humming like a top. It wasn't exactly an unpleasant feel, but it made sleep very difficult, and sleeping pills were banned absolutely in his chosen profession. Should any kind of balloon go up, the last thing wanted was a collection of important zombies being brought back to a decision-making state by pouring water over their heads.

Whilst he searched for coffee behind piled books and papers, chips still continued their momentary haunting. Now, in his ever-teeming mind, it was their birth, history, and development, as if an entire extra-human process were dreaming of all the cycles of its birth and death. He found his coffee, and remembered the day long ago when he first saw his father in tears. Fields Senior came home upset on the day all lists of equipment he dealt with in his War Office work had turned to 8-digit numbers. Fields remembered his earliest intellectual fear began with the sight of his father's devastated face. He remembered him telling his mother that nothing had a *name* any more. No-one knew who or what took such decisions in a society. It was certainly nothing to do with the faded arras of Parliament, or the doings of conventional institutions. His father's agony was that the creak of wheels, the clank and hiss of gear, camshaft, and track of all the British Army's vehicles had vanished into the first crude computers. He could hear his father's voice now, talking in complaining, almost heartbreaking terms to his mother. Now, instead of the immortal roll of *Bedford, Morris, Austin,* and *Norton*, there were rows of anonymous digits. It was a monstrous identity-crisis of unrecorded proportions; his father's generation never quite got over the silent explosion in all their minds, which had occurred almost simultaneously with an equivalent silent explosion in the world of machines. Fields supposed that the real moments of history were such quiet tremors like this; one day in the nineteenth-century, soldiers first changed from fancy-dress to khaki; on another day, in the early nineteen-seventies, the shop on the corner shut because electronic equipment could

27

hardly be repaired any more. Library shelves might be full of the formal proceedings of mankind, but nobody really knew who or what took such decisions. Fields supposed they belonged to a realm of orders of nature which grew through human machinations like brambles entering an old house.

As the hum and chat of increasing daytime activity increased beyond his fragile curtain, Dana Chong appeared again on the stage of his mind, to quite vanish his distraught father and his lost British names. Fields remembered being pleased and surprised when Dana turned out to be an ardent *StarPower* convert. Expecting boring professional questions, the doll-eyed, fairylike Japanese girl in her lemon-yellow dress, had bombarded him with questions of a very different kind. She came complete with a very un-fairylike interview technique, making her sound at times like young Barsby.

Stifling an image of a naked Dana Chong squatting on his huge paunch and twittering like a canary, he remembered again as he tried to straighten a tie, an impossible task, since he had absolutely no neck at all.

"How would you define the very essence of Entertainment State, Dr. Fields?"

"The complete melting of all intellectual resistance."

"*Old analogue friction* is another almost-amusing term you use."

"Oh, thank you."

"You say by transforming such resistance into merely another set of acts, eventually, the building of any kind of dominant structure which does not have anything to do with Entertainment would be theoretically impossible?"

"Exactly."

Amazing how much attention she had paid to his work. There was a Japanese hive-concentration in her brow which he rarely met in Britain these days. It was almost-amusing.

"All hard resistance would be outperformed before it could be realised?"

"Yes."

"Rather like a permanent *Life of Brian?*"

"What? Life of who?"

Fields reached for his chocolates and tried not to look baffled.

"The film."

"Of course."

His dread secret was that he had only ever seen two films in his life. This exposure (as he termed it) amounted to the first five minutes of *The Railway Children* (abandoned because the projectionist had a heart-attack), and *Passport to Pimlico* (abandoned after twenty minutes because of a bomb scare). Dana Chong continued with an urgent tone in her voice. Japanese thinkers did not, it appeared, have much time for European hesitations or uncertainties.

"I mean you say in Chapter IV that nothing objective would have time to develop, and hence dominate with what you call in Chapter III, let me see now..."

She opened a heavily annotated version of the Japanese translation of *StarPower:*

"...the kind of cancerous seriousness which characterises the most appalling twentieth-century afflictions."

Carefully closing the book, her eyes almost squinted at him.

"I think you have a very good point, Dr. Fields."

"Oh thank you."

"Pure *play* as you call it is a form of social control which like sport, has certainly been tried by various media sectors, but not really developed as a possibly complete social system."

"Except now in certain parts of America. They have actually turned out the very first cretin-films."

She smiled at this, as if she only partially-understood, and he noted she tried to avoid staring at the *Yorkie* bars he was steadily demolishing, as if they were a facial deformity.

"You have pointed out that in the postwar world, millions have begun to live their lives in a sleep of Entertainment stars."

"Quite so. A sleep indeed."

She continued with a strange mixture of part-quote, part-comment, and part-reverse-translation.

"Since the Arts appear to have long lost all functions of subversion and questioning, and electronic media never had or even recognised such a function in the first place..."

"What?"

But she was oblivious, a convert to the Great Message, as she almost-quoted partial-paragraphs at him.

"...you say such people only have their equivalents in the half-awake pod-people of lurid science-fiction tales, who are actually industrial units, milch-cows, a producing and pouring of endless repetitious consciousness."

"Where did you get that from?"

"Oh, its all in your book, Dr. Fields"

He began to relish the unstoppable ball of bastard ideas he had started rolling. It was a professional advertiser's dream. Such a complete grey-scale shaded from the most fantastic illusions to the even more fantastic illusions of the myths and reassurances of truth and solidity. He was proud of his intimidating software creation. Not only was he hearing himself coming out of Japanese as she spoke, but some of the stuff was somewhat new to him. He hadn't actually said what she said he had said. This was molecular growth of ideology indeed. He remembered thinking he must have a word with the Artificial Intelligence boys in Tower House about this. Much to the surprise of Dana Chong, to celebrate, he stripped a complete *Yorkie,* and threw it into his jaws like a tossed sprat to a dolphin. He supposed that he now had an ever-changing super-body, just like one of his Stars. He was becoming part of the Pantheon of Wonder he so urgently propagandised.

"Well, Dr. Fields, I think the *StarPower* blueprint utterly transforms the already existing elements of the first primitive universal entertainment systems."

"I think it does. Yes."

"How do you see this society? Do you see it like a kind of universal *Spitting Image?*"

For Fields, who had only ever seen television through shop windows, here was yet another bad moment. He vowed to get a copy of *The Television Times* and do some swatting. As an expert in deception, he hated lying. He would rather press the trigger and not see where the shell landed.

"Yes. That's right. A universal what was that?"

But she was too busy to reply, jotting energetically in a spiral notebook. She would perhaps have been horrified to know that he whom the world now called the Entertainment Prophet had hardly experienced any Entertainment in his life. Few people in Fields' day had ever come across someone who worked things virtually from first principles. It was an ancient method of thought and divination which had gone from the modern world with the gas-lamps, and the corner-grocer's box of broken biscuits. But Fields was like one of those geneticists who can build a body from the mere scrapings of fingernails. Give him a few minutes of television, and the history was foretold. There was no need to see any more television. This was a kind of thinking which ill-fitted twentieth century ideas of reasoning on the evidence of many samples. Some in Tower House said his mind was like a tapestry, or one of those paintings of an object which cannot be constructed in the world outside the painting. This gave him certain advantages, said others. It made him multi-mode, seeing possibilities of escape, life, and freedom in system-hopping. Certainly at times it looked like Fields conceived of life itself as a massive hacking operation designed to de-industrialise his entire imaginative faculties.

Dana Chong looked up from her jotting, her eyes wanting specific answers to leading questions.

"And what do you predict for the future?"

30

He knew he was much better prepared for that one.

"The death of seriousness."

The robot clatter stopped. Dana Chong stared, astonished, as if she had seen some spirit rising from the grave.

"The death of what, Dr. Fields?"

"Seriousness. All of it."

As he experienced yet another bout of impure thoughts about taking the slip of lemon-yellow off her in the nearest available private bedroom, he saw she was obviously ready to leave with the last bone he had given her. He would have given anything to have heard the Japanese version.

"You mean the death of the profound?"

"Don't worry. We'll love it. Get Entertainment-prone. Now. You know it makes sense."

If a Japanese face could ever go pale, Dana Chong's face certainly had done. She started writing rapidly as he continued.

"We are experiencing a great moment in history. We have now reached the Trashocentric via the Geocentric and the Heliocentric. And it is going to be great fun. And don't forget."

"What's that, Dr. Fields?"

"Keep taking the advertisements!"

Now a little frightened as well as baffled, she bade him a polite goodbye, and her child's form disappeared in the direction of a seminar entitled 'Information Systems and Very Large Scale Integration'. Well, he remembered thinking, they were going to have to get their skates on in Holland Park Comprehensive if they were going to catch up with 16-year-old Dana Chong's Japanese generation.

He was not to know it, but back in Tokyo, Dana hurriedly informed her TV-director brother of the death of seriousness at lunch that same day; within a week, *StarPower* sales had broken further all-time records. But the man himself, after further such impure thoughts caused by hemlines and cleavage in the lounge bar of the Hong Kong Hilton, caught sight of his huge bulk in a mirror, and thought about destiny.

But for the kind of destiny he had in mind, he knew he had to go on a crash diet.

There had been further such sensual moments during the past year facing lovely women interpreters in huts on freezing windswept secret airfields in Croatia, and even enchanting faces serving the appalling food in draughty official residences on Moscow. There were sleepless nights in Berlin hotels, with properly-printed whore's address-books on the beside table, and the endless shuffling of rent-boys and drug-dealers in the plush corridors. A frequent guest of MOSSAD, Fields slept happier

31

in Israel where there was still that old-fashioned sense of industrial purpose he was supposed to despise. He also had such ironic sleep in CIA-run suites in New York, and he certainly liked dining in the White House, where big-jawed dream-women smiled at him over the candelabra, and he was sure there were bugs in saltcellars, light-switches, napkins, and (he had heard) even in brassières. But the brainless American fashion-plates bored him, and although some of the European women haunted his dreams, his entire sexual energy was absorbed in supporting the divination of secrets just as fascinating as those behind an unbelievably beautiful smile. It was a different scale of sexuality was this, he often thought; his whole being was involved in the system he served. This did not prevent quite irreligious lapses, such as now, when he now put a hippo-eye through a chink in his curtain. Praise the gods, there was the magnificent young Ms. Hayes bending over by the shredder; she had a body that would have raised a stampede at a Zen-master's convention.

Fields froze now at a clipped and military voice outside his curtains, though a voice not without traces of humour and mercy.

"Hieronymus, I'd make myself scarce for half an hour, if I were you."

He stepped out, and was face to face with Harry Marshall. His boss stood with his sleeves rolled, his half-moon spectacles glinting, and a sheaf of ponderous documents in his hands. It looked like it was going to be a working day.

"Yes, Harry?"

"It's Wednesday."

"Good Lord. I forgot. Thank you."

Now flustered and terrified, he gathered papers to make haste to some hidden eyrie as the dread voice of Nelly Goby and the clatter of pans and brushes was heard outside the Main Computer Hall.

"Thank you, thank you. My goodness me, where is she?"

"Five minutes away. Morning Conference at 0930 sharp, mind."

"Of course."

"Oh, and leave your fried onion baps behind, this time. I'm expecting Sir Reginald to turn up."

"Of course."

"After your *Big Ben's Frankfurter-Sundae* effort of last month, I got an hour's dressing-down on Security and Sanitation."

"Not to worry, Harry, not to worry."

Leaving the Main Computer Hall, Marshall was handed a note by his Special Branch Liaison Officer, Christine White. Dr. Leonard Holt had been murdered. Marshall had his secretary cancel everything for quarter of an hour, and he gazed across the river at the sunlit city for a long time. Holt, a distinctly unpleasant individual, had been an important link and many-times-turned runner for all kinds of high-technology chemical interests. Everybody used him, and everybody tried to turn him, therefore to a casual observer it would seem that Holt's death could have been ordered by any one of a score of group-interests. But Marshall was not a casual observer. Not for nothing was he in a senior position in the sensitive organisation he worked for. In the back of his mind he almost knew. Holt had been killed by a privateer. A moral loose cannon. The worst kind of problem. Intermittent action. No connections. No pattern.

Never mind. He would loose some ferrets, and see what maverick creatures poked out their snouts, nosed the air, and ran for cover.

With the menacing clatter of mop-buckets in the distance, Fields almost ran to the washroom whilst his room was scoured. Here, determined to finish the last few pages of *The Quest for Corvo*, he perched unsteadily on a waste-bin, and scoffed pink and red chocolate-creams from a white box which trailed cut ribbons. Thus, he thought, apart from Nelly Goby, the day had started off well. He thought of his embryo Entertainment State as yet like the curious shapes of almost-there aeroplanes before the Wright *Flyer*. As a pure idea, it was still an impractical dream-shape which had yet to learn the laws of connecting its unstable power/weight ratios to other orders of matter and solidity. The engines of this half-form were revving mightily, and its airframe was shaking, eager to soar. But the last historical months of the preflight age had a few weeks to tick away before his creation could break away from the surly bonds of earth to the central blue.

33

IV

The Guest At The Penguin Hotel

Still alert for the sound of buckets and pans, Fields finished his *Quest for Corvo*, and plunged into Huysmans' *Against Nature*. As he did so, it was said by those living near the *Olde Brewery House* that the screams of the two children had been heard for a half mile or more. If so, then they might have been heard by the driver of a hired green Ford *Escort* who was reported accelerating rapidly past the village Post Office a minute or two after the screams were first heard.

If they were heard by the driver of this car, it is doubtful if he or she cared very much. For Dr. Leonard Holt, working late on a Friday evening two days previous, had blinded twenty rabbits, ten dogs, eleven cats, and two monkeys in his own commercial laboratory which manufactured a range of chemicals for the pharmaceutical industry. His action was to facilitate his noted researches on viscous flow of mucous liquids across the retina of the eye. The blinding of the animals was done by the application of a mild acid which took some hours to reach maximum effectiveness. The animals were to be conveniently left over the weekend without food or water, since these things could affect muscle-spasm conditions which might make later examination difficult.

As far as science went, all well and good. As far as British Law went, however, such experiments were unlicensed and therefore illegal. But this was how Leonard Holt earned his money. He carried out illegal experiments for companies with internationally known names. Some of the experiments were sponsored at a remove by various European military sectors, whose interests so dovetailed into civilian corporate interests throughout the world, it was sometimes almost impossible to tell the two apart.

Young Joyce and Peter, deep in shock, were now being heavily sedated in a local private hospital ward, with two policemen outside the door. In later years, the pair would doubtless go to fine universities and encounter impressive theories of existence from which Tragedy, that old metaphysical humbug, had been surgically removed as efficiently as the eyes and organs of their father's tortured animals. Tragedy had been replaced by the chromium-plated super-humbug of Facts and

Objectivities. Joyce and Peter would learn to play the Great Rational Evidence Game as well as ever their father played it. They could feel secure again, warm and safe in the pure sunlight of objective theorising as they once were by the blue pool before their discovery. They could feel out of reach of such terrors precisely the entire and complete education system had long ago thrown out any kind of idea that men and women were morally accountable for their actions.

Several hours after the village had seen more Panda cars in one hour than it had seen in ten years, the driver of the green Ford *Escort* booked into a small hotel in Eastbourne. Samuel Stone, the permanently harassed owner of *The Penguin Hotel*, could not help noticing the next morning as his guest in Room 11 walked past him and paid his bill, that for a man, this guest had a remarkably shapely bottom and slim legs.

He did not tell his wife.

In fact he did not tell anyone.

For Samuel Stone thought he was going a bit strange.

V

Trash Systems Are Go

In the first week of February, Fields and Marshall flew to a Joint European Security Conference in Paris. Marshall travelled as a representative of *Seelex*, which was a 'front' firm ostensibly doing business in 'specialised information security.' *Seelex* (which conducted authentic business, and took on private contracts!) was known to have had some considerable success against criminals as regards analysis of bank-account movement, identification, and origin. Marshall was to address a closed sub-conference of European police officials on the financing of the movement of ephedrene and sodium oxybate (pep-pill base-concentrate) from the Caucuses and Central Asia through Austria, Belgium, and Switzerland. He had also been asked to demonstrate models of specialised Intelligence analysis applied to corporate financial systems, on which recent international bank crashes had focused interest.

Fields, in his London University lecturing *persona*, had been invited to contribute to a seminar on Media Policy and State Security. Both men, as good members of the European community, made sure that the information they gave was of obsolescent procedures, and operationally useless, except as dummy loads for training and certain liaison purposes.

Both also noted that in the five years which had elapsed since their last attendance, something very interesting had happened to the usually subdued and somewhat conservative Joint Security Conference. Held in a palatial suite in the Tuileries Palace, the Reception on the first day was intriguing. Fields noted three known neo-Nazis bankers present, and Marshall weighed in by pointing out one of the best bisexual high-tech spies in the business; not to be outdone, Fields added one transvestite British Cabinet minister compromised by the Mafia, and several new drug billionaires; Marshall replied to this with a sighting of a veteran British paedophile, who was a leading figure in the European Economic Union. This urbane creature talked charmingly to a cluster of the very last gleams of Stendhal's France: a group of elderly pretenders and priests, one of whose father fought, when a young teenager, with Thiers against the Communards. In distinct contrast, both Marshall and Fields also noted the presence of two very young British business entrepreneurs who had been set up unwittingly by covert international interests many and various; this woman and man were popular national figures representing the very epitome of personal success, but were being run by principalities and powers of which their own rather gosh-golly horizons could hardly conceive. But as moth-figures in the dying of the afternoon light, at least they looked good, chatting merrily to some very fine brains from troubled African regions, to whom they were probably promising the world, and much breathtaking else besides.

To Fields, as a connoisseur of covert faces for nearly twenty-five years, a great many of this now multiracial throng looked absolutely scared to death; they were rather like the figures around Hitler he had seen in photographs. Only a successful capitalist culture could sculpture such terror on what were some very fine faces. He supposed that the Big Deals were always as dangerous as they had ever been, and the North-European super-rich, above all others, still looked traditionally as nervous as they did in the days when Krupp was casting his first breach-loaders. But in this highly educated and highly intelligent gathering, the many influential academics present were highest on his list of men filled with twentieth-century fear, higher even than the commercial sector, and that, to his mind, was saying a lot. Both Marshall and Fields agreed that the smell of many different kinds of sulphur here was enough to make any true child of nature run for its life. The fathers and grandfathers of the gathering they saw before them had created states and constitutions terrible and tragic enough. Both had an idea that this herd, frightened as only animals before thunder can be, were about to create yet more. Marshall himself supposed that somewhere beyond this gathering, on the wrong side of town, resistance would eventually come out of shock.

Gone now with the last coal fire and something called National Policy, was the old-style ultra-secret conference of weapon-faces in some refurbished bunker of the fallen Master Race. Seething before Marshall and Fields was the new post-Communism decision complex. This exotic creature had only tenuous connections with elections, still less the finite identities and unique processes of individual nations. What Marshall and Fields had in front of them was more like a fabulously rich fashion-show compared to its previous mask. Here, they were hearing about the financing of new-technology interactive media rather than Command, Communications, and Control; weapons-systems, long fashionable, were *out* in this season-furnace. Here, even security was about style. Without style, in this gathering, you were lost, thought Marshall, as a glamorous Italian neo-fascist girl looked for a second a little askance at his standard-issue British grey suit. Marshall thought of his father, driving his 8th Army *Sherman* from El Alamein to Cassino via Sicily all those years ago. What he would have said of the company his son was keeping, he dared not think.

Yet Fields, a huge rag-and-bone mess of crumbs and flying jowl-drops, had whatever it took. His fame spreading as the author of *StarPower,* he was obviously happier in this company than he ever was on his proper side of the channel. Up-and-coming young Czech and Russian blue-chinned entrepreneurs in *Amani* suits quoted *StarPower.* Old friends greeted him, women admired, reporters asked for interviews. Also very much to Fields' taste were the freshly baked Polish *babkas;* French onion rolls with Swiss sour cream; *strudel,* brought from Hamburg overnight, and fresh blueberry cookies, flown in by courtesy of the CIA. Fields spoke fluent German, tolerable French, hesitant Italian, and even some rather archaic Polish in the tearoom, whose continental atmosphere obviously delighted him. Here he circulated, enjoying the social swirl. In Britain he hardly ever left Tower House. Once, in a rare self-observation, he told Marshall that he loved the British very much, but he found them a little boring, and their very extremely few intellectual and artistic interests comically out-of-date. With continentals, Fields said he could pass quickly from Hegel to Einstein; then travel back through Rabelais, and Sartre, without horses, mincing thespians, parking problems, dog-shit complaints, or popular television programmes coming in between.

Feeling a little out of his depth for once, Marshall combed his hair carefully in a loo mirror, and had an attendant polish his shoes for the third time that day. Looking at himself as he straightened his tie, he didn't think he was built for this new evolution of the Great Game any more. He felt like an old man in a slightly old-fashioned suit, a keeper of equally old-fashioned temple secrets which nobody even thought about any more.

On the other hand, Marshall could see that Fields was delighted. Before him was displayed pure folklore in creation. Here was what Fields called the definitive grey-scale multinational animal, grazing on advertisement pasture of the very highest quality. Fields pointed out to Marshall an Italian Pretender, a descendant of Napoleon III, and lo and behold, even a Internationally Famous Face of Rock. Also present were one or two very odd characters who seemed to have appeared from nowhere. Marshall himself had occasionally come across a few of these men and women whose faces were known, but who appeared to have no personal history, security files, or identity papers. Fields, to the everlasting amusement of all in Tower House, named such completely traceless creatures BUACs, meaning Bits of Unadulterated Advertisement Concentrate. In his experience of only one or two of such folk in twenty-five years, Marshall found that trying to discover their history and obscure purposes was like trying to meet a person who was at the opposite end of a quantum-jump. BUACs simply did not have a before-and-after.

The Internationally Famous Face, obviously a blushing admirer of Fields, tried to strike up a conversation with him, but he did not get very far. Fields very politely disengaged the young Paddington ex-bricklayer after a few minutes, to plunge into a long and energetic conversation with an walleyed Hapsburg scion about the last days of the exiled Kaiser at Dorn. Marshall knew that it wasn't snobbishness, so much as Fields having a low boredom threshold. This, he thought, did not augur well for a future Entertainment Prophet. This incident caused a curious image of Fields to arise in his mind. He imagined him as a man who designed a digital TV-set from the ground up, set up a perfect test-card, then switched it off, and left it to gather dust in the garden-shed forever and a day. He was a bloody Athenian, was the Bunter, thought Marshall. After the thinking feast was over, with as much ease as tossing buns to monkeys, actual boring *constructs* could be thrown to the slaves to play with.

Marshall now found himself cornered by a very different animal to any Athenian. The florid features of the well-tailored and magnificently poised John Carlton, now hovered over him. A Junior Minister of Transport whom he had met several times, Marshall knew that John Carlton was notorious for assuming that confidences and loyalties were swapped and changed as easily as pressing a television remote. For some time, horse's mouths had whispered to Marshall that the *nemesis* of John Carlton's world, the Serious Fraud Office, was near, and about to strike. Coming to a grey-scale light were fraudulent logging and cement contracts in Rumania, Poland, and suspicious banking projects in the Far East. Too many loans had also been incurred trying to prop up a range of highly-wrought images. Yet this great blinded puppet of a man, a blown-up town-solicitor tragically out of his depth, still decorated his intentions upon Marshall by chatting of the swamp-fringes of the Great Suburbanite Facts Culture. Everlasting stuff poured out on mortgages, interest rates, holidays, clothing, and car-repairs; John Carlton lived in a whole continuum of consuming, buying, and owning. Marshall wondered whatever 'owning' meant in the Minister's fast-track world, where property, career and even life could be snatched away within the proverbial twenty-four hours it took the Post Office to deliver a registered letter from Chancery Lane.

Dropping Marshall as soon as he had picked him up, Minister Carlton was soon in much deep converse with Dr. David Barton. Now there was a meeting of like minds indeed, thought Marshall. Wherever there was any congruence of almost-hidden spider-webs, the almost-charming Barton was sure to be. Like the recently murdered Dr. Holt, Barton was a renegade biochemist of some brilliance, but he had been cast out of the BMA for gross malpractice. Barton, like the dead Dr. Holt again, represented one of the more sinister aspects of the strangely hybrid animal which was now international technological intrigue. Marshall answered Dr. Barton's blandishments with a curt nod, but the usually affable Fields refused even to speak to him.

Like Minister Carlton, Barton was trouble. Marshall knew that he now worked in a very private clinic not a dozen miles from Goethe's Weimar, a place supported by the whims of curious Hun millionaires. Everyone knew that here the disgustingly handsome Barton practised illegal genetic experiments on human embryos; far fewer knew that he also carried the experiments somewhat beyond the embryo stage. As with quite a few German medical matters during the course of the century, a description of both Barton's successes and failures could not possibly be committed to print.

Some of the many young women present, although almost all of extraordinarily high intelligence, made no attempt to distance the winsome Dr. Barton, who oozed charm over an almost fainting circle of international female admirers. Everybody knew what he did, yet everybody used him, for one purpose or another. As with Holt, Marshall was on occasion a rather shamefaced occasional user of Barton himself. He supposed that one day, like Holt, and many of a similar kind, Barton would disappear suddenly and forever. It would be anybody's guess whether all that remained of him was a slightly discoloured patch on the concrete stanchion of a new Prague flyover, or whether a stream of girls visiting a Taiwan villa led to a man with a different face and a different life.

But it was Mademoiselle Carole Arnoux who was to put all these rare birds to shame, and become the star of the conference. Like Fields, she was a fellow-travelling academic, and a well-known contributor to many respected centre-right newspapers and magazines. What was less well-known was that she was a specialist in Intelligence penetration of media, news, and current affairs. She made Fields' day by choosing for the popular Impromptu Lecture, the theme of *StarPower*. The author himself felt complemented; this was the very first time something called a Fieldsian System had been properly discussed at a semiofficial gathering of this kind.

Fields may have been pleased, but Marshall was wary. He suspected an irony. How Fields would survive an end-of-term leg-pull in front of this kind of audience, he did not know. Five years ago, the Impromptu Lecture had been on alien abductions. This was something which to

Marshall's mind at that time, was more absurd than any suggestion that German troops would one day once more drive through the Arc de Triomphe.

That particular impossibility, to his mind more outrageous an idea than a Fields BUAC, or even an alien abduction, he had witnessed that very morning. At breakfast in the Plaza-Athénée, forced by doctor's orders to nibble only a sugarless *croissant*, Marshall took a stroll and left Fields to vanish *consommé froid, toast de crevettes à la Rothschild, gratin de fruits de mer,* and *salade Niçoise.* To Marshall's utter astonishment, a long column of *Bundeswehr* 8-wheeled *Spähpanzer* armoured troop-carriers passed before his astonished eyes; they were on their way to the Place de la Concorde as a demonstration of European unification. He now suspected that there were many more such cosmic impossibilities parading in front of him at the Joint Security Conference. He vowed however, that if German armour ever passed through Admiralty Arch, he would throw a bottle of HP sauce at the first *panzer*, in the name of the guardian-gods of Britannia, or what was left of them.

To not a few bemused ears, Mlle. Arnoux opened her address by saying that the colour-magazines of major newspapers alone now served to show that a wide sector of the Western World's industrial efforts were now dedicated to a new main product: Entertainment Waste. This, said Mlle. Arnoux, strongly suggested that management, production, design, development, and expansion of Trash Culture would gradually succeed the main streams of industrial activity. Fields noted once more that his very phrases were proliferating; families of his scattered part-ideas were forming, breeding networks of dialectical resonance. The Fieldsian term 'Trash Culture' according to Carole Arnoux, now had dozens of curious translations, particular with regard to soaps, series, and game-shows. From the Far East she had gathered *garbage-make, camp-game*, and *bin-play;* from Russia came the harsh term *reject-construct,* whilst America contributed the hardly politically-correct term, *non-cerebral systems.*

The strident speaker then declared that a 'Fieldsian Philosophy of Entertainment' described what was probably the most interesting anthropological advance since salt-surf basking things hopped and popped and gurgled and splashed from salt shallows to the mysterious green depths beyond the mental shoreline. Such an idea as a Fieldsian Entertainment System was far more significant, she continued, than ideas such as Morphic Resonance or the Anthropic Cosmological Principle. Fields was delighted to see the audience give a smiling approval. A somewhat relieved Marshall supposed that after an extremely boring afternoon discussing sophisticated techniques of creating and managing 'legitimate' fronts of polling agencies, and phony joint-stock investment corporations, such light relief was most welcome. Carole then reduced the audience to ripples of delight by demonstrating what she understood was meant by Fieldsian 'Entertainment'. Blushing quotations from celebrated and extremely unfunny scientific books followed, two of which Fields liked in particular:

"Opinions differ as to what happened in the first 10^{-30} seconds of Creation..."

"Gell-Mann's conviction is that it is indeed possible to know it all...science will be able to explain absolutely everything, in a single coherent picture of how the universe works."

This sort of thing, and much else like it, said Mlle. Arnoux, led her to understand what the word 'trash' meant in a Fieldsian context. Trash didn't mean 'terrible' or 'rotten' so much as a something, which, as distinct from traditional industrial directions, was quite without the industrial analogue of spatio-temporal *purpose*.

Though the event had not turned out to be some embarrassing joke, Marshall now had very mixed feelings. That this inspiring French woman was obviously quite serious, was much more frightening than the prospect of a deeply embarrassed Fields. Marshall could see that the man himself was fascinated; he leaned over to him and whispered.

"It's alright, Hieronymus. She isn't a BUAC. I've got her address if you want it."

But the popeyed Fields did not reply. As if her own metaphors were now lodged within him, Carole Arnoux became one of the exotic new creatures emerging after a glacial age; her ideas were crawling up off the North European beach which seethed with intriguing possibilities of a new ideo-Darwinism. Seen against huge portraits of Clemenceau, De Gaulle, Lafayette, and General Leclerc, the vibrant young Frenchwoman giving forth from the lectern had a beauty which made both Fields and Marshall quite catch their breath. She forced the audience to focus on intense inner developments within a tribal mind, and the atmosphere was as intense as at any witch-doctor's meet. Mental interiors were restless, disturbed; a Paris April. was coming, and Big Brother Communism had died like a season. As yet, no-one knew quite what kind of world this flame-haired pale-skinned Gallic Amazon would help bring about.

She now spoke of developing fields of major research whose investors were beginning to catch Fieldsian straws in the wind. Desperate for survival, and ever-anxious for new gaming roles, the creators of a wide range of advanced technologies were already hinting that it might be possible to join a prototype Fieldsian System in a kind of blushing alliance. Already for nearly two decades, many defence chips had been identical with games chips.

Fields was in ecstasy. Philosophy in action raised its awe-inspiring head at the magical form of the vibrant speaker. The ancient walls of the stateroom, with its portraits of Louis-Phillipe, Emile Zola, and Victor Hugo, gave back Mlle. Arnoux's voice like an old barricade-ricochet from 1793, echoing through the nineteenth century. He felt his native country had never been like this. The audience was also visibly stirred. Since the four-hundred men and women here represented some of the most sophisticated and conservative interests in Europe, Fields' mind reeled at the thought of what Mlle. Arnoux could do with more susceptible folk. Since she was a world-renowned media-penetration expert, it wouldn't take many of those present long to calculate when her private opinions and her professional activity would become as one, if they were not that already.

The astonishing vision took a sip of water, gripped her lectern as if she were changing a car-wheel, and continued.

As evolutionary animals, great national corporate investments were becoming ever-alert for the next stage of what Carole called the great Fieldsian Performance Game. This meant to her that they were getting ready to sanction vast joke-creatures, abandoning responsible scientific detachment and objectivity, for the new disciplines demanded by the support base of what some Fieldsians now called the Junk Nirvana.

Amidst approving laughter, Fields relished this phrase as the astonishing woman continued. She became to him the magical imp on the July Column which through the window, rose up to salute the vapour-trails of *Luftwaffe* F16s exercising with *Mirage* 2000 fighters of *Armée de l'Air*. Over Saint-Gervais, and the Luxembourg, over the dome of the Tuileries, fled the mystical guardians, travelling east, as if fleeing the coming night of the hemisphere.

The roar of the aircraft died away, and the audience now heard of expensive weapons and space-technologies whose maintenance alone kept nations perpetually on the verge of bankruptcy. These elephantine structures were collapsing; recently, a conference in Brussels designed to raise international interest in building a huge space-station to 'manufacture medical drugs' had failed to arouse interest and had closed its doors. Sixth-form toys-for-the-boys science was on its last gasp.

Fields glimpsed the last of the fast-fading vapour trails beyond one of the tall windows, and was amazed at a new strain of slight bitterness in the voice coming from the lectern. He didn't think things had got this far. He began to realise that his ideas were only part of an unfolding pattern of energies which almost amounted to a rallying-cry throughout the planet as the speaker concluded. At this point, Mlle. Arnoux's fast and often spectacular French momentarily defeated Fields; but he had a thoughtfully-provided translation in front of him. He glimpsed down through his *pince-nez*. It read like a clarion-call. The particle physicists had disappeared up their own abstract backsides after the Bomb, declared Mlle. Arnoux; nuclear power had failed, psychiatry was utterly disgraced; now, the geneticists were having a go at trying to dominate the Main Feature, with the gods-only knew what horrors to come. For all its claims of superiority, all science had produced was the intellectual pollution of animal (and not a little human) experimentation.

Turned heads now stopped Fields rustling his paper, and he listened to the final words of Mlle. Arnoux. How long, she asked, was this fraudulent stage-show called science to go on producing its 'closer and closer' approximations to an 'absolute and disinterested' truth? How long was the *'déception rationale'*, the con-trick of *objectivism* to be practiced?

Thinking that these last ideas were delightfully French, Fields was indeed a little envious of such inspirations, coming himself from the only great nation which did not have a revolutionary constitution. As she concluded to energetic applause, Fields massive and weighty thighs were stirred, and he knew he would remember both the voice and the breasts of Mlle. Arnoux as well as her other inspirations.

Boarding the return flight with Marshall, Fields became momentarily depressed at the thought of returning to a country whose native food was universally regarded as being only fit for prisons, schools, and lunatic asylums. Whilst seeing two countries at once over a Channel scored with grey-scale light, like a Fields BUAC, Marshall let Fields' conversation put away from him for a while all thoughts of high-finance brokerage of illicit laboratories in Mexico and the United States. Marshall, like many others, used Fields as a kind of fix. He let what he called his 'mad talk' flow over him as a kind of mental balm. Fields liked this; it was the easy way in. Since most people thought that when Fields wasn't talking professionally, he talked delightful silly-assery, their defences were down, and a network of complex deep suggestions was powerfully injected, just like one of Dana Chong's doped defence chips.

Though he was beginning to see *StarPower* and its influences and origins more clearly, Marshall was always wary of Fields. He wasn't awed by a far-ranging vision, a superior education, and a mind which was his intellectual better, he was conscious of a street-fighting ability buried in all the gorging-display which equalled his own salesman's instincts. In one man this was a formidable and possibly dangerous combination. To make matters worse, Marshall never knew what his propaganda expert was really thinking. As a working pair, they were both top professionals in disinformation, constructing the most cunning

44

and elaborate falsehoods conceivable. When he asked himself therefore to judge a quite separate product of his partner, Marshall found himself in the somewhat disturbing position of not believing a single word of any of it in the first place.

Listening now to Fields, he guessed that he was up to something of which *StarPower* was merely a part.

"You see Harry, the trouble is conventional machines are linked essentially to analogues of purpose. Even the genius Turing's definition of a machine had the shadow of the nineteenth century upon it. As bundles of related parts of structured intellect, machines are designed to do work, solve problems against a background of a meaningful continuum of moral and cultural progress."

"What's wrong with that? What are you trying to tell me?"

"I am saying that the problems of human aggression and annihilating violence and evil in the machine-age could be avoided. What I call Star Structures could be built, because in them, sequences of analogue Questions and Answers, the programmed ability to solve problems, these machine-like things, are avoided simply because to a Star System they do not mean anything. Within such systems, Significances could be artificially manufactured, like soya. We have no need to be ashamed of such thoughts. In any case, History and Nature manufacture these things independently for group-control, like Communism, Scientology, Punk, or even the London Marathon."

"Freddy Starr ate my gardener. So popular culture is rubbish, and Entertainers are brainless. Tell me something new."

"If they are brainless, that is precisely the point I wish to make."

"You want leaders with no brains? We've got them already."

"Forget about leaders. Forget about brains."

"Well what should I remember?"

"Personalities."

"Personalities? Haven't we got enough of those damn things already?"

"Put it this way, Harry. In the old machine world with authority, purpose, painters covered canvases, and writers wrote books."

"Shouldn't that be so?"

"I am not concerned so much as whether it should be so or not, so much as noting that recently an internationally famous catwalk model, Sharon, was commissioned to write a novel."

"Why shouldn't she?"

"I am not concerned with whether she should or should not, so much as she didn't particularly want to do such a thing."

"How do you know that?"

"Because she said so."

"Alas, talent will out."

"In this case it didn't."

'Someone wrote it for her?"

"Of course."

"Did they have talent?"

"No."

"So what? When you were prancing around in an outsize-animal skin, you probably used the best-looking women to advertise the most comfortable cave-mouths. What, in the name of some approximation to sanity, Hieronymus, does this commercial tale of yours mean?"

"It means that there is a new category abroad in the world."

"What's that?"

"Fronting a novel. Not writing it. Fronting it."

"I don't care. Bless the girl. Good luck to her. I hope she makes lots of money. You're behind the times, Fields. Tell me, what do you read?"

For a second, Fields looked amazed. Marshall was pleased.

"Recently? -Er- well, I was reading about nuclear activators in a special memorandum."

Marshall waved his finger in the air.

"Fiction, please."

Another bad moment. The modern fiction on Fields' shelves was almost all American. He loved Mailer, and Tom Wolf, but what British fiction he came across seemed to him to be written by quaint pre-technological brains who liked such things as cat-detectives and quilt-conventions. As a call-to-arms, he thought the latter in particular was less than awesome. To Fields, this effete and high-camp wonderland was sleep, and sadly, Thinking and the Age appeared to have long since woken up and gone elsewhere. Reluctantly, he had to admit however, that he liked the way most women commercial authors said 'gorn orf'. Some around him had ventured to suggest that these views were unusual for someone as interested in Entertainment as he. His usual reply to that was a sharp reminder that electricity had been discovered quite some time ago.

"Not much."

Marshall rejoiced. It wasn't often he caught Fields out with a almost blushing confession of ignorance.

"I thought so. Cheer up, Hieronymus, Sharon's novel can't be as bad as the novels of breakfast-TV presenters."

Fields eyes widened with astonishment.

"They have TV at breakfast?"

"Listen: you'd better get yourself updated. They're writing schlock-

46

novels now about Diana and Hewett, and even novels based on television coffee-advertisements. But come now, it is no use getting worked up about this mass-industrialisation of British silliness. Our modern arts and farts have always been largely camp and kitsch, but just look what all that seriousness did for the Hun, what?"

"Quality is completely beside the point. In Sharon's case, a new order of nature has been created, and indeed accepted almost without qualm. A new idea is abroad. Personality as a total and complete arbiter. Not quality, skill, specialisation, but expanded Entertainment Concentrate."

"What?"

"Sharon is a bit of emerging high-nutrition Trasg-Protein which could construct a perfectly possible world in which relative technical quality is meaningless. That SHE did it is all that matters."

"What does all that mean?"

"Well it means that I could write to Bing Crosby and ask him to become author of my next book."

"Bing Crosby, bless him, died many years ago."

Another almost-blush.

"Did he? Well, say Sir Lawrence Olivier, then."

"He too, is long dead."

This time, a definite blush.

"Well It doesn't matter, Sharon is *supposed* to have written her book. A nice logical conundrum, that, you must agree. And you are *supposed* to believe that she wrote it. The fact that somebody else did is irrelevant. You are supposed to accept the illusion."

"What does that mean?"

"It means that the entire apparatus of explanatory causation could and probably is being replaced. Fact is irrelevant. You see the world through Sharon. For a moment, she has become the world."

These were the moments Marshall enjoyed. Fields was about to become excited.

"I tell you: this is the edge of your real new world, Harry. Hard workers, good thinkers, skilled writers, brainy folk, they are steam-age icons of old iron-age meritocracies. Not pressure, weight mass, acceleration, talent, but Sharon did it. Don't bother about objective Worth. Sharon's good to look at. Writers never are. They're difficult to package. They look at their feet and scratch their nose. And the ones with toothpaste smiles and good PR are no good anyway. Trust Sharon. Sharon is Pure Personality."

"Sounds like re-packaged Maoist communism to me."

"People like her are going to achieve more than Mao."

"She's certainly a lot better-looking."

47

"I tell you Harry, she's written part of the first chapter."

"Of what?"

"An Entertainment Book of the Dead"

"Stone the crows"

"Death and Life are to become a journey through the being of Sharon. Or Elvis. Or Presley. Or Lennon. Just you watch, Harry. Sharon will breed. So will her family. Eventually they will hold the bridges together, make the aeroplane engines work, until eventually maybe you don't need great solid macrocosmic things like aeroplane engines, bridges, or even authors. I tell you this is the new *mysterium conjunctionis!*"

"The what?"

"This is the birth of consumer-mysticism proper. Aren't you excited?"

"I am an Englishman. I do not like excitement, definite points-of view, and even less mysteries. Still less over-intellectualised nonsense. Tell me Hieronymus, do you ever talk about golf, or what is going to win the two-thirty at Aintree?"

"You must listen. Sharon and her kind are going to lead us straight through the advertisement. She and her kind are the new leaders."

"Straight through the what?"

"You see the advertisement is the ultimate looking-glass."

"The ultimate what? Hieronymus, as usual, I'm afraid you've lost me again. This is cult stuff. I am not interested. Not my department."

"This is more than a cult. This is a new culture."

"A culture of what?"

"Advertisements. This is the first such thing in human history. Aren't you excited?"

Mental excitement of any kind was obviously not Marshall's strong point, and he gave Fields an old-fashioned look and turned to his *Daily Express*, where there was sure to be no such animal. But to his great surprise, Marshall felt the beginnings of almost an erotic thrill as he savoured Fields' ideas. For a moment he felt almost young again. For strange ideas to penetrate such complete instincts as his was a formidable achievement. Marshall was a hard man. His enemies, most of whom had never been hungry in a reluctant *Cortina* on the outskirts of Middlesbrough with two-and-sixpence-halfpenny in their pockets late on a hard winter Friday, and with several crates of unsold 'shopworn' *Doris Day Birthday Goblets* to go, such men did not stand a chance against Marshall as far as double-take mental manoeuvres were concerned. The old Russian enemy, who thought salesmen last existed on the pages of Gogol, had suffered in particular with this esoteric management of part of British Intelligence based on the efficient organisation of trash-sales.

His eyebrows flew up when he came across an article in his newspaper which could almost have been written by Fields. At the University of St. Andrews, Phillip Bunson, a research psychologist, used computerised ASS (Advanced Scanning Synthesis) to show in graphic stages how each of Elizabeth Taylor's eight husbands really had an identical face to hers. Professor Victor Johnson, a psychologist at New Mexico State University used massive funds to create the characteristics of what he termed the 'ultimate beautiful face'. Considering the billions of sample-simulations, the result was unremarkable. Considering the state of Mexico, thought Marshall, this example of modern applied science was the most decadent he had yet come across. Marshall was both amused and inspired.

Taking the advantage of Marshall's obvious interest in the article, Fields continued his assault.

"You see those people you are reading about are building the new world, Harry. The Pure Performance Machine of any future Entertainment State would be the first real Artificial Intelligence. It would produce what I call Belief-Stuff, which could be woven into the texture of mass experience. The *prima materia* of Entertainment can be manufactured like soya-substitute. The mental level of TV soap-operas is already manufactured by a kind of molecular process equivalent to genetic engineering, and it can be subliminally sprinkled with enough Good-Cause Entertainment Additives sufficient to frighten the horses in the street."

"I don't like good causes."

"Well we're going to get them. Millions of them. The clowns are coming with baskets full."

"Is this the end?"

Fields paused in mid-bite as the aircraft hit some turbulence, and sent a bag of his sausage-rolls to the floor, much to the annoyance of a stewardess.

"Is this the what?"

Came from the floor as Fields tried to clean up. Marshall liked speaking down to Fields as he struggled at his feet with a pan and brush brought by the stewardess.

"Perhaps, Hieronymus, the thick books and the complicated questions are the wrong approach to history. Perhaps it wasn't the Vandals and Goths that gave us the Dark Ages. Perhaps some time a late Roman catwalk model was almost forced to write a silly tract, and it was all over. Civilisation could pack up and take to the hills. The butterfly's wing changing massive weather systems, and all that."

Fields stopped his sweeping and looked up.

"This isn't the end."

"Are you sure?

"This is the beginning."

"Always remember that the cleverest solution Hieronymus, is not always the best one."

At this, Fields dropped his pan of crumbs, the stewardess despaired, Marshall sighed, and Fields decided to finish his food in the lavatory.

During the noisy helicopter flight back to Tower House from RAF Lynham, Marshall resolved to take a closer look at this Entertainment business. For a moment, looking at Docklands below, he began to see the world through Fields' eyes. New skyscraper blocks stretched to the City, and a good proportion of these buildings were dedicated to leisure, arts, media, satellite-television, and new-technology communication systems of many different kinds. Their aerials, clearly seen on the tops of the towers, were radiating anything but analogue intelligence. They were pulsing pure image-stuff. Marshall thought he knew an operation when he saw one, but somehow he had missed this. It had risen all around him like a set of mysterious plant stamens in the night, a kind of junk-fungus.

The only good thing appeared to be that although almost all of it was conveying pure mental rubbish, it confounded the darker prophecies for mankind. Perhaps Fields was right. Populations didn't run from this spreading ectoplasm which didn't torture, burn, and kill. They sucked on it like an increasing part of the population sucked on the drugs brought in each night along the Thames now below them, and through the airports. Marshall had one terrifying thought that out beyond the rim of the city's fine buildings, rational intelligence was just beginning to falter. Schools were suffering forced closures, and to walk down any street in Britain with a *Rolex* on a bare wrist was to invite death or injury. To Marshall's mind, there had to be a way of controlling countless millions who eventually would be hardly able to read or write, never mind think in coherent terms. Perhaps what was forming in the costly buildings below the machine he was travelling in was the easiest and the humanitarian way.

Marshall shook his head and cursed Fields. He thought his own last leaps had been taken and he was ready for his boat-building on the river and a sunset cottage on his Dorset farm with his beloved wife, Mary. But here was this absurd 25-stone monster still at his side, now spouting obscure Latin texts mixed with Eddie Cochrane lyrics at the same time. It was too much. Fields strained Marshall's fragile education, exhausted his relatively undeveloped intellect, and in the bargain extended his imagination into almost laughable realms. Marshall didn't think at

50

fifty-five that he was ready for yet another new world. But he was far too intelligent to deny that he was deeply envious. Fields was uniquely multi-mode. Like one liquid being poured onto another, to Fields, reality and experience were both equally and utterly fantastic, even in their most prosaic forms. The Bunter never used the words *unreal* or *absurd;* not even *untrue,* or *factual.* Somehow, he had out-gamed the troubles that necessarily followed the concepts and confusions behind these words.

He was reluctant to admit it, but Marshall was pleased that someone had caused him to find something inside himself which wasn't dead yet; it was a something which pricked up its ears at the sound of Fields' curious phrases and ideas, like, he supposed, a first hearing of jazz, or rock n' roll. Certainly a whole geography within Marshall had heard the call of the Bunter, and for the first time in many years for Marshall, the world had no limit again. He was again hanging around at the back of the cricket pavilion waiting for the lovely June Besswick; assaults on the great infinite were possible again in some new quickening April of the world. Quick now, jump into the gap, said an imp in Marshall, jump before the darkness closes again, and complicated and ruinous games once more slaughter love, innocence, and cults of seriousness poison the sources of wonder. He cursed the Bunter yet again. Just when everybody was ready for a sleep of virtual certainties, the Fields bug started to move furniture around in everyone's head. And the bits and pieces could never be put back, indeed did not even fit any more. The Fields effect did something to the size and scale of the pieces themselves, and classical physics no longer applied.

Fields was the most dangerous of men. He could inspire. There are no men more subversive. But though cosmic inspirations had a chequered history, like love, they were almost always irresistible. Marshall shuddered. He was being slowly but surely reprogrammed just like the impressive dish-strewn crystal-structures he had just seen from the air. He supposed he should have been pleased. Others around him, though far younger, had long since slipped into the historical dark. They had been in complete control of their destiny. And destiny never likes being controlled.

'Through the advertisement' indeed. It was the most blatant piece of meaningless verbiage Marshall had ever heard. But despite its comic pretentiousness, and its wilful obscurity, it gave a part of his brain an itch like the well-known effect of pornography. Reject it as he may, its vital kernel contained a call to arms. Fields worked with the imagination. He could disinter a long-buried urge to know which might lead back to an old long-deserted address; here, there might be letters lying unopened on the dust-furred hall tables of the brain. There might be codes, missions, orders, journeys; he imparted a sense of all human beings as spies under deep cover. For some so inspired, the drab days parted only at a certain hour, when they had to do certain things before the grey suds of dross and strain closed over their techno-industrial heads again. This was the shining hour of deliverance to the believer. This was the time when the angels sang, and even earthworms rejoiced. Perhaps Fields was an anarchist at heart, thought Marshall, as the man at his side munched once more on generous amounts of French pastry, washed down with a can of his eternal *Umbongo*.

Marshall took a sideways glance at his colleague, now unwrapping a huge porkpie he had taken from a greasy bag. The man did not look like a source of inspiration. But those taking in his appeal felt that a blow had been struck, a genuine act of complete defiance had been made. Fields made something happen within the bedrock of perception that had a function far beyond the simple-minded heroics of the disgraced liberal purpose and fallen democratic ideas about roads, railways, good behaviour, and sound citizenship. But when Fields therefore appeared to be offering a practical plan for a new society, Marshall knew he could be sure that it was anything but that.

Tower House roof loomed up to take the helicopter. As they ran from the down-draught, Marshall was horrified to see Fields throw his waste food bags and chewed remnants into the airstream, where they whirled over the Thames, pursued by gulls who scrambled like jets from the roofs of Westminster. A big gull caught an empty bag, dropped it in disgust, swerved, and neatly scooped a bit of pie crust just before it hit the water.

Watching Fields laugh at this, as a salesman of old, it was then that Marshall knew. The fat clever vandal was trying to flog everybody something. Watching the coloured bags drift towards the city, Marshall still didn't quite know what it was. But he was not in a senior position within the Security Services for nothing.

He was beginning to form the eerie idea that the very last thing Fields was interested in was Entertainment.

VI

Dansette Days

Inspired by the Paris meeting, Fields went into full gear throughout February, filling his Dansette Den with increasingly receptive ears. Those who arrived for informal chatter in off-duty hours were both puzzled and worried regarding their personal and professional future. Many plans which had been the very heart and gospel of their lives had been shelved, and many viewed with dismay the camp-bed propped against the wall, and baked beans bubbling on his ancient primus. Perhaps this might be their lot if an envelope arrived at the end of the year, and they had to go looking again at window-cards in Ealing. To many therefore, Fields' ideas were beginning to be an intriguing and amusing balm in a professionally depressed situation. In canteens and luncheon-breaks, and even behind the sealed windows and debugged rooms of the conference chambers of the powerful, *StarPower* was used for much light relief during a period of intense gloom. The book was passed around by Tower House personnel as a kind of humorous intellectual pornography; it did not take long before the book was seen not just as another paranoid Great Paper Plan for humanity which would finish up inevitably with ditches full of corpses. Many came to see Fields' ideas as suggesting the possible construction and development of a quite original social structure; this, some pointed out, had in any case, been steadily building for two generations before *StarPower* was written.

Most were in awe of Fields' cerebral pyrotechnics, his phenomenal success on operations, his belt-size, appetite, and his old-fashioned patrician address. A few, however, regarded him as a giant Mr. Toad of Toad Hall, to be kept well chained down to earthly realms. There were even those who dared to compete, such as twenty-five-year-old Alan 'Cheeky' Benson, the young computer-genius of Tower House. Benson was renowned for his drainpipe-trousers, oiled *quiff*, and drape-jacket. He was also known for referring to Fields (out of his presence) as 'she'.

This evening, putting his head through the famous curtains like a pantomime sprite, Benson's character could be judged by his nervous attempt to give Fields a condescending look.

"Still cave-painting by numbers, are we, dear?"

"You can't cave-paint by numbers, Benson. They didn't have

numbers in those days."

Even smart-cards like Benson had to be careful if they wanted to swap lines with Fields, who now went on the attack.

"No, Benson: how real is ten to the hundredth power?"

"How *real* is it?"

"Put it this way, Benson. I think we're all the sperm of some cosmic Max Clifford, who is supplier of bimbo-ideas to the elite. Glamorise the apparatus. Create intellectual pornography. Make the accelerators bigger, the immensities more immense, the little things more little. In science, as in advertising, we must insist on accuracy. In my doorstep bag are some samples. How do you like your turn-on? Would you like *The First Three Minutes of the Universe* by Stephen Weinberg? Or, would you like what shall we say, something a little more risqué, sir? Well, how about this little hard-core number from under the counter: James Trefil's *Big Bang Physics from Before the First Millisecond to the Present Universe?* No? Sorry, can't go beyond the first millisecond, sir, we don't do anything involving children or animals. But wait a minute, sir. Don't go just yet. Something right up your street has just arrived."

Fields held aloft a notorious *Little, Brown &Co.* volume, and read aloud.

"'By a ten-billionth of a trillionth of a second inflation had expanded the universe (at an accelerating rate) a million trillion times and the temperature had fallen to below a billion billion billion degrees...' You like that sir? Enjoy your orgasm! Makes the Green Humanoid of Bradford I sold you last week look positively respectable, what? Tonight it is Science as show-business, folks! Roll up, roll up, for the Intellectual Wet Tee-Shirt Competition! The bigger the concept, the bigger the take, and a little bit of correlation goes a long way. Facts? I don't think they're worth an M.O.D. statement of non-culpability, what do you think, Benson?"

"I think facts are better than your Entertainment."

"Why?"

"All you'll get with that is mass oink-culture."

Annie, forced to lean uncomfortably leaning against Fields' tiny sink, snapped at Benson.

"That's what we've got already."

Benson snapped back.

"That's right, Annie. And thousands of powder-puffs waving their wrists about."

Fields rallied quickly.

"Call them Peter Pans. Just people who hate equations, don't know what a transistor is, and can't concentrate longer than a washing-powder advertisement."

"Peter Pans? You want to base a society on them?"

"Nothing would work without Peter Pans, Benson."

"You mean people who never grew up?"

"Yes, I suppose so. If you want to put it that way."

"People like you?"

Fields looked Benson up and down, from his oiled quiff to his winkle-pickers, via his flowered waistcoat, bootlace tie, and velvet-collared jacket.

"You're not doing so bad yourself, Benson."

Benson blushed. The company groaned. Annie saved the situation.

"What wouldn't work without people like yourself and Benson, Fields?"

"Image-making. Carving things of air."

"I'd rather have a bucket of bran-mash myself."

"Don't you ever imagine?"

"What's the imagination got to do with anything?"

"It's better than your ever-increasing accuracies. They're as phoney as silicon boobs. Like proper tits, innacuracies are much more interesting.

"Fields, I tell you the few Entertainment folk I've ever met were prime candidates for industrial retraining, you know that?"

Annie's voice now made Benson look as if he were facing a pack of hounds.

"What industry?"

Fields took up the hue and cry.

"Industrial retraining? For *them?* Do you want to poison, drown, and electrocute us all, Benson?"

"And what about the cost of all this, then?"

"Cost? Are you from the lower-middle-class, Benson?"

"People want value for money."

"Thank you for answering my question."

"Don't mention it."

Looking at his watch, Benson touched his *quiff* nervously, and slid towards the gap in the curtains like a cornered stoat, giving Fields a last baleful glance.

"Will that be all, Ron?"

Admiring Benson's courage, Annie thought to herself that if taxpayers could hear such exchanges, they might even be pleased. In popular novels, the image of Security Services personnel was largely of humourless and paranoid-grey public-school bureaucrats, devoid of all eccentricity and larger-than-life human features.

The conversation ended with Benson scuttling off, almost triumphant at his cheek, and Fields in a definite huff.

He had never been called Ron before in his life.

55

Apart from a few doubters such as Benson, to most men and women dedicated to unravelling endless layers of complex deception, Fields' illustrative performances began to sound reasonable enough. Often despite themselves, many good minds starting running his ideas as dummy programs in their heads, if only at first for fun and relaxation. The fine honed edge of a singular and very specialised machine hence slowly began to turn its aerial-like head towards the idea that here were things worth more than Benson's bucket of bran-mash.

Fields eventually captivated even the hard cases. The man himself, plentifully supplied with *ersatz,* continued preaching the doctrine that if even the great adventure of Reason had now begun to falter, if the universe was pure Zsa-Zsa Gabor, if all was therefore vanity, then what was needed was not a vanity-bonfire (humanity had enough of those), but vanity-management as a basis for a new society. He would set the Dansette Den a-rocking by claiming that whatever Nature did, the final product was Elizabeth Taylor, or some optional equivalent of Pure Advertising Concentrate. All control group sets in the limit became this good woman, or her associated group. All royal courts, and not a few laboratories, were her, or something like her. He theorised about a possible a pure Elizabeth Taylor Substance (or ETS), which was immortal, indestructible, the axle-tree of Universal Time. Fallen systems of science and socialism had tried to destroy this substance, only to come up with pure blushing Elizabeth Taylors themselves, such as the complete disaster of Nuclear Power, or the fellow-travelling and equally catastrophic Great Socialist Industrial Plans of the past hundred years.

By lucky chance, Fields had become one of the firm favourites of the Directrix herself, through almost making her smile. As her resident propagandist, at a boring reception for European industrialists, he described to her a possible physics experiment, to detect the said ET substance. This supposed material, would of course, be located only at enormous astronomical distances away from Earth, and in infinitesimally small quantities. The experiment would propagandise suitably intimidating technology, and be based on what he called 'credible designer-profundity'. He predicted eventual success, then doubts, then a quiet forgetting of all embarrassment, as with Gravity Waves, Black Holes, Anti-Matter, and Super-Dense White Dwarves.

But for once Fields was upstaged. The Directrix, looking him straight in the eye, suggested, of all things, that such a 'trash' situation as he described was trying to *outsell* the so-called 'real' situation. Fields gulped when she suggested that he try thinking of interfacing the two and letting them both mimic one another to death.

Even the Directrix had read *StarPower.*

Back in the lower reaches of his Dansette Den, Fields was pleased and surprised. All he could ever get out of the man the Directrix replaced were unprintable stories about old Cairo, and memories of the last polo match between the Bengal Lancers and the 12th Hussars prior to the Mountbattens leaving Durban.

Encouraged by his experience with Her Upstairs, Fields put new energies into proclaiming that the only human system which could succeed the comic accuracies, hilarious certainties, and ludicrous profundities of a tired science was the Entertainment system. At a dinner-party at the Russian Embassy, good minds which had replaced the paving-slabs of a dialectical yesteryear, listened carefully as he described Entertainment as a 'system' which did not have finite objectives to be achieved by the construction of sequential steps; it existed purely in and for itself, and was even complete, as a system. As such a structure, it knew no time in the industrial sense; it was not evolving, knew no struggle, and indeed no death. The response to what happened when boot met banana-skin would survive all technologies, all other systems of revelation and reference. Fields always said that he didn't see the point in staying in a 'catastrophic model' of a universe in which everything ate everything else, the rules being deliberately rigged such that all enjoyable things were in constant short supply.

More memorable nights were experienced in an increasingly crowded Dansette Den, when Benson, now christened the Last Doubter, made yet further appearances.

"But Fields, Entertainment people have no bloody depth."

"Of course not. That is why things are possible within their group. They are fundamentally unstable. Entertainment could not possibly work with any other kind of people. Solidities would never do. All you'd get would be Communist art, or German fun, and we all know what those bad shows did for sixty-million lost audience numbers in one Century alone. Not even Radio 1 could compare with that, Benson."

Benson turned to Annie and Barsby.

"Do you know something: he's frightened me."

Annie smiled, and passed the Bunter a fresh beaker of *ersatz*.

"Why do you use the past tense, Benson?"

"If he's the future, I'd rather be in Canada with our Fred."

Barsby bleeped-up from the back.

"Dr. Fields is the future."

"But does he know the animal he's dealing with, Barsby? His old *pince-nez* fairly gyrates at the sight of any well-endowed female bosom. Not exactly a suitable candidate for a showbiz prophet, know what I mean?"

Since everybody seemed to get this point but himself, Barsby blushed as Benson continued.

"But of course. I am being silly. He doesn't care. It's all just another bit of info-protein to him."

Fields was pleased at hearing one of his own phrases, especially as it was highly probable that Benson didn't know where he had got it from.

"And he'll sell it. That's what he'll do."

Barsby was alert again.

"As a what?"

Benson looked at first confused, then pleased with a sudden thought.

"As a sword."

Annie looked at Fields, who looked at Barsby. Benson stared hard at Fields. He was about to tempt him into a confession.

"Why are you using these people?"

Fields approached the nearest he ever got to a blush.

"Because they are virgins."

"With respect to what?"

"The twentieth century. And the nineteenth, come to that."

"Pre-industrial?"

"Quite. Most do not have a single contemporary analogue in them."

Annie was white as a sheet.

"Have we a right to treat people like bits of historical process on legs?"

Fields blustered.

"Who is hurting them?"

"Well it's a bit bloody behaviouristic, isn't it?"

"An Entertainment culture is the key to the future. Barsby, give Benson the sums."

Barsby leaped at the chance.

"Entertainment has no supply problems; as far as quantity goes, it therefore has no limit. It hardly costs anything compared with weapons and other technological systems; it uses hardly any raw materials, except for the comparatively minimal technology required to keep it going."

Fields soon overrode his acolyte, who looked glum.

"But above all, Benson, people *enjoy* the experience of Entertainment; this is more than can be said for the political and social systems produced by the over-serious and oh-so-clever po-faces of European Intellectual Time."

Benson hit back, desperately trying to straighten his bootlace tie as if it had width.

"But Entertainment has no moral core."

That word again. Annie was the only person in Tower House who was quick enough to sense a Fields hesitation, but this time she sensed something more; the Bunter was about to lose his temper for the first time in his life.

"Moral? Do you think the culture that produced the concentration camps and the atomic bomb and the Comprehensive School, has any right to use the word *moral*, Benson?"

Annie pondered: the culture? The whole lot of us, time present and time past? This thought was broken by Fields almost shouting.

"But now Benson, I bring the Good News."

"You're leaving us to run British Gas?"

"The Good News is that people are beginning to realise that Frank Sinatra has given more pleasure to mankind than Marx, Jesus, or even Miss Whiplash"

Amidst applause, Benson gave the thoughts of all.

"That's not bad. I could almost agree for once. Tell us another."

"The old industrial building-brick universe necessarily implied Brain. Therefore for new paradigms, Brain has to go. The only human system practically without *intellect* is the Entertainment network, in all its newly thriving life and variety. You don't need brains to be a performer; brains would a definite impediment. At the side of these new networks, the cerebral structures of science culture by comparison, have no evolutionary chance. Brain is a temporary phenomenon in Nature. Performance is eternal."

Benson's disturbed-look now returned.

"Eternal?"

"Yes. Style, Benson. That's what Nature is about."

Now Annie looked disturbed.

"But what about facts?"

"How factual is Cher?"

"Who?"

"Now there is an example of the way the world really works, Annie. A true prime cause, compared to rather ludicrous and extremely non-funny particles, the products of equally ludicrous and non-funny people. May I suggest the coat of arms of Entertainment State be a nearly-naked Cher Rampant astride the 16-inch guns of the forward-turret of the battleship *Missouri*, as on her video, *"If I Could Turn Back Time?"*

Fields clinched the point by producing from the floor-debris a picture of Atlas supporting the world on his shoulders, and then a poster of Cher herself, doing what Fields said she did.

"I challenge you not to see that both Cher and Atlas are as mythological as any fundamental particle, and a damn sight better-looking!"

Annie was unusually silent through the remainder of that day, and was later seen by a baffled Barsby in the General Library, looking intently

59

at a large print of old Triton blowing his wreathed horn.

As part of a constantly updated *aide-memoir,* from time to time, Fields and his colleagues were required to view the major events of the recent past. A few days after his Cher and Atlas outburst, Fields and a dozen or more of his staff sat before a screen and watched a new Europe running free, mad, and dangerous. The edits from many sources showed the overheated dreams of fifty years as bursting pods yielding a million windblown seeds of endless possibilities. A bewildering blur of unprecedented historical accelerations burst from the screen as archetypal borders and political philosophies flew apart from all points of the European compass. Dread ghosts flickered into life. The names of countries, institutions and geographies that had not been heard of since Versailles or even the Congress of Vienna, boomed out into the bland room, whose smug modern lines looked nicely frightened to death, or so thought Fields.

Even the overfed and the overprotected were momentarily chilled as the familiar outlines of Russian T62 tanks and BT series armoured personnel carriers of nearly three generations past tried unsuccessfully to stop popular uprisings and assaults in no less than five capital cities simultaneously. There followed many ancient monsters popping out their heads from historical dung-heaps: The Hungarian Christian Peasant's Party with a Nazi past, Croat Folk Dance Societies covered with a similar glory, the whole sprinkled liberally with some *Einsatzgruppen* old-timers in *lederhosen* and crochet smocks. The names of non-German SS divisions rang out into the room: *Prinz Eugen, Handschar-Kroatische, Lettische, Estnische, Galizische,* all with a history of shame and atrocities second to none.

Flicker again, and dole-drawing Tsarist and Prussian aristocrats were dug out of Brixton; handsome chisel-chinned fragments of the lineage of old Franz Joseph of Austria himself, gave interviews in beautifully-cut suits from palaces in Rome and bedsits in Ealing; all such were alive and well according to how fast their great-grandparents had been capable of running over borders in a time when both car and aeroplane had the same starting-handle. Even Stoke-on-Trent's Electricity Board offered up its director, Charles De Renzi, as the long-lost king of Albania.

To all present, Fields was obviously both inspired and hypnotised. Perhaps even the old god-kings might appear again, he commented, though not many of his young colleagues knew the meaning of the observation. Here in the enthralled silence of the half-dark, were images and calls from so many broken borders of Europe, reducing Tower House to a series of complex impostures, fracturing the clocks of the interior, utterly changing a preceding time of the inner and outer unities of a shattered collective oppression.

Later that day, Annie was passing by the closed curtains of the Dansette Den when she heard a sound she had not heard before. Viennese waltzes, mixed with the disturbing sound of Fields weeping. She told no-one, and kept all and sundry away from the place for the rest of the day.

These incidents took place in a busy month. Fields was in charge of organising various disinformation systems, analysing the media policies of friendly nations, and even carrying out *official* work on Investment in Entertainment Technology. When he found the time, he continued to perform and preach to callow youths with double-firsts in Greats, who often saved the beans from being burnt on the primus. Occasionally one or two visiting craggy SAS from the 'sharp end' would rush to the overflowing coffeepot, tripping over rare Latin alchemical texts, and the works of Paracelsus, and Eliaphus Levi.

Many could see for themselves now that in the outside world, impressive testimony to Fields' ideas was accumulating. *Cosmopolitan* magazine had created Fieldsian TECS (Total Entertainment Converts), and their succeeding generations, who would 'alter the implicit bias which caused piles of genocidal bones to form at the scratch of a nose or the wave of a flag'. In *Fortune* magazine, Fields was described as 'eventually
leading his people out from old industrial analogue slavery into a new Entertainment Time, where indeed the waves of the sea itself would part to allow them to escape.' Eventually, it was conjectured, he would construct an Attractor Region, an actual geographical area, a Fieldsian *Domain,* to be called Entertainment State. This place he would charge with the most potent of modern Entertainment potential that the world could muster. Eventually, with new Entertainment-dedicated technologies already on the horizon, the Warhol vision would come about, and everyone would have a show of their own. Eventually the old world would be cut quite loose. Performance Mirrors face to face, the shows would reflect one another until there was 'nothing but interviews, appearances, and acts. In full development, the whole industrial and technical base of contemporary society would be committed to support this new pyramid culture'.

But all mere resemblance to yet another super-Hollywood ceased when Fields declared that there would be Wonders. These would occur

he claimed, 'when the advertising concentrate reached sufficiently high a density.' Mixing his metaphors liberally, he described a moment to come when the control-rods would be withdrawn from this 'trash supernovae of a mass-advertising pile', and it would go critical. When that happened, said Fields, the world would see something it had not seen for a very long time.

Entertainment Fission.

When asked what that was exactly, Fields would give his famous mandarin smile, leave the Dansette Den, and disappear into the deepest recesses of the Main Computer Hall.

VII

The Elegant Solution

Spring came deceptively early to the first week of March, and Marshall took a well-earned week's break on his 1000-acre farm in Dorset. He wandered along the coast with Mary, the woman he had been happily married to just after he sold his last crate of *London Grill* on a wet evening in Ealing some thirty years ago. Together they explored pirate caves, and stopped young grandchildren from falling into dangerous crevices. He built a dog-kennel for a cousin, mended bicycles, and announced the numbers at a village Bingo game. Mary was the headmistress of a local public school, and she bathed Marshall's head with very English sanity whenever it had been clouted, which in the Security Services occurred often enough.

These were exhausting days for her husband. Mary knew that he trusted her with a lot more knowledge than perhaps he ever should. She also knew that for two years his main task had been the preparation of NIPP, meaning Northern Ireland Peace Programme. This was to be a plan for what that cliché-junkie of a Minister, John Carlton, had called a 'flexible set of options', should a 'permanent peace' in Northern Ireland *ever* come about.

Marshall knew that he was in his present position precisely because modern Intelligence was about management, and because the classic problem of all Intelligence systems remained the same: rapid integration of information, and the quick relating of the separate parts to a well defined whole. Such an approach, familiar enough for generations to the worlds of industry, commerce, and finance, had come late to the British Security Services. From the days of the home-brew electronics of Peter Wright, R.V. Jones, and Alan Turing, British Intelligence had gone through a painful process of demythologising a quite Edwardian attitude to systems-analysis and modern technology; Marshall had been typical of the new men that had been recruited in the late 1960s, not only to avoid being outmanoeuvred by the kind of folk who would certainly not be asked to dinner under normal circumstances, but to preserve tactical mobility.

To Mary, the intense inner preoccupations of her husband were the buzzing abstractions of an historical minute, as played against the timeless externals of cottage and lake, hedgerow, and barn. But she could tell those occasions on which he needed her involved close attention, those times when he was not pleased with his work. The complexities of a something which was not a peace, not a war, yet could turn out to be both at the same time, and quickly turn to yet further not-either states, were obviously giving him new and unprecedented difficulties. The Irish problems haunted and bedevilled hundreds of years of British history, and she knew that her husband felt, as others had done before him, that every single hour of this history was piled right on top of his head. He told her that for once in his life, he was impressing himself even less than he was impressing his ever-anxious superiors. Though he had a good team under him, the forming of a plan which would somehow suit the fresh shapes of endless teeming new possibilities (and impossibilities) in both Northern Ireland and Europe itself seemed hopeless.

Mary had heard the same story before in various forms. Marshall was being asked to form a semi-military plan within a semi-peaceful situation; he was also being asked to provide for differing levels of differing types of escalation within that situation; he was becoming the dump-bin for Ministerial problems; he was also being asked to draw up an entirely new Intelligence spectrum to fit quite often ill-defined perspectives. The result was that NIPP was becoming a mess to fit a mess, like every troublesome prototype which has had many gadgets stuck on it to try and make it work. Nevertheless, like all true philosophers, Marshall still dreamed a dream of the single, unified, elegant solution. This particularly twentieth-century nightmare haunted many minds, like a Mephistophelean offer of a pen and paper.

Walking on the cliffs in the early evening, their dogs running ahead, Mary was not completely satisfied with the idea that her husband's tensions were caused by a set of external pressures; no matter how painful, these things did not usually disturb her him to the extent that she could feel a very new kind of tension in him. She suspected that what he was now involved in was not just another task. Somehow it was the last job. The last fight. Everything was to go on a final single throw of the dice. She supposed all criminals, champions, and gamblers, knew the feeling.

He puzzled her even more when he asked about *StarPower*. She thought it would have been the very last thing he wanted to talk about. The book, which he had given her several months ago, underlined her previous astonishment on hearing that recently the Northern Universities Board had announced that TV soap operas would be studied as part of the GCSE syllabus to help 'analysing the realism, effectiveness, and

64

importance of setting.' She had known for a long time, because of preparing her sixth-form girls for scholarships, that even universities such as Sussex had now descended to researching soap-opera history and development; she supposed that this was the respectable academic equivalent of what Fields called Junk Culture. She had also known that the 0-Level Mathematics she took herself in 1960 would be now almost equivalent to an A-Level.

They sat on a flat rock which might well have seen those odd shapes which eventually became human species struggle from pools full of salt and sunlight. He was strangely quiet, only interrupting his thoughts to ask her about *StarPower* again. She was now alert. Somehow, here was the real problem. But she was still puzzled. This stuff was not in her husband's nature. But just why he had all this kind of thing on his mind along with all the other more serious pieces of nonsense, she did not know.

Just beyond the breakers below them, the sea showed multicoloured bands of sewage pollution. Beyond these lines was a channel of whitish yellow composed of oil-spill remnants and numberless types of illegally dumped industrial chemicals. Because of different specific gravities, these streaks were kept neatly apart in a tidal centrifuge, and were always at the same distance from the shore. Despite attempted official cleanups, and the occasional guitar twanged in anger, these new sea-marks had become built into the cycle of cultural expectancies; like *Coca-Cola,* soap-characters, and perhaps a high aerial appearing one day on top of a distant hill long ago, most had half-forgotten that these new and permanent sea-marks were not exactly a natural manifestation.

These half-memories of techno-junk were in her mind, like half-forbidden elements of recall, as she gave her opinion of *StarPower*.

"Most of it is pretty plain-cake. Over-obvious, almost. But there are other bits I think are the most baffling pieces of nonsense I have ever come across in all my life."

Looking a lot happier now she was willing to talk about it, he began to enthuse, and she listened closely, as if it all had a connection to something else, like the pollution, something very different to its surface nature.

"Before I read it, all I could recall about Entertainment was an uncle telling me stories about Max Miller that my father would not have approved of. Entertainment seemed to me to hang in a complete vacuum, like the ephemeral moment of a sweet or an ice-cream, taken for an instant of mildly pleasurable boredom."

"I liked some of the book. But I don't think many people are going to be happy about the way he describes science as a Disneyland for the intelligent classes."

"Scientists take themselves far too seriously. They need taking down a peg or two. They don't seem to realise that science will grow and decline like everything else. Fields is right. History is already eating scientific ideas and products alive, making them look as comic as Victorian ear-trumpets fixed into umbrellas "

"And that's not the only thing that's going to get him into trouble. Have you realised that he is just about as politically-correct as Bernard Manning? The New Order *fascisti* will have him for that."

"He's going to get caned for some things, but you don't know him. He'll swamp all opposition, just you see."

"As far as Entertainment goes, I think of it as the only thing TV is really good at: a few minutes finger-tapping whilst waiting for a bus. I cannot understand Fields' transcendental claims for it as a complete culture, still less as a quite original political force."

"What about the mystical bits?"

His companion of thirty years stopped by the cliff-path and roared with such laughter, that both their Yorkshire Terriers stopped and looked at them.

"Well, speaking as a practising Anglican, all that to me, Harry, is stuff for the brain-damaged, stuff whose peculiar comedy can only be afforded by the rarefied social class from which Fields comes. In any case, he's writing as a private citizen, probably ready for early retirement. Why should such things concern you?"

"Because when there are forces within a nation sufficiently powerful to cause a significant change of state within that nation, then they automatically become the legitimate concern of the Security Services, whatever their peculiar character."

He told her how, as the months passed after the publication of *StarPower,* he had tried his very best to reach out for a better understanding of what Fields was talking about. He knew of the launch of the troubled *Eurodisney* in France, a truly massive enterprise. His was a uniquely placed listening post, and he gradually began to discover the skeletal outlines of a massive live animal of an evolving brain of which Fields' book appeared to be part frontal lobe. She was not surprised to learn that Doctorates were now awarded for analysing television soap operas, and studying Madonna lyrics. Neither was she surprised that many other qualifications were given for researches into artistic interpretation, technical support, advertising, image-structure, symbol-interpretation, and the psychological nature of popular Entertainment appeal. The intelligentsia, it seemed, had discovered Fieldsian Trash Systems.

"But is the State in danger?"

"Its identity might well be."

"Should that concern you? Things are bound to change. They are natural processes. Should such things be the concern of the Security Services?"

He did not answer. Here were the dark areas within him she had avoided for thirty years; she still wanted to think that absolute reality was her sixth-form girls in starched tennis togs, getting Oxbridge scholarships, good jobs, and good marriages. Now, as he spoke, Marshall looked for a moment like a well-heeled top mobster, straight out of *The Godfather*. Hating violence, she didn't like to think of her husband as having anything to do with corpses in ditches; she even avoided the common knowledge that over the centuries, thousands of smugglers had died with slit throats in the caves beneath their feet.

"It could be used."

"Used?"

"As a weapon."

"What, *Entertainment?*"

She called to the dogs quite unnecessarily in order to catch her mental breath. There had been a time when all the secrecy had been fun; in this, she knew she was a little old-fashioned. Then, to her, what her husband did was still about Bulldog Drummond, fighting for old England against dastardly foreigners with strange complexions. But as a dark figure now, with his back to the sea, several protective assumptions of the years went from her; she knew now he had ordered deaths. She knew now that he had been involved in schemes which would have made the *mafia* blush; the most wicked social and political deceptions had certainly been woven by him; perhaps he personally had killed others. Perhaps she was married to a monster; perhaps there was nothing he would not do, no purity or innocence he would not contemplate destroying. She supposed all landscapes could be decoded like this; but the mind had to cut off somewhere, for the number of veils of appearance were probably infinite.

"A weapon against who?"

"Well not exactly a weapon as such."

"A means of persuasion?"

"Yes. Make it steerable."

"Towards who?"

"You know I can't tell you that."

"I think I could guess."

"I don't think I am doing anything particularly unusual."

This, from the mouth of a senior member of the Security Services, convinced Mary that something most bloody extraordinary was going on.

"Nothing financial networks are not doing."

The financial world as a moral example, she thought. Well, wonders would never cease.

"You see you have to try and keep ahead of the game."

"Oh, of course."

"The universities and the big corporations are already in on the first stage of the software planning operations. Fields is providing them with a hell of a lot of useful theory. This is Entertainment State in embryo."

"Have you discussed this application of his theories with him?"

"Yes."

"He knew that they would be taken up, of course."

"In all certainty he did."

"What's he like, this Fields?"

"Quite a character. You'll see him soon. I think we may be about to open the cage door."

"That's a good way of getting rid of him. Make him one of his own Stars."

"Getting rid of him? Oh, we don't ever want to get rid of him."

"Oh, you'll still be around?"

"Yes."

"Running him?"

Marshall could not help a smile at the phrase from popular books. "Just about."

"Is this what he wants to do?"

"Wants to try, put it that way."

"He must have Entertainment on the brain."

"I don't know about that. I'm not completely convinced that he really likes his precious heroic actors, singers, and film-stars, for all his professed worship. Although he hums and taps his fingers to a few ancient records, he's only seen television through shop-windows, and I don't think he has seen a British film for twenty-five years."

"Sounds lucky."

"He is lucky. Over the past twenty years he has been vitally involved in every single major cover operation, and with terrifying success. His stock is high, to say the least. There is practically nothing the Service won't let him try."

"Is he married?"

"No. His wife Alice died in 1968."

"Is he you-know-what?"

"You must be joking."

"That doesn't sound like a promising background for

Entertainment, these days."

"Neither does the fact that he's never been to a concert, or met many Entertainers, although I know he's read a few books and magazines about a few of them."

"Why read a book about Entertainers, and not see or hear them work?"

"You tell me."

Marshall now listened carefully to an expert on lightning fluctuations of teenage mood, ambition, motivation, and opinion. A good model for Entertainment psychology was being made in his mind as his wife continued.

"Mark my words. When he's finished with his actors and his Entertainers, he'll drop them. He's a philosopher. He'll go on to describe the next snowflake in line."

"I hope he doesn't drop his mental pantomime just yet. The entire world is screaming for Fields' appearance, but we'll make them wait just a little longer. I tell you Mary, I can't wait for his first world-entrance."

"What's he look like?"

"A gorged Fat Owl of the Remove."

"He'll be absolutely adored. Pity he's not grey-area, you'd have a rave on your hands."

Her husband missed the dryness of the Anglican sarcasm.

"And he comes complete with steaming tuck-box, shirt with bits of dinner on it, half-mast corduroys, odd socks, and often a Bill Haley kiss-curl plastered down on a huge globular forehead."

"Sounds worth dragging the little black-and-white out of the attic for."

"I don't think we've got an aerial, have we?"

"I don't think so."

"There's always your brother's house."

"He's just thrown out his television."

"We must stop all this sales resistance."

"Don't worry. They're on cable, *Internet*, and they have three video-players."

As she laughed, she noticed he smiled to himself, almost oblivious almost of her presence. His relief was obvious. He had at last told someone about the way his mind and ideas were moving.

"Do you know Mary, I have an old forest-feeling that I haven't experienced since I took my last breath of leatherette from a Company *Cortina* thirty years ago. I know I am being sold something. It is my one infallibility. I know the fat clever bastard is putting out some kind of bait."

She knew now why he was here. There was something about it all he could not focus. Of course, the mystical bits. They would worry him more than anything.

"The small print. There's something he isn't telling us. I'm damned if I can figure it out; there are times when I curse the strength of my innate pragmatism. But I have a feeling. All surviving salesmen know it. It is the same feeling that risks a journey after closing time with two crates of 8-oz tins of *Celebrity Pork Roll With Stuffing* to a store thirty miles away to find the place still open, cash in the hand ready and waiting, and the exact tins that were desperately wanted. And the right number. And the right price."

She laughed, but he was gone from her again, gazing out over the sea as she spoke. She knew that he had decided that his life was not yet finished. There were still mighty unresolved conflicts within him. Sometimes she wished there were some in her.

"He's taken you, has this Fields. He's revived your fighting instincts. You are young again, hungry for some action, on the road once more in your battered car, anxious to beat the System, the Bank, and the Devil if necessary."

But he hadn't heard her. When he spoke again, he was dropping like a stone. She had never known such mood fluctuations within him before.

"Fields is right. Nothing can be done. The Stars are about to take over the fairy tales, broadcast them from their very own mounds and towers, quite different from those you and I work in. Resist, and it would all be as hopeless as ancient screams against the Enlightenment, the Industrial Revolution, or indeed protests about the slightly chipped *Doris Day Birthday Goblets* of my first world, which were probably just as cracked as any great world movement."

"But probably a damned sight more useful."

"Do you know, I feel an excitement of which I am almost ashamed. But now, probably for the very first time in my life, I can't quite decide whether I am being offered a good or a bad deal."

"He's offering an exciting plan for a new society. That explains everything. Or does it?'

"After thirty years working for the Service, I only know one thing about explanations."

"What's that?"

"They make you go away."

Making their way home, the pollution streaks gave off wonderful reflections under the quarter-moon, but Marshall had never liked being in the countryside at night. He felt naked, stripped of his skills and power. The primal dark threatened to smash all the deceptions and hypocrisies of all the years; it was as if the old immensities in the night over the sea were a gathering death-reckoning because they remembered everything. The supposed the age of tide and nightfall beyond the city's temporary refuge in history was the source of much rational fear, like infinity, or the square root of minus one. The idea of having lived and died more times than could be imagined, perhaps even before Man appeared, aroused naked elemental awe. Marshall felt changes in him even older than the sea, and wanted to run to the city and pull the city's human voices over him like a cloak of forgetting. She almost read his thoughts as she spoke, as if she understood all this far better than he did.

"It's old. Very old. What he's doing."

"Older than what?"

"Explanations."

"Am I the man for this sort of thing?"

"No."

"Now she tells me."

They both laughed, and Marshall felt closer to his wife than he ever had been.

"It's too late now, Harry. You're hooked."

"I thought so. Yes. I thought that's what it was."

"You're in love."

"You don't say?"

"Don't worry. It's not the Fat Owl."

"Thank God for that."

"It's what he's talking about."

"What is he talking about?"

"I don't quite know, but I would watch out for the small print, if I were you."

"The small print?"

"There a tiny whirl of chaos there."

"Whirl of what?"

"Chaos. He's designed it. He's using Entertainment as molecular biology. He calls it himself systems-protein. Here's your new techno-man for you. And probably something else much older."

Marshall, his brain reeling, heard a robot voice come from his own throat.

"What's that?"

How could she describe something which she didn't know whether she even believed in herself? How to describe to a hard, practical man, a something in the back of her mind which the century had long since thrown out of the cultural window? He shrugged his shoulders when she

71

did not reply. She took his arm as they walked home along the cliffs under an almost white quarter-moon.

Voices were urging, pushing him on to the last mile. But his mental lungs were screaming. He was too old. Simply no more wind. He wouldn't make the mountain top now. His mind was panting so fast he thought his whole being was coming apart. As night came over the river shallows behind the pig-sheds, where otters were now back, the changes and the challenges within him became incomprehensible.

"Mary, tell me, is he talking rubbish?"

"Rubbish is the key."

"What key?"

"He wants to show that it works as well as anything else."

"What an equation."

"You're telling me. The best of luck."

With these thoughts in mind, Marshall caught the milk-train to London from a station which hadn't changed from the time it received the first Somme casualties for the surrounding convalescent homes. As the pollution bands gave off shades of dusky copper in the early morning light, he thanked the gods that in his late middle-age, he was still mad enough for anything.

Back in London that same day, Marshall turned once more to his work. But he could not concentrate on the matters in hand. *StarPower* was taking him over; his mind was become one big sleepless night in which a wild chattering sea rose up and consumed him. He felt he was being taken apart and rebuilt. His one independent thought was that somehow he was being religiously converted, but to what, he didn't quite know.

His thoughts ran on, quite unstoppable: Entertainment State was pollution-free, independent of slaughter. Already generations were taking their values from massive institutionalised Entertainment systems. Bland, lightweight actors, and facile, superficial show-business people dominated anything and everything. Silently, in the night of only a few generations, there had arisen a culture of advertisements, which was really all that any true Entertainment Culture could be.

It was essentially an Acting Culture. Like the great Banking Systems of the planet, and indeed like the organisation he worked for, everything in Entertainment State was achieved by complex imposture. Perhaps Fields really had rediscovered a previously forgotten state of Nature. Perhaps the illusion of substance itself really was a zooming array of advertisement-stuff.

To his own great surprise, he burst out laughing.

Expertly stubbing out his roll-up on the lid of his tobacco-tin, Marshall was worried. That was the fourth time he had laughed that day.

He laughed yet again as he recalled the previous conversation with his wife. Entertainment a *weapon?* Of course. Since war had become mechanised, for generation, societies had toiled at building the great megamachine of the weapons culture. As the supporting weapon-systems fell away, with their tanks, guns, ships and aircraft, there at the top of the pyramid was the ultimate in super-weapons: the Entertainment Bomb. He had overheard the ambitious young Barsby, Fields' convert number one, chattering at breakfast, tea, and supper: 'Authority was carefully re-advertising itself, changing utterly from The Leader frothing at the mouth before parades of tanks and marching men...'

The Entertainment system could be some final development of weaponry. No-one would suspect this all-powerful entity, with its perfect camouflage, and its irresistible imaginative appeal. It was a common assumption that wars were always fought largely in terms of the previous conflict. But always along came the almost-inconceivable: the aeroplane, tank, or nuclear bomb. But that the tip of the megamachine's pyramid could be an amusement arcade, that from the tip would pop out a floppy clown instead of poison gas?

Yes, he liked that.

In any case, it was a lot better than dull old NIPP, which to Entertainment State, was like a muzzle-loading cannon compared to a cruise-missile.

A weapon. Yes. A weapon needed a target. It was a good story. And it was getting better. He had heard far worse. And he thought he knew one or two who would appreciate the fun.

The leathery Scottish hunting features before Marshall were wreathed in smiles. Marshall was lunching at his club with a Senior Assistant to the Directrix, Richard Gayton. Gayton knew well the Bunter, and thoroughly appreciated his apocryphal ideas and methods, all of which were invariably successful. Fields' innovations also had the advantage of leaving not leaving a trace of blood; or none they could see, at least, which was what really mattered to Gayton. Only that morning, by an edifying example of one of those coincidences he felt the Bunter would appreciate, Gayton told Marshall that he had noted in

The Sun (both Fields, Gayton, and Marshall were proud to describe themselves as examples of those politically-incorrect scum who had the nerve to confess publicly that they obtained great pleasure looking at photographs of naked women), that the students of a northern University had changed the name of a new hostel from Nelson Mandela House to Benny Hill House. Marshall responded by quoting from his own private collection: on a southern housing estate, Arthur Scargill Road had been changed to Frankie Howerd Street. The Pantheons were on the move. Both men smiled at one another over their excellent *Beef Wellington*.

"Yes. My goodness me, Harry. What an idea. No heads banged together, and nicely tailored-made for the conga-line of Them Upstairs, don't-you-know. An elegant solution. Great class. Congratulations. And nicely air-born enough to appeal to Herself. Few risks. Almost no intrigue. Just a wee push here and there, and the thing would run itself, quite unstoppable. A perfectly blended natural state. No possible comebacks. Good egg! And no politics; no endless mouse-men conferences; no weapons; not even religious arguments. Just one mighty tinsel cosh, old boy. And money, pots of lovely money coming in for once; money not flushing out by the million over the years in rivers of wasted liberal concerns, bad investments, and yet more military commitment. Of course, some snotty little ponytails will no doubt write of self-financing and self-generating repression (Gayton was proud of his talent for forming what he thought were good Loony-Left phrases), but this time the lentil-eaters will be swamped with the world become one mighty great Good Cause. There won't be the time, never mind the need, for the ring-nosed ones to snort a single *didgeridoo* in anger, don't-you-know."

Gayton gave a rare grin, and as a libation, they ordered another round. After an hour of further toasts, a red-faced Gayton said to a swaying Marshall that he would arrange for both of them to see Her Upstairs herself.

The Directrix was a sleepy, blinking chameleon on a sunlit river-bank. When impressed, which was extremely rare, her dark eyes with a hint of blue on the lids closed completely for a long time; this was quite an unnerving experience for any enthusiastic petitioner. She was a Chief admired and liked more than anyone since Furnival-Jones, and Marshall felt that if Entertainment State were to stand a chance at all it was with this popular and attractive woman in front of him. She had also had the courage, brains, and bottle to force herself in the late 1980s through further degrees in Mathematical Physics and Electronics; These qualifications shamed some of her colleagues, who would have preferred British Intelligence to stay where Fields always said it had begun: on the river banks of *The Wind In The Willows*.

74

Tower House cynics said she had done this to avoid becoming the kind of the witless pre-electric Bohemian relic who, in Marshall's opinion, had not only paralysed the British brain before the Somme and before Dunkirk, but had also caused the total Intelligence disaster between 1945 and the defection of Philby.

Gayton and Marshall turned and looked at one another; the eyes of the Directrix had been closed for at least two minutes. A smile then began to spread across the features which lapped around the still closed eyes. Gayton was extremely alarmed. The woman had never ever been known to smile, never mind anything else. The astonished pair almost cowered before the gales of laughter as merry eyes appeared beneath the blue lids.

"The Bunter! Just what the Micks bloody well deserve. Well done, chaps. Let's DO it!"

Back in his office, Marshall could not wait to tell Fields the good news. He knew he was expecting a positive decision anyway, but now planning and organised moves could start. NIPP would bow out, and Entertainment take the stage. Here was the elegant solution. There were many questions flying through Marshall's brain. He was about to contact Fields and arrange for a first meeting when he received an urgent report.

Dr. David Barton had been murdered.

VIII

Dinner with John Carlton

The charming Dr. David Barton, last seen by Marshall at the Paris conference a month previous, talking to the equally user-friendly Minister John Carlton, had been found garrotted in his girlfriend's flat in Eastbourne. Marshall just had time to read the report in his flat in Tower House just before he went to bed. Apparently, the previous morning, 25-year-old Julia Church, a newly-qualified research biochemist, was moving along Crayford Road, Eastbourne, at a bouncing rate with the sea at her back. She had told friends she was in love, and to prove it, she had showed them a set of intriguing lingerie she had just bought. She thought that Dr. David Barton, a charming thirty-something she had recently befriended, might already be waiting for her at her flat, having possibly arrived from the airport sooner than she expected. She had the highly specialised and fabulously expensive biological samples he wanted, stolen from the research laboratory she worked in, at considerable risk to herself.

But she was surprised at seeing her flat door open. David must have let himself in somehow. She smiled. He would pay for this. She would have his trousers off before he could even think about making a cup of his precious mint tea. Shouting his name in mock anger, she almost ran into the living room.

Julia was of sound constitution and good nerve. But she was hardly prepared for what she saw spread out on the new carpet, where she had planned to playfully seduce her lover before he had a chance to put on the kettle. David Barton's handsome head had been replaced by something which looked by a blue ball surrounded by red and white spittle, and his neck was as wide as his thin wrist.

Before her mind had time to shape a scream, something which she could only later call a shadow, hit her with annihilating force, collapsed the entire side of her right cheek and part of her right forehead, and she knew no more.

A young man witnesses later described as being of slim build, was the one person police could not eliminate from their enquiries. The trail went quite cold after a brief report of a glimpse of such a person at the local railway station.

Several times, Marshall had to interrupt his reading of the details of Barton's murder with a stiff drink. The investigators were very interested in the wire found around the neck, which had to be severed with a pair of Eastbourne Fire Brigade mechanised wreck-cutters. Marshall gulped down his whisky and shuddered. He never really liked the sharp-ends of the chess game he worked within. He knew that the garrotting wire popular in films was a complete fiction. It was always shown as being a simple piece of bare wire which, when looped round the neck and held tight, cut the windpipe and caused the collapse of the victim. In practice, such a piece of wire would be useless. It would require almost King-Kong biceps to twist and hold the wire around a healthy person's neck for the time required for collapse. The reserves of strength summoned up by a healthy victim in terror of death would almost certainly break the hold, particularly if the target grabbed downwards in the right places, or smashed shins by back-kicking. Even if the wire were fitted with pegs (as shown in many a film), to twist beyond a half-turn would be impossible, due to the crossed wrists. The truth, the report reminded Marshall, is terrible. Garrotting wire proper is serrated, and fitted with a small tubular locking device which cannot be released (except in the case of the training version). A five-year-old could playfully put the loop round a neck, pull tight, and the serrations would lock. It would be quite impossible to release the wire unless a pair of good *Lindstrom* bolt-cutters were handy, and they would have to be plunged at least a quarter-inch into the neck in order to get a grip on the surface-hardened highspeed steel of the wire.

Marshall poured himself yet another double. First Holt, now Barton.

Somebody was bumping off the bad guys.

He downed his drink, climbed into bed, and was soon asleep. He dreamed of Fields in one of the first aeroplanes, and Tower House become one infinite supermarket, with Carole Arnoux undergoing cartoon-adventures best left untold, in every aisle. As Fields flew to the moon on gossamer wings, and Carole continued her similar adventures in stone-age forests, in a small hotel near Victoria Station, a young woman of slight figure changed from being a thin man to a rather dumpy housewife. The following morning, she caught the first plane she could to Belfast.

There is nothing more disturbing to a secret agent than to

contemplate the baffling process of information leaks. There were times when Marshall thought it almost provided evidence for a kind of ESP. When Marshall got back behind his desk the very next morning, he found an invitation to dinner that evening from Minister John Carlton, 'to discuss this terrible event...' as Carlton put it. Meaning of course, the death of John Barton, whose corpse was still warm.

At dinner, Marshall was not surprised when Carlton dropped the Barton business rather quickly, and went on to talk about the possible launch of Entertainment State. Though only tentative discussions had been held, Carlton was in full possession of alarmingly sensitive information. He bore in mind Fields' remark that Carlton's dinner guests always checked their wallets, and even spare change, never mind their secrets, well before they got to the soup.

The florid face leaned forward.

"I wouldn't want you to break a confidence of course."

Saying that to a member of the Security Services as if he might well do such a thing at the drop of a hat, was a measure of how this tragic animal did business.

"It's just that certain recent developments *on,* and indeed *in* Northern Ireland might well turn out to be what shall I-e r- say, *unusual.*"

Marshall marvelled at how quickly Carlton had got hold of Entertainment. If only he were as good in the Cabinet, he thought, we might have another Winston Churchill.

"I wouldn't want you to make any leading statements, you know that."

He liked the plural. Saying that to a member of the Security Services, was like warning the commander of a nuclear-powered *Trident* missile-submarine not to get his feet wet.

"It is just that I may be in a position to help."

He meant of course, that his two failing construction companies in Northern Ireland were in need of work.

"I might be prepared...but at the moment perhaps you may not know of real confirmation...If only I knew...well, you know, whether the situation was going to stabilise in that particular unusual direction; if so, I might be able to prepare for any extra industrial effort required in that sphere. To our mutual advantage, of course."

Which meant that if he did get to know what he wanted to know, he could buy in suitable cut-price stock. Like his great heroine, Margaret Thatcher, to John Carlton, the world was a markdown store, and the identities and moral obligations were just about as deep. Marshall, being a grocery salesman himself once upon a time, knew the feeling well. Marshall also knew well the method of moving the intention in and out of the florid chat, the reasonable points made in a nicely modulated tone.

78

"Of course I can't ask you professional questions, I know that. And I am not going to solicit you for information, even as a private person."

"That's very nice of you."

"Oh, don't mention it."

Marshall was astonished. A private person? What the hell was a private anything in John Carlton's world? His wife owned his mansion, his girlfriend owned his cock, the European investment companies owned his shares, an elocution teacher owned his accent, and the Hong Kong banks probably owned even the hairs on his arse. But still the target-intention of this expensive lunch at the *Athenaeum* wove in and out of the glowing domestic proscenium arch. It snaked through talk of the growing children, it slithered through the condition of friends, relatives, colleagues, and the great screaming English menopause: staid and worthy British art; popular TV series; the problems of travelling to work; tax burdens, price-ranges, and the yob-scratch on the *Volvo*.

"If at some time you see yourself needing help..."

Marshall almost laughed out loud at the masonic cliché. Then came Carlton's other mask. Now, in a second of costume-change, he was affable executive-commuter Man making jokes about brunch, house-buying, and the difficulties of driving through The Hangar Lane Gyratory. Marshall now understood the chapter in *StarPower* entitled *Advertising as New Natural Selection*. The good-natured smiles flashing before Marshall were auto-cued from a world of simple rationalisations about improved housing, the restructuring of the National Health Service, better motorways, various pension schemes and the Party Policy on Europe. In a Fieldsian moment, he felt as if he were drowning in time-wasting and energy-absorbing cartoons made of interacting bits and pieces of failed meccano-mythology.

Summoning up a little nerve, Marshall looked Carlton straight in the eye, and thought of an address equal to his companion's character and station.

"And what you got for me, John?"

Carlton's eyes hit the ground. They did not do that very often.

"A woman killed both Dr. Barton and Dr. Holt. Her name is Nora Harcourt. Master of disguise. Most likely anarchist. Cross-dresser. She is a native of Northern Ireland. A pirate. A pro. Belfast is her base. You'll find her there."

John Carlton took his leave as if he had just launched a great ship, and was anxious to speed back home with police escort. Seeing the Minister keeping his pecker up, as another citizen of Shakespeare's nation, Marshall almost admired, and almost forgave.

Fields was right.

The world at times was pure Entertainment.

IX

Nora Comes Home

The woman John Carlton had spoken of gazed up at thin white trails of USAF *Starlifters* stark against a high, cold blue. These marks of the Nato milk-run were all she remembered of the late afternoon light before fast rain whipped across the derelict aerials of the now abandoned British Army Lookout Post at the corner of Bream Street. Sections of tired ancient street lights flickered in salvo as if in reply to the vertical onslaught of the frozen water.

Hunched and hooded in a duffle-coat, her slight figure moved into the maelstrom of Spokes Road, between a brightly lit Off-License, and cracked Victorian drains sluicing down railway arches. She carried a cracked cardboard suitcase and an *I Buy Anything* carrier-bag, overflowing with waterlogged newspapers. Passing a just-closed Co-Op, she glanced back towards the old Lookout Post, and caught for a moment the nostalgic battle-smell of damp ashes and scorched rubber blowing from kid's rubbish fires still defying the downpour beyond the cracking plastic banners of *Bob's CarMart.*

Nora Harcourt had come home. But in a country where many names were still as brittle as the frostbitten edge of a late-winter city, her name might well be as temporary a half-substance as John Carlton's honesty, a Fields BUAC, or indeed the Paraffin Man's momentary cry caught from a far twilight corner of Lee Road.

The rain stopped as she turned into Peter Street, and the front of a boarded-up betting-shop showed the blanketed forms of two milkmen, their fragile vehicle upturned, bleeding gallons of milk into the blackened Tarmac. By a still-burning *Hillman Estate,* paramedics examined another inert form, a roadsweeper, whose upturned Belfast Corporation dustcart lay toppled amidst scattered sweeping brushes. She breathed hard; just a traffic accident. A striped tape barrier was being put up by four soaked and miserable RUC, who looked corpse-white against their camouflage jackets. A woman in a yellow nylon pinafore came out with a jug of tea; Nora skirted the tape, fingers crossed against being pulled in for a 'questioning' session, a reaction which was now part of history. The

RUC looked young, scared, and not particularly healthy or disciplined. Though there was never any distinguishing insignia, their sporadically-drilled nerves always picked them out from the fit and lofty coolness of the British Army.

All kinds of psychological expectancies were still present. She surveyed the scene again. No craters. And no weapons in evidence. But just the same still forms under blankets. She missed certain things about the past; she missed wanting to correct the bad tactical habit of forever focusing the 4x1 sights of SA 80 rifles into misty obscurities which changed both sky and land to many shifting planes of grey and white, and from whose changing angles anything might emerge. At that time, in the country of her birth, by the time a target was acquired by the cross-hairs of a telescope sight, it was far too late to press the trigger.

Some things hadn't changed. An expert RUC eye quickly focused on her suitcase and carrier-bag; keep moving. As if she were still in the London Tube she had left only twenty-four hours ago, she made sure eye contact was almost nil. There were far more shadows on the boarded shops and cracked road than thrown by the evening light, now almost gone. Above the dead, on a hill full of rhododendrons and neat driveways, the lights were just coming on for dinner; as ever, the fat cats were still safe and dining well. She caught the RUC mind as it scoured her. Poor wet piece of rubbish. Wino. Probably mad. Probably done something in her trousers. Go away. That's right, she thought; always look like a complete dirty, idiotic piece of nothing. It had saved her life more times than she ever cared to remember. Nothing apparently still came out of nothing.

She bought a carton of milk and a hot potato at a small corner store. With the rain gone as quickly as it came, she squatted on the damp pavement edge and watched a flying squad of 12-year-olds throw half-bricks at beer bottles propped against a healthy weed in the middle of the lacerated road. From a badly drained and swollen earth base, hastily laid concrete slabs marked 'London Brick Company' rose up before her to form Möbius strips of lost and drowned fragments of British and Irish industrial Time.

A complete film-unit passed her, their custom-built smart vehicles contrasting with Town Lane, a fifty-yard stretch of stillborn blueprint which ended abruptly just short of a forlorn rusting bulldozer whose spare-part raiders had probably got there before the repossession company. Town Lane had gone to quick ruin through lack of predicted heavy traffic from yet another fallen scheme of 'urban renewal'.

The kids disappeared smartly as a battered RUC *Land Rover*, appearing as if from nowhere, slowly crunched over broken bricks and bottles in low gear. Seconds later, from the roof of a burnt-out clothing store, bottles soared in a high arc and shattered on the bonnet of the prowling vehicle which expertly reversed from the high throwing angle. For a tense moment she sipped her milk, and chewed her potato; carefully studying the ground in front of her, she was thankful that in these calmer days, the kids didn't appear to have any petrol handy. Gulp, nibble, drink; don't try engaging the eyes behind the darkness of the sinister armoured slits. Don't kick against this examination by a wheezing, robot, or you could still be beaten half to death, Peace or no Peace.

No door bangs. She was lucky. The crew were still wary. Kid's antics were standard decoys of immediate past. Great satisfaction to know that the vehicle crew were also probably afraid. The sun was down now, and they wanted to get back to their circle of covered wagons a mile away across the sea of rubble and broken glass which made road, gutter, and pavement almost indistinguishable. The scowling armoured-car changed reluctant gears, and lumbered off to join three others, which were lurking by the far main road. The group of vehicles then shot off to the high beyond at great speed, sirens screaming from a doppler-mix of angles and directions.

If this was peace in Northern Ireland, it didn't look or sound like it.

A mile beyond, she passed no less than three huge concert platforms being built by hundreds of scaffolders. She saw more tents and new structures as she passed muddy acres of abandoned half-built housing estate along a road split and shredded by the heavy traffic of many more building projects. This place was the renowned EuroDump, which in the past, had bred long snaking queues of hypnotised investors, seemingly ever-anxious for a thrashing. Some ritualistic beat brought in every Peter Pan project, any amount of Mickey Mouse money. Indeed, it seemed that everyone in the world thought that the one thing a Northern Ireland now at a fragile peace needed most of all was some vast clown project as a 'solution', such as another gull-winged car or a funny-money aircraft. For insane projects in Northern Ireland it seemed that there were always countless millions of pounds available, together with a great sacrificial planning-up by the Great and the Good, who inevitably left with bleeding hearts, broken dreams, and frequently exploding company cars and machine-gunned account books. The place was a sucking-bog for every suspicious corporation, every over-subsidized crank-scientist, and every clever manager and canny engineer who gulped as they saw immaculate computer-planned projects veer towards the impossible faster than finance companies could disappear.

She looked at the stillborn part-robot shapes around her in the gathering dark. This was an indeterminate country of the not-quite born,

83

and the not-quite dead. Her country was every brittle edge of every insecure dream. Giants of mental sinew would strain and break under sudden mighty unforeseen fluctuation of cost, technical analysis, supply, planning, transport, raw materials, shifting investment, or design; women and men would wake in their sleep, waving arms at airy ghosts, shouting at mounting insubstantialities.

Rounding a corner, she had the surprise of her life. A young woman jogging past her had an unmistakeable world-famous film-face. Even Nora, a woman of great alertness, thought for a moment she had entered some cartoon, or sketch. Only three months away, and already she faced much readjustment. From a car-park Europe whose mall-brain, in her opinion, was now trying to run a permanent flickering version of the Eurovision Song Contest. she was back to an unceasing mental hurricane, she had to remember how to cling to a rail for dear life. Catastrophe, achievement, despair, contradiction, those wild cliff-face contrasts of inspired absurdities that had created a mighty Irish Literature, these dreams were a kind of antimatter; they split and sundered anything and everything in this country, as if there were arguments between the very sea, and sky in his place called Ireland.

And still, for the life of her, she could not put a name to the famous face.

Passing *The Clonard Bar*, she saw it was almost empty. This was unusual. She remembered the talk in the ever-crowded bar sixth months ago had been intriguing. Then, according to freshly minted local legend, the very foundations of the EuroDump had yet once more collapsed in a firework display of definitive fraud, corruption, bribery, and drug-deals. Also intriguing had been the charges made by a red-haired man with a face like a stewed prune: he claimed to have witnessed cannibalism, human sacrifice, plus UVF coon-hunts, and all under a full moon. Fortunately (as a stout woman in curlers straight from an ancient TV soap-opera had said), the *white man* was running out of money. This was a good thing (said she), otherwise coons and cannibals alike would be drugged, raped and strangled by the skip-full, to be buried under British South Bank stained-bunker-culture before you could say EuroCurrency. The landlord, a massive ex-farmer from Kerry, agreed. Yes, redevelopment was a wonderful thing. But only if you wanted to die laughing, added Stewed Prune, buying another foaming tankard with several of what *then* were known as Protestant Portraits, but *now* had become Peace Portraits.

A rumble and thump from the direction of the UDR barracks in Cadogan Road. The horizon streamed pockmarked smoke, a section of the ancient street-lamps flickered out, and of a sudden the air stank of almonds, stewed cabbage, and burnt asphalt. She sniffed approvingly. Probably what was euphemistically termed a controlled explosion. The place still had atmosphere. Here, as the curler-woman said, the *white man* still watched his step. She had added with toothy venom, that three private rent-collectors and two of the universally-loved social workers had been shot over the past twenty-five years. A large companion with beehive hair pointed out with glee that the last 'Windsor Family Money Collector' had been kneecapped in '82. If this was the New Spirit in Northern Ireland that the Traffic-Cone Man talked about, thought Nora, she would be better off in the Balkans.

In the face of such charity, she had thoughts that a voyager might rest up for a time in such a half-forgotten hole in nothing as this area, where the roofs looked mediaeval, the plumbing almost nonexistent, and the kids had the last snotty noses in Europe. Stewed Prune had said it was a 'liberated area,' though it didn't look like one.

She hid in such scars as these all over Europe whenever she could find them. They were beginning to be easier to locate, were more dense, and gave good cover from he who was now known universally (she had heard the phrase in both Germany and France) as the *white man*. She assumed that this mythological creature was the one with everlasting Plans, Fresh Initiatives, and nonstop cries for more labour, more prayers, more money, and an ever higher level of ritualised consumer-death.

She had not wished to join the few customers in the *The Clonard Bar* because, at the moment, she did not want to be contaminated by what was known locally as Familiar Irish Noise; a returned traveller could be almost eaten alive by this natural hazard before they even had time to unpack. Dazzling arrays of manufactured dishes from all the different holy supermarkets were always on offer: Murder and Virginity; Blood, Soil, and even *Fidei Defensor;* there was also The Deep Designs of God in the bargain-basement. As an almost-free gift, the Big Flickering Cartoons of the Great BBC Television Janet and John Meaningful Book of Politically Correct Life minced out from the 36-inch *Sony* above the bar-counter.

To Nora, it was all a perfect image of a EuroDump in the head. Religious culture here, she thought, was a continuous-process industry making endless versions of monstrous joke-structures of mechanised belief-robotics. Only three months away, and already there was a complete new growth of fresh images: the *white man* and Peace Portraits indeed; and even coons and cannibals. The land of her birth grew cartoons and games like a Frenchman grew grapes. In her experience, these natural growths had their own seasons. The Great What Happens Next Game would succeed the List of Wrong Doings Game; then would come some repotted trestle-table MK XIV Improvement of the Freeing Of The Peasants Game. When she was very young, she remembered thinking that perhaps Paradise was an escape from the web of this crazy anthropology of God's castoff part-sketches.

But like Paris, and even New York, she thought, at least here in Belfast, a citizen moved through epic; in Manchester and London, a citizen moved through precisely nothing. The British, to Nora Harcourt, had lost everything: all sense of themselves, all purpose, all ambience and character. In Berlin, Tel-Aviv, Moscow, Tokyo, there was at least some attempt to form a kind of sulphurous destiny; but in England in particular, she saw the population as almost disappearing with a six-pack and beer-gut through the TV screen to vanish from the face of the Earth. They had become so soap-opera-blandified, she doubted if they could even smell their feet in a downwind. The inventors of steam, the discoverers of electricity, the makers of the first locomotives of the world, now couldn't even make a light railway to the docks. The last time she took this train, two doors had fallen off, the computer jammed, one carriage caught fire, and hundreds were almost asphyxiated by toxic smoke from the smouldering seating material. Somewhere along the historical line, the British brain had lost its technical focus. She would never ever try the Channel Tunnel. She did not like this situation. She had no great liking for the British only because they appeared to *let* this shameful suicide happen. To see the nation that produced Shakespeare drop to the ground like a magnificent old lion, dying of old TV series, *Carry On* films, and a headful of high-camp British dolls, was an unprecedented moral and cultural obscenity.

She cared for Britain. It took a lot for an Irish Catholic woman to say that. But she thought it was better to live in the agony of a permanent mental and physical cauldron than die slowly of television. Her own country was a least a permanently seething maelstrom, whose own natural weathering seemed to know her. It sheltered, protected, listened, and whispered. As others put their ears to native earth and blended with tarn and mountain, so when world-cities screamed or blossomed, burned, sweltered, or lay locked in snow, she was still dangerously unremarkable by *Woolworths* or by the Convent of the Sacred Heart. On the Piccadilly Line, by the docks at Antwerp, and occasionally in downtown New York, as one of her other faces and names, she would listen to a similar trembling web of day, ears pricked and ready to jump between hairline possibilities faster than a boxing hare. This secret time of cities was her element. She could see seasons of natural growth and decay in tunnel, vehicle, and a manifold electrical life; she could read spore of splintering bang, siren and crash-reverse; she knew quick herd-sensing and could track the first signs of systems-strangers along brilliant avenues of changing light. This world of human structures was to her as natural as wind on water, sunlight on field and crop. She could read the centres of this other life as others might detect a first unease in ruminating beasts, or some vital change of natural minutiae in forest gloom. And after her uncoiling strike, the nights of the cities would take her back as their very own; she would be vanished as if she had never been. Several cloaks of impossibilities would wrap themselves around her as if she were the city's sacred child, avenger, and guardian spirit; she rode the high waves of a natural antidote system of city mysteries for which rites, language, and devotions had long been lost.

But what was now happening in the city of her birth? She passed more film-crews, endless channelling for cables, floodlights for all-night builders and scaffolders; many huge tents, and there, on a rise, a nest of huge dish-aerials flanked by at least a dozen stretch-limousines. She skirted a tower-block along a broken strip of narrow cracked paving lined with bulldozed rubbish, and stood still for a moment, as if instinctive of some near danger. Surprising even herself, she did not scan for external threats, but examined her vocabulary; Cartoons? Sketches? Belief-robotics again?

This was not herself.

Something was entering the woods.

She looked at the tower-block again, and saw it was peppered with small dish aerials, clustered around windows and walls like flies around the eyes of starvation. As stamens of image colonisation, Nora supposed that the satellite-dishes squatted on the buildings as the churches had once sat on the goblin-mounds. Still wondering about her strange new bits of vocabulary, she passed more lines of long-dead street lamps, all at different comic angles. Now came the last light of day over half-sunk rusting skips full of uncollected EuroRubble. Half-completed endeavours gathered round her. By abandoned bus-stops and mournful graphics of forgotten scaffolding. Out of these twilight cartoons, loomed *The Biddles Rooming House,* whose open door threw a beam of fractured light into the half-geometries of the oncoming dark.

She had never seen a room like this before. A lone fly-spattered bulb trembled into light, revealing a room plastered with photographs of famous stars, past present. Each wall was covered with cutout images of famous film, television, and radio personalities of the past, and even one or two from old music-hall days. A tiny model in varnished wood of the famous Val Doonican in his rocking chair marked 'Kilkenny Souvenir Company' perched on a bedside-table, and seemed still quite ready for lights, cameras and action of some pink oval-screen TV show of yesteryear. A knock at the door, and Mrs. Biddles wheeled in a fine beast of a TV set. It was a 24-inch *Mitsubishi,* with enhanced colour, new high-tech flat screen, and the latest remote which could handle many kinds of bar-coding and digital programmes. Various decoders sat on top of the attached video recorder. Mrs. Biddles smiled furtively as she pointed out the equipment.

"They're putting coin and cable next week. Subscription applications are still a bit slow, but they're working on it."

This, from a 60-year-old woman who could have come straight out of the Ireland of Robert Emmet and Wolf Tone, this gave the ancient room, with its curling images and its shining technology an eerie dimension.

"You had a lodger keen on show-business, Mrs Biddles?"

Mrs. Biddles replied as if she had not heard even a sound. Of such stuff are absolute invisibilities made.

"Don't worry."

"Worry?"

"There's a free-installation motor-drive 6-foot high-gain parabolic coming next week, but don't worry, there's a temporary fibre-optics hook-up tomorrow, so you can still have fun."

"Fantastic, fantastic."

"But some of the smart-cards still won't work without the motor-drive, so I'm afraid you might not get your Red Hot Dutch for the time being, my dear. But I can bring you a nice cup of tea, if you like."

"Thank you. But Mrs. Biddles, how about the shopping channel? I must have that."

"Oh, that's alright. Install the software in that box over there, and you'll get a 12.896 Gigahertz automatic lock-on, with some very slight attenuation. Any problems, Entertainment Helpline will down-load corrections straight to your main memory. By the way, The old analogue FM channels are OK, but there's a bit of a VHF dip in this area, and sometimes the line resolution is not properly modulated, and the mid-frequencies are a few dB down. Damn that mountain. It's full of iron, you know. Plays hell with the soaps, sometimes."

Nora mentioned she had seen a famous face.

"Oh her. Yes, they're all here now."

"Making a film?"

"Oh not necessarily, my dear. You'll see hundreds of those people. They all live here now."

With that intriguing remark, Mrs. Biddles left the room.

Nora looked at one TV with disc-drive, one definitely illegal decoder, one almost-illegal descrambler, and a grey-area smart-card slot, probably for the continental porn channels. Jesus Christ, thought Nora, *The Biddles Rooming House* sure gave good television. Big as a sideboard, and with stereo speakers either side, the thing bristled proudly with its impressive controls, and digital displays.

Mrs. Biddles came back with the tea, and stood gazing at the set again, as if puzzled that it was not switched on. She said that there was now such a set in each room. She told Nora that there was some sort of thing called the Entertainment Scheme in Belfast whereby such wonders could now be obtained almost free of charge. Nora had no opportunity to ask her about this strangely charitable offer before the woman disappeared, muttering about similar such Entertainment schemes in town about which she would tell her tomorrow, when she had more time.

Celebrate homecoming with a piss. Good God. An outer wooden corridor made for dwarves. Incense coming up now with the sound of an accordion and a comforting chorus of *The Belfast Brigade* from below. A cupboard. Utter dark. Strike a match. Stub of candle. Jesus, Mary and Joseph! What was this? Looks like loose 18th century boards laid across 18th century hole. Thoughts of Alexander Pope. Careful, or she might never be seen again. One of the Biddles was good at the toilet-paper: neat squares of old daily papers were stacked, exactly 7"x 7", going to back to Mrs. Simpson and fast-forward through the Nurembourg Trials to IRA campaigns of the 1950s. They were pitted sheets of long-stored cartoon-time, neatly torn by some conscientious historian and carefully threaded with baling wire and looped on a six-inch masonry nail, rammed into the ancient crumbling plaster.

She squatted, tore off a sheet, and as she gazed upon the leaders of the Third Reich, a stream of her urine fell into a soundless dark, and the past of Ireland returned to her.

High-tuned high-revving military engines of clutch-surging heavy vehicles; Boots on wet rocking pavement slabs; A million flashing lights. The bang and clank of tailboard, armoured doors, and small-arms. 6th February, 1971. And Nora Harcourt was five minutes old. Shouts along street and entry; A tiny wrapped bundle; A rush to the Mater hospital in a taxi. Endless alarm bells, splintering glass, and jammed car horns. Through folds of sheets and stitched blankets filtered the key tones of the city and the century. Bullets. Armour. Flight. Fire. Rushing soldiers.

Nora's first fragment of torn Ireland at this age of five minutes, already old for the time, the era stamped her with its lore before she could even breathe properly. Carbon 14 dating of her pysche could have got her to within a split second of a decade in the twentieth century.

Ferret armoured cars of the 17/21st Lancers closing the bridges across the River Lagan; baton rounds streaking across Clonard Gardens, Kashmir Road, and Odessa Street; brick and glass shards covering Getty Street and Cairns Street junctions; Leeson Street jammed with flaming buses, upturned milk floats and hijacked council trucks; shots, petrol, and ammonia bombs against the Ist Royal Anglicans. Brits receive many incoming calibres and velocities: snub-nosed lead rounds slow as bumblebees from turn-of-the-century low-velocity long rifles disinterred from cellars at midnight, now banging away above Kelly's Bakery. Saracen and one-ton Humber Pig giving piteous moans from overheated Rolls Royce engines, and pouring gallons of slimy moonlit oil by a collapsed wall. By Falls Road, armoured glass vision blocks of Ferrets penetrated by unexpected armour-piercing rounds from 1940 Boys half-inch Anti-Tank Rifle. Wounded driver on stretcher by the last grocer in Europe with blended teas in wooden drawers. Crackle of wireless sets as a Land Rover skids into a street lamp. Unarmed RPG rounds float through the windows of the Prudential Insurance Head Office and nestle on the deep-pile carpet; a single half-inch Browning opens up from the Halifax Building Society, fires ten rounds into the mountain profile of the street's end, then no more from its jammed 50-year-old breech.

Now a smell of acid rain on opencast working. You had to laugh. Female in still-life squatting position. What? Hole so deep cannot hear pee strike water; now wipe vagina on the mad Hess, and dab a drop for Reichmarshall Goering at his side in the dock. Can hear a woman singer in Room Number 10 trying to rehearse; another final dab, and pictures of Clem Attlee, the first mushroom cloud, and a picture of the ITMA cast flutter down into the utter dark; now pull up pants to Mimi's solos from *La Boheme,* coming from a trying amateur somewhere above her head. Now quick zip, and vamoose. Talk about Entertainment Helpline. Definitely not a place to spend a lot of time in.

But back in her room, seeing her face in the oval mirror of the old dressing-table, the past refused to go.

15 minutes old. Already she was watching, observing. A mask over her face and the semi-realisation of a speeding vehicles full of bars, straps, steel fittings of all kinds, rows of incomprehensible technics and a great howling from the roof.
Attempted arms-search near the Clonard monastery defeated by a screaming phalanx of brick-throwing buttress-bosomed women the like of which the young Brit squaddies never dreamed. Nail bombs and sticks of commercial gelignite force back 1st Parachute's patrols in Butler

Street; tribal Amazons with fresh perms, hairnets and beehives and Bingo-swift hands tearing up paving slabs and cobblestones with slight dark men in flared trousers, Sergeant Pepper shirts and long hair of just time past. Still some old valve No. 19 wireless sets in Saracens, and a single blushing Saladin at the corner of Leeson Street, with no ammunition allowed for its 75mm. Fresh spotty faces of poor-diet British youth still in pre-camouflage-jacket khaki, wearing old-fashioned shiny helmets, their Belgian FN rifles sporting equally shiny bayonets, and still capable of Full Automatic, more dangerous to rifleman than Rebel.

32 Heavy Regiment moving down Lepper Street. Gunner Curtis falls dead, hit by automatic fire from Templar House Flats.

The first soldier to be shot dead in Northern Ireland.

6th February, 1971.

Nora Harcourt was two hours old.

The circles of dead stars on the dressing table were momentary pleasure even from a paste-up universe from which the live juice had long gone. This focus was a rare moment of reverie, a brief time when her concentration wasn't locked on to some extraordinary scheme of complex vengeance whose detection was now beginning to absorb more person-hours than the servicing of the National Dept. George Formby. Flicker, flicker. Frankie Howerd. The pulsing advertisements, though old, were still powerful. Films. Rock n' Roll. Dancers, actors, singers.

Giggles. Non-threats.

Throwaway stuff.

She laughed at the *Mitsubishi*. It laughed back, daring her to switch it on and get wired-in.

Junk cartoons.

Sleep.

X

The Old Curiosity Shop

In the last week of April, Marshall was able to have the first Full Team Conference on the situation in Northern Ireland. After getting the green light from the Directrix, two months of almost 24-hour work had succeeded in making a fine nest for Entertainment State to breed. A front organisation, *Entertainment Enterprises Unlimited* had been formed as a cover to help launch the new Fieldsian vision in Northern Ireland. This front, lovingly designed by Barsby and Annie, was a conglomerate consisting of international business men, many Famous Faces, and interested slabs of American and European corporate muscle. *Entertainment Enterprises* included two subsidiaries within its framework. The first was *EAT-I* (Extremely Advanced Technology Indeed), which had become one of Fields' favourite grey-scale hybrid animals, whose power and interests threaded through Defence, Security, and the Military. This particular organisation, as pure twenty-first century Prototype Control, had been designed by Benson, and in his own words, made both Westminster and Congress look like fire-sharpened sticks to poke the hide of a woolly mammoth. The other subsidiary was *The Most Unusual Aeroplane Company*, an almost-failing business which made light jet aircraft of quite brilliant, but most eccentric design. This business was promptly bought out by *Entertainment Enterprises*. Turned round quickly with extra investment, it soon made a small profit, which gave great authenticity to the entire cover operation. *The Most Unusual Aeroplane Company* had factory test-sheds, an assembly-line, and a landing strip near the EuroDump, the strip of waste land which was the assembly area for all incoming elements of Entertainment State.

The aircraft company made the *Black Mountain Bird*, a fly-by-wire aircraft whose revolutionary form appealed to Entertainment folk in particular. It was basically four 12-foot diameter transparent spheres connected by thin struts to form a diamond-shape. One sphere contained the two engines, and small jet-thrust stabilisers were mounted on the struts, which were computer-managed for stability. The computer itself was located in the middle of the diamond. Already, the fascinating shape of this craft was the unofficial symbol of Entertainment State on badges, flags, and letterheads, just below the picture of Fields himself.

There was still much work to do, but when all was ready, Fields would leave Tower House forever, go fully public, and eventually, after a few weeks, travel to Northern Ireland as President of *Entertainment Enterprises* to unite his kingdom. The Tower House organisation itself was looking forward to the coming operation, and there was confidence that the operation to dose the troublesome Irish head with beautifully-engineered glitz would be successful.

Whilst happy with progress, Marshall knew that the Entertainment Bomb MK 1 had now reached the inevitable stage where it had to be discussed by the dreaded Committee. This was the nervous moment when the broad particulars of an extremely secret operation were required to be revealed to a panel of rank outsiders appointed by Parliament. The Grace and Favour Mob, as The Committee were better known in Tower House, were a hybrid collection of Them Upstairs who were supposed to act as a caretaker buffer between Parliament and the Security Services. Predictably, most were from the Second Chamber, the Privy Council, and the traditional dining clubs. The Services, Westminster, and Oxbridge were well represented. The Committee was only usually convened when Most Serious Matters needed to be discussed. These usually involved the absolutely required termination of lives (the Gibraltar Three, Hilda Murrell, Rudolf Hess), nuclear matters (the suppression of information about radiation leaks, nuclear plant security, and the ever-increasing threat of terrorist use of nuclear weapons), and any immediate sabotage threat to major strategic installations such as oil platforms, ports, and nuclear-weapons storage. Most Serious Matters also included all 'close' assassination threats from whatever quarter. With these things in mind, the thought of what The Committee would make of Fields' ideas about *Take That* or Kylie Minogue with respect to Northern Ireland, certainly lightened the heavy working days of Marshall and some of his colleagues.

All in Tower House disliked The Committee intensely. But the continual problem was that inevitably the Security Services frequently had to be connected to both muscle and money. Unlike the United States, they did not have the physical and financial resources to carry out such operations as Marshall proposed purely by themselves, and The Committee had also made it very clear in the past that they would never be allowed to do so. This was to prevent the Security Services getting ideas above their station, as certainly tended to happen when any such organisations were both over-financed and under-regulated, such as the CIA.

The unheated room in Westminster had an odour of stale beer and fag-ends. Marshall had not been surprised, when some weeks ago, the ubiquitous Minister John Carlton had been appointed head of the members of this august body were now arrayed before Marshall, and looked like something out of a stoutly constructed British film of long ago. The semicircle contained a stout squire who favoured beatings and red-hot irons, and an old soldier, ready for the portrait in the dining room, who had in past days recommended bringing in the tanks and heavy artillery from Rhine Army and 'doing' everything that needed to be 'done' in Northern Ireland in the course of a single inferno-evening.

To John Carlton's right loomed a great hairy Scottish bear with a permanent scowl; to his left, was a terrified token socialist from the Privy Council who looked as if he had just dropped in to plaster the ceiling. But, Marshall reminded himself, you had to be careful. There was always someone on The Committee who was bluffing. He (or she) was the dope who was taking it all in, but who appeared hardly capable of boiling an egg. In this case Marshall put his money on the Privy Councillor. As he often told Fields, in his *Cash N'Carry* experience, no-one who looked like Norman Wisdom on amphetamines was likely to miss a single thing.

Marshall seated himself as comfortably as he could before the crescent of faces. A renowned horse-breeder present sniffed the stale air as if he expected Marshall to arrive with steaming onion baps in a *Tesco* bag, as Fields had done on several legendary occasions in the past, to utterly terrify the assembly. Yes, Marshall saw Fields getting nought out of ten from this Committee, who usually fought clever men from *any* social class with just as much elemental savagery as any swarthy enemy from beyond Chelmsford. Fields was that nightmare of the Spitfire-Britisher: a lone-wolf Bohemian intellectual who not only had the infernal nerve to go to Eton, but who wrote marvellously incomprehensible books like *StarPower* in the bargain. The Bunter also trebled his infernal cheek by making a fortune thereby. To add insult to injury, Fields' was almost a foreigner, and in the right light, his *pince-nez* glinting, he looked as if he might just have emerged from Lambeth Synagogue around 1900.

As a elementary professional precaution, Marshall made sure his presentation of the *Entertainment Enterprises* Plan was a sixth-form journalistic affair, a smart pragmatic little essay which he assumed the Committee would seize and waddle off with like a dog with a juicy bone. He was also careful when speaking not to indulge in anything but singular end-stopped telegraphese. Anything else gave the Committee unprecedented intellectual difficulty. As was usual on such high-level British Committees, both the technical command, and scientific qualifications of the Grace and Favour Mob were nonexistent. Of the men who might have the level of ability to understand modern military intelligence and associated technologies within the very special context

94

of Northern Ireland, there were none present. The members of the Committee had all been chosen on a level of a deliberately cultivated neo-Edwardian idea of Trust. Like the Officer Corps of the First World War, these men would never crack, certainly never betray, but then they would never ever really think, analyse, investigate, study. It didn't really matter whether they cracked in any case, thought Marshall, longing for a roll-up, because possibly not a single one had any idea at all of the depth and perspectives of modern military and civilian Intelligence operations within an advanced industrial society. A good selection of the fathers of the ramrod backs and clipped moustaches before Marshall had actively resisted mechanisation of the British Army in the 1930s. It seemed to Marshall that unfortunately the moral honesty and solid practicality of these sons of the Great and Good and Brave and True had long ago defeated any radical intelligence they may have possessed.

The only thing the members really had in common was their anti-Irish sentiments, which reached back through cultural infinity. In the past, Marshall had often been rudely interrupted and given a brisk Baden-Powell type lecture on the Irish being 'cowards' which seemed to mean that the Irish had the infernal nerve to absolutely refuse to flap out from the heather and have the honour and privilege of being shot down wholesale by decent types. Marshall often thought that Philby was allowed to escape from Beirut long ago, to avoid the existential gymnastics involved in trying to define exactly who he was or what he did. He had the impression from previous meetings with The Committee that the Anglo-Saxon mind still had unprecedented difficulty with the idea of *political* crime.

The nature of cultural time was such that these men, who after all had been born in a technical age, these men were somehow nevertheless become their fathers. This was a manner of psychic throwback which was little understood. Great DNA Entertainment, thought Marshall, noting how nicely John Carlton got on with everyone here. It was always a perfect wonder to Marshall that an exact tribal syntax and accent were wonderfully preserved in an essence of tribal robotics which could only be called pure Fieldsian Performance. Or perhaps, he often joked to himself, the men assembled here were not even human. For light relief, when before the Committee, Marshall would often imagine that he could pretend to leave, but return almost immediately to see multicoloured smoke issuing from the eyeless heads of slumped Fieldsian BUACs.

They were talking about Fields going to Northern Ireland when up popped a six-foot-six toothy blinking owl who belonged to one of the oldest families in the land, and who always appeared to have read the glossier and more enthusiastic Hi-Fi magazines.

"Will you be in touch with him by VHF satellite?"

Marshall stifled the comic image within him of anyone at all attempting to speak to Fields by satellite, and decided to try terror tactics as a return favour.

"Would you like the technical details?"

The blinking owl, who happened to personally own a quarter of the south of England, paled at the prospect, and was rescued by the massive grizzled Scot who happened to own a different quarter of the same said area.

"How you going to get him in there?"

"He'll go by himself. Literary success. Early retirement. Going to his promised Land. Buy his own train and boat ticket."

"Label around his neck?"

The Committee gave a good-natured roar, which was quickly stifled by John Carlton, being today surprisingly protective towards Marshall, who noticed Carlton's laser glance at the foppish individual who had made the remark. This character's sense of humour was acknowledged to be somewhat more underdeveloped than even his Grace and Favour brain. However, this thin rake, who had the inspiring nickname of Doggy, was a successful breeder of fine racing mares; this, apparently was the elegant way of being absolutely forgiven for every sin Marshall could think of, including that of being discretely dismissed from the Junior Officer's Course of the Parachute Regiment. The reasons for this dismissal resided in a pink folder 349/3x in a nuclear-proof bunker sunk hundreds of feet into the ground beneath their polished chairs. Marshall hoped he would never have need to open the folder, although he thought he could have a rather a good guess at the contents. He now decided it was time for a shot across the bows.

"Would you like to take the risks he is taking?"

John Carlton almost smiled as a blush crept around Doggy's family nose, unchanged for well over ten plush generations; this prompted the balding ex-Major-General to leap to Doggy's defence. Poor thing Doggy must be protected at all costs. Marshall wondered what was being protected.

"See here Marshall, your man could disappear like a kipper in a furnace."

"I am hoping there will be less of a furnace."

"Why?"

Came from Skull, to the left of Doggie, whose private family fortune was of a size quite beyond any kind of rational estimation.

"Money."

Skull responded as if Marshall had spoken of excreta. Marshall had a feeling of falling down a well made of so many DNA jokes he would soon meet Henry the Eighth via Gladstone and Walpole.

"Money?"

Said Skull, with a sneer which gave him his name.

"They'll start earning. For the first time in their lives. Particularly the youth of the province. It's the one thing any paramilitary element would have extreme difficulty in coping with."

"Earning?"

The interrogative came from a new member Marshall had not seen before. He was a fresh-featured individual sporting a Household Brigade tie, and whose astonished features certainly expressed terror at the idea that working youth should earn anything significant at all. The atmosphere in the room quickly became one of horror that (particularly Irish Catholic) working-class people should obtain any kind of real earning power. The idea seemed to arouse such depths of loathing equivalent to a threat of pollution or radiation, or the deliberate spreading of some absolutely devastating plague or disease.

"Yes. Earning."

The new member looked at Marshall as if he were Eliza Doolittle. To actually suggest giving people freedom and pleasure instead of a new and varied form of banging them on the head caused hateful rays to be directed at Marshall as if he were the very devil, or totally mad, or both. For a moment Marshall saw the world of his cracked *Doris Day Birthday Goblets* as a world of innocence from which he had fallen. He also hoped his old salesman's skills were intact, just in case the Committee turned really nasty and dumped him on the Parish.

The technique of the single-question-then-silence continued. On these occasions Marshall always felt like a child about to be punished in a world in which there was no such thing as good news, and even less of such Transatlantic dago-nonsense as encouragement, or enthusiasm, and even less technical interest. No, not even a look in the eye, not a grin. It wasn't that they could not forgive his cleverness, so much as they despised his lack of style. That Fieldsian word again. And the idea of someone getting something for nothing other than dire punishment was obviously going to cause as grave a difficulty as any sentence with more than one clause.

"*Entertainment,* d'ya say, Marshall?

This came from the owner of a faraway prewar accent who looked at Marshall as probably one of those funny little squirrels called ordinary folk who just happened to run around the high street and clog up the pavements and roads.

"He wishes to establish an area where Entertainment reigns supreme."

"A kind of permanent amusement arcade?"

"Yes."

"Good God."

Pause. Don't overburden them, thought Marshall, laughing inwardly at the thought of what Fields' more spectacular and esoteric objectives would do to the minds assembled before him.

"How you going to control the bounder?"

"We have formed *Entertainment Enterprises Unlimited* as a management team."

"Entertainment, d'you say? How does he feel about it?"

"He believes in it."

"Good God. Does he really? Poor fellow."

Giggles all round, and even a shy little squeak from the Privy Councillor, who looked as if about to serve double sausage, egg and chips all round. The faraway prewar accent sounded again.

"Why do you keep him?"

Keep him? Was Fields a zoo-creature? For a brief moment Marshall was thrown. Why did he keep one of the most brilliant minds in Tower House? He would tell them.

"Because he is successful."

The fruity chortles stopped, and Doggy became Lady Bracknell.

"Success?"

The General blew his nose. Doggy coughed. The Privy Councillor looked down at the floor.

"He is very good at selling things."

"Selling?"

That was enough. The meeting was quickly concluded as if interrupted by a National Declaration of War. Marshall the salesman had mentioned the ultimate vulgarity. That was sufficient burden for one day.

Limousine doors softly clicked shut in the ancient courtyard below, and the guardian spirits sped rapidly back to their more comfortable tumuli; Marshall speculated that what he had experienced was the close proximity of a complete intact Fieldsian world. The Committee was pure Entertainment Texture. It couldn't die because it wasn't alive. It couldn't grow, wasn't going anywhere, was somehow eternally frozen in the midst of a Victorian nursery afternoon. The poor creatures were incapable of even minimal evolution. They were all like cats, showbiz, or the Wizard of Oz. But when the last brain-cell in the world had died, the Grace and Favour Mob would probably still be perfectly composed, preening themselves in some eternal sunlight; or featuring as themselves playing themselves in some inconceivable version of cartoon-flicker produced, directed, cast, and certainly paid for by somebody else.

In almost every other land of Planet Earth, the poor Committee would probably all have been shot generations ago; or else he, Marshall, would have had sordid and embarrassing files on each of them which would have had all their Entertainment dignities shaking like dried peas in a cocoa-tin. This was not a situation which Marshall would have liked or enjoyed. The men before him were some of the last fleeting heartbeats of his nation. He should have loved them, but all he could summon up was a mild nostalgic affection, and little else. A terrible thing had happened to them: *they had forgotten their mission.*

Marshall knew what that felt like; at times, he thought he had almost forgotten his. But he had no alternative but to try and deal as best he could with this fastidious blindness hot from what his rude American colleagues were wont to call 'the old curiosity shop at twilight time.'

XI

Enter the Apache

By the end of May, the first big accommodation tents of *Entertainment Enterprises* had been pitched on patches of newly filled and graded areas, of the EuroDump, just by the hangers of *The Most Unusual Aeroplane Company.* This area had rapidly become the main assembly point for all incoming elements of Entertainment State. Already, there were extraordinary scenes. Each morning started with the orchestrated shouts of the mass callisthenics sessions, and parade and carnival rehearsals; these were often led and conducted by Famous Faces, who took to their new sergeant-major roles better than anyone ever thought. With the arrival of such great Stars, the camp-following tentacles of money, influence and technology were spreading the body of Entertainment State through the city. The *Eat-I* organisation was saturating Belfast with any and every aspect of modern Entertainment technology Marshall noted with great satisfaction that now these much-admired constructions were in place, his popeyed American colleagues no longer referred to his native country as *the old curiosity shop.*

With this satisfying thought in mind, Marshall commenced his morning's business by opening a Red Box which contained four single-spaced sheets of A4. These were part of the regular ultra-secret General Index for the first week of June, distributed three times a week. Each issue usually consisted of some thirty or more pages circulated to Heads of Departments only. In his hand were reports on the hundreds of spider-lines which radiated from Tower House to an astonishing range of the world's compass. Anything in the slightest way relevant to Northern Ireland might be included, from a remark heard on a Madrid railway station to the tracking of a major arms shipment, a certain face in an unusually expensive restaurant, a postal worker's tip, or a railway driver's phone-call. Times were changing very rapidly, and those Intelligence analysts who still had managed to retain a sense of humour called most of what they were now engaged in 'The Watch On The Self'.

Each item in the General Index had been filtered a score of times before being taken from a log-jammed river to its appropriate significance section, that choice being an art no machine could yet match. Only then were the computers really put to work. What was the strategic-materials talk in Stockholm or Rome this particular week? To obtain, pay for, and transport weapons, and strategic nuclear material across Europe was not easy. Good experienced operators might well get the material through, but the manufacturing base of tactical, never mind strategic, hardware was narrow and unique; it involved relatively few highly specialised interest sectors, most of which were crammed with inbuilt alarm-channels, both human and material. Such a channel would open and flicker just long enough to enable a Hamburg GSG9 computer to tell the *Sûreté*, *Guarda*, or Special Branch, where and when to catch hold of a fast disappearing tail. The main-frames would then be let loose, their extensive linked networks being the only hounds fast enough to work up the inference speed required.

His thoughts were interrupted by his secretary bringing in yet another Red Box. He looked up, surprised. He had not had two Red Boxes in one day since the Gulf War. Alex Spencer gave him the faintest of smiles as he caught her eye. He opened the battered case as if it might contain a cobra. A single sheet of A4. An Apache Signal. Direct from Her Upstairs.

He gazed in wonder at the report. Although he had heard of such things, he had never received such a signal in his entire 30-year career. John Carlton had been correct. A privateer was on the loose. Rare in Intelligence as he once heard Benson say, 'as a sighting of a foot-high hobgoblin in green hose and pointed shoes along Westbourne Grove.' Here was Minister John Carlton's Pirate. And to generate an Apache Signal, a bloody good one. A loner amongst loners. Amazing, he thought, reaching for his cigarette papers. Most such buccaneers got wasted before they stepped out of their back-bedroom. His breath whistled through his teeth. He didn't think there were any of these comic-strip heroes left. With an Apache, what was being looked for was not just another isolated clandestine arms or drugs shipment, but the very highest measure of human skill and determination.

And this one acted apparently for pure moral and political idealism, now supposed to be the rarest of commodities, whether amongst innocent or guilty. Motivation without profit was the wildest of cards. Yet all the major assassins (left, right, and anarchist) of the past forty years had something of such motivation. They were very different to conventional criminals, who usually had a record, could easily become informers, were not the brightest of folk, and certainly not the most disciplined. Most such had a sentimental streak, and could usually be caught by the net-full, flashing and shouting and spouting, their blond girlfriends all

101

over the front pages of *The News of The World.* The police loved this largely working-class game-show. It came complete in itself, with TV stars, fallen boxers, drinking clubs, and nightclubs crammed with informers and policeman enjoying themselves, a lot of whom finished up in gaol alongside their underworld friends and associates.

The first sign of a true Apache being active was the deafening silence from this heaving stew, who usually knew anything and everything there was to be known or told about anyone, from roadsweepers to Royals. The first spore of a very different kind of creature stalking Europe was the complete absence of trails of misappropriated property, money, passports, myriad licenses, tax returns, and the inevitable social security records. To achieve twentieth century invisibility proper was a quite unique art-form. Every kind of contact-life had to be cast off or reforged, changed and reforged again, then further changes and forges were again scattered, split, shredded in their turn before further false paper-trails could again be laid.

To continue to remain invisible in the twentieth century was to some, Marshall supposed, the only interesting game. The compensations were the taste of real blood, some equally real action, and the sound of Authority falling, which to some peculiar folk was far sweeter music than any mass of beautifully harmonised string instruments.

In his experience, most assassins were pre-Freudian creatures. Despite the efforts of popular psychiatrists and the press and media who would have them as psychopaths or maladjusted middle-class trendies, almost all assassins were quite sane, and drawn from a broad class spectrum. Some lived secretly in a private land where valour and moral purpose were not yet sullied by overprotective democratic rationalisations. In what Fields called The Great Age of Clerks, he was always surprised to realise that there were still many who secretly dreamed and lusted for the simplicity of the assassin's view, with its complete dedication, and its resurrection of genuine mystic purity of moral purpose. This, he supposed, was part of an anarchist religion in which all the old lost codes of righteousness and rites of Old Testament vengeance appeared to be very much alive and well.

If the Apache trails didn't plunge deep into the criminal forests, they nevertheless led to a world which to Marshall was just as fascinating. With the sound of the trains in the night, the ennui of what he called the Hidden Ones was at its most painful and acute. Some were simply too old, many were completely thrashed out, others had lost their gun-nervelittle known outside the Intelligence services. The broken hearts of hardly-known old subversives tended to beat again when the almost inconceivable smell of sulphur was again detected on golf course, in and there were a few whose many covers in the past had so confused them, they didn't really know who they were any more. This was a society boardroom, on factory floor, or before mirrors which revealed the belly hanging over the gut.

This was a college as secret as any himself or Fields belonged to. If the Hidden Ones really believed in anything at all any more, they still served to open doors, arrange a journey, help with bundles of used notes, clothes, transport, new documents, food in tins, or a place to lay the weary plotting head. Often, in Northern Ireland in particular, a bloody plotting head needed a surgeon, a nurse, and a well-scrubbed room at the back of the suburban garage. Here was a subterranean community only partially known even to the conspiracy theorist and the professional investigator. Such coast-watchers were often rightly baffled by the incomprehensible movement of weapons and information by shadowy figures at the limit of the focus of the discursive investigating eye.

When the Apache moved, Marshall conjectured it would be through this particular forest. He imagined by now the whole of the globe was pulsing with her electronic ghost: *Sex: female. Country of origin: Northern Ireland. Motivation: moral. Age: mid-thirties. Appearance: master of disguise, cross-dressing frequently suspected....*

With Fields about to go public under the guise of early retirement, and *Entertainment Enterprises* getting underway in Northern Ireland, this was just what he needed. How long would it take she who was known as Nora Harcourt, to detect Entertainment State?

Not very long, he guessed.

Not very long at all.

XII

A Pirate Ship

On a morning early in June, with a sky the blue of a fairytale, Marshall sat facing two colleagues for what he knew might well be the last time in any foreseeable future. By Fields' side was Benson, whose brothel-creepers and oiled *quiff* nicely contrasted with Fields' half-mast Oxford bags and Bill Haley kiss-curl. Marshall tried to cast out of his mind a remark from a particularly humourless superior that the *Entertainment Enterprises* package now appeared to be designed around two of the biggest clowns in Tower House.

Judging by the expressions of the two men in front of him on this important planning morning, it was obviously going to be a difficult meeting. Both sat with their noses almost in the air, looking away from one another, like a rival pair of Dames at a pantomime audition. Both reminded Marshall of figures modelled in pre-Regulation ultra-inflammable plastic he had last seen packed in cardboard boxes in the back of his *Morris Minor Estate* in 1965. He remembered The Pissing Gnome and the Very Rude Monk as going up like phosphorous grenades should any *Ronson* flame, or lit taper from a book of *Go-Go-Girl* matches come even near them. But, he thought, perhaps the more esoteric parts of modern civilisation were always custom-designed by such figures as Benson and Fields; perhaps there were hundreds of other such modern elves who wore slippers and slept in alcoves, or who sported winkle-pickers and regularly ran pink plastic combs through glistening waves of jet-black hair. Bunkered men, bunkered thoughts, men building systems as defence against a world whose low-key practical ordinariness probably terrified them.

He supposed that the pair now talking warily to one another were brilliant loners who knew only deep night, intense speculation, and the sustenance of snacks machines, the only really bright and warm things within their life, smiling theatrical presents in dark corridors, little pantomimes of welcome in the deepest night. Such things were designed for nocturnal coast-watchers like these, he thought; they consumed such trifles as they worked all night in their laboratories and workshops as if on their knees praying to the one true genie of the lamp: the Correlation. This, he supposed, was always the alchemical heart of the forming substance of the endless vigil within some Great Project. For the men in front of him, and their kind, he imagined that this was sufficient in itself, this old and beautifully rare ecstasy of the Ancients. Perhaps, he thought, such intense cerebral activity would eventually almost vanish from the mass-world, like Keats' Psyche, or the Beast of Bodmin; perhaps, like Fields said, Brain itself would be cut adrift, disintegrating to become semi-abandoned hulk-thoughts, drifting in and out of disintegrating levels of perception, and eventually left to founder on the rocks of the television dark.

But if Fields always appeared almost too happy, Marshall knew that Benson lived in a reign of complete personal terror. Perhaps the man with the carefully folded white linen handkerchief protruding from the top pocket of his velvet-collared jacket had, like Marshall himself, come at last to realise that knowledge had almost started to travel back from whence it had come, back into elite survival cults within such tumuli as Tower House. He supposed that at some instant within the lives of all men such as these, clocks older than formed iron had begun to count the hours back to mound and barrow time. When he thought of such things, he thought of the Security Services as one of the few institutions preserving something of infinite value, just as the monasteries had preserved the precious texts of Antiquity.

Almost at the end of a long career, to Marshall's mind, from the days of the Cavendish Laboratory to Los Alamos, from Harwell to MIT, the brilliant had steadily become more bunkered, isolated from an outer culture. But Fields' ideas appeared to have had leapt right away from the controls of their own culture dish, to become an elemental firework display; they were now unstoppable, a kind of essence of pure proliferation which moved in all directions at once like a bomb-burst. He imagined that the structure of the first nuclear critical mass must have been something like Fields' singular idea, exploding as it did through the mind as an equally unique solution to a dreadful human predicament. Within Tower House the awesome term 'The Entertainment Bomb, MK 1' was circulating, although no-one had yet had the nerve to put this on a document heading.

As the discussion commenced in earnest, an ever-tense Benson shot low glances at the closed door, as if calculating that it was the only means of escape from the room. If he was the Mod, Fields was the Rocker. If Benson's mind was ahead of most others in his field, Marshall noted that nevertheless, as a figure, he might have been sold with Coronation Mugs and sticks of Blackpool Rock, although Benson could not have been more than thirty. Fields seemed aloof to Benson's shifty glances as he lapped at a wobbling curiosity which was a mass of red-and-yellow shaving-cream substance squirted into a shocking-pink Barbara Cartland hat.

Marshall adjusted a small fan as Benson's aftershave mixed with the intense aromatics of something Fields had in a stained *Bargain Town* carrier-bag nestling at his huge feet. This morning the Bunter wore a pair of what looked like black-tarred felt boots which, thought Marshall, probably no-one had seen in Europe since the death of Tolstoy. God only knows where he does his shopping, he marvelled, but nevertheless he admired the anarchic symmetry of this twin spearhead of the 'Faction Force' of *Entertainment Enterprises.*

Despite being pleased and inspired with the intriguing possibilities of what was to come, Benson was in a dreadful mood. Fields was against all he ever stood for. Marshall cursed inwardly. He had let the discussion get off to a bad start. Benson had been in Japan a month previous when a noted theatrical psychic, Tonto, had apparently stopped two of Tokyo University's Physics Laboratory computers in a very impressive demonstration of what some called psychic powers. Benson was an intense sceptic, he belonged to that increasingly defensive movement, and Marshall's head quickly became a tennis scorer as Fields spurted in mid tongue-lap.

"You were there, Benson weren't you? Were you impressed?"

"Impressed? Should I like frauds?"

"Was it an official fraud or an unofficial fraud?"

"There's a difference?"

"Which was the dominant falsehood? Which magic is the fallen magic? Which aftershave means success?"

"This is fantasy."

"There is no such thing as a fantasy. Talk about a grey scale of realisations if you like, an octave of appearances."

Marshall smiled at Benson, who did not smile back.

"Fields doesn't have fantasies, Benson. He's having such a good time in reality, he doesn't need them."

"He's a very lucky man."

Fields licked his lips and looked away from Benson.

"Only a simple mind needs a reality. They pair up, like religion and suffering, Denials and Leaks, or TV and death."

"Do you do this for a living, or are you just a pretty face?"

Fields snapped back into pursuit-mode.

"How did Tonto shut down those computers?"

"Only he knows that, Fields."

"Shouldn't we?"

"Not really. What for?"

"You disappoint me, Benson."

"I belong to a profession of disappointments, Fields. They stop us getting excited and making claims we can't back up. My profession is the art of the mundane. I refuse to apologise for there not being awe-inspiring semi-animalistic mysteries behind every curtain. Your ideas are pure childhood, Fields. Like your food. You must be a very happy man."

"How did Tonto do it?"

"By a trick. He's a magician."

"Bloody good trick."

"He's a bloody good magician. I must say that in my opinion, the cosmos is a far less interesting place than you ever suppose."

"Did the computers have a history of instability?"

"How should I know?"

"You were over there. You might have asked."

"No man can shut down computers like that. Sorry to disappoint you."

"Actually, you amaze me. Because he did it again on three succeeding days."

"He's a fraud. The whole thing is a fantasy."

"What is weight?"

"Mass multiplied by the acceleration due to gravity."

"What is mass?"

"It doesn't matter."

"That's nice to know. What is gravity?"

"I don't know."

"Don't blush. Neither did Einstein. What's an electron?"

"I don't know."

"That phrase again. I love it."

"All these things are conventions. They leads to a million and one integrated consistencies throughout Nature. Electrons light the cookers and heat the homes."

"I am warmed by a convention?"

"God forbid, Fields, I am talking to another scientist, aren't I? You have to be careful how you name things."

"*Name* things? Now that's very interesting."

"People can get confused."

"I hope so. Confusion has saved me from insanity many a time. It is also very enjoyable. You should try it in you circuits sometime, instead of all that Boolean colonialism."

Benson now lowered his voice and looked as if he were in a bad spy-film. Considering what he was, and the place he was in, Marshall thought this rather amusing.

"You aught to be more careful with what you say, Fields. You can easily begin to sound like some kind of nut. The vocabulary can go all wrong The language becomes so fuzzy as the shouts get louder and louder, and the happy-nut finishes up like the drunk at the end of the bar-counter muttering about ghosts, UFOs, and metal-bending. People take liberties, believe you me. You want to be careful what you say. You could be professionally dead within twenty-four hours, talking the way you do. I mean who the hell are you to talk like this here?"

"A storyteller."

"Nice to know. Nice."

Benson noted that Marshall always showed an improving mood when he asked Fields questions.

"You say that there is an element of fantasy in everything? Where does it begin and where does it end?"

"It begins more-or-less in any story at the point where we get near ourselves. I took a young son and daughter of a friend to the London Museum. There were the stocks, the ducking-stool, the whipping block, and the rack. They laughed. There were the seeping walls and chains and red-hot pokers of the dungeons. The laughter got less as we worked our way towards our own centuries. Then some clever museum-designer had decided to call a halt. Round about 1800. Very clever. Round about British Christmas-Card time. That's probably the last time we were happy. Beyond that point the children got a bit disturbed. They were learning to remember. I took them out into the sunlight and bought them ice-creams. They danced around, feeding the pigeons. They were learning to forget. Between learning to forget and learning to remember is the seam between realisations."

Benson gulped.

"A nice story. What does it mean to me?"

"You mean to say that the sliding scales of such a waxing and waning are not present in your circuits?"

"That's irrational."

"I'm not a rationalist."

"Well in that case, perhaps you shouldn't be working here. I haven't time for this. I thought we were here to talk about *Entertainment Enterprises.*"

"Do you think your circuits are made of anything more than Athenian debates? How do you think the genie could ever get out of the bottle? He escapes through the assumption-stuff of which the bottle is made."

"Is that how you escaped?"

"I don't know whether I have escaped. You see I have a big

problem. I don't quite know whether I'm alive or not."

"You're looking well on it."

"Tonto escaped. That's how he shut down those computers."

"I've got bad news for you, Fields. Nobody escapes, nobody."

With the discussion now rapidly becoming more conventional, Benson imagined that outside the building were ordinary men and women going about the pleasant and normal business of the day. However, as always in Tower House, after two hours of extremely boring planning details, even Benson found Fields light relief, as he again picked up his endless thread.

"Tonto shut down those computers because a piece of him was in there. Everything we make is a mirror of everything we are. That's the channel. He merely told a piece of him to go and do something. It heard. And it did. He mimicked an action. And the impurity mimicked him. The old laws of Performance, Imitation. Mimesis. He was in there with the chips."

Benson, with a nervous attempt at a condescending smile, looked at Marshall as if for sympathy.

"Good this is, innit?"

He did not get any sympathy. He turned to Fields again.

"Why are you telling me this?"

"I'm telling you this because within this operation, when the Advertising Concentrate reaches a certain level, your computer circuits will be affected."

"Why?"

"Because Advertising Concentrate is what they're made of."

"What a piece of crap."

Marshal winked at him.

"There never was a new initiative like this one, Benson."

"I'm not sure I can take the pace."

"And it's going to get worse."

"Without advertising, Benson, your circuits and programs could never change, become something beyond their present selves."

"There you go, Benson."

"It's all too much for a Cockney of Quality."

The discussion stabilised quickly again, but nevertheless for the next hour, Benson felt as if he were trapped in a downtown bar in Sumatra, faced with the prospect of having to cut his way out. Never had he conceived of such conversations within such a place as this, judged to be more conservative than the Jockey Club. To him, something here in

109

Tower House had slipped badly out of gear. The impenetrable Marshall had been penetrated. Somehow, they had all relaxed, and as a consequence the place had become a plague house. Some info-virus had made all their protective logics flip their lid. How such a conversation as he had just had with Fields, could possibly have taken place, Benson did not know. What had happened here was something he felt he didn't have the language for.

As the multi-mode Fields now mercifully turned to more rational aspects of planning, Benson's thoughts returned to *StarPower,* though he would never admit to anyone that he had read it. It seemed to him some kind of elaborate joke. But as he now watched Fields dipping into his disgusting bag for more victuals, he was aware that some fantastic mythological animal had come to birth. Benson imagined the cracking of a shell, a tiny piece of protruding claw, a moist nodding beak, a twisted sodden feather or two, a pushing foot; then a first blinking, baffled walleye; then the first moment of exhaustion with sucking lungs and feel of a new gravity. With a final crack, the massive egg that was Fields had apparently exploded. All the cakes, pies, rolls, trifles, loaves, and *Brandysnap Fools* that Fields had ever eaten all his scoffing life had mushroomed up through Tower House into the sky above the city. It was an H-bomb burst of a great host of cultural confectionery. It seemed to Benson that this ideological delicatessen full of amazing bargains formed an invisible but inescapable field of influence beaming out from a Temple of New Belief, whose rays sapped both brain and the will to escape.

Listening to Fields now speaking of Entertainment possibilities, Benson realised that he had built his new church of tinsel. According to all the serious rules of the grownup universe nothing made of tinsel worked. Except models. And as the afternoon sun caught Fields' scoffing features, the new Entertainment State became to Benson one super-dense model, pregnant with undiluted advertisement concentrate, a tumultuous nest of imps and images and dreams about to break out into super-stuff of the Entertainment Edge. Benson was terror-struck. If Fields was right, his programs, languages, and circuits might become pure parish-pump overnight.

As Marshall now summarised Report Number I of *Entertainment Enterprises Unlimited,* Benson looked at Fields, with his 'Neil Sedaka Lives' badge, his new Max Wall trousers, and egg-stained *Bay City Rollers* tartan waistcoat. He was in a madhouse. Or within screaming distance of those American and Japanese techno-dons completely beyond academic recall, who were beginning to whisper about 10th Generation Games. But Fields couldn't be that far ahead. Benson had heard the vaguest of tales about what he was ultimately trying to do. No, Fields couldn't be that far ahead. His own verbal repeats struck him like the dread chords of his worst nightmare. The fear of obsolescence. The fear of himself and his blessed super-computers passing out of Advertising Time like a brand of washing powder.

Now he had the equivalent to Marshall's *Cortina* itch. He was being quietly reprogrammed, that was what was happening to him. What new stage of technology was this? The quest for answers commenced within him. He knew that such a process might take hours, days, even months. Especially for that question. But his inner mind had stood him in good stead before. Most knew the feeling, Benson supposed. Strike a match, tie a shoelace, and up shot the answer to a question asked maybe months previous. The answer would come superimposed over any prevailing situation; it would often come as a shouting advertisement which had the power to severely interrupt any conscious time, demolish a face, a conversation, or a complete set of developing moods.

Fields himself took good note that Benson was now paying more attention as Marshall continued summarising Report Number 1.

It appeared that predictably, most had ignored the more controversial and mystical chapters in Fields' book, and looked upon the Entertainment movement which had sprung from it as a something which although slightly odd, brought in much-needed investment and employment. One thing was certain, this early Entertainment State was no set of puritanical little gnomes who scratched away in cults from Scientology to Socialism. Some of the very top names of the world of show-business, films, theatre, and rock and pop were actually seen digging irrigation channels, delivering Entertainment State mail, and even carrying messages on bicycles. The result of this was an amazed state of rejuvenated conversation in Belfast pubs, clubs, and bars. To have mail delivered by a Famous Face broke all the laws of psychological expectancy, and appeared to appeal to an Irish sense of humour.

Two or three times a week, representatives of *Entertainment Enterprises* would go into town to batter officials with questions and requests for which there were hardly technical or legal precedents. There were ranges of pressures and implications for which officials and civil servants were hardly prepared. The same went for roads, buildings, power-lines, railways, water, and hard-standing for the erection of permanent accommodation and concert platforms within the EuroDump. All these questions and proposals could easily have been smashed to pieces by the average bureaucrat, were it not for the terrifying realisation that in the particular case of Entertainment State, immediate cash-down was always available. Any amount of it. The absolute demanding *now* of such a situation was terrifying for the civil servants of any legal or administrative department. It meant that things were possible. There could hence be no delays whilst heavily mortgaged interests were organised; even the British love of endless Dickensian complications, legal, or financial and corporate, was powerless Many such questions and issues were beginning to be ignored by a City Council and a UK government which was in dire need of the kind of success in Northern Ireland which such multiple projects promised. The infinite delays and complications with the applications to print Entertainment State stamps, and establish an Entertainment State Investment Bank and broadcasting facility were hence short-circuited by government structures which found themselves ambushed from all sides.

The marble-mausoleum City administration, always desperate for money, of course welcomed the sudden inward flow of many different currencies. What it was getting in the bargain was just as irresistible and just as hypnotic. It had to be admitted that most conventional political movements were essentially unimpressive, boring, or unpleasant things. As Fields often said, almost all were attempts at meccano-set interpretations of the world on different levels of sophistication, twisting the world and human lives into estranged perspectives. As with science and socialism ('those two twentieth-century incestuous harpies' as Fields called them), both Nature and humanity were tortured until they fitted some phony set of palsied equations which became the absolute 'truth', until advertising changed. After that, hands, and not a few whole heads were usually found trapped in the greasy till, full of the spare change of compromised singular ideologies. As for the numbers of deaths caused by the incestuous harpies both, well, said Fields, that was anybody's guess.

As Marshall continued his summary, it became obvious that the joy and laughter and enjoyment offered by Entertainment State put the few critics on a very slippery slope indeed; it restricted them to making mainly sheepish remarks about the breaking of bye-laws and the sudden arrival at Aldergrove airport of rather large numbers of most un-Christian folk, who moreover, were not United Kingdom citizens. The answer to these criticisms came in the form of a survey by *The Belfast Telegraph.* Some ten-per-cent of the visitors were near-millionaires! The rest, well, somewhat more comfortably off than the average citizens of Great Britain and Northern Ireland, to say the least. The sheer level of the sudden cash avalanche smothered any and every argument. Of a sudden there was money for everything and anything. And the biggest fall in unemployment for many decades. Without a drop of blood, even prototype Entertainment State had, in the space of just three months, begun to solve at least some of the cancerous problems of hundreds of years.

Whilst Fields was commenting on these things, Benson did his best to try and concentrate on the matter in hand. But his proper responses were stifled by the inner questioning which had started within him and was going its inexorable way. The process was familiar. First, it would go through the subjectivities. They would become in turn more intense, whole arrays often being completely meaningless, except for some cross-referenced scraps of possible anagrams stitched across the images which went by so quickly he could hardly ever retain them.

Meanwhile, in the world outside Tower House, it appeared that Entertainment State was just what the world needed, since the world was exhausted, and chased its tail in a maddening frenzy. During the five hours the trio talked and planned, global warming had replaced global freezing, and the Chief Clerk had tried to launch a Dustbin-User's Charter. In the universities, papers had been given on Dinosaur flatulence, the folk-roots of soap-operas, shaving techniques, the proper storage of spare tyres, and a Nobel Prize winner had declared that very soon, science would know Everything.

At Hyde Park Corner, a strange man declared that with Entertainment State being born, the Junk Nirvana had arrived.

Fields would have said that there were those who agreed with him.

Benson watched and waited for his mind to answer as the morning became late-afternoon, with endless changed plans for The Entertainment Bomb MK 1. Secretaries and assistants came and went, fresh tea was served, notes taken, plans and outlines copied, discussed, and redrafted. Introductions were made to various members of the *Entertainment Enterprises* Planning Team who would eventually 'insert' Benson and Fields (both noted the American Special Forces term) into the Northern Ireland situation. Future meetings were arranged with Military Liaison, and both Fields and Benson the next day would be given something called a General Security Briefing by British Army Intelligence.

Throughout all this, Benson could feel a robot part of him making the right and proper responses. But the mounting subjectivities eventually became intense, almost literally exploding across Fields' face opposite as Benson saw him bite he bit into the vileness of a steaming-something whilst making a point about something called Entertainment Belief. Benson popped what his doctor called 'stabilising pills' into his mouth. Just let it ride, he thought, just let the mind feel free to play with fascinating rubbish until it disentangled itself. He shuddered. Entertainment? Performance. Play. Theatre. The Entertainment Bomb was ticking away the hours to midnight in his head. His mind-machine was getting the measure of Fields' ideas surprisingly early. Both faces of Fields and Marshall leaned towards him. The endless productions of a vastly extended self raced on within. He hesitated. His two colleagues were looking at him, waiting for a comment. Now the feeling wasn't pleasant any more. The machine within him was accelerating. If he wasn't careful, he knew he was going to have a panic attack. He listened with increasing inner vertigo as now Fields, in turn, now gave his own Belfast Briefing, compiled from his own sources.

The Famous Faces had changed, said Fields. Gone were the days and dinners of twittering and plumage displays; gone was the endless talk of drugs, perverted sex, psychoanalysis, divorce and parties; and gone was indolence, and also the endless need for ever-costly security systems as a defence against the cast-out ones who wanted more than a audience-piece of the action. In Belfast, even the Extremely Famous Faces were directed to packaging departments, the new international telephone exchange, the Entertainment State broadcasting station (Radio Entertainment State FM, 97.35 Megahertz), or the myriad jobs on the increasingly busy airfield of the nearby *Most Unusual Aeroplane Corporation.*

Some Faces had never worked physically in their lives, and the small hospital was busy with sprains, pulled muscles, and exhaustion cases. Fat and dissolute Famous Faces were stripped of dope and booze, and put on a compulsory health course before attending whole series of lectures on *StarPower,* or on courses with such terrifying titles as World Media Systems. Breathless Faces were seen red-faced, jogging in the many surrounding country lanes, causing mouths to drop and cars to swerve, especially when they came across renowned glamorous women Stars with politically-correct looks, their hair blowing astray, and no make-up. Previous fashion-plate Faces, who had never had a thought in their vacant heads other than screwing educationally-subnormal surfing-boys, writing cunt-and-cooking novels, and having continuous tired and emotional outbursts, were frequently put to what was called essential Persuasion and Propaganda work. This frequently meant their turning up without notice and charming the heels of the City Council members with regard to such requirements as the sale of land in the EuroDump.

The City Corporation was used to quite different methods of persuasion, more often than not vicious and murderous stuff, which they had no problem at all in handling. But this was a very different kind of siege. When there appeared in a Council office three or four Faces which had been seen in famous epics on the silver screen within the previous few months, the psychological pressure was somewhat intimidating. Say no, and any anonymous civil servant could find his picture throughout the world within twenty-four hours, accompanied by some copy which made him a laughing stock for all opposing factions in Belfast, a city which specialised in having as many opposing factions as the Balkans.

Benson shook his head as if to free himself of all these thoughts, and quite by mistake reached out and took a deep draught of Fields' *ersatz*. Coughing, gulping and swallowing, he was inside and outside Tower House at one and the same time. Marshall patting him on the back and Fields' fruity buckshot brought him back from vertigo.

"Don't worry. Come alive. These are the last days of the last engines, Benson."

"Well wicked, I am sure."

"Forget your calculations, my boy. Audience figures are what matter."

Benson swabbed his lips.

"You are so right."

What a conversation, thought Benson, He had never heard scientific and technical questions placed in such a macaroni context. There was definitely a touch of moonie-flying about it all. Perhaps they should all take their clothes off and scream. He wasn't surprised at Fields. He was capable of anything. But he was surprised at Marshall. Of all people, he usually had no problem in sticking to the known, the singular, and the specific. Benson coughed again, straightened his tie, and pushed a comb through his shining *quiff* as Fields launched into another polemic about something called Entertainment Engines. Benson noted that now, for some reason, Marshall was giving Fields his head.

Benson had acute nostalgia for his Polytechnic womb. Clean-line monks in cells with quite set functions. Don't rock the boat. That was the way to deal with intellectual fear. Cut the bastard off. None of your old wide-ranging liberal waffle. That had all gone with the dying of the old light. Trouble was now he was strung between Entertainment, Rationalism, and the funny-farm. But sooner or later he had to jump. Not two ways, but three, possibly. Or, working with Fields and Marshall maybe four ways. Maybe more. Fuck it. Leave it alone. Have a good time. God only knows, there was plenty enough to do without getting stuck up some mad Limpopo without a bleeding canoe, never mind a paddle. Another sigh. He should resign. Get a proper job. Stick to specialisations within specialisations and count himself king of infinite space. Wonderful. Except for the despised and totally rejected lunatic rumours from the edge of fairyland. The banging on the padded walls. Blast Fields. One thing was certain. He never let anyone rest for a minute. If you wanted to keep up, you had to jump. But now, listening to Fields, Benson realised what a bloody great leap it was going to be.

"You see Benson, Christ was seen again amidst rocks, caves, and in a beautiful garden."

"Christ? I knew he wouldn't be far away."

"And Presley and John Lennon are seen again in supermarkets, in Disneyland, in children's comics, cartoons, corn-flake packets."

Marshall thought he might ask a question at such a fascinating point in the proceedings.

"Why *there?*"

"That is their country."

Marshall may have been laughing, but Benson was reeling. This was the predicted death of Seriousness. All this meant no more or less than that. The idea of human beings as pure cosmic paste-up. Advertisement Science meets the Jesus and the Aliens show. The Profound going down the plug-hole with Marshall, and perhaps the whole of Tower House. The song-and-dance God who frequently fell off the stage. Stone the crows. If Seriousness went, along would go its card-carrying acolytes: Accuracy, Precision, and Objectivity. What a party!

Fields' voice now came to Benson from far away.

"You see Resurrection-Control is Advertisement Control."

Benson couldn't resist it. He spoke to the air.

"I always find a good dose of salts does the job, myself."

Despite Marshall obviously loving all this, and equally obviously disappearing fast down the Fieldsian rabbit-hole, Benson thought it was time to try and call in the boats from the lake.

"Does anybody know the price of seed-potatoes this year?"

The men in Room 23a were a good triangulation of modern implicit and explicit conspiracy. They could not have been more different in personality, age, background, and indeed appearance, but all three were professional tricksters, with a common total concentration on the levels of manipulation of spirit, matter, technology, and national policy which each represented.

From the beginning, Marshall knew it was no use trying to confine the talk to The Finite Package. He had to let men like this play, and now, at the end of ten hours managerial mode, the relaxed talk drifted to definitions of a machine. All had different ideas of what a machine was, exactly. Benson, always at the frontiers of materials technology, told of how he had often been intrigued by how one state of desirable affairs, say in the physics of electronics, was only achieved by tricking that particular state of affairs into posing as quite another. Fields spoke triumphantly.

"An acting culture. The only real way to build a true artificial intelligence."

Benson now had the answer to the question he had programmed his mind with some hours before. It hadn't taken long. Film-stars and such were not what Fields was at. This, damn it, was a bloody great new

116

machine Fields was constructing. Marshall blinked at Benson, as if reading his thoughts. A final stage of development, thought Benson. A machine with no hardware. Marshall thought he almost heard Benson's heart thumping fit to burst as he slumped into his chair as if completely exhausted. The computer freed from its circuitry. Muddy Mildred!

In the hour of intense discussion that followed, Benson and Fields would individually drift off from contact, as if to consult the gurus of some intensely secret interior. They would then return with possible sets of solutions to a matter ten minutes and four items gone. The pair now sitting quite silent in front of Marshall could freeze into pure thought within an instant, quite vanish the room away, quit all localised situations, people, and concrete events. Fields would even stop eating, stare at the floor, his mind quite flown to far astral regions. Benson's eyes would close as if fast asleep. Marshall marvelled at the strength and intensity and scope of great mental geographies of which he knew he did not have a tenth of a part. Never mind. Here were his two extended hemispheres, and for once, somehow it felt good not to be like them. There were definite advantages. The pair had no explicit moral direction. Like the Los Alamos physicists, the thrill of the endeavour was all. Let the clerks and pygmies clear up the moral niceties afterwards. He could not imagine either Benson or Fields voting for anyone, arguing about the price of socks, or knowing what was on at the local *Odeon.* He was glad of the comforting proximity of his normal frame of hard-nosed reference as a ready retreat from these two alienated and sometimes chilling mountain-brains who were to form the two main parts of the super-machine of *Entertainment Enterprises.*

But could he control them?

Not one of the three men would have admitted it in their wildest dreams, but politically, they were more like anarchist freebooters than anything else. For the very best historical reasons, the right-wing impulse was little understood. Certainly all three sincerely hated racism and fascist psychopathology. Marshall and Fields themselves, after a mighty effort, had introduced the very first black and brown faces into the British Secret Service. But each was nevertheless an occultist in his way, accepting that it was very possible the world was stranger than could ever be imagined; equally, each believed secretly that democracy and collectivism were deceptive and dangerous fantasies, born of the same kind of existential desperation as was every other projected system of cosmic order. Each also believed above all in the very different realities of the subjective Self, and the power of these levels for interpretation, inspiration, and transformation. Unlike the outer world, their secret private Self had never ever betrayed them. In an Age in which nothing but the Great Popular Ordinary was sacred, not one of them worked really well within the world of so-called normal folk. This was a natural disposition for which each secretly gave the uttermost thanksgiving.

But in the face of superior intellects, and better education, Marshall was proud that he had something fundamental over them. Neither of them could sell a somewhat crushed box of out-of-date *Mita* laser-toner to a manic-depressive one-legged dwarf of an office manager on a rainy Friday to save their clever lives, though no doubt all had seen equivalent primal things in their own way. But for the first time in his life Marshall was worried. Most might think so, but The Entertainment package deal wasn't totally pragmatic. Ever since he had graduated to the British Security Service, the mechanics of uncertainty fascinated him. Like most men, he only really feared what he didn't understand. And there was something that the ever-joking Fields still wasn't telling them. Salesmen like Marshall were great tellers of jokes, but they didn't like them in the card-pack of possible order-forms. Selling was about exorcising such joker-demons. What was that thought? Fields was near.

Night came, and the trio shook hands all round, as if they were about to step into a huge experimental space-rocket. The three left Marshall's office, and walked along to a conference room where they met more members of the *Entertainment Enterprises* team. These men and women were young, questing animals, at the very top of the first division. As a typical late-Century Security Services swashbuckling crew, they came complete with the simplistic politics of all heroes. Each still had the perceptible smell of sulphur about her or him, each was dangerous, amoral, ready to risk all, and with lean fighter's instincts still carefully preserved. David Stirling, Oliver North (and perhaps even Margaret Thatcher, or at least her son) would have loved the hellfire original machine they were constructing.

If, as Fields claimed, Tonto the magician somehow threaded through the Tokyo computers, then threading through these plotters was a graded shading which moved from the solidity of Benson's machines through the ghost-mechanisms of Fields, via the managerial super-software of Marshall, the Great Planner. Free of socialist guilt, democratic compromise, and petite-bourgeois morality, in the eyes of the normal world they would have been judged a pretty wicked bunch, and historians would inevitably judge their types against such characters as the British arms-export conspirators and the Watergate plotters. But that the world-structure was probably more like such creatures than it was like anything else, gave them the combat advantage of being able to communicate and live with the Amazonian river bank that was Western science, technology,

Intelligence, and government. To the everlasting despair of those who looked for grand and formal philosophical order, those who tried to find in Nature a respectable well-adjusted harmonious regime, the formidable *Entertainment Enterprises* team were part of an ultimately disreputable alchemy from which most things taken for modern realities were forged.

The transcendental, the physical, and the mundane middle-earth were the bones of the systems-animal threading through such groups as theirs; some parts in crisis, some parts undergoing painful enforced change. The group was a perfect mirror-complex of all the uncertainties in the psychological structure of a treacherous technological materials base; as Benson said, this science had to coax and seduce, trick, and manage, and frequently re-colonise. The protection of this activity was their one single vital national function.

As they talked late into the evening, the Entertainment compass was starting to swing wildly in the great outside. In the early morning, yet another genocidal Balkan massacre had been discovered; by lunchtime, an all-Asian riot in Bradford had replaced the massacre; eight hours later, as the trio headed for the Staff Restaurant for late dinner, both slaughter of the innocents and riot had been replaced by the Chief Clerk putting sun-cream on his gold-fish.

As the three tired men dined, Fields claimed that advertising time was gone exponential, and image-fission was near. Marshall, still remembering the Winner garment, was now almost convinced of this. To him, the outer shell of world was in such a state of collapse it would soon be reduced to the cultural and social level of the outskirts of Mexico City. Containment and avoidance were the only tactics possible in his view, in the face of a muscular decadence which rampaged through the TV twilight of the land as a virulent madness which must essentially be tricked, diverted, kept drunk with meaningless work, or drugged by carefully engineered and intense amusements. To his mind, now, they were all the world really had, these covert planning groups, unless there was to be a collapse back through Bugs Bunny to oxen-ploughed Mickey-Mouse dust. To Marshall, whilst an outer body slept an Entertainment dream, the mighty ancestral equations of the *volk* were to be kept here in these towers in which he worked, guarded in these modern sealed mounds by prætorian aerials whose eyes never ever closed.

They were not men to be swayed much by emotions, but as the meeting ended, all three were aware that they would not meet again for some time. Fields and Benson left to pack their cases. Both would now leave Tower House, perhaps forever. From this moment, Fields was to enter the world proper as President of *Entertainment Enterprises Unlimited*, and similarly, Benson was to become Director of *EAT-I*, the technical operations subsidiary. *Entertainment Enterprises* now had a Headquarters (Fields refused to have it called 'Head Office') established on five floors of Bayswater Meadows, a high glass rectangle, just behind the *Odeon* cinema in Marble Arch. Operating from here, for the remaining three weeks of June, Fields would speak at meetings, and give lectures and broadcasts in Britain. It was then planned that the three, together with their full planning teams, would go to Northern Ireland for the official inauguration of Entertainment State.

Though exhausted with the months of preparation, the three were nevertheless excited. They knew they were about to board a freebooting ship for a journey to a dangerous horizon from which quite a few previous voyagers of their profession had not returned. But now summer was here with all her inspirations, and theirs was the irresistible subversive thrill of the true pirate. The sun was on the running tide, the fair vessel was pulling at her moorings, and Marshall fancied he could almost hear a Jolly Roger, cracking in a fair breeze above the turning aerials of Tower House.

Chapter 2

1

The Higher Disturbance

Getting Fields ready for his great world-appearance was likened by many in Bayswater Meadows to the launch of the great prewar liners. On hearing of his fame, a distant and ancient cousin from Golders Green promptly dispatched on loan a creaking family manservant, known as the seething Elmon, because of his permanent bad-temper. Fields and Elmon would sally out from HQ to perplex the best tailoring skills in London. A Greek shirt-maker crossed his heart, and said it was like trying to get Rasputin ready for *Blind Date;* a famous Jewish cutter threw up his hands, and said it was like trying to get Adolf Hitler ready to burst out of a cake. The much-abused Elmon almost despaired as designer spectacles, shoes, ties, and trousers all spun into discarded chaos, finishing up as expensive piles on the best West-End floors and counters.

"I can't wear that suit, Elmon. Makes me look like a queer Sicilian ponce-doctor."

"I agree sir. See you in that, they'll think the loans are being called in."

"That's right. There will be suicides all over the Home Counties."

"But what about this pair of trousers, sir? They've been specially tailored for you."

"I can't wear those. Look at them! Just think what the old Dean would have said about this attempt to make me look like some kind of bloody solicitor."

Only once, to his cost, did the baleful Elmon remind his master of the expense of his constant rejections.

"Can we have less of this constant working-class wailing about how much things cost, Elmon? Think about Destiny and the Soul, or something. I'm fed up with this modern kitchen-chat about the pennies and the pounds. You'll be talking about evening classes, social services, local amenities, and even popular television programmes next. Talk to me about the latest UFO sighting, conjuring up Cleopatra, anything but peasant-culture. That seems to drop on everyone these days like drops of pus from a gangrened fetlock."

Stifling a momentary thought that these were hardly the thoughts of the originator of a new populist philosophy, the unsmiling Elmon persevered in his efforts to find a way to modify Fields' appearance so as not to strike terror. But to no avail.

"Elmon, have you seen this jacket they've sent over?"

"Yes. You'd look as bent as a Channel Four winter-schedule in that, sir."

"Looks like something left over from an incest-crisis conference. Who designs these things, Islington Social Services?"

Finally, Elmon had to accept that the *Thunderbirds* chipmunk assurance beloved by television was impossible to achieve. Fields would just have to be transmitted as he was, and take the risk of viewers thinking something had wandered in from beyond the rim of the cave-mouth fires.

Tower House had whistled in admiration at the 'magnificent escape' as it was called. But a sign outside the now deserted Dansette Den announced sadly that 'Mr. Toad is not at home'. Colleagues felt that yet another spirit had departed, as now the Main Computer Hall no longer echoed to Earl Bostic's *Flamingo* or Little Richard's *Good Golly Miss Molly*; there were no more cocoa-mugs forming rings on open pages of *Face* magazine; no fried-eggs book-marked Nietzsche's *Zarathrustra*, or Schopenhauer's *The World as Will and Idea*; no rotting bananas resting on *Degeneration* by Max Simon Nordau, and no old cuttings about the Sex Pistols adorned the open pages of Kant's *Critique of Pure Reason*. Despite the protests of Nellie Goby, who wanted to turn the Dansette Den into a broom cupboard, the place was kept as a shrine. The niche however, still retained something of the presence of the absent man, and those very few of a religious nature in Tower House, said that a shrine always witnessed a Return, although now how he could ever return, no-one dared guess.

There was much interest in seeing how the Bunter would perform in the great Outside. At the end of the second week of June, many were gathered in various *hovels* in Tower House, looking forward to his first live prime-time appearance on Jean Harrison's show, *The Big Top*. On this BBC 2 programme, the anti-scientific views in *StarPower* were to be challenged by Professor Henry Wagner, a 'distinguished' physicist. *Entertainment Enterprises* rumour had it that the 'distinguished' addition was there because Wagner had, in past years, managed to torture more young monkeys to death in 'space-acceleration' experiments than any other honourable savant of the Enlightenment.

As the theme music commenced, the screen showed Mr. Toad was in fine form; but though his suit, shirt, and tie now at least looked decent, his peculiar frame so spread them out, that he still looked like a river-bank washing day in East Timor. To add to the visual interest, a couple of the now world-renowned stained brown-paper carrier-bags were propped by his feet.

Marshall, together with Annie, and a few dozen others, crowded a large-screen viewing room in Tower House as the introductory music faded, and Jean Harrison introduced Fields and Professor Henry Wagner. Wagner, whose views were diametrically opposed to those in *StarPower*, was a well-known media science-pundit. Part of him was still a pure Edwardian dream of a string-and-paper-bag science. Over-promoted in Government science for years, he was now in decline, downgraded to sixth forms, to whom he demonstrated 'facts' with scale-pan and thermometer, mirror-galvanometer, liquid oxygen, and Wheatstone Bridge. In Fields opinion, Wagner's philosophy of 'facts will save the world' fitted such fast-food TV-simplicities extremely well. That the 'facts' he 'demonstrated' had about as much relevance to modern science as a water-wheel, was alone a guarantee of stardom. The other guarantee of such was that Wagner was a brutish vulgarian, and his ever-ready popular scientific simplicities had in the past scarred the screen-reputations of many better minds.

Fields noted that Jean Harrison was a nice Bristol girl whose face had been tarted to look like an air stewardess, circa 1955, seemingly the eternal image of all television women. Someone had done an expert job on her, he thought, particularly on her pleasant and natural public-school tones. They had been transformed into standard television Dalek-cum-Lady Penelope, which somehow lower-middle Britain thought was much more classy, especially for discussing compassionate gaslight novels with sensitive and extremely serious 'ethnic' and 'alternative sexuality' themes.

Prior to introducing her two top guests, the evening had not been promising. The latest tabloid find, a prostitute turned 'dancer' gave heavy hints that she had 'known' he of the Committee, Minister John Carlton; a diseased actor and an inarticulate black football star who had just been 'married' followed a baffled and almost panic-stricken lottery-winning pair of pensioners; there was even a prizewinning 'literary novelist' who had the Kenneth Williams synthetic-hush beloved of the type, although Fields could not decide whether the voice had come from the same bottle of *Hawaiian Tropic* as the superb tan.

Tower House now tensed as the gym-teacher tones, familiar to the nation, introduced Fields and Wagner.

"Well, we've had the mini-series of the post-industrial age, now get ready for the doubtless many instalments of the post-scientific show. Take my tip: this one is going to run. As most of the world now knows, Dr. Hieronymus Fields has written a book..."

In Tower House, Annie pointed out to a surprisingly nervous Marshall that from the waist up, the twenty-two-year-old Jean wore the weeds of a sixty-year-old, apparently obligatory for young women television presenters. But this evening, Barsby and Benson, watching in the Bayswater Meadows HQ of *Eat-I,* noted that from the waist down, there had been a change. Changes of any kind were almost unheard of in British television, whose clock was difficult to move past pre-Suez Britain; but when changes did occur, they were quite original in their potential for disaster. Some department brain, presumably thinking to make a salmon-leap to 1965, had put Jean in a red PVC microskirt. The result was that even before the programme started, this remarkable garment was already giving Yours Truly problems from Bath to Cardiff, as Jean turned to Fields.

"Are there possibilities for a different kind of society using the Entertainment principles you have outlined, Dr. Fields?"

The beaming Fields was a child given a bag of popcorn just before the start of a main-feature.

"Oh indeed. Some old-fashioned folk are still talking about economies, class-structures, and industrial developments, whilst all around them the new world of Entertainment State is being born."

"But you still need an economy to support it."

"Entertainment will become the economy."

"What will it produce?"

"It already produces almost all our experiences. You want more than that?"

Jean wobbled a little on the world-famous settee, but came out with a decent punch.

"I can't eat the imagination."

Marshall made a mental note of her name. Jean would go far.

"You eat it already. 95% of what we eat is pure technicolour trash, like all cults of personality. Massive technical resources are committed not to making food more nutritious, or more available, but more Entertaining. Same with breast-implants, Royalty, and cruise-missiles turning left at the traffic lights, don't you think? Trash culture is here. Let us welcome the Pop Holocaust."

"Is Entertainment trash?"

"Many Entertainers are quite brilliant. Some even have great genius. By trash systems, I mean by using Entertainers there is a possibility of constructing a society which has no industrial direction. I use the word *trash* merely because, like lollipops, you can throw Entertainers away and immediately replace them. You can't do that with Isaac Newton. His Laws of Motion act sticks around like a contamination. As a performer, he would not have lasted longer than a Yorkshireman on Second House Saturday night at the old Glasgow Empire."

"Entertainment is somehow going to be the new social contract?"

"Of course. It's unstoppable. Entertainment exists in an eternal Now. It doesn't have friction, losses, inefficiencies, prices to pay, all those WASP negative-entropy hang-ups. With Entertainment, you can drive sideways, explore the inner space of the jokes, go anyway, which way. And who knows, we might just get something for nothing, as happens already within the Windsor family, the National Lottery, or the nuclear furnace."

"Will Entertainment become a major social force?"

"Let us forget these old metaphors. In Entertainment State there will be no force, just personality."

"Isn't that what the Nazis had?"

Jean was punching very hard now. Back at Tower House, Marshall changed his mind about her good promotion prospects.

"Technically, I agree. But does it always have to end like that, in unimaginable evil?"

"Personality cults usually do."

"But Entertainment gives. It doesn't take. Oh, in any case forget Nazis, forget that Royalty and actors and pop and film-stars have little intellect, education, or intelligence. That's all the dead past with its problems to solve, its formulas to remember, its social hierarchies, its doom-laden oppressed lives, its endless murderous industrial product-tasking from the cradle to the grave. Get into Jimmy Tarbuck, Hermione Gingold, Betty Grable, and Lady Di. Become a child. Stay a child. Enter the BAFTA world. Admire yourself to infinity. Why shouldn't you?"

"Why shouldn't I?"

"Just let go."

"I can't. I still need solidity."

"That's guilt."

"I still need something to cling to."

"That's all Anglo-Saxon school vegetables, and Bertrand Russell's bad breath. But never mind, you'll soon come to understand all this, Jean. That is because you have the higher disturbance."

Both Tower House and Bayswater Meadows braced themselves. The higher *what*? Such was the nature of Entertainment State, minutes after Fields had produced this intriguing phrase, it was whipping via satellite and the World-Wide Web, through San Francisco bars, causing fights in Australian car-parks, puzzlement in Moscow, and suicide pacts in Paris. It was also causing catastrophic translation, dubbing, and subtitle problems from Thailand to Alaska. In Tower House, Annie said Jean looked as if she had been given a good beating by the politically-correct Thought-Police as she looked at Fields with a puzzled frown.

"What is the *higher disturbance?*"

"It means you are elect."

"What does that mean?"

"Special. You are chosen."

The phones were soon starting to ring from throughout the sceptred isle. Nobody had been *special, elect,* or *elite*, never mind *chosen*, since the last demob suits were issued. The Producer and the Assistant Producer, watching from the outer ring of the cave-mouth fire, were terrified. They thought they had so carefully tailored the nation's favourite presenter to be obviously quite indistinguishable from a *Marks and Spencer* face advertising thermal vests.

Jean, momentarily at a bit of a loss at her unexpected elevation, was grateful when Fields helped her out.

"You see Jean, in Entertainment we have a great historical opportunity."

"What is that?"

"The recreation of the old magical gods-state."

Marshall's mind reeled. Had Fields gone mad? Meanwhile, as Professor Wagner quietly fumed, Jean's mind wrestled with ideas she had last come across in her A-Level Tolkien.

"What is a gods-state?"

Professor Wagner, up until this moment entirely ignored, fought hard to get into the act.

"Load of old cobblers, Jean. That's what it is. Not worth a bucket of well-boiled senna, if you ask me"

To the horror of her two Producers, Jean completely ignored Wagner's agitated figure on her right. Fields replied as if the Professor hadn't spoken.

"A state of wonder."

"My goodness me, Dr. Fields. What is that?"

The professor jumped up and down at the back of the class, his arm almost raised.

"The flat-earthers are coming in large-sizes, this year, Jean. Put some ribbons around this one, he'd be the finest fellah in the Easter Parade."

"The imagination in action, Jean, that's what a state of wonder is."

Jean, whose idea of the imagination in action had been bounded

126

by prudence-kitten *Virago* novels, and extremely solemn women's workshops in Stratford East, had now quite forgotten her staid influences. Fifteen minutes still to go in a live prime-time interview is no time to forget anything. She backed off, gloves in front of her face as Fields followed through.

"It is therefore Entertainment in action."

"What does that mean?"

"A load of rubbish!"

Fields turned to Wagner with a smile.

"Precisely"

Jean moved in before the astonished professor could reply

"Trash culture?"

"Yes."

"What exactly does that mean?"

"Nothing! I tell you all here and now, this man is a masturbator."

For a moment, the dumbstruck Jean looked like a character out of one of those French art-films the British always have great difficulty in understanding.

"True. I have a taste for both the shadow and the substance."

"There you go, Jean. A regular tosser."

"Abuse ye not the flag of Onan, Wagner. On it is written: *'everything shall come of nothing'* "

The audience might have loved it, but Jean and her production team winced. They were paying the price of hiring a street-fighter like Wagner to try and maul Fields down. Jean struggled for control.

"Dr. Fields, what is trash culture?"

Wagner leapt in.

"Anything daft as the proverbial brush."

"True. It means the social resurrection of a powerful set of ideas so long forgotten by the world it is as if they had hardly ever existed."

Wagner scowled from off.

"You can say that again, Fields."

But now the fascinated Jean made Barsby's eyes pop by actually sucking a finger just before she spoke.

"Such as?"

Her Senior Producer closed his eyes at this teen-time response and made a note to his Assistant Producer, who was agonising by his side, his terrified eye on the gradually elevating hem of Jean's short skirt, which was now keeping the metaphysics warm from Wigan to Waco. Both were relieved when the skittish control room (manned by imprisoned 1970s techo-subversives) filled the screen with Fields' face.

"You see Jean, the great Stars of the world are the natural inheritors of the traditions of a fallen race of original *shamans*, the first holy-men of the world."

Astonishment in Bayswater Meadows. Benson spoke first.

"Did you hear that? Mother's got one on her tonight, Barsby.

In Tower House, Annie couldn't resist it.

"Is this the small print you mentioned, Harry?"

For the first time in his life, Marshall almost blushed. By this time, Jean had decided to be her natural self as the only solution to the situation. As her prime-time knitting-pattern mask dropped, her Senior Producer was on the verge of running to the Gents and being sick. He had spent six months trying to transform this Oxford First into something which looked and sounded like as if she were selling Motel Time-Share Weekends, and he had been much-praised for this. But now his fragile masterpiece was collapsing before his eyes as Jean continued, gazing in fascination at Fields as she spoke.

"As *Time* magazine said, you as 'new secular mystic', have managed to do the quite impossible in that you have introduced a sacred element into something which was previously considered to be anything but sacred. Do you agree?"

Sacred, secular, mystic? The Senior Producer sweated fear as he thought of all the dictionary pages turning from Bosworth Field to Glencoe. This would never do. The Assistant Producer winced at the thought of the infamous sarcasms The Department Head would inflict when he heard of a programme which sent people searching for information from books. Meantime, Fields was in his element.

"You see my idea of *performance* having fallen from some previous pre-science historical ideal and function has appealed to many. A great psychological impetus has been provided by a new-found desire to unravel the traditional threads of modern acting, something which has been previously considered to be a much more simple manifestation than I have revealed it now to be."

A gulp from both Producers. The vocabulary alone, never mind the grammar, had probably not been heard in prime-time since the days of meat-safe microphones, and things called *talks*. Marshall had a vision: somehow, perhaps, the Bunter was fooling them all. He heard Annie's voice from a great distance.

"If this is Entertainment, it's got a very old-fashioned Oxbridge feel to it."

Marshall nodded.

"True. The sod is out there selling like mad."

As Fields continued, Marshall admired, and his envy almost turned to jealousy at the mouthwatering technique.

"You see the transforming power of the beat of the *shaman's* foot has been forgotten, it seems. There has been a Fall, and Entertainment has descended from its original high throne to become a mere throwaway consumer convenience provision for an affluent society."

The obviously inspired Jean went for it.

"But thanks to *StarPower,* Entertainment now sees the dimensions of what some now call a religious revival?"

"Yes. As *Time* magazine explained, empty formal religions have, in the past, pushed aside this original *shaman* function, with all its drama, emotional variety, mystical sexuality, nature and animal relationships, cosmic connections, and humanity is a lot worse for it."

"You see the Star as New Entertainment Priest?"

Jean was getting interested in her guest. This meant professional suicide. Authenticity of any kind did not look good on television. Usually, the guests were led to the lift by the Assistant Producer, Jean stepped back, the doors closed, and they were gone from her mind forever. The Senior Producer caught this whiff of genuine enthusiasm as he reeled back, wiping his forehead desperately with pink *Kleenex.* He leaned against a wall, sweating. His dolls-house-style was in shreds as Fields continued.

"Of course. There are now calls for a new priestly caste of Great Stars to arise. They will go on a path of pilgrimage to the shrines of dead Stars, who of course are not now 'dead' in the strictest sense. This will enable us to make a complete rediscovery of the character of the original western *shaman,* whose earth-thump of feet brought rain, and whose actions, rhythms and dances initiated the great cycles of regeneration of land, soul, and idea."

"Shouldn't the Arts do this anyway?"

"In becoming merely a service industry, the Arts have become mundane, rational, hardly rising above the mental level of concerned social workers."

"Surely that's a bit elitist isn't it? What about democracy?"

"I am not a democrat."

Jean nearly slipped from her fragile perch as if Fields had said something obscene. Her gas-showroom voice, useful for selling caravans through a Tannoy on a draughty Wembley forecourt, had almost collapsed now, and her public school accent came cutting through. The two Producers (of a similar strangulated ilk themselves) looked as if they were having a simultaneous heart-attack as Jean spoke.

"What do you mean by that, Dr. Fields?"

"I said I'm not a democrat. And neither should Arts or Entertainment be such, for that matter."

The cheering audience responded as if this was a call to arms. Professor Wagner, straining at the leash, saw his opportunity. In an increasingly tense Bayswater Meadows, Benson commented that there hadn't been a non-democrat on television since test-card transmissions of Errol Flynn's profile in 1938. Pointing a finger at Fields, Wagner now jumped up like a frog onto a stone.

"It was rubbish like you ruined democracy."

"It was tat like you ruined science."

The Professor sat down to laughter. Little did he realise that in ideological consumer-time, democracy (and probably science) had probably just passed their advertising half-lives, as Fields might have put it. Judging by a half-chorus of the *Marseillaise* from the back of the raffish studio audience, that time had come not a minute too soon. But now the Producing pair had another problem. Jean *was lighting a cigarette.* The Senior thought of suicide. The Assistant thought of Lisson Grove Labour Exchange on a black Monday morning as Wagner jabbed desperately from off-camera.

"This man is talking absolute rubbish!"

Fields, after imperiously looking around to see where the voice came from, focused on the professor.

"Rubbish? Would that be like the last three projects you advised on, professor: the *Nimrod* radar, The British Rail Advanced Passenger Train, and the Stock Exchange computer?"

These projects had been the most catastrophic and expensive failures in the postwar history of British technology. Momentarily deflated by jeers, Wagner sat down.

"You were a bit young for the TSR2, but somebody else took care of that, what?"

"You don't know what you're talking about, Fields."

"Well in that case I'll have my money back."

More cheers. Fields was becoming master of the popular response. Taking a deep breath, Jean became synthetically defensive, trying desperately to be democratic.

"Now don't you think that's just a little uncharitable, Dr. Fields?"

"I didn't come here to talk about charity. I came here to talk about the loss of the third grid."

Marshall imagined a momentary silence throughout the land. Even Wagner's mouth gaped like a fish. Jean inhaled deeply. Tower House viewers leaned forward. The studio camera-team were silent skaters, catching Fields body as it moved like a badly-patched carpetbag full of large conger-eels. Jean coughed out smoke as she spoke.

"The third grid?"

"That's what I said."

Quite carried away, Jean's uncomfortably short and tight skirt had now risen to heights which were causing excitements untold through the nation. Her voice was a croak.

"What's the third grid?"

Both Producers gave hand-signals to Jean to pull down her hem as Fields replied.

"The third grid is the actor."

To the two Producers, what had been a simple-minded dog's-breakfast slot with perfect salon-brat smiles perched above permanently greased rectums, telling of Martin's reconciliation with Julian, was now out of control. To Marshall what had been a purely pragmatic plan for social engineering was also out of control. Jean, now apparently unconscious to everything but Fields' presence, and with untold phones ringing about her gusset, was also very nearly out of control as she wheezed on.

"The actor?"

"You see we live now in a fragmented world fallen to such concepts as 'luck'. In Christianity there is practically nothing between God and Man. The European Mind has lost access to a rich world of half-realised forms, a bubbling sea of rehearsals, almost-theres, and partial-creations. This was a transfer region, the third control grid between thought and creation. It was a region of elementals. Without the Actor to traverse and interpret this middle-earth, we are lost."

Waving like a bookie, and on camera at last, Professor Wagner smiled his media-pundit smile. Desperately wanting to be liked, he was like the pratfall actors of West End theatre. Managing to take his eyes off Jean's spread-legs, he roared at Fields.

"Really, Dr. Fields, what gobbledygook all this is."

"It sells a million. Like your stuff, professor."

"Just who do you think you are?"

"I never ask people who they are, just who they were."

"I don't know where you've parked your reindeer, Fields, but you're never going to get down chimneys with this particular sack of dreams, I can tell you that. Let me tell the world here and now that there is absolutely no experimental evidence..."

Wagner must have carried on alarmingly for a full five minutes. Everyone had heard it before. He sounded like a lost boy-scout from the 1930s as he talked of social improvements, and the 'lamp of knowledge' casting aside 'mystery and darkness'. To Fields, it all trailed historical deceptions like a living minefield. The smooth surface of Wagner's face was the beautifully structured trick of the voodoo-mask. The Mouth opened. Weather Forecast Culture came out. There were certainly no secrets. And absolutely no mysteries. Take notes, compare evidence, reach objective conclusions based on common-sense, experimentation, and factual verification. Great Entertainment, thought Fields, as an inspired Wagner rattled on something called rational evidence. Fields always thought this kind of prep-school pre-quantum science was like the piano-music before a Charlie Chaplin film. After a full four minutes of Scientific Faith, Hope, and Charity, the professor concluded.

"Science works, that's all I know."

"Of course it does."

"Well there you are then."

"Because you've won an historical round."

"Thank you for admitting defeat in front of the nation, Dr. Fields."

Jean swung her long legs round to meet Professor Wagner, the sight causing near-chaos in pubs and restaurants from Watford to Glasgow, and thoroughly disturbing young Barsby, who sat by a slavering Benson.

"He said a round, Professor Wagner."

Swinging her legs back to Fields, she caused even homosexual regrets in darkened bars from Chiswick to Newcastle.

"Dr. Fields, how long is a round?"

"It's as long as the Professor's customers want it to be."

"How long is that?"

"I don't quite know. You see the trouble is he doesn't die. More like he's re-sold. Re-packaged through generations. Our only chance is to try and slip in between one of his reincarnations."

The young audience were warming to Fields now. Science, so obviously the religion of twentieth-century Authority, was momentarily on the run. But Wagner was a tough old bird.

"What is all this stuff about commerce? Science is the truth."

Fields turned a massive head towards the uneasy twilight beyond the gat-toothed circle of expensive lights around him, as if something was moving out there in the great dark beyond.

"The truth, Professor Wagner?"

"That's what I said."

"The truth that the new experiments in the new laboratories will be better than the old experiments in the old laboratories?"

"Well, yes."

"Sir, If you believe that, you'll believe anything."

"But what about facts?"

"Facts are the greatest conspiracy of all."

Jean turned, eager for more.

"You don't believe in facts?"

"As an advertiser, I've never come across one, myself."

The audience roared. The professor's voice was now high-pitched.

"You're here now, aren't you, isn't that a fact?"

"Are you an advertiser?"

"I don't advertise anything."

132

"You must be joking."

"So now we know what you really are, Fields. A shopkeeper!"

"Nobody's the shopkeeper. We are all customers."

"How can a customer advertise?"

"Through what he buys."

"From a nonexistent shopkeeper?"

"You leave what you can on the counter, and hope that the reckoning never comes."

"That depends on people's honesty, Fields"

"That's why my system is superior to your facts, which depend on people's dishonesty, Wagner."

Jean decided to end this metaphysical-bazaar talk from two wily old birds who perhaps could have carried it on forever. Perhaps, she thought as she turned to Fields, they should be given their own series.

"Dr. Fields, what exactly is an advertiser?"

"Someone who does not believe in objectivity."

"Such as yourself?"

"Indeed. I think objectivity is the best piece of multicoloured political dog-jollop ever sold from the back of a quack-professor's covered wagon."

Waving a copy of *StarPower*, Wagner spoke as if he were addressing Europe in an hour of peril.

"I warn you all: this book is evil."

"Can't be evil, Wagner. The word 'social' does not appear in it."

"And I will now tell the nation something else."

Wagner beamed to a silent audience. This was obviously going to be his masterstroke.

"The author of *StarPower*, the man you see before you, is a senior member of the Security Services"

Wagner leaned back, beaming. But never had a man so miscalculated. The audience hit the floor. The idea of the man seated to Jean's left being any such thing was ludicrous.

Tower House faces almost turned blue. Hearts thumped in Bayswater Meadows. The audience were silent as Jean turned to Professor Wagner.

"Do you have any evidence for that statement?"

Fields, wiping a tear of laughter from an eye, spoke.

"He doesn't need any, Jean."

"Dr. Fields, are you joking?"

"Only the advertisement is true."

The popeyed Wagner's words came out almost as a choke.

"What does that mean, for God's sake?"

"Well, as the sorcerer said to his apprentice, 'the game may be

133

rigged, but it's the only game in town."

Fields waved happily at the cameras.

"Entertainment State is a security services operation from start to finish. The whole idea is to erase a community's identity by smothering it in Entertainment! I bet they are all watching in Tower House tonight. Hello, Sir Harry Marshall and Annie Lloyd!"

Tower House and Bayswater Meadows breathed easy. In a few seconds, Fields had turned all such accusations into a joke. He was now safe. It was another popular masterstroke. He now had the audience almost eating out of his stained brown paper bags propped against his chair. Oh, said the World, from Brisbane to Moscow, he wasn't half a card, this Bunter. From this moment, all accusations of being a member of the Security Services were to be greeted by universal laughter. In succeeding days, fans would come up to him and with a smile, ask him how the Security Services were today, and he would reply, giving them the latest details on how things were preceding. He would name names, give actual plans, so detailed, and so accurate that when they were absolutely verified, nobody believed them, they were so *true*.

But these 'security services' jokes became a kind of sideshow to the entire circus built around such phrases as *only the advertisement is true,* and Fields' remark about the sorcerer's apprentice. What did it all mean? Kettles boiled over in Zululand, feathered red-indians pondered in wigwams, arguments were started even amongst world-series cricket fans, who had been made to change channels. In Dorset, Mary Marshall squinted at her black-and-white from the attic. Cursing its blinking 1960 horizontal-hold, and its incorrect line-standard, an instant-phrase entered her head: *the third grid?* What was that?

Wagner turned with a desperate look to Jean.

"This is a battle between Good and Evil."

Fields tried to give him a wink.

"I think it is a battle between different kinds of magic, myself."

At the mention of magic, in order to bring the nation to both intellectual and sexual relief, Jean wrenched down her hem and signed off *The Big Top.*

"Thank you for your input, gentlemen."

In the taxi back to his new Belgravia flat, Fields felt a rare pulse of fear. Wagner's face in his mind became the brutal architecture of a city-centre. Talk about summoning up. A physical blow was one thing, he thought, but attack the seething ideological base of the Explanations and Objectivities, and a thousand guardian trolls awoke in cave and forest to hit back with so many invisibilities as would never be believed. The great Reasons Why were guarded as only the holiest centres of mystical belief were guarded. Touch the wired jaws of the Great Facts Machine, and thunder-sheets bellowed alarm through the stage-flats of body and mind and tribe. The routes marked by structures of almost-collapsed Reasons Why were modern lays, access channels to the points of uneasy union of flesh and spirit. He saw *facts* as half-ruined castles along the line of extended being, though where the flesh ended and the spirit began, he supposed even the half-forgotten guardian trolls had almost forgotten that.

With that thought, and calmed by Elmon's cocoa, He slept sound.

The next two weeks swept Fields off his elephantine feet. The media and press raved on. The *higher disturbance?* The *third grid?* The *magical gods-state?* After the broadcast, the entire fashionable media world was trying to beat the proverbial path to his door. Anything was better than the difficulties of the Labour Party, or the doings of the Chief Clerk, anything. And that his philosophy appealed to the great Stars themselves did not surprise anyone. Ritual theatre? Occult power? Back to the Roots! Of a sudden even the most obscure professional on the verge of dole-despair in Ladbroke Grove became rain-dancer and *magus,* plugged into a super-accelerated credibility machine with the power of forgiveness, transformation, and transcendental understanding. As an overnight millionaire padding about in ancient moleskins, and demolishing *Maltesers* by the carton, he still found it all somewhat difficult to believe.

But he certainly liked his new life. And years appeared to have dropped from him. As soon as he had *escaped*, as the term went, he suffered an astonishing loss of seven stone. His GP almost screamed with ritual disappointment when he could find absolutely nothing wrong with him, who finally stabilised at 18 stone, and eating one green salad a day.

The sudden loss of both appetite and weight was a mystery to the man himself. He saw it as if a great body of spirits had fled from him to a new resting place. The success of *StarPower* seemed to have turned ancient locks within him to rust, and myriad spirits had run free to some external region of his vastly expanded imagination, where they patiently awaited his arrival in the flesh. He knew all their names. He knew all their songs. Their dances and films and musicals formed an angelic order in his mind. He had written a book. Books were not exactly unassociated with the invoking of both angels and demons.

At first he had been frightened for his brain. He felt it might lose its power as his body had lost its flesh. Each day he checked his brain for efficiency points as others might check their body for cancer lumps or swollen glands. He would harass puzzled and bemused colleagues in Bayswater Meadows to set him difficult partial-differential equations, most of which he managed to solve without difficulty. Lately, it appeared to him that his brain was not contracting, but expanding. He would awake astonished at the sharp intensity of his dreaming, whose recalled frame-speed was accelerating in many overlapping directions at once.

He had also an overwhelming sense of something being built within him, and quickly. There was an urgency to the putting together of streams of what he could only call pure advertisement-stuff, or *image-protein*. His brain still remained the headquarters of his departed spirits, still the control centre of what was being built by them somewhere in the great out-there. And still they sang to him in their absence the old songs in the same old way, as children might sing to a father to comfort him in their absence. But the music within him was now changing. It was become the chanting of legions in the far distance; the battle-cry of a newborn State on the march. The dreams were not painful, doom-laden, frightening. They were dreams of pleasure, of glamour and adventure, in which everything came out right at the end. He felt rescued from Freudian patterns, harbingers of doom, guilt-feelings about pure and unadulterated enjoyment; there were no panic-levels, traps, inescapable labyrinths, he had been cleansed of the doubts of middle-age and the terrors of youth. But if he had broken free of such primal fears, it was only to experience the most lonely and ultimately terrifying thought of all: that the universe could actually be a success. He dreamed that the biased nature of life, in which the most minute split atom of goodness was only created at the expense of unimaginable horror, he dreamed that this tendency to spin out of control could be corrected in the redesign of the structure of the advertising interiors of Mind as a *product*. He began to conceive that this bias towards destruction was hence a semi-mechanistic illusion, a barrier which could be outsold on some deep level of communal giving, of which he was only just beginning to have the faintest conception.

After his television appearance, towards the end of the second week of June, public speculation was raised to fever-pitch. The cheeky Fields now had acquired *two* adoring girlfriends. Like bright-hued tic-birds on the back of a hippo, young Alison and Mavis (both of whom Fields said had the *higher disturbance),* appeared never to leave his side. That both were only seventeen years of age raised further intense speculation in the tabloids, who called them 'the twins', though they were not related. But definitely not amused was the ever-furious Elmon.

136

Scandalised, he at first refused to serve tea to the twins, and only spoke to them in monosyllables.

Mavis and Alison were terribly excited when Fields said that the three of them (plus Elmon, plus Fields' utterly silent and almost invisible bodyguards) were going on holiday together for a few days. When they learnt that paradise was going to be a tour of the old V2 sites in the Cherbourg Peninsula, and not a suite in the Tel Aviv Hilton, as promised, the twins gave a sigh, and changed disco outfits for camouflaged overalls and 'Dr. Martens' boots

At Watten, the party picnicked by upended 3000-ton concrete blocks split by 1000-bomber raids of 1944. They travelled on to Wizernes, and the girls peeled off their camouflage, to sprawl in swimsuits on top of a *one-million-ton* dome cratered by 20,000 Ib 'Tallboy' bombs. Seeing female thighs in the sunlight against the rusty wire frames of shattered slices of reinforced concrete of the old V2 assembly area, Fields confirmed a long lingering suspicion about camouflage. Scientifically-oriented Intelligence operatives like himself, he supposed, were old enough now in the cultural tooth of the century to have taken on something of the role of the leather-featured navigator, with his glimpse of headland or rock through a wall-like obscurity of raging elements of artificially-generated confusion.

Seeing Elmon turn his back away from the twins to eat his sandwiches, and a craggy man with a gun blend into the shadow of a derelict tunnel a few yards away, he was fascinated by the power of a system to advertise that it was *something else*. Blending almost imperceptibly into sunlit French hillsides, these splintered domes, shafts, and tunnels had been built by tens of thousands of half-dead *Tödt* Organisation slaves from concentration camps, prisoner compounds, and elements of disintegrated armies from all over Europe. Yet their beaten bones were a first part of a path to the moon. In a world turned as upside down by mighty blasts as these first rocket-sites, nothing was as it seemed, neither science nor fact, nor politics; neither history, nor achievement, nor morality. It came to him as he plodded about in khaki shorts and straw hat, that the history of ideas was as much camouflage on camouflage as these old torn wounds of Europe. The contrast between the flesh-tones of the sunlit girls and the weathered strands of reinforcing wire forced up through the scarred old dome, finally convinced him that slavery, the craters of the moon, and the craters of Wizernes, were all connected *simulchra*, mimicking ideological, sexual, and political *deceptions.*

Sandwiched between young and limitless female flesh that same evening, he thanked the gods for this pure and ancient intellection which was still indeed miraculously preserved within him. He guessed it was now summoning up its powers for that brief historical moment in which it would run up off the beach and leave the clear sea-shallows for the first time.

To the great delight of the twins, he now sprang his surprise. The party now travelled on to Cannes, where a two-million-dollar Entertainment State party was being thrown, mainly by international film interests. Fields marvelled. The Entertainment sector was the only business which could now even think about affording such things. On the second night, he left the equally exhausted young girls snoring loud in the hotel room, to walk along the shore. In the half-dark, he looked back at mini-Vegas of light, bubbling over the sea like the rising of a neon-goddess. A night-tide alive with the distant reflections washed glittering sand though his fingers, and the grains became ideo-cells within him. These cells, he thought, could possibly remember a time which was mightily concealed from himself, as their fragile and finite host-creature. They had waited long for the correct pulse of their historical time-code. For a moment he saw himself as a mere incubator, who, if the cells were not careful, might encounter every squirrel's heartbeat from the earliest time there were things such as squirrels. Then he knew that the man called Hieronymus Fields would not survive for long. And that tiniest of beating grains on the smallest of forest floors was not the most diminutive of infinities.

As if he were trying to make the girls swoon with contrasts, he now led the party on to Sword Beach in Normandy, where Elmon's father had piped ashore Lord Lovat's commandos sixty years before, on the early morning of 6th June, 1944. On the outskirts of Ouistreham, Fields and the intrigued twins bathed. As the tide pulled out, he came ashore, and looked back to see the girls appearing to be walking on water. Laughing, they swam back to the beach as the receding undertow revealed a steel stanchion. Then a long steel girder. Then some faded grey riveted plating covered in brown bladderwrack, as an old landing craft revealed herself like the old *Dutchman* of nightmare history, coming brimful of wonder out of the dark, ready to vanish again on the tide-turn. The young girls, silent for once, gazed in wonder. Elmon wept. Fields himself stood up and saluted, and two of the craggy men bowed to the sea, their shadows lengthening across the beach. Alison and Mavis bought flowers from a nearby stall. They threw them into the sea by the wreck, which the tide quickly took back for its own. Fields felt that the advertising cells within him had come through such a similarly hazardous journey as this rusted craft. But the journey was of multiple lifetimes, and such a virus was not going to risk anything now. The struggling sperm of ideologies within him were running unstoppable, up off the warming beach, dragging their dead and wounded with them, ready to bring havoc to the cities of ideas deep inland. In his dreams, Fields heard their battle-cry.

Forward, they roared.

Attack, attack!

II

Nora Finds the Plot

When countless screens all over the world were filled with the sight of Fields and Wagner raging at one another, parted only it seemed, by Jean Harrison's outstretched limbs, Nora became invisible in yet another house which according to all rational calculation, should have been bulldozed scores of years before she was born.

The almost-impossibility of the building she was in fitted the equal almost-impossibility of herself as a human animal. Her dens were in such obscure places they were virtually holes in conceptual space, sculptured purely out of the gap between old and new expectancies. The city which hid her hadn't changed much in three decades, apart from a little cleaning up of the military act. The warlike *Saracen* armoured vehicles which provided manic TV viewing of the seventies, had long been replaced by much-modified *Land Rovers,* their engines straining under heavy layers of unobtrusive *Kevlar* plastic armour. The city centre was no longer deserted at night, but though trendy night clubs and wine bars with smoked-glass windows had appeared, many of the water tanks, lift-shafts and generator rooms of the main hotels were often still searched with as much diligence as ever they were.

Resting within this new and often nervous growth meant reading her beloved Flaubert, between intervals in a ruthless daily routine of situps, press-ups, and consecutive spinning kicks with left and right legs into a pillow suspended on a string from the ceiling light chord. This was mixed with at least two hours of lifting a broom handle above her head with four house-bricks lashed to each end. Then came hop-and-head-butt, elbow chop, hand strike, straight kick, then palm, wrist, and finger strengthening using two pieces of quarter-inch padded spring. Then breathing exercise. Wind down. Then again, until thighs, biceps, arm-muscles and hands were fine spun iron.

This evening, after hours of such steadily controlled pain, she collapsed into a tin bath after taping *The Sun* (her favourite newspaper) carefully across the one small cracked window. Sluicing water on every screaming muscle from a Florence Nightingale dream of a saucepan, she emerged, and swathed in towels, she switched on a video recorder and inserted a cassette.

140

The man who had delivered the video was also such a quiet dweller on a similar silent ocean floor, drifting through the holes in the nets of the surveillance systems, with equally minimal engine noise, magnetic trace, or acoustic signature. Both the man and Nora were deep-sea fish, quite beyond the light of day, just sucking and stealing a little sustenance now and then. From the dark would come to them travellers from other such silent hidden worlds as theirs.

Alarms would also come. Words, quickly filtering through the coral, would tell that dragging nets were near, and these shadow-fish would lift slowly on deep-current thermals, letting the undertow hoist them through interstices of systems-tentacles. The man and Nora were super-particles so small that the world hardly felt the infinitesimal pull at its teat until they struck. Their raid would then come up from the obscure deep so fast and back again, that the world's advertising focus could rarely resolve down to the cracks in the sunless gloom in which they lived.

Since she had walked out of Nazareth Lodge orphanage at the age of sixteen, Nora had for all social intents and purposes, disappeared from all earthly maps in the Irish turmoil of the early 1970s. Long before Fields wrote a word, she lived within the powerful first stirring of intense media influence, but in the vision of the new electronic power in the land, she had hardly a counterpart. The new scale of seeing and assessing everything in terms of *actors* and *personalities* and *performers* of one sort or another was such that there existed hardly anyone who believed that she could possibly be.

Such cultural warping was ideal natural camouflage, and gave her a great tactical advantage. She would hide within the folds of belief-assumptions to gain admission. She would charm, hypnotise, befriend. Since she did not (except in gross facsimile) exist as a media type, the first thing many knew about her was possibly when they themselves were hovering above their body and looking down to see either their head or feet several yards from each other, and hair still neatly combed for a date with the beautiful girl they had only met the previous evening. This female would have no resemblance to the hag a lift attendant saw leaving the building some time later.

Nora operated under yet another layer of almost wilful invisibility. The more cynical operatives of various Police and Intelligence sectors called this moral ecology. They, and others (and there were many others, in far less definable sectors), were damned if they were going to commit valuable resources to finding out just exactly why one corrupt swine was murdered as distinct from another. They would note an unmourned passing, and maintain a coast-watch, for so many other ghost-ships passed down the same straits in the night. Such half-guilty twinkles in the eyes of professional hunters were rarely, if ever, revealed or reported.

This of course gave Nora a great operational advantage. Not only did she only half-exist, Authority was only half-looking for her as a killer of some highly unpopular people. She was therefore a kind of human Loch Ness Monster, a piece of half-realised substance operating in the corner of the investigating eye. As an ever-changing partial-form, a model could hardly be made of her, and any searching energies could not therefore proceed through that spider-web of metaphors called coincidence to form a narrowing cone of searching concentration. In the bargain, she had re-invented moral certainty, a pre-TV something which, in the opinion of most, had disappeared somewhere between Joan of Arc and Julian Clary. In her eyes the men and women she killed were not fit to live.

She had never been interested in The Troubles. They were absolutely beneath her contempt. She was pre-Luther Time, an anachronistic crusader, battling against an idea of evil in a sense which had almost completely left modern Christian thought, compromised, and visionless as it was to her. Compounding her several invisibilities was that she herself thought in terms of a kind of one-dimensional moral simplicity. Such a thing had almost disappeared as the world had grown so complicated that its capacity for outright moral action had long vanished into the mists of the existential uncertainties of the liberal-democratic view.

Tearing narrow strips of newsprint from the tiny window, she peeped out at the city which had formed her youth and vital inspirations. The harsh late midwinter had vanished almost overnight, replaced by limitless blossoms of heat and light. But she frowned. As a Belfast native born and bred, this wasn't the city light she knew. The electric shimmering had an artificial quality, as if some great high dome of floodlit artificial pleasure had been clamped over the entire province. Even the Mountain had a theatrical quality, a manufactured mall-dimension as if even massive geographic features were part of an emerging film or theatre set.

Turning from the window, she pressed a switch on the recorder, and Fields' face appeared on the screen.

The edit ran 'Restricted Conference, Chimo Industries, Vienna, 7th May', and a Dr. Hieronymus Fields was speaking in decent German, glossed with excellent French. Listening, she was immediately alert. Chimo was a half-animal, like herself. It existed in that area where the military industrial complex shaded into conglomerate unity. Succeeding sections of the video were of carefully-edited recordings of similar such meetings from all over the world. Threading through the edits was this new hippo-face to be watched. The international webs along which she ran had trembled for an instant at the sudden global appearance of this Dr. Hieronymus Fields. All investigations into his life had disappeared under the hill. His front as an obscure university lecturer turned popular cult-author stank. It was an operation alright, but all signal systems were quiet. This meant deep background. But for what purpose this part-comedian had appeared suddenly on stage, no-one knew.

The video had come through several hands from John, who had a chalk-white villa in Cannes, and who Nora fancied like mad. On the high rocks above the harbour they would talk of who was Next as easily as they drank themselves silly and screwed until they were almost insane. John was so rich that he hardly existed in terms of any world scale. Quite the opposite to Nora's microscopic life, John's existence had been enlarged to such vast proportions that practically nothing at all was registered in any frame of perception. He was of a Middle-East complexion, certainly, but she knew that even for her, it would have been difficult and certainly highly dangerous to enquire who her occasional lover was exactly, or where he came from originally. He was typical of those who belonged to the kind of circuit which hid and protected Nora. Like BCCI, or EMI, or indeed Nora herself, this control of psychic scale ensured invisibility of a kind, just as something is searched for whilst it is actually held in the hand. On both these macrocosmic and microcosmic scales, it was as if utterly fantastic animals were struggling in invisible mortal combat. Only occasionally did a distant crashing of forest or scream from torn flesh enter the normal scale of perception to pose as a solidity in the form of police investigations and smoking guns.

She dried her hair, put down the towel, and focused a ray of diabolical concentration on Fields' face. Her head cocked to one side slightly as ideas she had never come across before began to penetrate her brain.

'Moreover, Entertainment has no relative sequential development, and therefore the possibilities for mythological engineering are far beyond anything Brain can offer. Brain has patently failed as an experiment. When clever brick is piled upon clever brick, there always comes a fixed time when it all falls down. Brain is the great Humpty-Dumpty of the mental universe. With pure and endless Entertainment texture, all this constant and inevitably tragic up-and-down motion is avoided.'

Most curious. A storyteller. English cultured voice, with the very faintest suspicion of some foreign accent. But Englishmen hardly ever thought like he did. And he certainly didn't look like one. She knew English stories when she heard one. As an Irish girl in Belfast, she had heard enough of stories, English or otherwise. She had seen what they could do. Often, as a girl, when she awoke, she found that during the night, the stories had been out hunting. Like prowling gangs, the stories had territories. Like sharks, they had feeding-frenzies. Even in this uneasy peace, it was still possible to stand on a street corner and be crushed by two different interpretations of the same Creation tale.

Who was this Dr. Fields? She certainly didn't like him. Somehow the face on the screen brought back the indoctrinations of childhood. She felt an injection of the blood-vessels of half-alive story-creatures who were ever dependent on mankind, like the tic-birds on the back of alligator and rhino. From Christ to Michael Jackson, such animals to her were metaphor-vampires, sucking pure image-concentrate from imaginations to flesh their super-bodies. Such figures would encourage and develop ranges of belief as mental crops, a kind of farming of eternal pulse and counter-pulse of binary yes and no.

Binary what was that? Image concentrate? What did these words mean? Who was this Fields? She opened a cupboard. No sugar. Metaphor-what? Blink. Cough. Look through window, see if Christine's light is still on. In a pool of lamplight, a drunk sang his heart out as the distant horizon flashed with a rising column of rose-coloured light. By good old Irish instinct, she flew from the window as the frames rattled and a great hollow rumble in the earth raised dust from every crack and hollow of the old house.

It could only be a traffic accident, but within minutes the night was full of lights and sirens. In this country, history was never far away. She could remember when such a noise meant legs, arms, and families gone. She could remember the hospitals, the lamentations, and the endless funerals of the endless Irish agony. Once, long ago, in a night-school Eden, she had thought it was all about jobs and wages. But not now. No paragraphs or percentages could ever arouse the elemental fury of a war of dog-fighting stories. No question of living conditions or wage-levels or any other part of the apparatus of community *sapiens* could raise up the berserk level of violence aroused if certain basic stories were ever interfered with, insulted, ignored, or, worst of all, denied. To Nora, they ruled a large part of humanities higher instincts did these tall old tales, they frequently had the cruel beauty of deified gods, and they did as much mischief. They were perpetually at war between themselves. They were the jokers, the original tricksters were these visions on mountain-tops, and they enthralled for thousands of years. The greater part of humanity became brainwashed battery-hens plugged as galley-slaves into these story-machines, which caused individuals and sometimes whole cultures to fall in love with rocks, visions, mirages, moral tales, bits of bones, bits of doctored storybooks, and priests who to Nora all looked like seedy, down-at-heel drag-queens, as indeed many turned out to be.

Another video clip. 11th March. Fields popeyed at a private meeting of the Hamburg Group, a powerful right-wing think-tank.

'A social system based on Entertainment would make all other social models look as obsolete as the cavalry regiments in 1914. Coming soon to Britain was the first non-political Entertainment Prime Minister. He or she would command the high frontiers of information, image, and performance. Politics, like literary fiction, would be replaced by a plumage-game in which all information was seen as Entertainment. This change was inevitable. It had been so ever since the now dish-strewn African villages could tune into the first fitted kitchens of *I Love Lucy*. No other cultural paradigm stood a Darwinian cat-in-hell's chance of even thinking about standing against it.'

She froze. Of course. This man was right. There wasn't going to be any opposition to this. She supposed not even Marx or Jesus would have been daft enough to tell folk to turn off the television, even if such a thing as an off-switch now even existed for anyone at all.

She thanked the man with the hippo-face. As he had updated the story-machine, he had now updated her. Everyone, she supposed, now lived within a kind of electronic story-fluid. As an ex-Catholic, she was suspicious of all stories. As Dr. Fields continued, she became alert to them as complete animals with complete brains.

'They are very good at camouflage, are stories. One particular story, could, just like a virus, pose even as a great demystifier of other stories. It could even stoop so low as to make the claims of all good salesmen: *don't listen to that lot: my goods are BETTER in every way.*'

His words reminded her of how, long ago, she had absorbed the tee-shirt tales of oppression, starvation, and torture. Here, in Northern Ireland, to disappointed and frustrated political minds, such things had rarely been found. Here it was still all about the dread influence of a magician, an old storyteller; like this Fields, this story-magus appeared during the late crisis of the Ancient World to tell simple tales to the peasantry. Though no doubt an advanced occultist of genius, to Nora, his youthful innocence, mystical folly, and absurd claims of divine lineage had brought social and cultural disaster to entire regions of the planet, and still continued to do so.

Another clip. February 11th. The same Dr. Fields, appearing slightly drunk, almost floating in an armchair, apparently at some dinner party in palatial surroundings.

'After a million years of natural selection, people really love not Christ, Mohammed, or the Buddha, but the Stars, those half-gods who rise above the ever-quaffing herd. Democracy, rationalism and non-performers will eventually sink back into the historical morass from whence they came. People finally hated these cultural molesters, whose only contribution is medicines that don't work, irradiated concrete from Pole to Pole, a mass of one-GCSE nose-ringed paedophiliac bisexual social workers, and the equally semidetached thoughts of the wey-faced Chief Clerk. Of this post-industrial wreck, humanity will keep the toothbrush, the bicycle, and *Grecian 2000*. Also retained for a while will be the already ancient technology of the vacuum-tube television set, and its even more ancient programmes, until the new generations of Entertainment Super-Technology came along.'

So, a bit of a comedian, too. She liked the bit about the social workers, and she would love to have known how *Grecian 2000* came over in Swedish. But still she did not like this Dr. Fields. His story-machine had the morals of a bazaar on the wrong side of town. Her mind, far from resting, started to move into gear. Stories were dangerous. The stories were the pure essence of Advertising. Advertising? Where did she get that idea from? Sometimes she thought ideas came and went as if they had an entirely independent existence. She often saw herself as a mere factory batch-production manager, always walking corridors inspecting these limitless rehearsals of ideas and stories in their separate little mind-hatcheries in which they were endlessly breeding and cross-fertilising. Everyone knew the feeling, she supposed. Wake up one morning, and something had been in rehearsal overnight.

She lit a cigarette. Stop. Essence of *what* had she just said to herself? *Advertising?* A strange phrase. She must have read it somewhere.

In the next room, Christine, a notoriously humourless girl, with braided hair falling down a long dress from a just-past era of stories, glided silently through clouds of incense as she rummaged in cupboards.

"Sugar should be an illegal substance, you know that?"

Ignoring the snapping feminist tones, Nora pointing towards a flickering TV set.

"Don't you think that crap should be, too?"

Christine turned, tossed her long braids, and was silent and fuming, standing almost protectively by the TV set, her fists clenched. But something within the sharp girl told her that it would not be wise to attack the particular non-person in front of her. Over her shoulder, hundreds of photographs of Entertainment stars laughed at Nora. as if they too, would have liked to attack but dare not.

"I haven't got any sugar."

"Alright."

"Why don't you use the alternative?"
"What's that?"
"Go and suck on your own gut"
Nora pointed to the pictures on the wall.
"I'd rather suck on that, than them."

Back in her room, she felt for a moment she had almost been part of a B-feature. The storybook girl had almost immediately detected her as one who had not yet been converted by the alien image-virus. She wondered why people attached themselves so intensely to such storybook characters. Humanity was herded like pigs by these depictions of purity, suffering, miraculous interventions, these highly engineered images. All these forming games wanted was a bit of pain, a tiny giving up, a little pulse of suffering, and humans were sent on their way again, spinning and turning on the fairground rides of semi-mechanised belief. She imagined that she herself, like Christine, was part of such a story-lair which would in turn wither and transform, be born again perhaps, like the old magician whose extended brain was forever fighting itself to death out there in the Belfast night, and in many others places the whole world over.

Back in her room, with her last match, she lit another cigarette, and with her only other stimulant boiling on the stove, for no reason at all, she thought about Fields again, and switched on the video.

No date this time. But most likely quite recent. A private meeting at the United Nations. A transformed Fields appeared, smartened-up considerably, and with a much better delivery and microphone technique.

'The trash universe of pure Entertainment would have texture, but no direction, no moral arrow. It was a state of mind, and not a endless series of industrial products. The troublesome and betraying illusions of conventional theological revelation and the falsehoods of the ideas of quite purposeful destiny would be cast aside by Entertainment Culture, as society had cast aside the coach-and-four, the armoured knight, and the tin bath tub. There was no *When, To Be,* or *If* in Trash Universe, which was Fun Unlimited in the eternal *Now.*'

She cursed. The match had burnt her fingers, breaking all her reveries, and disturbing the conscious disciplines which taught her how to detect that almost molecular thinness between averages, which in her chosen profession, was often the difference between life and death. Somehow this Fields disturbed her. In doing just that, he removed a vital element of that deep concentration which kept her alive. He was a very dangerous man.

She certainly needed such a state of high alert. A year previous, she had been returning to a flat in Paris when she noticed that the greengrocer across the way had a new healthy-looking woman assistant who seemed unfamiliar with tills. A minute later, the debonair M. George, the husband of the concierge, did not for once try and stick his tongue down Nora's throat and take off all her clothing as he passed her on the staircase. Nora knew a trend posing as a fluctuation when she saw one. To the everlasting admiration of the concierge, a woman whose admiration was somewhat difficult to arouse, she tore through the back kitchen and cleared the dustbins in the yard with a flying leap. One second later, a fair amount of something very nasty under her bed blew her favourite pot-bunny hot-water-bottle across to the greengrocers, together with a large piece of the outer wall, and a not unsubstantial piece of M. George. The fumbling assistant was nowhere to be seen as patched-jean pieces of the concierge's husband were draped over the till, the bloodied light of its pulsing digits still signalling a time of prices, change, and molesting kisses the poor man was no longer a part of.

She looked at Fields' image on the screen again. She must get rid of this storytellers influence or he would destroy her. Already his language was on the edge of her mind. But with an immense efforts of will, she replaced his troublesome image with that of Alan McNaughton.

McNaughton was Next. The Catholic McNaughton. The same McNaughton of the Far East logging corporations. The same man who had recently been received by the Pope, and whose *Phalanx Corporation* was now active in destroying the Earth's last lung of the great Siberian forest.

This powerful entrepreneur was now intent on building MANNA LTD., on the outskirts of Derry. This was to be a massive food-irradiation plant described in the lush brochure before her as designed to serve the '21st Century Food Needs of the New European Community' using the 'latest technology,' a chilling phrase which in the opinion of many, was already carved on every twentieth-century gravestone. She read on. 'Genetically engineered foods...an ICI-developed tomato that does not rot. By removing the enzyme polygalacturosnase, a vegetable is created that is tastier, cheaper, and lasts longer than the natural one. The Food and Drugs Administration says it anticipates the new genetically-engineered food lines will displace conventional husbandry within 15 years throughout the West.'

There was already a certain amount of liberal outrage, but as always, it was far too late. The arguments about the absolutely determined cancer-clusters which would appear, the arguments about genetic damage,

148

the arguments about the poisoning of water, sea, and air, all these words were over, long gone, finished, the last remnants spluttering about in university debating societies, TV documentaries, and the columns of *The Guardian.*

But now Fields was back in her mind. And she had taken a decision.

McNaughton had to wait.

This Fields must go.

It was a calming decision. Pulling the sheets over her, she slept the sound, with healing liquid dreams of sun, forest, and eye-blue waters stretching to the moon.

Forty miles to the south of her as she slept, a horse pulling a rubber-tyred farm cart stopped by a yellowing washed-stone cottage half sunk by the road connecting Dundalk and Newry. A hundred rounds of hand-tooled 7.62 mm match-grade ammunition for a *Steyr* sniper's rifle had arrived with the morning milk, packed under cartons of new-laid eggs, and butter fresh from the churn. High explosive rounds were duly stowed with the now fully-assembled gun, under ancient floorboards beneath a dresser. Above the dresser was a window which some years previous had added the sight of the incinerated crew of a mined *Saracen* to its memories of the local Irish colour of nearly two hundred years.

A new weapon was on its way to her.

But now it wasn't pointing at McNaughton.

Its target was Dr. Hieronymus Fields.

III

Explanations Under Siege

What the *Daily Telegraph* called the 'chattering classes' had to have a lecture. Nothing as common as television would do for them. Praising lowbrow culture to the skies, they made sure their offspring went to public schools, where they were effectively shielded from all manifestations of such a thing. With this thought in mind, as soon as he saw the *Odeon* ballroom, Marshall realised that someone in *Entertainment Enterprises* had an equally ironic sense of humour.

The *Odeon* was the venue chosen for the well-advertised event, entitled *A New Theology of Entertainment.* The response, two days after the Jean Harrison programme, had been beyond all expectations. Relays of loudspeakers carried Fields' posh bass to outer corridors lined with curious *cognoscente,* anxious to see scores of Famous Faces arriving as if for an Oscar presentation.

The man himself was on top form as he stood before an illuminated pink-plastic female nude supporting a scrolled lectern from which hung a gold-lamé banner announcing 'Bingo every Friday Evening at 7 o'clock.' Under a silver *Mecca Dancing* reflector-globe flanked by the music-stands of a dance-band of yesteryear, he looked thinner now, but with a good shave and smart haircut, he showed at least some of the results of the massive efforts made to smarten him up. His *pince-nez* alone was now sported by countless thousands of trendy young fogies, ever since a popular fashion magazine had said Fields 'Eisensteins' were *the* spectacles to wear. Camden Market even sold a cracked-lens 'Odessa Steps' version which was very popular. Brown paper carrier-bags were also a sellout on the Portobello Road, full of small plastic models of an endless variety of junk- food, and grease-stained to a customer's requirements. The famous *Rock Around the Clock* kiss-curl was now imitated throughout the world, and Carnaby Street, ever-sharp, sold a squeeze-tube of 'Authentic Fields Egg-Yolk'. Apparently this was to drip down lapels and waistcoats, and it came with a free packet of plastic crumbs and beans, and floppy strips of rubber ham and bacon. Fields enthusiasts could also buy a sealed enamelled beaker full of 'Genuine Hamburg *ersatz,* 1943, to be heated over a very hot flame'. According to urban legend, under-the-counter versions of this beaker were available

150

either with RAF roundels or swastikas, according to political taste. The received image of Fields himself was now of a lovable Michelin-diapered Sumo-god. He dispensed spells, rituals, was surrounded by glamourous Faces, and due to the twins appearing quite naked arm-in-arm in *The Sun*, he had even acquired sex-appeal.

Fields commenced speaking against posters advertising 'Hire Purchase Time-Share in Torremolinos', and 'Low-Interest Loans for Three Ethnic Self-Catering days in the Morocco of the North of England' by Pork & Pickle Tours. To Marshall, observing from a Ruritanian balcony above a sea of intent and worshipping faces, the opening was equally heady stuff.

"The corporate Entertainment systems of the world are already in themselves models of operational virtual realities, vast simulations of pure advertising experience which serve for megalopolis-culture as carved images served for communities in the forests and caves of long ago."

Marshall admired. What a salesman. They were already eating out of his podgy hands. The designer-chords began again. Careful execution. Slowly amplified developments. The Advertisement was become sonata-form as the Bunter continued.

"What is Entertainment State?"

The audience practically sat at his feet as they were taken on a journey way past Chaplin, Radio 2LO, and the first abrasive squawks from wax cylinder, crystals, and horn-speakers. Fields took them to where the video and film trail ended, and photographs began. They travelled on to where photographs ended in turn, then back past lute-players and leaping Fools, back to the infinitely longer trail where paintings and monuments disintegrated and collapsed into cave-daubs and scrapes of earth. Then back still, to the old stone gods before Cuchulain, Thor, Zeus, back to the 'Entertainer's Time' as Fields put it, which was the true, aboriginal dream-time of all races and cultures. That Time was Entertainment Eden.

Marshall looked at the audience closely. Here was the middle-ground Fields had to capture if he was not to disappear into history as yet another hero with a perpetual-motion machine made from cocoa-tins, bicycle clips, and a Message from God. He could see where the vulnerabilities lay. Most of the disciplined faces here were creased with the typical deep anxieties of an industrial culture; they were minds half eaten alive by the Deadly Serious Truth game. Quite a few, he suspected, were now anxious for salvation from, as Fields now put it, 'an industrial time of corrosive factual anxiety'. Of course, like Fields, Marshall knew that the chattering-classes loved anything to do with actors to the point of sickness. The floppier performers in particular were their favourite darlings. Marshall supposed they were ready to follow anyone like Fields, who appeared to worship actors. Though Marshall knew that he privately referred to such as 'proliferating brainless morons', he was now nevertheless placing actors on such a dais as to mightily confirm the deepest middle-class beliefs and expectations. Quite a cool schizoid, Marshall thought, as he listened to him now describing these favourite pampered offspring as guarding the secrets of Time, Art, and Life as fervently as the last English corner-shop jealously guarded the very last jar of orange marmalade. In yet another private remark, Marshall also remembered him saying that after that jar was gone, it was time for Alice to start playing in the middle of the nearest eight-lane motorway.

Marshall admired again the way the Bunter had nicely calculated the depth and extent of an implicit conspiracy. He supposed that most present in the *Odeon* were now hearing a voice their dreams had wanted them to hear for a long time. Here was rapt attention, shining eyes, and thirsty minds. On the front row, a twelve-year-old albino junior-genius-manikin blinked anxiously and checked his cassette recorder. Pens hung poised. Some clasped their hands in the almost sexual atmosphere. It was pure intellectual eroticism of a kind which Fields was expert in arousing. A Professor of Psychology, whose face Marshall knew well, took extensive notes. Some research graduates he knew were present, together with a noted Reader in History, and row after row of Extremely Famous Faces from the world of Entertainment.

Marshall sensed that many of these minds had been carefully prepared. He imagined that most of them would be surprised to know that. They had experienced a gentle, subtle nurturing, ready for fertile reception of the first pollen of a joke-system. This had drifted in as if from nowhere, like a Fred Hoyle Space Flu, or the hundreds of horse-molesters of this hot mid-June, none of whom were caught.

Fields continued, to a most attentive audience.'

He described 'ponderous, weighty, and over-serious intellectuals' of the past, as 'products of narrow, betraying specialisations'; they were always 'brittle, dangerously inflexible, puritanical, and never very good-looking'. He declared such 'iron-age thinkers' were 'wrecks of latter-day European Time', and accused them of building systems of destruction of any and every kind, such that all Europe ever knew was pain.

A hall silent with rapt attention now heard that the 'spiritually-ruinous tasking time' constructed by these 'great strapping Easter Island faces of Europa', would now be abandoned for a rediscovered Entertainment Time. This dimension would replace the whole *why* apparatus of explanatory causation by the elements of a deeper Entertainment Past. This would be a time without a troublesome *why*, a time flexible and liquid, a time personalized and ever-listening. It was a rediscovered old garden-gate time of Will Hay and Frank Randle, Gillie Potter merging as a *continuum* with Tommy Steel, Freddy Mercury, David Bowie and Tommy Handley, as well as *Take That, New Kids on the Block*, and Boy George. Moreover, this Time had a human face. All these people and all these things had actually given pleasure rather than gas, flame, genocide, or mouthfuls of nagging chalky dust from seriously depressed old analogue white-men, who could not kick a jiving leg to save their depressed and puritanical lives. This last image raised dusky cheers from many black faces at the back of the *Odeon*. Even the most severe critics of this 'secular theology' found it difficult not to agree with Fields that Duke Ellington, Count Basie, and even the *Rappin' Black Pigs* had given more meaningful pleasure than Jesus Christ.

In the coffee break, Fields was besieged by autograph hunters, and not a few glamourous young ladies, whose intentions were foiled by the ever-watchful Alison and Mavis. Marshall quietly circulated, taking careful soundings of the varied human scene. He felt a great gulf between himself and the well-dressed young chorus around Fields. Marshall had been born in 1939. One of his first memories was when four years of age, his father lead him by the hand into a dawn garden to see a sky almost black with droning aircraft. His father's hand pointed: black and green *Lancasters* to the left, blue-hulled B 17 *Flying Fortresses* to the right. And lower, right over his father's head, countless camouflaged C 47 Dakotas taking 6th Airborne Division to the Orne and Caen bridges on the left flank of the Normandy beaches. The history of every blast, bullet and scream, every nightmare of the unspeakable was somewhere faithfully recorded within him. Nearly half a century later, the roar of ghost aircraft still shook him on occasions when he had the one drink too many. He knew most of the people in the ballroom had not been witness to such primal stuff. The Strontium 90 face of 1945 was hidden well within their younger bones. He supposed that the super-sharp Fields, over ten years younger than himself, knew that he had been born near to such a cosmic shock, but he never spoke of it. To Benson, ten years younger again, Marshall supposed it was an almost unacknowledged set of mysteries locked in some museum of his teeming brain to be visited occasionally on long lost rainy afternoons, a set of historical curiosities considered briefly in a rare pause between mind-bending projects of the roaring present.

The deep hollow boom of a 747 almost hanging in the air over the *Odeon* brought Marshall back to 1944 yet again. Behind the stream of glider-pulling *Dakotas* was the body of a live culture. To him, in the hall here now, there was a body of almost nothing. No-one had painted Armageddon like this; in 1944 nothing could crack his beloved island.

Now it could come apart at the seams in the time between two TV advertisements. Once, as a fifteen-year-old school army-cadet, he stood guard at the Cenotaph in his home town. The sense of community he experienced then was unspeakable. The sense of community he saw before him now in the *Odeon* he would not have wiped his arse on.

Marshall gazed at a moon rising up over the city, and began to understand the meaning of the word *game*. To his generation it had meant mere toys. To the present generation it was one of the highest concepts of activity. Now the moon sped behind a cloud, and for a moment the great Thames was once more aflame by the docks, and the air over St. Paul's was full of throbbing *Daimler-Benz* engines at 25,000 feet.

The fires in his mind across the darkness of the memory reflected back to him the question of what would happen if the world ever kicked again, and gave all those assembled in the *Odeon* something real to do.

As the lecture resumed, Marshall noted that the audience were not tiring. Now, claimed Fields, Entertainment, like Rationalism, was a religion of Advertising. Systems of facts were merely powerful suggestive invocations to induce belief. All systems tried to buy time-share into the mainframe *realisation* of the dominant conscious experience. That way lay immortality, for re-selling was re-birthing. A belief-system in decay would do anything to try and revitalise itself: it would destroy, lie, deceive, even produce and sell off bits and pieces of prime assets to a downtown market where its various manoeuvres and deceptions were just about ready to be downgraded to magician's tricks. It wasn't a question of whether UFOs or the sawn-in-half circus-lady were *real* or not, said a perspiring Fields, so much as which particular near-bankrupt circus was trying to beat the bank by juggling the figures of now-you-see-it now-you-don't. This process produced things as 'real' as 'gravity waves', or even a Parliamentary statement of Declaration of Interests. It was also as 'real' indeed as such-under-the-counter Entertainment Cut-Price Value as a return from the dead with nothing much interesting to say.

Marshall admired the technique again. All the best-seller iconography was in perfect operation: the good accent, the well-modulated voice, the main points delivered as sensibly and carefully as if Fields were giving a lecture on politically-correct social responsibilities to an audience of grim-faced feminist lesbian academics from a tee-shirt polytechnic. He sat back, and enjoyed a master-class in the propagandising of a grey-scale of almost-truths as Fields continued

Since in the late twentieth-century, the shadow-play of Conspiracy Theory had replaced metaphysics, Fields went on to outline his First Law of Conspiracies: 'There is a true conspiracy when explanations are more unbelievable than that which they would explain'. Therefore, said he, let there be no more accusations of eccentricity, or even occultism. To further amused and mostly appreciative murmurs, he added that what was 'real' was only this week's winner of the big intellectual game-show, and was about as Permanent and Profound as an Hot Line for Stray Traffic-Cone Spotters.

As an ex-seller of *Popsicles* and *Post-Toasties*, Marshall saw the technique was sound. It was all beautifully worked out. The man was become fashionable bourgeois credibility *par excellence*. Now, as he continued, he didn't cast doubt on the validity of previous intellectual discovery, so much as its *style*. The discovery of the existence of a magnetic field created around a current-carrying wire, said he, didn't really cast light upon the way the world worked so much as change the presentation of information. In such a process, various causal links were merely re-mythologised, their inner character remaining just as mysterious as ever. Thus the undoubtedly great women and men who pottered about with magnets, coils of wire, and jars full of chemicals, were, in the final analysis all *advertising*. At this point, become a master of ironic timing, Fields announced a forthcoming new book, *The Last Days of the Last Engines*, and left the platform to thunderous applause.

After any Fields lecture, Marshall never knew whether he was coming or going. But some salesman's subtlety within him said that this was exactly what was intended. As popular man now circulated, signing copies of *StarPower*, Marshall looked again at the flushed faces. He was a witness to changes in the very record of the rocks. The entire audience was now one great unified thought, one of Fields' 'systems-animals'. Marshall was sure a powerful part of the middle ground had been won, to become a unified collective thinking fabric calmly ticking away under the streamers and balloons still suspended from gilded roof specially built for the previous night's *Come Dancing* television broadcast.

Watching the audience leaving, they were become a procession of seedlings to Marshall's mind; newborn, a little breathless, but precision-balanced like a wrestler searching for pivots, pressure-points; they were new information-bases ready for rendezvous with other networks, amplifying, selectively filtering, getting ready for what he had heard Fields describe as the big push up off the beach from the ultraviolet basking shallows, to the tree-lines and forests of Entertainment State. Marshall supposed that as Fields had suggested to him, most gathered here in this ballroom had now come under orders to a process dedicated to determining the shape of the next serial-frame in historical line. Each shift in frame entailed leading the great Explanations, by trick or treat, to a region of uncertainty which would break up that bedrock of which fundamental assumptions were made.

But these ideas now quickly vanished from Marshall's mind as he now saw a tall and thin young man waving a pistol, and struggling with two Special Branch men in something called a *Neapolitan Alcove* just by the *La Vie Parisienne* bar. As more police rushed over to help, the man was brought to the ground, and Marshall saw a face which had just started to appear in his files.

It was Jack White.

White was a thirty-year-old ex-corporal of the 2nd Royal Tank Regiment. Two years previous, he had been court-martialled and dishonourably discharged from the British Army for driving his 65-ton *Challenger 2* down Warminster High Street without benefit of crew, knowledge of his superiors, or permission of Her Majesty. The tank was not the only sensation: his black girlfriend, Donna, happened to be sunning herself stark naked on the turret at the time.

After White left the army, he had rapidly acquired an equally spectacular personal history, traversing as many belief-structures in five years as he could possibly manage, absorbing anachronistic ephemera from all points of the compasses of belief. Many voices had spoken to him: voices coaxing, persuading, convincing, until he paced the narrowing cell of his life with increasingly angry and bewildered steps. Hunted by Hell's Angels, drug-dealers, and favour-collectors many and various, he had moved from Islam to the British Ku-Klux-Klan, from there to apocryphal encounters with British Israel Society, flat-earthers, nudists, communists, and even something called the Elmbourne Road Church of Aphrodite. He was prime conspiracy material was Jack White, a genuine back-bedroom hero, whose pistol had now dropped to the floor, kicked away by a Special Branch boot as his hands were manacled behind him.

Marshall, identifying himself by a daily code-word, looked at the weapon now being examined by the almost-blushing Covert Team.

The gun was made of wood.

He was told later that Fields called this pistol a 'theatrical weapon'. The phrase disturbed him, as he realised it was probably intended to do. Apparently Fields added, probably more thrilled than disturbed, that Oswald's gun, though admittedly better than White's, was almost equally as theatrically useless as far as *that* particular job was concerned.

The next day, looking at the photograph of the expertly-carved toy in *The Sun*, Marshall felt that the small-print of *StarPower*, ignored by almost everybody, was near, brushing against his mind as lightly as a fairy wing. The mass of almost unconscious suggestions buried in the footnotes at the bottom of each page of *Starpower* was first sunlight on primal pools. Within these beach-shallows there stirred a world of sprites, elves, and Universal Jokers. Marshall almost laughed out loud at his own thoughts. Some of these elementals, like BUACs, would soon be ready, he laughingly assumed, to step out of their cartoons and press their toy-triggers.

But Marshall did not smile when he heard that the police found one such half-cartoon when, after Jack was safely locked up in Paddington Green, they burst into his Notting Hill Housing Trust flat in All Saint's Road. The place was an Entertainment shrine. Fields' face was plastered all over the walls, together with hundreds of great Stars. The trouble was that poor Donna was almost plastered all over the place in the bargain. She lay securely trussed between unlit candles on a kind of crude Entertainment altar, and for the first time in an extremely difficult life, was most pleased to see the boys in blue.

But if Entertainment religion had not quite achieved its first sacrifice, it had certainly produced its first anomaly. A few days after White was arrested, Carol Davies, a cleaner who had swept the *Odeon* stage every morning for twenty years, was doing her duty with brush and pan, when she found a bullet. At least it was something that looked like a bullet. The thing was wedged near the navel of the illuminated pink-plastic female nude which supported the scrolled lectern from which Fields had given his speech. A Special Branch report on this eventually reached Marshall, two days later, but he was far too busy to attend to such minuscule obscurities. One thing, did, however remain in his memory.

The round was made of wood.

White was almost immediately released by a magistrate on account of his 'difficult life' and also Donna's decision not to press charges. The whole affair would have ended there and then had not the tabloids nosed out Jack White's history. Some months back, true to form, White had made clumsy attempts to get into Buckingham Palace several times, and had been arrested and charged on each occasion. In response to this, using the kind of peculiar logic known only to social workers, it had been decided to send White on holiday to an African village for 'creative recuperation'. Here, he promptly caught full-blown AIDS from a

157

prostitute, nearly died of food-poisoning, and was thrown into jail for drug-dealing. There, he was promptly buggered by inmates, obligingly tortured by the staff, and nearly died again of infected dressings and polluted drinking water in the rat-infested prison hospital. Within the environs of the prison (and also the hospital), he witnessed the mass-murder of countless thousands of African men, women, and children, almost all innocent victims of tribal conflicts gone berserk. Eventually, both gaol and hospital were burnt down around him, and holding his own drip, he found himself dodging bullets amidst approximately 8000 festering corpses. He was rescued by a team of French and American paratroopers, sent to protect a United Nations medical team.

As a just-alive White trembled on his hospital bed in St. Mary's Hospital, Paddington, these soldiers shot and killed fifteen drunken renegades who were about to burn down an orphanage containing 270 sick and wounded black children. For this action, they had been labelled 'fascists' by White's ever-attentive British social workers, gathered around their hero's bed.

This threatening history had taken its time to get to Marshall. He was frantically busy, and he could hardly concern himself with nutcases and police matters. White was quickly released from Paddington Green after dire warnings, and all Marshall could do was keep a watching brief. He was fascinated however, to see the growing correspondence and documentation about what should have been nothing more than a bit of a nasty laugh for the tabloids, and little else. A Home Office laboratory had requested the 'wooden' bullet from the police. It had been misplaced. The laboratory complained. There was an investigation. The 'object' (for now it had no specific name) still could not be located, but in any case, a reply stated that despite signed statements to the contrary, the *missile* (the reference had changed again) was not made of wood, but of a 'strange metal'. Marshall suddenly felt old. There were so many preposterous professional mistakes and presumptive technological blindness in even these few statements, it all reminded him of something with which he had once been most familiar.

Between 1970 and 1980, he had been part of a watch on the investigations into the finances of Robert Maxwell. In 1971, in the face of the complete failure of the world's mightiest accountancy brains to prove fraud, 'the man unfit to run a public company' had thrown a dinner-party in celebration. Marshall supposed that he had been invited as an disturbing indication that the Security Services were as accessible to Maxwell as goods on a *Woolworths* counter. In his after-dinner speech, Maxwell had told a story. Marshall remembered the booming voice, not exactly unlike Fields' own.

"A man who definitely does not believe in fairies wakes up one morning and reads in his morning paper that a milkman has seen one of the said creatures trying to hide behind the empties on a doorstep. Formed by the outrageous denials of the first man, and the outrageous claims of the second, is a half-form."

The foreheads of many of the now long-gone power-names of Britain in that period still glistened in Marshall's mind. He remembered the drunken voices of that summer evening two decades ago, as a peer of the realm responded. This man was not exactly out of the woods himself as far as City investigations were concerned.

"What's a half-form, Bob?"

He was one of the few who had the nerve to call Maxwell by his Christian name, if that is what it could be called.

"Something which half-exists, John."

"Like a corporation?"

"I was thinking of yourself, actually".

Foot-stamps and jeers. The peer blushed. Even an experienced member of the Second Chamber had to be careful if he wished to swap lines with Cap'n Bob. However, the old soldier let Lord John off the hook for a cost far less than the price of the shares he had just sold him.

"Don't worry, John. All we part-forms live in the seam between mass accusations."

Tables were banged. Bread rolls flew.

"What does all that mean?"

"It means the late crisis of rationalism."

Cheers, table-thumps, and not a few catcalls.

"How much you pay for that line, Bob?"

"That's a half-secret, John."

Now plenty of grudging applause as Maxwell turned his terrible eye upon the titled one.

"I leave you all with a question: which is the greatest terror: the terror of what wilful deceptions reveal when they collapse, or what they reveal if they hold fast?"

The peer turned pale and sat down. Fortunately, another such was flying top cover for him.

"Too clever by a half, Bob, too clever by a half."

Feeling the need for air, Marshall took a popular book about Maxwell from his office shelf, put on his Jacket, and walked across Vauxhall Bridge to a small local park. Sitting on a bench, he practised the salesman's trick of accidentally switching off his mobile phone. He then practised the much older commando-trick of totally emptying the mind before setting the key-signature of a thought.

Both still worked well. Soon, into the forced silence, suitably cleansed thoughts crept back, their billion useless acres of modern noise momentarily dumped. What was a half-form? After all these years, he felt he had only just begun to understand what Maxwell was talking about. He now supposed that the 'bodies' of modern mythological animals were built of such things Maxwell's investments and accounts, the pattern of Jack Ruby's intriguing telephone calls in the first three weeks of November, 1963, the mass of similar telephone calls before and after the death of Vince Foster in July, 1993, or Marilyn Monroe's many extraordinary visitors by car, ambulance,and helicopter, on Saturday, August 4th, 1962. Or perhaps such a Big-Foot creature as a half-form was now a wooden bullet which had never really been a bullet, and apparently wasn't made of wood, but was a kind of April snowman built of information-dumps, and strangely and quickly melting away, like a Yeti, Harold Wilson, or the Black Puma of Shepherd's Bush. Marshall also bet that if cleaner Carol Davies ever took it into her head to write to the Home Office asking about her find, then she would not get a reply.

Advertising as sonata-form again.

And why had it led him here?

From where he sat he could see a row of shops whose bright and colourful displays of sweets and chocolates looked frightened to death by heavy iron grills. The shops were flanked by the intimidating structure of the *Maxillian Community School*, a place known nationally for banning all fairy stories, and even the violence of Odysseus. The Managing Director (previously Headmaster) had designed the The *Free Association and Relating Area* (previously the playground), himself. This was a wide concrete tank-park surrounded by barrack-style blocks, and this lunchtime was deserted of tiny dancing feet as the moon and socialism. Marshall assumed that in the classroom-bunkers, the escape-doors were locked, barred, and bolted in the manner all such British doors, ready for the *News of the World* lead-article and photograph of fifty small charred corpses. But this lunchtime, the children to have escaped their benefactors. Where were they? The spikes, edges, torn stanchions, and rusty poles of the *Free Association and Relating Area* looked as if they had long masticated any wandering innocent, of whom there was not so much as a torn sandle-strap of a sign, But somewhere he could hear laughing cries, as if the young played in those spaces between young time and old time, dimensions either lost, incomprehensible, or barred to adults. Marshall imagined the children, as always, had sidetracked the plots against them using the banned stories as their secret guide. He imagined that fleeing the now obsolescent sirens of group dialectic, they had escaped with their good-fairy guides through the darkness of 'crawling tubes', steel frames, springs, traps, slides, split tyres, and twisted steel of new stories which beckoned to them like old witches from the battlements of fortified schools such as theirs. He fancied the children had found the lost street, the old brambled gate, the hidden cottage, by brook, wood, and had been guided past dark ideological groves where prowled the predatory dimensions of mass intention.

He stopped this flow of association and gripped the handle of his briefcase. These were Fields' thoughts, not his.

He was already a half-form of someone else.

Hurrying back across the bridge to Tower House, and almost at the end of a long career in investigation, he knew he wasn't supposed to think like this. He was supposed to think like the Chief Clerk, that tea would be served at the usual time, and officials would explain everything that needed explaining, should there ever be in the United Kingdom that almost inconceivable need for questions of any kind, still less explanations.

In his room in Tower House, he took the Maxwell book out of his case, and read for twenty minutes. He entered a Fieldsian world in which any simple concepts of reality and truth had been replaced by constantly varying forms of solidity, differing planes of action, policy, and experience. Marshall had an idea that Maxwell's 'half-forms' were dust-devils of varying orders of matter and thought within this structure. They were part-realities scavenging a part-life in an almost-region sculpted by the plastic locus of accusation and counter-accusation, of fact and counter-fact, an area into which poured all the fears, doubts, and uncertainties of an Age.

He quickly put the book back on the shelf as if it were spreading a contagion. The terror Maxwell mentioned he assumed was the terror in the face of the inability of any human to put even a single millionth grain of experience into absolute rational perspective. He pulled the book back out of his case, and opened it at random. The dinner party had been updated. It was now 1990 as he read.

'There was a notable difference between Maxwell and Murdoch. The Australian owed the banks so much that the banks could not afford to allow him to go broke without bankrupting themselves.'

161

That night he dreamed of firing a rifle on a range. There were two kinds of target popping up at random. One was called the Man on the Clapham Omnibus, the other was called a Power Centre. When he fired at the first, he hit the bull every time. When he fired at the second, his rounds took on such a life as was never ordained for them by any respectable gunsmith. Up, down, in circles, anything but in a Euclidian line

In the morning he was forced to forget such things as dreams. Her Upstairs ordered him to fly to Northern Ireland at once.

The Apache had been located.

IV

The Hunt

Nora twisted and turned on a mattress whose consistency and geometry seemed as impossible as the lumpy body of her newly intended target. After a few days of filling her head with a copy of *StarPower*, and reading newspaper reports of a madman trying to attack the author with a wooden gun, she was more than ready to snatch some sleep in the lost attic of yet another small boarding house by the abandoned bus-station in Garfield Road.

As from many high towers an ocean away, tentacles of ideological protein reached out for her, feeling for her name and her substance, she again dreamed of eye-blue waters stretching to the moon. Yet more towers and turning aerials on old hills sent pieces of digitised brain after her like baying hounds. In the night, the dream architecture of twenty decades containing half-living stuff created before her great-grand parents were born, was reaching for her like many hands from many graves. Robot ancestors hunted for her face, as the blind would try to decipher the character of inhabitants by the touch of furniture. These clusters of half-ancestors were everywhere, in the ideas behind the computer's hunting circuitry, in her extended electronic body, which was full of the night-thoughts of centuries. Hunting for her was a beast made of the mad logic of troubled endeavours, the shame of fraud, the despair of mistakes and confusions, and the most subtle of scientific insights.

In the half-life which possessed her before she saw waters stretching to the moon, her last thoughts were that perhaps this Fields was right. Perhaps the idea of inanimate matter was a deception of first magnitude, a conspiracy in itself, and the plot had a quite specialised function: the flood this piece of rationalist chicanery was damming up would be instantly catastrophic for a unit mentality. Before drifting away, she saw all the sequential steps of the search structures trying to detect her slender self, as having a personality. From resistors to entire computing languages, from programs to tapes and magnetic discs, each shape was the history of an idea within a piece of architecture of mind. The technology of the search operations carried a burden of inheritance so wide and so deep that to it, conventional ideas of life and death meant nothing. In her half-sleep, she had never seen herself (or anybody else) like *this* before. She thought people were enclosed, finite; she thought that nothing of their mental life extended beyond the surface of the bones of the skull, never mind extending before birth and after death. The history of each separate visionary facet of her pursuers (and she assumed, her protectors, too) was an ever-widening estuary of voices and faces which were still pieces of conscious tissue of active memory and invention. Each step in the sequence of the material development of the electrical apparatus which was stalking her had torn something from the heart of someone; each fumbling truth which gave the hunt coherence and integration had needed some original tiny pulse of suffering, a little giving up of some loving metaphysical fluid to blood this flexing of mighty computerised muscle.

Looking for her was a half-form.

Sleep showed her eye-blue waters stretching to the moon. The waters became a phalanx of secular devotions connecting hunting machines by countless aerials, transmissions, and cables. Like old sepia ghosts drifting before her, were some of the men and women who had pushed themselves to spectacular and often tragic limits for the prowling technology. Her dream showed her an experiment here, a piece of circuit theory there; she saw much earlier crude sketches of faces and pieces of ideas and minds reflected in the *realisation* of rubber and plastic and steel and silicon. Here was developing technology as a temple god being prayed to, being given gifts and sacrifices, being stroked and loved, being bribed and threatened. She saw whole electromechanical systems forever being asked to behave, being pushed to new limits, their bits of old time and new time being experimented upon, being asked to grow, being asked to cooperate, and being measured and tested and calibrated and checked.

Alarm. She sat up in the tiny room and fought for breath, as if waking under a pile of heavy black sacking. Only a distant car-horn and the sweep of headlights beyond the dusty window by the broken gas-meter brought her back to the world. She lay back exhausted, in a no-man's-land of consciousness. This dark border was full of the history she had once been, the lives she had not known she had lived. The 19th century hovel she was trying to get some sleep in was the 19th century itself, with all its fears, its collapsing certainties, all the half-bits and pieces of what she once was. Perhaps this Fields was right. Perhaps *objectivity* was the greatest cultural deception of all
Sleep.
If objectivity was a deception, it was a protective trick. Certainly now reaching for Nora's face and name and location, were vows and blood-revenge, victories and failures and suicides of which she could not, thankfully, have had a conception. If *psi* ever really reveals itself, it will be by an opening of channels of implicit memory within shape, purpose, and function. In

principle and discovery, in research and investment, there were ruined lives, silent curses and pacts against the gods now hunting for Nora. Each circuit board and pulse, each grasping piece of hard-fought-for advance in concept and operation was a set of evolving stories, an inferno of names and days and books and nights, and somewhere along this spectral line of visions would be faces which recognised, hands which guided, and voices which cried out to Nora: *run as fast as you can.*

Such voices were now reaching her through the very crystal lattice of the mechanised corporate structures of the great city half-asleep in the night around her. The voices were everywhere in her dreaming, as if they too were programmed, were part of stylistic retrofit, change of frequency, modification, redesign, or prototype test to destruction. There were counter-voices babbling in the interstices of the half-dreaming city who paid a lot of the interest-quanta to maintain the management of an ecology of inspirations within whose denial-schedules, none heard any voices at all. Any sense of mission was a lens for all these mouths, an amplifier through which Fields heard disputing theologians, Marshall heard Nazi bombing squadrons, and now, to Nora Harcourt, came warnings within a singular delta-mouth of naturally-selected purpose.

Alarm. Awake. The image-streams within her were now a flock flying in all directions, sheep looking for any shelter in night and storm. In some deep-sea level of organisation within her dream, a clock had skipped a beat. Tripwire touch. Some commando-virus had cut a way straight through the first barriers of early significance. Alarm. Coincidence. Start the countdown. A watching clown outside Fingal's Bar. Thousands of such were in town, but only this one took his eyes away quickly from her. Clowns *never* take their eyes away. In Nora's world there was no such thing as that shameful intellectual excuse called the *random*. Staying alive as long as she had done, any alert guardian process had to be completely automatic and twice as fast as any evolving technology. Pull on pants and vest. Tie shoes. Scratch of armpits. Scan. Count. Estimate. Tick-tock. Alarm. Another clown by the post-office. Coincidence was the crack of a twig in the night-forest. Another scratch. The mattress must be alive. Waking, she reached for her cigarettes. The match-flare blinded her in the half-dark, and the skin of her arms and legs felt as if scraped raw by sharp invisibilities.

She looked out of the small window.

No lights from the rooms across the way. Drunks struggling home under the street lamps brought her to the window. Lights moved within the distant shadows of the Turf Lodge housing estate. Heart-thumping now. A solitary clown propped against a building skip, looking up at the moon. The figure was quite still, head upturned, as if it were in some fine engraving of a past age. And the house was quiet. Far distant threads of powerful music caught on a sudden shift of damp air around the old building, making the window frame rattle as if the not-so-distant past had returned.

The image-circuits were humming.

Tie back hair

Something was entering the woods.

And whatever it was, it was different to anything she had met up with before.

And the house was quiet.

Take off pants and vest. Secure weapon-lanyards.

And no light in Mary's room across the way. No sound of chugging water pipes, radios, baths running, no smell of cooking, no children crying, no doors banging, no windows opening.

Just a foot on the stair.

In one move, she threw herself into the 1870 fireplace hearth, and swung herself up through the chimney like a pre-Factories-Act soot-monkey. Making her blind way, the silenced *Uzi* and two fragmentation grenades dangled down across her naked backside like the *dildo* of a cross-dressed gargoyle. To the astonishment of two SAS troopers covering the roof, she shot out of the broken chimney-stack of an abandoned wash-house some five hundred yards away. They looked down to see the faintest of naked shadows pass across a tiny cobbled space before their bullets streamed towards a great splash into the dark and oily waters of a canal which wound through an old industrial warehouse area. She was gone then, even from the water, vanished into a multi-angled Victorian murk like a striped convict running from press-gangs and transportation. She had the soldier's admiration. It took some cool to gamble that even the SAS would hesitate for just one second before shooting down a stark naked woman. Five seconds after her dive, the ancient wood of the door of the attic room became a crumbling furnace as *M16* ammunition poured through it, and a high-explosive grenade was thrown towards the narrow bed on which, seconds before, she had dreamed of history and the waters of the moon.

166

Marshall stood by the doorway, watching the squad check out the still smoke-filled room. It was eerie to be this near to her, yet still so far. He stepped inside, nearly choked on soot, and noted the badly decayed outer wall, now almost blown away by the grenade. Somehow she was still here. Miraculously, vapour still rose from a mug of coffee on a small bedside table. The bed itself now hung half-out over the courtyard below, and would have fallen had one leg not caught on the single cold-water tap in the room. Barsby and Annie appeared, and started quickly putting items in a tea-chest before the Official Version of Events arrived. A torn blouse, a burnt shoe, a bit of smouldering bedding which Barsby tried beat out, receiving the curses of the coughing SAS for his troubles. Into the case went improvised hand-strengtheners, several wigs, male clothes, a box of make-up. Feeling for his roll-up tin, an historical vertigo possessed Marshall. He'd definitely been through this one before. Apart from holes from the automatic rounds, it could have been any downtown room in Europe from 1832 to 1870, back via 1848, and onwards to 1968. Perhaps countless more such hovels as this, straight from the pages of Gorky or Dostoevsky, still existed, tailor-made for those million manifestoes which created and yet still fed the bleeding and ever-restless European heart. Marshall noted a crushed tin bath, bricks tied to an exercise pole, and even a shoe-box which contained nibbled crusts. He sighed. What a life. He was getting old, and the world hadn't changed. He picked up a devastated copy of Flaubert's *L'Education Sentimental*. It was open at a page she had underlined:

'Soon it will be winter, the season of balls and dinner parties.'

God help us all, thought Marshall. The woman would have been far happier as Editor of *Harpers & Queen*. He turned to the SAS officer, who spoke covered in ancient soot as he looked up the fireplace outlet.

"You'd need Bill Sykes' dog for this one."

Barsby chimed in.

"She must be built like a ferret."

Annie, black from head to toe, snapped at him.

"Well we'd better bring one next time, hadn't we?"

Marshall's sarcasm silenced the blushing and disappointed company.

"Probably be more effective, wouldn't you say?"

On their way back to the warehouse which was their temporary HQ, Marshall became convinced that something was had happened to their basic perceptions in this place of intense Entertainment influence. The operation this evening had been a bungled, amateur affair, almost as if time was forgetting, pushing such actions into some lumber-room of experience, and not bothering to make them consistent any more. Perhaps, he thought, as they all tucked into Army pack-meals and dreadful coffee, resources for a new world-picture were now flowing elsewhere. And perhaps a something was no longer interested in keeping up appearances, and Nora Harcourt's attic would go unrepaired, just as similar dwellings in the house of experience fell inevitably into decay.

On the flight back, hardly a word was exchanged. Annie sulked, Barsby played mini-chess by himself, and Marshall read his favourite Tom Clancy. If the shamefaced team now feared the edge of the tongue of the Directrix, Marshall now also feared the edge of the small-print of *StarPower*.

Crawling into his Tower House cot at four in the morning GMT, he didn't quite know which was going to be the worst.

V

Shoot-Out at the Albert Hall

A week after he had returned from Belfast, Marshall, somewhat still disgruntled over the failure of the expedition, decided to cheer himself up. He took a taxi to the Albert Hall, where Fields was speaking at one of the now legendary Entertainment State Performance Marathons. He had only been able to get into the meeting himself by a colleague making a personal phone-call to a Fifth Columnist, as the jocular term in Tower House went. Travelling through a London which seemed to be full of sirens, he realised that in truth, he missed the conversations over the years with Fields, whose latest name was the Michelin-Man. Though now Marshall could hardly contact him, he looked forward to hearing him speak.

The Albert Hall was packed. Despite pouring rain, a great crowd blocked Kensington Gore to see the inevitable arrival of the hundreds of famous faces. The Marathons were very different to the *Odeon* gatherings; they were steamy anarchic jamborees which lasted sometimes a day and a night, and featured 'New Performance Talent' from what Fields called 'the Four Corners of Advertising Destiny'. These popular sessions were still far too hot for staid British television; there were fainting fits, screaming protests from religious groups, controversial 'acts' and a generally sulphurous atmosphere which frequently exploded into violence.

But still the Famous Faces came, drawn by the hypnotic Fields and his message.

Such were the almost riotous scenes on occasion, that the much-feared Inspector Roy McCork and his merry men were frequently ordered to attend and keep good order. McCork and his own almost private group of constables were a law unto themselves, and their 'loyalty' and racist politics were rooted in the murky corners of an increasingly uncertain Britain. A permanently restrained explosion, McCork was an anachronism who saw himself as forever on the *strasse* with Himmler and Streicher, covering the pavement with the blood of Yiddish Bolsheviks, or with the old *Bunde,* teaching them there blecks a lesson they would never ever forget. All McCork needed was a sabre-scar to compliment the permanently puckered brow and eyes which were so close together his nickname was Cyclops. His flexing fingers seemed permanently curled around the handle of what his more subtle friends called a *schambok,* ready to strike right across the features of any bog-wog-liberals and dervish-shrieking poets who dared to pass in front of his flattened nose. Predictably, with McCork and his gang, the Jews ran the banks and the cities, the niggers ran the drugs and the brothels, and only a milk-white thoroughly de-yidded Christ held the pure provincial earth free from contagion.

The many Famous Faces in the audience were surrounded by their court retainers. But the circles of muscular guards around a Face on these occasions was often the only means of telling a them proper apart from the many imitations that Entertainment State had now spawned. Throughout the world there were now Clone Clubs, whose members appeared as perfect Hugh Grants, Elizabeth Hurleys, and Mel Gibsons. By the ranks of assorted near-perfec t imitations of famous Stars, Marshall noted McCork was almost smacking his lips. He was obviously inspired. Judging by some of the company, tonight it looked very much as if there was a good prospect of a nice skull-banging and hence bringing a few people he could name back to a proper God-fearing reality of chapel, ferre t-breeding, and *The Daily Express.*

Alison and Mavis now waved incense sticks as if the occasion were an Alan Ginsberg love-in from the heroic past of what he had heard Fields call The Ancient World. The incense was to announce Napoleon Smith, First Comedian of Entertainment State. Dressed as the Emperor himself, Smith rhapsodised on the theme of the evening: Entertainment Religion.

"Entertainment, when you think about it, is the only thing we've got left. In this floating sludge of whale-breakfast which the theological fast-food managers call Creation, the nearest you ever get to God is when you hear him laugh. Mind you, the joke, whatever it is, might appear to be doing nothin' for you, particularly when you suddenly find yourself listening to the divine mirth when you are dive-bombing the bed of the North Sea minus bow-doors and parachute. But the thing is, Entertainment is still there to comfort you. Just think: you're still clinging onto your half-drunk can of Hospitality *Cola.* Even though you know you're soon going to hit the reprocessing stack, you've still got your *Convenience Pack of Iced Nerds,* so you know God has had another Good Day. You might even have been luckier than that. Your very last memory could well have been the face of some Great English Toe-Sucking Whore of Yore before you are sucked through the ill-maintained hull like an extruded piece of missing pension fund."

Listening to the popular Napoleon Smith, Marshall took in the scene around him. The hair styles and motley of many movements and generations were a seething camouflage before his eyes, some of which was anything but familiar. On one flank before the stage stood a silent, and forbiddingly statuesque swarm of Hell's Angels; they glared malevolently at a line of jeering and bullish skinheads, who had already thrown a firework or two at them. These two factions were held apart only by lines of McCork's men, and also by a mass of their more modish and colourful mutual enemies, who occupied the middle of the hall in overwhelming numbers.

Grizzled fragments of the over-forties old guard of the avant-guard were packed alongside Marshall at the back of the hall. Communists from Ealing in black berets who had known Poetry & Jazz in Soho, glared nastily at bewildered and slightly deranged walking-wounded from other long-lost movements of an heroic bomb-banning Bohemian past, such as Fringe Theatre, Agitprop, Free Shops, and Claimant's Unions. Anarchist veterans in flasher's macs, who had known Ladbroke Grove in its cocoa-drinking days, stood uneasily by a group of recently violently defrocked Jehovah's Witnesses from Lambeth. Remnants of Socialist Collectives scowled at Travelling Folk. New-Age Christians shook their fists at chained Punks as Inspector McCork himself arrested one of a knot of elderly geldings with bare tattooed torsos and rings through their noses. Assisted by a favourite pair of what he called his hatchet-men, he also pulled down from the stage an adventurer in a Homburg hat clutching a tightly furled umbrella. Protesting loudly about alien abductions, and asking for a ban on female fighter pilots, Homburg joined his comrade, a pre-Munich Hampstead crone, hot from Speaker's corner, who held up the placard *Use Lentils for Lest Lust.*

Fields himself, offstage, appreciated these nice cosy British touches in the broiling host. Sprinkled throughout in nervous clusters were ranks of fallen Oxbridge, Special Branch men in size ten boots taking painstaking notes, and once more the ever-present ten-year-old white-haired genius-manikin, now yet again proudly unfurling his cassette microphone-lead in the front row. He only really loved his country to death at times like this. To him, these gatherings were the only bright spots left in what he considered to be one of the most completely featureless and deprived cultures on planet Earth.

In the weeks since he had 'escaped' as the Tower House term went, he had developed into quite a performer himself. Marshall noted that he was much slimmer, but still looked like a cross between Charles Laughton and Margaret Rutherford. As an image for the young, he confounded all possible Public Relations predictions as he toured Britain, filling stadiums, making hundreds of thousands of Entertainment converts, and in Wigan and Ealing causing the first Entertainment riots.

171

Marshall almost began to enjoy himself as Napoleon Smith continued.

"No, an open bow-door is not a bad Entertainment deal, you'll all agree, for the price of as much flat Sellafield Roentgen-Hot Spring-Water as you can piss out, and *The Mars Bar That Ate Santa Claus* free video stuffed in your case next to your County Court Judgment Papers for refusing to register to vote for the bastards. Oh yes, you've just got to enjoy the Advertisements with The Lord. So act now. Buy an sea-ticket, and get to Jehovah's Technological Joke Emporium before denial-time. Become the Messiah of your Entertainment ghetto. Feature in your very own technocratic holocaust as a mini-series. Do it now. There are no hidden charges. The death is free! And don't forget to be objective. That way, its not you doing it."

There was now a hushed expectancy as Napoleon Smith now banged a gavel, like a music-hall master of old.

"Thank you, and now the moment all you Entertainment Citizens have been waiting for. Now all you advertising saints, Fieldsian systems-animals, trash junkies, and fuzzy sets, give a big hand now for the man who liberated theology like the Tories liberated plastic macs and *satsumas!* Here he is, ladies and gentlemen, that engaging, egalitarian, eponymous, epicyclone, Mr. Entertainment himself: Dr. Hieronymus Fields!"

Riotous and seething admiration as the Rolling Stone's *Can't Get No Satisfaction,* announced Fields' entrance through the crowd, for all the world like world-class prizefighter, ringed by male and female minders in baseball caps and black shell-suits. Roars, stamps, and clenched fists, V-signs, Milwall supporter's chants, some seig-heils, a punk leap, a late-hippy swirl or two, and even a short exhilarating burst of *The Star-Spangled Banner,* which Fields thought, as he entered, was most inspiring. His brain spun as he gazed upon delicious pieces of pure image-concentrate popping up and down in front of him like corn on a hot griddle. Only *StarPower*, he thought, could serve up such a edifying feast of deep-pan advertising for the connoisseur.

Marshall saw that *Entertainment Enterprises* had done a good job. Though his clothes still tended to make him look like a blanket-bath gone wrong, the man of the hour was more relaxed than Marshall had ever known him to be. His microphone technique was superb, with an assured tone and a practised delivery, as he commenced speaking to a now almost silent assembly.

"What is trash? Most miracles are trash. Not untrue, or false, but half-forms of Fuzzy Entertainment. To multiply loaves and fishes and to do that only once is a trash-act. Someone, or something is joking. Christ, like Communism, forgot that the peasants have to eat on the second day

172

and the day after that. Christ cocked it up. He forgot they needed Tea and Supper. What a clanger. I don't reckon much to that, I really don't."

Topknots and bald scalps swayed; skinheads grinned, Angels spat, and Christians hissed.

"Miracles are the very purest form of Entertainment Concentrate. Miracles, like Royalty, are the purest form of Performance Trash. Tinsel food for an hour, miracles are the most superb form of phenomenological junk-food. But they give good value, because like the very finest of advertisements, they are always invariably comic. Miracles had the best script-writers of their day. Always the tongue-in-cheek Divine Ones seemed to forget that the *untermensch* (and quite a few others), need three meals a day, not one every few hundred years, thank you very much. A single serving of cobs and herrings with nothing but condescending, pompous, and boring little parables about the correct moral life served up as afters, doesn't seem like the best culinary deal exactly that could come from the brain that made Niagara Falls, or the legs of Sharon Stone. If the gods can't do better than a cold fish bap every few millennium, then they are either only part-kosher cherubs, or are deliberately taking the piss."

Roars and applause. A few fist-fights started at the back of the hall, but were enjoyably dealt with by McCork's men as Fields continued.

"Miracles remind me of something. Throwing out sarnies from the back of a truck to refugees is what *we* do. The natives look through the palm-leaves and what do they see? The first big ships of the New Age. What gods are in that long-boat coming ashore? Clerk-Maxwell, Faraday, Dickens, Proust, all bringing you the glory of the 19th century? More like a psychopathic Bosun, a cannibal Cook, and a one-legged alcoholic Mate spewing over his stump and wishing he was back screwing press-gang backsides in lovely old Portsmouth. Back on board, a thirsty Something looks for loopholes, discarding as many religions as it discards snake-skins and snowflakes. What I say is this: *don't trust long-boats putting out from big ocean-going advertisements. You might find yourself buying something you don't want.* Hence, ladies and gentlemen, my Second Law of Conspiracies: 'The only question we can ever ask is not what is true or false, but *what shall we allow ourselves to experience?*'

A few fainting fits at this, a New Age surge or two, one firecracker, and a dead animal something thrown right across at Fields.

"Don't misunderstand me. I think Jesus was the right stuff. At least we got one free meal out of him, which is more than you could say about the other sublimity salesmen. But as for his stories, rather like that other story, Communism, nobody ever got a single brand-new shining tractor. The heart of all the stories is The Wait in Time. The Wait in the Queue before you get Served. Because the Stories never give you anything at first. The Stories want you to go through a certain little dance before you get what you think you are going to get. With the Saviours, like with your communist tractor, you've got to wait just a weeny-while before you get the Good News. That's for the little bit of suffering there's always got to be. The little drop of real blood to sign with. That's what all the Advertisements want. But don't worry, the blood's not necessarily yours."

Hecklers silenced and thrown out, several cases of panic-attacks, claustrophobia, and hyperventilation. Marshall saw paramedics struggling through to reach a man who was having hysterics, though whether he was ill, or laughing, he did not know.

"OK: what's this now? Now here's a message hand-crafted on stone for you alone from the far holy hills: YOU'VE WON! Oh lovely, praise the gods! And look: you've got yourself a nice little butter-dish and some cigarette coupons. Come on: give the Saviours a big hand now! They're all real nice, are these religious Time-Share stories. But nobody ever gets the new *Daimler.* Come on: give all the Saviours a big hand now!"

Seeing the violently energetic appreciation of the completely advertisement-conditioned young in front of him, Fields was again delighted. Before him was his child, his creation, his true family of ideas made flesh. Here was home. Here was the fertile seminal nucleus of his original vision of a complete story-machine which could be steered into manifold dimensions of alternative creations. From this hour, he was convinced that all software of social engineering was obsolete. His equations had been correct. Here in front of him, forged by his inspirations, were all the predicted holographic sets coming out of store like a complete DIY pantomime-kit for experience itself. He loved this crowd. Though their intense preoccupations had probably ruined their lives, they were still mad enough for true philosophy. The deadly liberal virtues would not plague their death; unlike most of the *Odeon* crowd, they would not be taking *hara-kiri* jobs with Channel Four.

Encore! Encore!

Fields moved calmly to the microphone again.

"Mind you, the very best stories, the classiest stories of the lot, don't cleverly offer you any nice prize. No such vulgarity. They offer you a beating. A regular thrashing. Now how about that, folks? No Prize Holiday getting ripped off on a polluted beach under acid rain for these boys, these little story-weavers. Oh no, you get First Prize of living without food and water for six months in a hole in the ground, biting your loincloth and wishing you were even back in some good old Costa, with Carlos pinching your wallet, Luigi pop-eying your girlfriend's tits, and you getting bottled Continental drinking water you wouldn't wash a prize heifer in, never mind your feet, how about that? Come on boys and girls, give all the Saviours another big hand!"

But now, at the very back of the hall, there was real opposition forming. McCork's men were only just managing to hold back a screaming pack whose clothes and accents suggested that they did not usually scream at anything at all. Fields, oblivious, continued.

"Oh yes, they're a good game-for-a-laugh are the Stories and the Saviours. The only thing you've got over 'em is that they can't do without you. Brothers and sisters, do they need you. Sweeping, cleaning, starving for the Cause. Oh yes, every Saviour and every Story and every Advertisement has a Cause, but that's another Story. So don't forget: keep taking the beliefs!"

Yet another band of Entertainment enemies of various kinds who looked as if they were hotfoot from swampland, now worried the Famous Faces as they threw unmentionable things towards Fields, often hitting fellow-sympathisers, who protested vigorously. This caused McCork's Munich beer-bellies to wobble threateningly above size twelve ammunition boots. Within the minds of McCork's best men, terribly sensible statements of fact and moral purpose came back, together with terror-dreams of wives and daughters taken away and ravaged by dark, handsome gypsies with long black locks and Semitic blood. McCork minds became the image of the face of monosyllabic swine-logic: lock, shot, slam, gaol, knock, block, strap, bang, kill, crack, rope; the countdown chant of the old brown-shirters had begun, guts pulled in by stout service belts.

Fields voice now bellowed above rising chaos.

"And remember one thing: in the Information Explosion, the last thing you're going to get is Information!"

The microphones howled as three or four paying customers fell to the floor, blood pouring from shattered mouths and fractured skulls.

But of a sudden, a hush fell on the assembly, and even Fields froze as lines of ham-pink English-Bavarian faces swivelled towards a wedge of space widening quickly in the centre of the assembly. An identical Fields clone had appeared, and firmly gripped in two outstretched hands was the biggest revolver anyone could recall having seen anywhere. Terrified eyes gazed at a 1900 Model German Naval *Luger,* complete with an original lanyard attached to the huge ribbed pistol-grip; the contraption looked as if it had just been unhooked from the wardroom of the old *Emden,* prior to some East African boarding threat in distant colonial days.

It was Jack White, dressed and padded as Fields. But this time his pistol was not made of wood.

Far faster than he could ever think about pressing the trigger, the pseudo-Fields that was Jack White became a convulsed puppet as a full magazine of M16 rounds sliced up his body neatly as any butcher's knife. *Entertainment Enterprises* had done a good job again. A tall statuesque blond in dark glasses, shell-suit, and black baseball-cap calmly and expertly changed her magazine once more, the stiff clicks being the only sound in the two seconds before pandemonium.

She then disappeared.

The *Luger* hit the floor, a two-foot flash springing from the barrel, and a bullet over one hundred years old sped to no-one knew quite where. The black-powder igniter, from a time closer to the *Königsberg* than the *Emden,* gave a great hollow report of dying history which seemed loth to blend with the drawing of horror-struck breath.

A few feet beyond the heaving pool of gore which was now the well-cloven Jack White, few noticed that Inspector McCork had acquired a neat round half-inch hole just above his close-together eyes. Looking for a moment as if he had suddenly developed a three-eyed squint, McCork staggered forward, dropping heavily on top of what was left of Jack White. The gap left by the absence of the Inspector's considerable frame showed an open-mouthed Clone-Club Jimmy Saville, Bruce Forsyth, and Perry Como, gazing upon Jack's several parts, which now bled like butchered meat by the side of McCork's quite still upturned backside.

If White and McCork were permitted such a thing as a last moment, they would have seen such a fleeing of heroes and pseudo-heroes and beliefs and pseudo-beliefs as if an air-raid siren had sounded in some great Bohemian Beyond. A screaming wave of motley disguises, some daubed with gore, stamped over McCork's astonished team, streaming to the great outside for all the world like a gone-double-mad video-loop.

Napoleon Smith, still holding his gavel, turned to a slightly pale-faced Fields, who was cowering behind his lectern.

"The *shamans* are jumping tonight, Ron. Another show like this and they'll bill you at Vegas"
Fields managed a smile. He was beginning to like the name.
These events were followed by what most Fieldsians called an authentic twentieth-century litany-form. The ejected cartridge case of

176

the single fired round could not be found. The 9 mm *Luger*, when examined, was defective. It could not be fired in tests due to a quite inoperative trigger mechanism. Yet otherwise the ex-soldier Jack White had cleaned and correctly maintained his weapon.

A bullet (9 mm) was found in the timber of a wall-support, high above where Fields had been standing. The point was made by several different investigators however that this bullet was 'another' bullet, an 'old' bullet. A bullet with 'different characteristic marks'. The *Luger* had only been fired once, and if the bullet in the timbers somehow *was* the bullet which had entered McCork's head, this single round would have had to traverse an immediate turn of 90 degrees and almost simultaneously another upward angle of at least 20 degrees since McCork was quite a foot taller than White. This same round would then have had to traverse yet another 90 degrees in an upward direction from McCork's head in order to finish embedded in the said timbers.

The trouble with this theory was that not only was Newton's first law denied, but like the head of President Clinton's Aid, Vince Foster, and indeed President Kennedy, McCork's head was also denied an exit wound. True, there was a bullet found in his skull. But it wasn't from White's *Luger*. It was from a vintage *Stirling* machine-pistol the property of McCork's Number One, the trusty Sergeant Dean. Though Dean should never have had such a thing in the first place, he avoided all possible charges and accusations because at the time in question, his weapon was wrapped in greased sacking under the driver's seat of the Tactical Weapons Squad Van; according to his enlightening testimony, the gun had only been fired at 'gypsies' since Dean left the RUC some years previous.

Yet *another* bullet (7.62 mm) was later found on the floor of the Emergency Ward of St. Mary's Hospital, Paddington, to where the still-breathing McCork was rushed by helicopter. And so found later *was* a slight wound in McCork's head in the spot where the bullet *should* have exited. But like this 7.62 mm pseudo-bullet, this half-hearted lesion was a pathetic pseudo-wound, a half-thought from nowhere which appeared off-cue, slightly out of puff, and late for even the second act.

At the end of another similar Entertainment Meet at Wembley Arena, two nights later, an attendant child of nature was distributing pamphlets, and one of these finished up in Marshall's office. The blotched offset, complete with mispellings, pointed out that White's *Luger* was pointing towards Fields; it also pointed out that no investigator was intrepid enough to make the point that in firing at Fields, White, as apseudo-Fields, was almost firing at himself. Marshall breathed hard. The mad folk certainly were intriguing. He was glad his own daughter's eccentricities had been limited to listening to *Emmerdale*. The half-torn pamphlet (complete with dusty impression of trainer-shoe sole), added that since the round didn't want to damage its first-cause, it simply jumped out of the way. Whilst Marshall roared at this, his laughter rapidly diminished when he read the last paragraph. This stated that since they were all boiling-up beliefs in the Albert Hall, and indeed plenty of other places in Entertainment State, neither actions, nor events nor bullets indeed, quite knew what to do, where to go, or even how to form.

Marshall reached for his tobacco-tin.

Perhaps this was what Fields had not been telling them.

VI

The Mysterious Mr. Mellow

After the extraordinary events at the Albert Hall, there were those within *Entertainment Enterprises* who were beginning to agree privately that Fields had indeed created what the man himself called an Attractor Region. This he defined as an area of *sympathies* rather than objective forces. Certainly, in the experience of most at Bayswater Meadows, most actions and events within the centre of what Fields called the 'intention field' of Entertainment State appeared to move into a super-efficient performance spectrum. Telephones always worked well, mail arrived promptly, and schemes of difficult and controversial ideas seemed anxious to be realised, and most ready to demolish any opposition with explosive force. Benson and Barsby had quickly found, often to their surprise, that traditional human difficulties of communication, personality clashes, jealousies, rivalries, all melted away within a scheme which united both mind and mechanism to one Entertainment end. As Fields explained to the many famous visitors to his room looking out over Hyde Park (where he still secretly demolished boxes of banned *Brandysnap Cream Horns* on occasion), these most positive effects were due to many things were looking for loopholes, gasping for escape, all anxious for rebirth into the cycles of the next life-extending game.

Such was the pace of events that Princess Diana, like Princess Grace before her, placed centrally in what Fields called the 'magical transfer region' between Royalty and Film Stars, had graciously accepted the title of *Entertainment Defensor.* She had become a good friend of Fields, though the *Evening Standard* said that rumours were not nigh. Such powerful influences were telling. Entertainment Sermons were now beginning to be written exactly according to Fields' theory that the disembodied spirits of Great Stars of the Past were still part-present in the world, and could therefore interact with the human and animal worlds in the manner of the Greek deities, one of whom (said a scurrilous magazine) Princess Diana thought she was.

The aristocracy and the nobility took to Fields immediately; the middle-classes, who had some difficulty with the mystical bits, took a while longer. Fields' comment on this to Barsby was that they mistrusted anything which did not have a meritocratic price-tag on it. To help everyone along, as President of *Entertainment Enterprises*, Fields would write syndicated articles for the serious dailies in which he described Entertainment Time as being:

"...much more complex than the relatively linear continuum in which Pre-Entertainment industrial events existed. Consequently, within Entertainment State, as in ancient Egypt and Greece, death itself could become something quite different again, a spiritual progress indeed, through to many other states of being."

That this appealed to the upper-crust was not surprising. It rediscovered their role as mystic leaders, linked them again to forgotten mysteries of those hierarchies which constitute the roots of national destiny. Led by the Princess, they were not at bay any more; conversely, Intellect, that great enemy of both the class-system, and Entertainment both, was now on a slippery slope. A popeyed Barsby and scowling Benson frequently heard from Fields that for the first time since the fall of Empire, the titled classes now had once more a world-view. He also added that there was also a prospect of a new kind of colonisation which would yield far more than even tea, diamonds, gold, and numberless cheap servants.

Benson in particular knew that this kind of class-credibility was given tremendous muscle by breathless electronic advances. Already he had heard the faintest of whispers from the labs of possible Entertainment Wars; of old-fashioned 'wasteful' physical explosions being replaced by warring information-fields, self-constructing virus-bombs, intelligent nano-machine locusts, cytoskeltons, and microtubules. Many of these still-in-the-lab ideas he knew had been originally intended for military or scientific purposes, but were all capable of being put to good Entertainment use. Moreover, as such, they could yield tremendous profits, which was something science and the military rarely offered.

In Benson's words to Barsby (who seemed to have put on more years than even Benson in the past few months), from Greenland to Antarctica, all people wanted was an alternative to conventional violent death in the form of limitless Entertainment channels. As Barsby, terrified by almost treacherous views, tried make an excuse and leave, Benson pursued him up and down the corridors of Bayswater Meadows. Barsby wanted to stop his ears as he heard Benson saying that all the world wanted was sports, arts, pornography, music, and as many of what he called 'the new American cretin-films' as could be stuffed in those ice-cream cones which he said were rapidly replacing minds.

As far as Benson himself could see, much more than Gump-films were on their way. Due to such techniques as morphing, complete feature films were about to be made from computer-cloned 'samples' of previous classic performances. No one knew what the rules of Entertainment, or

180

indeed many other things else were going to be if Marilyn Monroe and a few hundred great stars of the past like her, continued to make films indefinitely. As for documentaries, well, if a faultless film or video could be made of Churchill dancing with Hitler whilst Stalin played the saxophone, it was not a lot of good trusting documentaries any more. Where there was no moving image at all (such as in the case of Jesus Christ, or Karl Marx), actors could integrate with the morphing, and therefore all reference points to what was previously termed 'reality' would be gone; Princess Diana could have an affair with Julius Caesar (complete with mobile-phone taps, nicknames, and denials) and Harold Wilson could marry Lucretia Borgia (complete with sub-texts, strange resignations, and similar denials). Fields pointed out to Benson that given the continued advance of such technology, and its spread through digitised world-webs, individuals would eventually make their own Diana-Monroe-Stalin-Caesar films, giving the inevitable under-the-counter business a tremendous new area of operation. Given also the continued development of virtual-reality systems, morphed films could be created by scripts written by countless individuals. Benson had even heard whispers from the laboratories of *holographic* morphing, coupled with Artificial Intelligence systems. Stalin could be seen in three-dimensions even *in his youth*. Where that would lead, no-one knew. Already the first few minutes of video footage had been transferred to a holographic plate. This promised the power to have John Wayne and Joan Crawford (at any age) walk as almost-living flesh into a room and perform an *interactive* script. Such things were even beyond the imagination of 'Entertainment-Junkies' (as *Horse and Hound* called them), or even 'Fieldsian TECs', meaning 'Total Entertainment Converts' (as *Country Life* called them).

If Fields now had mass support for such ideas, many were still critical in that they saw such a proliferation of what they called Entertainment dolls as a new kind of Orwellian nightmare; but Fields saw all these things as something wholly positive. The man himself talked of image-spirit (meaning 'Entertainment Presence' in Fields' terms) as being no longer remote, inaccessible. The (Fields' term) 'Entertainment Dimensions' of the past could now be permanently preserved, entered into, and were spiritually alive in every sense. In one of his frequent *Daily Telegraph* articles, entitled *Consumer Mysticism - the Entry to Inspiration,* he wrote:

"Furthermore, these Entertainment Dimensions can be legitimately appealed to as the much more remote and conventional Saints of the past were once appealed to. The force and nature of our new fledgling religion is warm, welcoming, and it contains a growing recognition of the power of imagination and human sexual nature. Suffering and deprivation are absent from all its initiation stages. As in a supermarket,

Entertainment Baptism is cheap, easy, pleasurable, and immediately effective. Let 'Down with Suffering' be one of the earliest and most effective banners of Entertainment State."

Fields often told Benson and Barsby that given the rapid development of AI subsystems, soon there would be no telling where the border was between Entertainment and a previous something which could hardly be remembered. A TEC could live with the Stars as mythological companions forever and a day. The object of Entertainment State was to blend Entertainment and technology into one mystical union in which the *only supreme deity* was the human Imagination. As regards the past, pre-Entertainment experiences were costly, said he, wasteful, and difficult to unify. Then (he always used the past tense) life was one long miserable work-schedule from cradle to grave. These past days were painful, tragic, full of disease, and the failure of human and mechanical components. A world without Stars was lonely, painful, and merciless. There then being no possibilities of what he called consumer-transcendence, in this previous world, the physical body, straining with frustrated desires, could only destroy, rampage, and conquer; it could go nowhere, and therefore it either went berserk, mad, or became suicidal. In its quite impossible predicament, the human body, with its (Fields term) bad design, everlasting economies, narrow nationalities, its painful aging, and its ever-unsatisfied lusts, hungers, and dread of death, was one big Darwinian dead-end. Of late, even science, the great liberator, had turned into a system of implicit political tyranny and oppression.

To those who attacked him by saying that the kind of technology he talked about needed vast economies, Fields replied that technology itself was only needed for the new cultural *launch stage*. When asked exactly what that stage was, he would give one of his famous mandarin smiles and wander off to meditate. But Barsby and Benson always knew he was either in the Science Museum, or taking extensive notes in Whiteleys Store in Queensway. where he would drink his favourite *cappuccino*, and demolish plates of diet-banned chocolate cakes when he thought no-one was looking. But even when found, he still would not tell anyone what the *launch-stage* was.

Even in these early days, there were claims that this new Entertainment Religion could work miracles and cures, that it contained a power which recognised individuals, had a recognisable live voice and face (and even a roaring laughter) which had long disappeared from almost all of the official religions of the world. An Elvis portrait in Graceland, Tennessee, was reported to give miraculous cures for muscular complaints. Even cancer cures were already being reported at the gravesides of Jimmy Hendrix, John Lennon, and even President Kennedy, all three now recognised as Entertainment Saints.

Fields wrote a long article in *Rolling Stone Magazine* in which he said that Entertainment Thinking caused such a tremendous and willing suspension of disbelief which so astonished any cancer monster within that it fled for its life; it ran to more predictable horizons and events which could be nibbled away and digested much more easily than the anarchic contrasts in Entertainment State. Cancers, according to Fields, only really thrived in the conformity and predictability of a dying industrial time. Drama, joy, change of pace, and above all the 'maintained astonishments' of a constantly revived sense of wonder seemed to place cancers under such burdens they ran out of town never to come back. In the ideal Entertainment State, all such astonishments would be free of charge. This, said he, perhaps worried the cancers even more than the astonishments.

There were other effects of mass Entertainment thinking which even Fields found much more difficult to account for. It seemed almost-complete sets of possible worlds were beginning to assemble themselves from the extraordinary box of which he had taken off the lid. Pop-up characters straight out of nowhere were appearing from that area where Fields claimed 'the implicit shifts down through the octave of appearances to become the explicit'. He himself had come across such things before, outside an Entertainment context. He had last seen such traceless creatures at the Paris conference, some months ago, when Marshall had laughed at his idea of BUACs, meaning Bits of Unadulterated Advertisement Concentrate.

Like some fundamental particles, many Entertainment Prophets disappeared almost immediately after they entered the focus of the world, as if they had only been screen-displayed from some memory-store in the first place One such was Professor Cantillon, who looked as if he didn't have a blood-vessel in his entire body. He could not be found again by anyone after he gave one lecture at the Oxford Union on what he called 'Entertainment Semantics'. Others lasted a little longer, like the seven-foot Dr. Anne Clark, who preached something called 'Consumer Transubstantiation as Metaphor'.

A Mr. Mellow appeared, though no-one knew where he had come from, still less where he disappeared to after three weeks of preaching The New Entertainment Gospel on American TV. After watching the videos of Mr. Mellow, he became one of Fields' favourite 'instant' stars. The meek Mr. Mellow was good value while he lasted, and he didn't use the word 'folks' once:

"The guides to the New Journey of Spirit within Entertainment State are to be the great Stars themselves. The gap between the immortal and the mortal, long ago banished to theological absurdity by Christianity, is now steadily being rebridged to create an area of half-realisations, an area of pure cheek wagging its finger at tyrannical Absolutes of Life and Death, Truth and Fiction, buying and not-buying. Let there be a one minute's silence for Janis Joplin; let there be a prayer to the gods of Rock n' Roll for Elvis Presley; let us have ritual thanksgiving days in the Entertainment State Calendar for Douglas Fairbanks, Marlene Dietrich, and Charlie Chaplin."

Ever since he had heard Dana Chong's Japanese translation of quotes from *StarPower*, Fields had been fascinated to hear these extensions of his own mind. As he watched and listened to Mr. Mellow, he saw that his ideas had grown like resonant structures of verbal crystallisation, spiralling out from his own head like molecular or protein structures:

"These are the First Days, not those terrifying Last Days of the old religions. The first Entertainment Churches have now been built, and have been consecrated by playing copies of a recently discovered ancient wax cylinder recording of Buddy Bolden, the first recorded jazz trumpet-player. His horn, it is claimed, could be heard for five pre-electronic-village miles down-river on a clear summer night in New Orleans. At that time, the sound was said to rival that of massive fairground steam *Calliope* organs and the sirens of distant Mississippi paddle-boats. Let us now make this elemental trumpet the very ram's horn blast of Entertainment State!"

As Fields told those closest to him, Mr. Mellow, Dr. Anne Clark, and Professor Cantillon, were, in his opinion, almost two-dimensional strips of advertisement-substance; they entered the very interstices of the intention-field, where they left but their shadows, as in the intense flash-stage of the Hiroshima bomb. In late July, there appeared a second crop of BUACs. Much more solid, were this lot, as if there was a self-activating implicit learning-process which had almost got it right, as with Joyce and Ben.

This perfect soap-opera British mother and son, presumably arrived on the scene from the same nowhere as Mr. Mellow. They preached that Fields had liberated theology as the salesman of Western capitalism had liberated supply lines. In the Old Town Hall, Chelsea, 60-year-old Joyce, in full Barbara Cartland splendour, with her rhinestone-collared terrier Sparkie in her lap, spoke to the massed ranks of the equally extraordinary in strident northern tones:

"You can win. You can have what you wanted. Previous religions

184

were tyrannical, humourless, terribly mean with supplies, and as bad Acts, they couldn't even make the back room of the *Cock and Bottle* just before throwing-out time on New Years Eve."

Young Ben would chime in, wearing a white bolero jacket, black flared trousers, and Cuban heels:

"With these traditional Performance-cults, you always went to bed hungry, sick, fearing the morn, that is if you had time to feel the luxury of fear at all before your head came off. With Entertainment State you can pay on the never-never. Eventually, you might not even have to pay at all, which is the most revolutionary religion anyone on the Earth has ever heard of."

Watching this priceless pair then move into their song and dance act, Fields was delighted. Once more, he saw his equations had been correct. What super fun. Here again was his holographic DIY pantomime kit. The reality-game could be played like a yo-yo. After all, he reasoned, there was nothing odd about BUACs; they only represented the different levels of unreality in everyone; there had to be such, otherwise people would instantly crack, like tall buildings constructed without any allowance for elastic movement.

Like winged ants along a summer pavement, scores of other Entertainment Prophets faded away throughout the world, some after a period of mental confusion, as if they were only partially-created in the first place. With the looks almost of *Thunderbirds* characters, or types illustrating slightly old-fashioned bargain catalogues and packets, such as the 'Bisto Twins', BUACs looked towards the end as if they were very happy to disappear forever and go back to being faces on sauce bottles, cartoons on cans of beans, and crayon and charcoal faces on fashion advertisements. To Fields, they appeared to become some scrap on a workshop floor, some fast-ideo-food reject of an accelerated natural selection of trash-thoughts.

Like those Fields called 'almost-real' humans, such as Oral Roberts and Tammy Baker of American gospel renown, these first Entertainment preachers and prophets had their equivalents in China, France, Germany, and Hong-Kong. Like most group-clones, such as feminists, nudists and communists, they all had a similar tone of voice, and a remarkably similar ritual intonation. Many looked like white-collar suburbanites of a decade past, and Fields noted that a faint 50's aura clung to them, as if a process hadn't got the present era quite in focus. After only a few weeks, many of this first crop were very difficult to find. Journalists were just as baffled as detectives who struggled to catch the scores of phony social-workers who had tried to collect young children from suspicious parents some years previous. As soon as some hidden project was secured, these BUACs all tended to disappear, as if sensing dawn and the crowing of some extraordinary cock. All BUACs had, in the language of the new physics, High Strangeness. Addresses and telephone numbers of BUACs were more often than not, complete dead ends.

Using the massive resources available at Bayswater Meadows, Both Barsby and Benson tried to arrange a meeting between Fields and Mr. Mellow several times, but they found it was like trying to photograph some legendary animal. Mr. Mellow's being was a spread of molecular thinness, so worn in places that parts of him appeared to be of no substance at all. All that could be found was a grainy photograph, a few rumours, a couple of newspaper articles, a few minutes of shaky video-tape, some badly-printed pamphlets from meetings, and a recent slim volume entitled *Entertainment Prophecies*. But shaking hands with the meat-and-potatoes was difficult. Mr. Mellow moved so fast that like H.G. Well's invisible man, his progress left only a smoke-trail of anecdote, innuendo, dead lines, and empty rooms.

Delighted with his lighter body, Fields could tie his shoelaces for the first time since his childhood, and could almost touch his toes. Using this new found social mobility, one early summer evening of bright moon and clear stars saw him track down Mr. Mellow to a hired hall in Brixton which was packed with Entertainment State enthusiasts. He noted that Mr. Mellow was well-schooled in Entertainment Theory as the slight beige-complexioned corn-haired figure spoke, moving more like a marionette than a man:

"In Entertainment State, individuals were no longer alone, cut off in mechanical singularity. Their being stretched through many areas and dimensions, and they were still developing at many levels, rates, and directions, this was because they belonged to a far less tyrannical Time than any industrial or Judaeo-Christian continuum. The good Dr. Fields' prophecy was that this new form of Entertainment Time was a developing New Time which could turn and wonder at its very self. This emerging Entertainment Eternity had a face, and in the gradual re-orientation of mass belief that was now beginning to take place, the static worlds of both Christianity and of mechanical causation were slowly but surely being unshackled from determinism, and the world was being recast, made fluid once more, becoming a magic mirror brimful of all kinds of transcendental possibilities. Entertainment State has ripped latter-day democratic masks from the face of Performance to rediscover Performance as Primal Joke, Mystic Vision, and Occult Healer. Let us remember Dr. Fields' immortal words in StarPower: 'Only when the universe becomes fantastic, does it become merciful...'"

Walking slowly back to Tower House in the hot evening, Fields decided not to call at Mr. Mellow's address in Hampstead. Like the Surrey Puma, he thought Mr. Mellow would probably not like company. Not that it mattered. He now knew that the appearance of these BUACs meant that the mimicry had been kick-started, and the Entertainment intention was now beginning to run itself.

He had often thought of trying to interest some of his colleagues in this curious phenomenon. But apart from some momentary interest from Benson and Barsby, the dour and practical minds of *Entertainment Enterprises* had taken their fill of his theories. Enough for one Generation, said some. Enough for ten Generations, said others. Fields knew he was really alone with the BUAC idea. But then everyone had a personal secret college. As small child, he had once remarked to his psychiatrist mother that he found the 'factual' programmes on TV more utterly fantastic than the fictional programmes. His child-thoughts came out in breathless telegraphese, as if they were too early, too soon:

"Look. Mother: masquerades!"

Since they were watching a programme about space-science and nuclear physics at the time, this did not go down well in a family with very serious intellectual interests. Though his father almost laughed, his psychiatrist mother did not. It was his first chilling experience of what he was later to call the minefields of perception. The hills ahead were occupied. There was something called High Seriousness, and it appeared to be the last inviolable frontier. Once that was cracked, apparently all would be lost. Hence he knew from his earliest days that as far as things called BUACs and indeed all ideas like that were concerned, he was going to have to fight his way through. He remembered thinking long ago that perhaps all cultural resistance and hence all revolutions began with such back-bedroom thoughts as his: a curious light in the sky; a shape in a cornfield; a vanished Mr. Mellow; a second Oswald; an Entertainment Bomb.

But young underground fighters keep quiet. They don't tell. Because they knew that if they did, both family and tribe would not hesitate to nail them up. And that, he thought, *that* was perhaps the greatest conspiracy of all.

With such thoughts, on the morning of the last hot weekend of June, he made his way to his favourite *McDonald's* in Whiteleys Store, for his last illicit One Pounder Breakfast in London for some time. He was in mid-bite, and half-way through a newly-launched *Telegraph* colour-magazine which was a brilliant Entertainment essay in selling the most crass English dullness, when his mobile screeched.

187

It was the *Entertainment Defensor*.

Carefully dabbing his lips, and wiping his shoes on the back of his calves, he left the store, and casually strolled through the park to Kensington Palace to have a *bon voyage* lunch with Her Majesty.

He found the Princess excited about an invitation to address a prestigious literary society. Fields, happy with the news that even the country's top intellectuals had turned to Entertainment, amused the *Defensor* by telling her that even Oxford University's latest super-computer had now joined the game. The 'characteristics' of the Princess had been fed into it, and also the findings from a country-wide questionnaire about who would be her perfect lover. Though it used the latest Artificial Intelligence techniques, the perplexed new-technology couldn't decide between two 'ideal' choices: Max Bygraves, and he of the underpants, Michael Winner. Amidst gales of the *Defensor's* laughter, only broken by unprintable remarks, Fields added that should anything come of this idea, then the Succession would be in good advertising hands.

In a very good mood after fond farewells, Fields took a cab back to Bayswater Meadows and prepared to leave for Northern Ireland the very next day.

VII

Entertainment Goes Up-River

The day after Fields left with the entire staff of Bayswater Meadows, Marshall was relieved to know that despite the messy Jack White business, and the catastrophic attempt to trap and destroy the Apache in Belfast, the Directrix was nevertheless pleased. It was now the first days of July, and in Northern Ireland, *Entertainment Enterprises* was having great success, and had prepared the ground for Fields' arrival. As the only protesting newspaper in Ulster had said, Entertainment had 'come near to the objective of all political and religious and scientific systems: the annihilation of all alternative resistance.' Which, said Her Upstairs, was not a bad beginning at all. As Report No 2 described, despite this attempt at irony from a minor local newspaper, most folk in Northern Ireland thought something glorious had happened. According to reports, Belfast and a wide swathe of the surrounding countryside was becoming one huge interlinked stage-set and concert platform. Come night, and the city was beginning to glow and sound until dawn with thousands of watts of concert-music and countless performance troupes. Balloons and airships blasting sound and song surged and hovered over newly-constructed drive-in cinemas with hundred-foot screens; legions of one-wheel white-faces flooded shopping precincts, parks, and swimming pools.

But above all it was the pantheon of Famous Faces which was the most spectacular. They were often seen shopping, carrying their children, with not a single stretch-limousine in sight. But still citizens felt awed by the sheer psychic dimension of these faces, young and old, fat and thin. It was extraordinary to see a fairy tale riding a bike, or a piece of pure Western World mythology emptying a wheel barrow full of wet concrete into a trench. The Faces moreover were now scrubbed and shining, muscles female and male browned in the endless summer sun. The great Stars had always had power. Now they had a focus for the millennium. The EuroDump was Israel, 1948. Dig for Victory!

And within the promised land, the Star's position was unassailable. Exhibiting great commitment and sincerity, they visited orphanages, hospitals and old peoples' homes, and poured money into charities and organisations for Senior Citizens. Most were convinced that the Stars did a damn sight more than official 'serious' organisations had done in many lifetimes.

There was also another element in the general air of exhilaration. For generations it had been only Socialism which posed as the system which got things done, but now Socialism had gone into the joke-museums with Cold Fusion and the Sinclair C5. Some said it had been replaced by Field's Entertainment Dialectic, which some said was as daft as a brush, but at least it wasn't as daft as the Class Dialectic, others said.

Few cultures, never mind cities, had any experience of defence against this kind of invasion. There was no precedent to creating an antidote to an Arts, Media, and Entertainment explosion. The forces and demands and pressures which had been tightening their grip for nearly four months before in these early July days, were beginning to be beyond all terms of reference as regards local civic understanding and legal requirements. These fractured scales of seeing became effective degrees of invisibility as far as live processes were concerned. They broke the dam wall of what was possible through which flooded the Impossible. This in turn bred the Quite Impossible.

Things were done which were mortally forbidden within human bureaucratic systems. Rushed through on the nod were land contracts, and complex loan and investment schemes. Broadcasting and television licensing were freely granted, and frequencies were allotted with unheard-of speed. Passports and Citizenship requirements were all practically demolished, as were most Civic Planning Requirements. The Klondike rush of '48 and even the 18th century South Sea Bubble were dug out by the Press and Media as models to try and build a picture of what was happening.

There was rejoicing in the land. The voice of the utterly boring drama of conflicts of Protestants versus Catholics, in which window-cleaners gunned down garage-owners, and road-sweepers blew up fish-and-chip shop proprietors, was for once silent, buried and choked almost to death under a slurry of powerfully engineered Glitz. All sides stood hypnotised by a blinding light which dwarfed and ridiculed their previous intensely serious preoccupations, making the issues seem absurd, out-of-date and extremely provincial.

Entertainment Enterprises Report No 2 suggested that it had not been realised there would be so little psychic defence against the Advent of Toy Society. Nobody had a developed vocabulary of defensive responses in this direction. There were defences against nuclear weapons, racists, fascists, Japanese high-tech companies, defences against the rat, the bug, and even the infestation of the common flea, but there was no defence against the mass plague of actors, film stars, singers, dancers, theatre and opera companies, film crews, dance troupes, rock concerts and a thousand and one 'alternative' clowns, who, in the words of one still doubtful journalist, now pratfell throughout the city 'like a mobile acne'.

Surveying the opposition, Report No 2 concluded that even the most skilled Doubters had difficulty getting any kind of critical grip, if only because liberal thinkers had been rapidly won over. According to their view, Entertainment State was the only really powerful movement emerging which was not recommending the physical destruction of a set of 'evildoers' on the grounds of race, religion, class, or the incorrect political size of the left ear.

Marshall was pleased that all this had been judged by the conga-line of Them Upstairs as being a Very Good Thing Indeed. Entertainment Culture thus gave the appearance of being a pacifist movement, in essence. The end product was that the Belfast latheworker, or shop-girl saw themselves as part of the Entertainment process. As in a mediaeval court (which some critics described Entertainment State as being), ordinary folk were part of the chain of being leading to the Great Lovers, Cowboys, and Space-heroes, and even Royalty in the form of the ever-visiting Princess Diana; for this was her country, some said, in more senses than one.

The non-glamorous simplicities of Chapel and Mass couldn't cope with this effusion of the 'compliment culture' as one famous American commentator put it. As Fields said himself to various colleagues, here was a New Theology hardly concerned with stopping laughter and the covering up of cock and cat's face. Theology (not exactly the Century's most popular and vital subject), had changed. The debates flowed over in the gymnasium, school halls, and pub rooms: what were the politics of Entertainment Technology? In what image was the technology made? What did this Fields mean by *cosmic advertising?* What was meant by role, image, performance? A leading Ulster journalist wrote Politicisation had become Entertainmentisation, suitably abbreviated to P=ET, the latter two letters being by coincidence, some noted, the initials of Fields' great love.

Amidst all this, it appeared that Christ had taken a holiday for once, for which most apparently were secretly and eternally thankful. As the whole scale of mass-experience gradually changed, poor Jesus, with his little peasant homilies, was as out-of-date as the Royal Variety Show, the Warsaw Pact, or a Channel Four AIDS documentary. As *Macho Magazine* put it, the 'Great Fieldsian Leviathan was starting its first unstoppable advance'. Everything, literally *everything*, was beginning to be seen as some aspect of Entertainment. Film-stars and stage-actors and (yes!) comedians were being asked for *medical* advice; dancers and

191

singers were asked for help on personal and family affairs. The Stars were the New Astrologer-Priests giving meaning, coherence to lives, and above all providing a solution to the problems of personality and existence which previously were the province of what Fields called the Men in Nightshirts And Funny Hats.

Popular opinion was that here in Entertainment was a fancy-dress mob who did at least a bit of sweating on stage and screen for a living, as distinct from the usual mob, whose dresses were just as fancy, but who did nothing at all for anybody, least of all sweat. Gradually the mechanics of the old reference structure controlled by what Fields called 'the Not Very Glamorous Person With the Well Modulated Voice and University Degree being the Great Scientific Controller of Experience' was being replaced, to the relief, it seemed, of all concerned.

It looked as if it was far too late for any significant opposition to form. Pay packets were full, and as Fields had forecast, that was the one situation any opposition would have great difficulty in handling. As far as *Entertainment Enterprises* were concerned, the beaches had been rapidly secured, and Entertainment forces were moving fast into the interior, keeping the enemy quite off-balance, blinding reconnaissance, and causing rumour and panic in rear areas. Poor humanity knew little about the diseases of happiness. People were used to living with heavily reinforced definitions, a war, civilian strife, starvation, not a release into a wilderness of rapidly changing performance-masks, the intellectual and artistic equivalent of fast food. Everything was an *act?* All actions were *roles?* Was a nurse in a terminal cancer-ward *acting?* This caused some confusion in minds which assumed there were things called Fictions on one hand and things called Facts on the other. The idea of there being an infinity of choices of identity led at first to much existential bewilderment. It was thought by many that through all the layers of experience, some kind of objective consensus could be reached, at least a bit of a shelf to reach, to catch a half-breath on within an almost-life.

But the diseases of affluence and freedom were relatively uncharted areas. At first, the mechanism was just too overwhelming, too powerful, too concentrated. There were no controls at all in this first Entertainment State, this ur-society was on one-hundred percent high dosage from the start. Relentless, disturbing, all-demanding, there never was any question of reaching for the OFF switch. Simplistic conventional politics had yet to discover that in any electronic culture, there was never any OFF switch in the first place. The last liberal dream of there being an escape channel had been shattered long ago. Trying switching off Michael Jackson: it was impossible. But in any case, as Fields pointed out, the very idea of *switching off* itself was a 'old directional analogue, an illusion of

192

democratic and objective vectors.' All compasses of choice were meaningless in a universe of pure Entertainment Texture.

A very thin crust of resistance was beginning to form on the far edges of the whirlpool. Enlightenment? Possession, more like, said some. This was the nature of the almost imperceptible murmur just beginning on both sides of the Christian divide. The more perceptive defence-lines were beginning to come out of shock, alarmed by such statements in *StarPower*, as 'the limits of the Impossible can be set precisely where we want them to be set'. That, some said across the religious divide, that would never do, that would never do at all.

Fields, as the uncrowned Head of Entertainment State, travelling to Belfast aboard a luxury yacht loaned by a Saudi Billionaire. Marshall, a little envious, put Report Number 2 into his briefcase, once more brushed down his scuffed grey suit, assembled his *Seelex* staff, and set off on what the RAF call a bucket-seat flight to Northern Ireland.

At 40,000 feet, in an RAF *VC 10* weaving a white trail against the evening sky, Marshall was feeling an uncontrollable excitement. He simply could not maintain his famed concentration. He supposed that Fields' theories were beginning to nudge an entire previous world aside, and his expanded being was beginning to spread up-river like an uncontrolled virus. He had a feeling that he was following an entire circus as it prepared to begin a long journey hundreds of miles up-river. It was to be a journey along a great river of tribal games. Already an older part of him felt fowl, feather and fish were trotting, flapping, diving, nosing under rocks and mud, running and leaping, urgent to get away, get upstream, before being taken over by a spreading algae of hallucination and hypnosis of a flying Dumbo terror. The entire bush was alive with running claw, tooth, paw, and tail.

He sensed hidden eyes watching the ship of *Entertainment Enterprises* as she moved up-river with Fields as Captain. Sooner or later, deep inland, the Indians would be gathering in the higher crags above the falls and rapids. And you couldn't see them. You couldn't hear them. As the Entertainment Big Show organised, so did the jungle thicken either side of the gaudy flotilla. Marshall remembered the red-tabbed signal on his desk some months ago. He supposed the Apache on the distant high uplands had already caught the first notes of a propeller which was now become a great bass throb below the mountains. Sooner or later the brains of animals and Apaches alike would combine far upstream to generate an antidote to Entertainment.

His mind had never ever worked like this before. He had caught a piece of the Fields virus as easily as catching a cold. He looked down through gaps in the cloud cover and imagined a sudden comb of wash along a primaeval river bank, disturbing the sleeping atrophied detritus of a million years. Small creatures hopped, looked, squinted, cocked their heads, and fled into the darkness of the interior as the bow wave approached, pushing aside slick and sheen, branch and leaf and rotten trunk. He sensed that up-water, eyes behind scattered rock and scrub would narrow, focus, measure range, speed, and course. Wraiths of signal-smoke would flutter up from tiny crevice-fires, and horses would stamp the ground impatiently, and know.

The strangers were coming.

Chapter 3

1

Benson's Last Breakfast

Despite *Eat-I* having become the envy of many computer technologists throughout the world, Benson was an unhappy stranger in a strange city. He was made even more miserable one fine morning in the first week of August, when upon arriving for work, Barsby gave him a rolling-eye version of the arrival of a steaming John Carlton, of all people; wonder of wonders, The Committee had just appointed Carlton as Director of *Eat-I* over Benson's head, and the man himself was arriving within the hour for a tour of inspection.

Failing to join in the universal fun which this sudden ominous visit had seemed to arouse, Benson saw immediately that things were very serious indeed. Whenever there was a real panic, all Page Three Calendars disappeared faster than a Denial followed a Leak. With slowly-clearing brain, he saw in the middle distance of the extensive open-plan area, those tight, unsmiling features of his staff that were used to give that universal professional illusion of order and control. Not quite up to these kind of masks at this early hour, he was rapidly brought into full consciousness by seeing John Carlton appear, department-hopping like a great bullfrog in season, poking all and everything with his tribal wand of a forefinger. This notoriously compromised individual appeared to be quite fraught, as if he now knew that he had not long to reign before being cast down to the higher regions of the BBC. Coming towards Benson and waving his hands in the air like a sun-priest of Baal, Carlton streamed a terrified entourage, hotfoot from Mary Poppins land; these harpies became nodding and eddying swirls of mud, bracken, and water behind his webbed feet.

The notorious Junior Minister had changed over the past few months. Once the quiet sinister smoothie, he was now a roaring lion, with ideas about Efficiency. Trying to address Benson as the Duke of Wellington might have spoken to Sam Weller, he told him that *Eat-I* had to be more Efficient; such a thing could, according to Carlton, be obtained through a little application and diligence, just as the Staff Manager of *Eat-I* ordered teacups, scrubbing brushes, and photocopying paper.

195

A furious Benson, restrained by training, self-discipline, and the Official Secrets Act from commenting on Carlton's tricky deals, was asked to assemble his Executive Team. Before them, the junior-league Carlton then had the nerve to threaten tea breaks, lunch breaks, and even the loo break if things were not made more Efficient. To everyone's horror, he addressed the Executive Team as if they were some woebegone unskilled part-timers of one of his near-bankrupt industrial enterprises. Not that Carlton saw it that way. In his new role as the New Man from High Upstairs, he spoke like Satan before leather-winged hordes of mutants upon a burning lake of sulphur.

After Carlton had abruptly about-turned, and streaked back hot-hoofed, to his hotel opposite the *Eat-I* building, the ever-thoughtful Barsby brought Benson a cup of tea. The tea was welcome, but what Barsby had in his other hand was not. This was a sheaf of what cynics in *Eat-I* called Monkey-In-The-Space-ship Tasks. These consisted of 300 pages of all kinds of paper buttons to push, most of which to Benson, had Fields' face on them. The prophets of doom had been wrong, he thought. Not a rubber truncheon in sight, just the tinsel cosh. And the last monkey-button was death. Benson, depressed, now sipped his tea as if it was a merciful thimble of oblivious poison through the rubber feed-tube before the space-capsule finally spun out of orbit to infinity.

The memory of Carlton had created a terrible ache in Benson's head as he looked at the work he had to prepare for his mighty computers. Multidimensional analysis of the work of influential actors, film-stars, singers, dancers, filmmakers; their careers, politics, family connections, and business interests; then Entertainment-income investments-analysis; then detection of the 'vulnerable' parts of the business profiles of worldwide film, video companies and TV conglomerates. There followed integrated analysis of cable, satellite, and landline potentials in terms of developing new technologies and their investment, sales, and organisational patterns; then something called a media content and policy-index to be compiled, together with new programmes for yet further investment analysis and developmental control of Entertainment State. Other schemes were to be developed by *Eat-I* for image-analysis of content, style, and emotive structures. Throughout all this, in addition to John Carlton's voice in his head he now heard Fields' mighty bass: '...using evermore powerful computers, pop & media-stuff could be culture-dish developed, cloned, and designed into disposable protein for the megalopolis society, whose literacy and mental grasp would be near catastrophic levels by the turn of the century.'

He looked up, and his eyes met the slogan on Barsby's baseball cap, perched on top of a console: *'You'll come to love interviewing yourself'*. He looked down. He was a slave. Just kept alive in the pyramid

196

twilight by electric flickers on the impenetrable walls of the tomb.

He supposed he should have been pleased. He had been asked to help design the Entertainment Bomb MK 1, to take his computers into a New Age, and not waste time playing old-fashioned Intelligence games. On paper, the job he had been given should have the most exciting intellectual challenge of his life. But Barsby's baseball cap laughed at him again, a voice formed in his head, and Robert Oppenheimer's beautifully tragic features appeared from nowhere, to say: *'cooperate in this and you are damned'.*

In a sudden acute attack of nostalgia for his beloved Westbourne Grove, Benson almost ran out from the smoked-glass front of the *Eat-I* offices, to try to find what locals had told him was the last bacon-butty grotto in Belfast. As he walked, the early-morning city looked like an archaeological site in Hell. Crews sweated by roaring drills and generators to channel pavements and roads for various competing experimental TV systems. Roofs sprouted countless odd-shaped aerials, and every second shop was being refurbished as a cinema, a video and record store, or a small *studio,* or *studio-theatre,* 'studio' being a word that he thought, proliferated throughout the city like the myriad *blobs* of science-fiction tales.

Finding the legendary place at last, he perched on one of the cramped and slashed car-seats of *The Atalanta,* squashed between road-sweepers and bus crews. *The Atalanta* was a half-caravan half-tent, parked behind Central Station. The place served what veterans called the last decent Giro breakfast in Belfast, and was also one of the few places which had a reasonable chance of being free of what were popularly termed 'luvvie-clones'. These, like the plagues of old Egypt, were now spreading as if from nowhere; even at this early hour, Benson had passed two identical Dean Martins, one Michael Jackson, a Charlie Chaplin, two Rod Stewarts, numberless Danas and Sineads, and even a blacked-up original from the Shankhill Road who called himself 'The Rapping' Al Jolson'. Most were making their way to the new Entertainment State sponsored courses in schools and colleges, courses entitled 'Film, Personality and Media: A Creative Way of Knowing,' and 'Art Lifestyles: Studies in Performance.' He remembered Orwell saying that *only the proles were free;* at this rate, he thought, they were not going to be free for much longer.

One of what his cynical colleagues called Entertainment Victims now sat by his side and introduced himself by saying, like a Jehovah's witness, that he had recently had a religious conversion. Bored, Benson was about to get up and leave when it became obvious that this was a very different kind of conversion. As if confessing sin, thirty-something Michael told Benson that he had absorbed all the beautifully-written-up schlock-horror ideas of the political paranoid-industry from the 70s to the 90s which advertised catastrophe-consumerism. He had believed that race riots, traffic gridlocks, and mind-drugs in the water-supply would ravage the nation, and there would be one sex by the turn of the century; he had also taken seriously the old left-wing polytech-cartoons about the coming systems-apocalypse: pollution would reduce life-expectancy to 50 years, and electrical power systems would suffer multiple breakdowns. He had also taken in limp-wristed *avant-guarde* films about tanks and SAS killer-squads slaughtering long-haired youths and pink-tinted maidens in the burnt-out centres of British cities. Of late however, said Michael, he had recovered from what he called all these diseases of affluence; he had discovered, through what he called Fieldsian Mechanics, something called *High-Kitsch Transcendence.*

As toast, brown sauce, and good Irish bacon hit Benson's solid British taste-buds. Michael told him that much of the present Entertainment grapevine talk was of a recent find of boxes of old discarded cuttings in a forgotten basement of Pinewood. These shaky scenes of long ago were now offered up as a kind of religious host. Originally smuggled out, and illegally copied, there had grown up a thriving blackmarket of often poorly-copied pastings of *Ghost Train, Genevieve,* and *Love on The Dole.* In these modern equivalents to holy British relics, Famous Faces of the Famous Past could be seen for a few seconds scratching their noses, changing their socks, even having a pee behind a hedge. After a quarter-hour of joyous descriptions of what Michael called New Worship, Benson started to laugh hysterically, and was immediately admonished by Michael.

"Never laugh. You only conceal your despair."

"What despair? I've won."

"Nobody wins. Except the Stars."

"I've already escaped. In my head. None of this crap affects me."

"Only Stars escape."

"Fuck Stars."

"How can you say that? What is the object of your life?"

"To forgive God for repeating his jokes, Michael."

"Would there be anything else?"

"Yes. I want to hear Him say he's sorry."

"For what?"

"For the Doll-folk. All of them. I wish God would stick to things he's good at, that's all."

"Such as, may I ask?"

"Forests, leaves, sunsets. The rest is shit. Especially Stars."

"Have respect, will you? Go home and pray for forgiveness."

"That's no good to me."

"Prayer is no good to you?"

"No."

"Why not?"

"Because I want too much. The good Lord would go bankrupt."

"You will become reconciled to Stars. If not, You'll be sorry before God, the greatest Star of all."

"I'm sorry for him."

"God will laugh."

"Wait until he gets my bill."

"Hasn't he paid enough already?"

"No. He's been living at my expense."

"Aren't you satisfied with his Creation?"

"I've told you: God's good at skies, and seas, but he's not so good at the exhaust system of the human body. It could have been designed by an unsuccessful pig-farmer don't you think?"

"You're not happy?"

"No."

"Why?"

"I want more. Much more."

"You're talking about the God I love."

"Well I wish you both a happy life together."

Seeing him an obviously hopeless case, Michael then dropped Benson to talk to a pair of baffled bus-drivers about George Formby and Jimmy Edwards, both now official candidates for Entertainment beatification.

Leaving *The Atalanta,* and nearly tripping flat on his face on a kerbstone, an utterly lightweight feel of everything possessed Benson. Happiness was difficult to resist. Particularly Entertainment Happiness. This was a feeling of careless pleasure whilst a live creature picked the soul clean as bleached bones, and replaced the pilfering with almost dimensionless forms of goods, which were endlessly reproducing subdivisions of *performance.* This word he saw on every wall-slogan, poster, and piece of graffiti. All the apocalyptic threats and militant boasts of a previous time, all the scabrous religious wall-insults about the Pope, the Rhythm Method and the supposed strange sexual habits of good Catholic Mothers, all these had been gradually replaced by the products and slogans of what Michael had called 'the clown-machine.' Benson was glad that he was not yet converted. But he was severely depressed. He had to admit now that his one hero, *Microsoft's* Bill Gates, had always been much more interested in Entertainment than computer-science. He supposed any future Einsteins would be working for Hollywood, if they were not doing so already.

In the blizzard of fun-intentions around him, Benson could see that the original community was beginning to lose sight of itself. From his work in *Eat-I,* he knew that visitors from the as-yet relatively uncontaminated areas of Northern Ireland brought back alarming reports. Belfast was becoming a city of Entertainment zombies. Just one Barsby idea was the distribution by the 'commercial' department of *Eat-I* to 'deserving' families, of four or five free TV sets, with different new-technology aerial packages, and any amount of associated video-control and Hi-Fi equipment. The sales of a quite expensive single console designed by *EAT-I* to integrate and control all this equipment had been astronomical, bringing in enormous profits for *Entertainment Enterprises.* For front-organisations, such profits were embarrassing, not to say dangerous, but rapidly becoming the rule rather than the exception.

In the Entertainment-struck city, life was beginning to gradually slow down to a work-and-view and view-and-work rhythm. Whilst there was certainly a lot less drinking, by all accounts there was also a lot less screwing. Irishness of all kinds, both sacred and profane, merciful and murderous, mystical and non-mystical, had stopped in its tracks, quite image-swamped. Most family time was spent programming and reprogramming the video-recorders until the dark night of the soul was reached in which mental shifts of reference which had previously taken hundreds of years now probably took five minutes. There were many reports of cultural dysfunction: of people solving the constant absorption problem by watching programmes in fast-frame or stop-run-go sequence, or automatic-edited sequence, or even by using hooked-up multiple screens which shook to pieces eyes, brains, and families alike. The only alternative to this onslaught were the limitless live concerts, plays, films, sports, pageants, and countless rehearsals.

A catch of breath. An middle-aged man passed by Benson dressed as the film character, Rambo. An M16 rifle rested against his blow-up rubber muscles, although out of the barrel poked a white flag, which Benson assumed was still essential in Belfast if he wanted to get wherever he was going in one piece. As this vision joined a Ninja Turtle, for once in a chequered career, Benson felt quite completely out of his depth as key words of what Fields called Image-Time sang in his brain an endless song of Era-advertisements: Chaplin. Atom. Hitler. America. Time was become pure media-substance. He leaned momentarily against a lamppost like a drunk from some old-fashioned theatre sketch of long ago. His head spun. Lenin. Coleridge. Mickey Mouse. And a wall-slogan: *Everything Means Nothing which is Everything and Nothing.* Round went the video-wheel of the clown-machine. A young man passed by dressed as a perfect Val Doonican, even down to proudly carrying a miniature rocking-chair, that vital symbol of Doonicanism.

Sitting on a park-bench, his mind reeling, Benson recalled seeing Fields at a great banquet some nights previous.

Fields had been a perfect Henry VIII, sitting in state at a high table, crowned, shrouded in ermine, and flanked by world-famous Entertainers costumed as Elizabethan courtiers. All were digging into their 300-Portraits-per-head dinners, and raising up a big head of candy-steam for this night's discussions on the new-found fortunes of the yellow brick road. In the foreground, Benson could see dozens of FTTs (Fabulous Top Toys as another phrase had it), and in the cheaper and roped-off beyond, some Fanatic Club parties cashing in their hard-paid-for 50-Portrait Entertainment State dining checks. The Fanatic Clubs were groups of folk who dressed like one particular Star. Benson remembered memorable collections of Terry Wogans and Mel Tormés, and even a complete Robert De Niro choir, of all things. In the far distance of the great banqueting hall, he remembered with alarm that staring right at him were three identical Val Doonicans, complete with miniature rocking-chairs.

He recalled the scene with horror. Though the average mental age of the Top Toys couldn't have reached single figures, here was unlimited money and power of the New Fields Leviathan. But the mechanised warmth of the tainted jollification disturbed him. It smacked of the calculations within a nutrient dish. He knew a fairy story when he came across one, and there were plenty gathered here. To him, a hothouse of stagnant darkness was within the power and display, an unspoken nursery horror of dwarves in the toy-cupboard, an infant threat of strange men at the school gate, and the shuttered house down the road where an old woman sat in the gloom and where children were said to have gone never to return. Benson was overcome by a powerful and hypnotic melancholy, as if some vital protective amulet was being wrenched from his breast by powers and principalities so old, he gasped with historical vertigo. Here was no thrill, inspiration, excitement, nothing but an awesome feeling that here in this chortling grotto his sense of time was slipping, and the time back to home from this chilling mobile waxworks was gradually becoming nothing to do with distance divided by velocity.

He had thought all threat was objective, mechanical, and he realised that here he had almost missed the trick. Before his eyes was the very pulsing lifeblood of a process which had captured the high-frontier of metaphor, presumably to contribute to some vast psycho-industrial restructuring, the planned mass-manufacture of some imitation of an imitation. The cloned half-forms in the far distance were being farmed, their memories reprogrammed, and new circuits installed. For one moment, he didn't have the faintest idea of what a human being was any more. He supposed others were being milked of other angles and shapes and memories to contribute to some universal cull of all human resistance to some inconceivable project in the great historical beyond.

Stealing another glimpse at the technicolour throng, he imagined at key points in the formation of cultural time, people found it especially difficult to understand what was happening to them. Now he began to realise that for the first time, like a semi-intelligent monster of science-fiction, *Eat-I* was helping to create incredible bough-plumage, or rather helping it to organise itself, since he felt now merely an arm of a super-organism.

He walked to the shipyards, where he wanted to try and soak his brain in the last of the great analogue things: real working men building great things of steel. But Prince, Elton John, and Michael Jackson still stalked his brain like strutting post-industrial harpies. The effect of just *three* of what a Dublin journalist had called 'human Christmas-decorations' was inimical enough. Never in his life had he found it so difficult to concentrate. The trick was, he supposed, that after the first panic-stricken gulp of the radiating waves of the Entertainment influence, the experience wasn't exactly unpleasant. It was as if there had been a quick death through drowning, only to find that it was possible to breathe through the wave. A convert's intellect in particular was gone with the coach-and four, and he was effectively dead, but entering the Entertainment Pyramid, he began not to care. Nature was nothing if not original. Not the trenches, or gas-chambers, this time, but an infection by legions of jinxed barbie-dolls.

He imagined what the mind of future Total Entertainment Converts would be like. Perhaps they would be authorities on the house-moves of the distant relatives of the first girlfriends of Val Doonican, Harry Tate, Flotsam and Jetsam, and k. d. laing. Benson imagined himself travelling along the endless scenic generations of this game-wave, in a geometric proliferation of life structures which opened from all angles at once. He had read no books on Val Doonican. Like Fields, he had hardly seen any television programmes, nor heard any popular songs. The esoteric computer-circles he moved in were as likely to mention films, videos, or Tina Turner, as fly.

His mobile phone screamed constantly, but he ignored the sounds as if they were signals from a world he had finally decided to escape from. The visions of his youth now lay broken about him. He would have liked to have taken a job in the great sea-workshop he saw before him, start a new life as a welder or a driver, but it was all too late now. He could never be an ordinary bloke again.

Benson despaired. Ideas of knowledge as a definite function of input and output, of patterns of finite time and precise concrete experience, now lay about his mind like broken eggshells. To flee was not an alternative. He had been irradiated. Quantity, as with all radiation, was meaningless. Just a touch would do to push his soul towards a universe of personality-stuff in which the Star was king, and there was no such thing as information, this being replaced by what Fields had already called Entertainment Relativity. In this new world, all Stars were everywhere, transmitting from all spatial points at once. As in a mediæval court, there was really neither *in* nor *out*. While there was breath in the body, it was the breath of the Stars, down to a coat-colour, the shape of a shoe, even the slightest thought. Even if the particular Star hadn't been heard of for generations, the half-life of the personal influence was still within human dimensions of experience. Benson was now almost shuddering at the thought that he would carry this stream of new sales-lines within him until he died.

He remembered Fields again at the banquet, as television cameras swivelled, journalist's recorders hung poised, rosaries were counted, and countless female hearts pounded as Fields performed to the world.

"The Earth was pure Entertainment. Some bad, some good, some indifferent. Illness and murder were jokes gone wrong: nobody laughed. Other than that, there was every kind of half-completed laugh in this nursery for half-monsters of giggle and dream. There were creatures who could hardly breath, yet they had great mouths and lungs; there were animals who had massive brains, but could hardly think; there were some so heavy they gradually collapsed under their own weight; there were countless others with half-forgotten wings, and quarter-legs; there were even animals who were virtually nothing but petulant fractured crayon-thoughts of a lazy nursery afternoon, deserted with the chalks and pencil-boxes when the nurse announced high-tea."

Benson shivered as the morning grew suddenly cold, and he started to make his way back to *Eat-I*. But there was Val Doonican again in his head. A non-cerebral world? There was a piece of good old English flint in Benson which shouted no! Whatever would the mind of the Total Entertainment Convert be like? Perhaps the days (if there were days) would become consumed by a proliferating pond-weed of the imagination which ate time and individual will in a manner which knew no law of conservation. Perhaps such TECs would give up their jobs and go around asking ancient proprietors of long-gone lodging houses, garages, cafes who perhaps blinked several times and thought they had seen something of *any* young embryo Star. The merest piece of her or him would do; either past or present. They would look for forms so thin and vaporous they could hardly be called ghosts; there might be interviews of an early friend who hadn't seen the Star since the Star was eight. Old attics might be ransacked for bills, receipts, signatures; flat cigarette cases and tiepins and false handkerchiefs-in-the-top-blazer-pocket time of a Star's youth. Some might be arrested breaking into old rooms, searching curved drawers of ancient dressing tables, with their folding mirrors, their sets of brushes, box-camera snapshots, and chipped pots full of combs, hairpins, bracelets, and cuff-links and collar studs. Searching for a tiepin time of not-so-long ago, some TECS would ransack Pensioner's Rest Homes for the merest piece of knowledge, shake the faltering memories of hometown ninety-year-old tram-conductors slumped in chairs; they would wrinkle their brows at the endless questioning. Did they see something? Did they see HIM? Or HER, if only just for a moment outside some pink-lit old *Granada* strung with fairy-lights? Could they remember, even sepia in the mind? Or could they remember in washed-out late-60s *Carry On* technicolour, different frequency-standard pastels; was the recall in film-processing tints the colour of mum's birthday-blancmange, the hue of Cliff Richard's early chipmunk-cheeks? Had they seen the Star searching a satchel in a lost moment outside the Grammar School? Did he or she stand there amidst the first discarded leaves of the generation's autumn, as the No. 15 passed, in what some possible eventual last philosopher would trace as the very last hour of British strength and innocence before *le deluge?*

As the *EAT-I* building loomed before him, Benson saw individual TECs as choosing their own particular molecular game; they would only be concerned with cinema preferences, inspiration, sadness and elation of, say, Val and his billion latter-day cloned harpies. The structure of the world would not be boring molecules, atoms, corpuscles, waveforms, or particles, but the achievements, failures, successes and humiliations in a great expanded body of the Val super-family to the end of the universe. Money, property, ambition, relationships, love affairs, marriages, even the details of the mortgage-loan deals of a second cousin, even a journey down the very grain of Val's left sock in 1962, would form a new Old Ley Track to discover some inconceivable Entertainment Grail.

With the *Eat-I* staff bar closed for a week as just one of John Carlton's ways of disciplining bad boys and girls, Benson lingered in the small hours of the succeeding morning in the dimly-lit and totally deserted main office suite, swigging neat whisky by the cracked-cup full, and seeing the shapes and outlines of various apparatus as roads to a personal nowhere. In the half-light, he was a shadow almost indistinguishable from the gloom. His mind was become the shadow-thoughts of Nazca lines. Patterns to nowhere. Logics, programs, the switching simulations he had spent his entire life designing had now quietly slipped into museums. That was all that Fact ever did for you. Put you to rest in your coffin before you were born. He felt like a cavalry general who had just glimpsed his first tank. Not only his life, but his very being was now short-circuited. And there was more. Much more, if he guessed at some of Fields' theories correctly. But he wasn't going to stay around for the small print. The main text was enough.

Barsby's baseball-cap still laughed at him from the top of a console. He tried it on, looked at himself in a reflection, but no, it didn't suit. He could not change. Not if he tried for a lifetime, could he make the jump. He wasn't built for it. It needed a different animal. Even a different species. It was all a sad triumph of a nonsense he had always despised, a plane of rubbish which defied everything he ever thought or stood for. All that was left to him now were the motions of pure pastiche, ceremonies for the dead in a cultural sarcophagus. Trumpets may sound in dreams, but he was no longer on the front line. He had a dread suspicion that Fields was right. Entertainment was going to move through walls, and if it could do that, it was not much use building them any longer.

He caressed the cabinets of the main-frames. Built as animals of the third eye, his chargers had been blinded in battle, were lost and vulnerable before machine guns, armour, wire, and a dimension of tactical thinking whose geometry he could no longer grasp. Increase of electronic consciousness was a monstrous illusion, a circus of cheap sustained flickers around the sorcerer's apprentice which the master magician had produced to see if his pupil would take its appearance as something of value, a sign of true initiation and progress. Magician's laughter was something Benson could not live with. A bunch of damned peasants kicked shit out of the Forces of Fact in Vietnam. The High Frontier. The Forces of Fact. There was nothing more comic in this world than a dated advertisement. Magician's laughter was now everywhere throughout the circuits and the equations, through the semiconductors and the wiring, through the software and the very principles of technological conception themselves.

Was this the prelaunch stage Fields talked about?

Taking a last full cup to the window, the shutdown lights of the city now emphasised a skyline which even at this hour, was alive with the sound and lights of a machine which made his own machines seem childish and amateur. A machine beyond hardware. The first real programmable artificial intelligence. The MK 1 Myth Engine. And all it needed was a little electricity. Here, of course it could still fail. But it would breed before it died. And now, like the world's electromagnetic transmissions, it could never ever be switched off.

He dimmed the room lights and stood by the window. On the steel cabinets of the main-frames danced the lights of ancient fires. *Eat-I* was surrounded by drums. Fieldsian animals were near. To be obsolete was to be almost dead. To be almost dead was to hear the young snigger at a worn phrase, and to see the old give the half-fallen ones that patient, sympathetic look which was an unbearable accusation of failing on a mission, and not having the bottle taking the proper path of *hara-kiri*.

Turning from the window, Benson felt thin, wasted, of no substance. The legions of the bodies of Belief were leaving the outer walls of being. He was almost dead. He turned from the window and looked down at the floor as if looking right into himself. He drained his cup. He must prepare now to travel the Performance Path, that grey-scale octave of being and appearances which led to the darkest chambers of the pyramid. In that timeless gloom where death became pure information, he would reorganise his shattered forces. There would be rumours in valleys and hills that he was still alive, and one day would come back along what he had heard Fields call the Octave of Appearances for the next stage of the assault on infinity.

Before Benson finally took a terrible decision, he remembered his last conversation with Fields.

"My watch has stopped. What time is it, please?"

"The twentieth century."

"I need it a bit more accurate than that, Fields."

"You want to scare yourself to death?"

Benson wondered. Sometimes Fields sounded as if he were made of a host of voices at the bottom of a well, crying out for rescue. But now, both accuracy and the twentieth century had indeed scared Benson to death.

Time to go to the next game.

After patting his life's work like a dog, Benson put down his cup, climbed steel ladders to the twentieth floor of the *EAT-I* building, took a running hundred-yard jump at the fragile netting on the rim of the windblown roof, burst through it, and hurtled into space.

The stuff which contained the mastery of seven ages of technology, as well as his last perfect image of a first pair of shoes, and also the luscious thighs of seventeen-year-old Janet Campion, landed on John Carlton's *Rolls Royce*, which was parked outside the hotel which was just across the road from *EAT-I*.

Benson's body smashing straight through the car-roof caused two

206

porters to drop a large trunk which they were about to put into the boot. This was promptly clouted into the air by a speeding lorry. The trunk burst on hitting the ground, and a high wind sent thousands of photographs of a bondaged John Carlton in frilly knickers, stockings, and suspender belts, all over Belfast. His partners in these pictures were all very young males, and equally male Famous Faces. Within minutes these pictures of the extremely well-known Carlton were providing collector's items for further generations of subversive Irish folklore. Another contributor to this epic tradition was poor Benson, who even in death, had not been able to avoid Entertainment.

As John Carlton's staff, like a bomb-burst of rabbits, searched for the lost items whilst poor Benson's body was still warm, Nora pondered in yet another nameless back-room, where she now heard many sirens howling towards a dead Benson and a hysterical John Carlton. For four days, surrounding concerts had penetrated her head with a bass-boom whose intensity left her skull full of cinders and her kidneys feeling like mangled prunes which had been in washing-up water for a week. Looking out to a laser-flashing horizon, she despaired at this utter waste of time indulged in by the luxury organ inside human skulls. Human beings, thought she, must be the most inefficient and directionless animals in the entire cosmos, more useless than basking worms, often less intelligent than drifting ocean mites.

Boom, boom! She was now convinced that these terrible beats were the incantations of a first stage of ritual death. Out there in the night yet another story was evolving. Entertainment Time was ruining the roads of literacy, shrubs were growing over the old tracks and ways, and many were being left behind, trying with difficulty to focus in old industrial time. She imagined a few stronger spirits would clutch at trees within the torrent for a short while, but she had absorbed her Fields Dialectic well. Resistance within the expanded body of a Fieldsian Entertainment Attractor was extremely difficult. All thought tended to be of an Entertainment Eternity, the last and first joke being that there was no coda, and there was really no such things as facts and fictions, but a mere variation of anthropological performance-texture.

As what was left of Benson was slowly extracted with some difficulty from the steering-wheel and dashboard of the *Rolls,* Nora made her tenth cup of strong coffee that night. She had walked back to her lair a few hours previous past a new range of shrines, relics, and various new Entertainment devotions which were beginning to push aside their equivalents in the old world. Such previous things were beginning to lose their spirit, that mystical entity which, when it travels, leaves an empty shell, looking for some new body. She supposed that a previous system of mechanised beliefs had been out-advertised, and had blundered and fallen, become a half-blind prehistoric animal unable to find its proper food-swathe. The loss of spirit was the loss of capacity for transforming the world, and the elements within the old games were shutting down shop, ready to drop like autumn leaves as a new season of changes began. For herself, she could only hope that Doll Culture would eventually gorge itself to death in an orgy of incestuous Star-eating cannibalism. But this Fields must go. She did not want her country to become like the car-park country across the water: a lobotomised Scandinavian mall, its engineers gone to clown-stuff, and its mind full of diseased actors.

This Fields must go. But his mere death would make a first Entertainment Martyr. It would unify his creation. Dead, he would be the first Entertainment Saint.

Somewhere in the mind of the man who had created this mind-numbing swarm around her, was a key to the game-generator. If she could find it and turn it, she could possibly collapse the source of his inspirations.

She would find this key.

Field was in the business of loosening concentrations. She would see if she could loosen his a little. She would become a virus, trick her way into the interstices of what she guessed was the thin membrane of Fields' sense of the Present. To do this, she would become one of his precious advertisements herself, and release the damned-up mounting pressures of Time within him.

But first she had to do some research.

II

A Meeting In The Hanover Café

After Benson's death, Marshall, always keeping a close hidden watch, had the definite impression that Fields wasn't enjoying himself any longer. The smiles were still there, but there were no more snatches of Madonna, or Elvis Presley. Summer and the great Entertainment Experiment were growing old, he supposed, and he also took good note that he now appeared to spend no time at all with his beloved performers; rather he talked to any good minds he could find at the local university, and what was left of them at *EAT-I,* after poor Benson's world-renowned leap into the digital beyond. Marshall thought that if Fields were ever to have a permanent place in Entertainment culture, it would be in such an organisation as *EAT-I,* where he drove 14-year-old thick-spectacled and blue-chinned American geniuses mad with such hair-raising questions as how to get digitised holographic images to 'talk' to one another.

Despite such rarified fun, he guessed that Fields' decision path was narrowing. Sooner or later, the Bunter would try and get back to Toad Hall. The last train to cerebral-land was hooting at the station, and the brave man had his ticket. But the train would not wait forever to take him back to the mounds and barrows of the elite to design yet more original programmes of mass-cultural irradiation. Marshall sensed a fall. The truth was there wasn't really a collective impulse in the whole of Fields' being. That was probably why, in the iron-age past, he had been such a successful operator against Communism. Of late, he spoke privately of his ostensibly loved Entertainment folk as 'habitat brains', pure 'kitsch concentrate' for the test-tubes of the charitable dictatorship of his ruthless ideo-technology. To Marshall, Fields now saw his actor-gods as mere garden-gnomes, whose artificial manufacture could be used to control and manage a great new media What-Happens-Next-Game. He had suspected from the beginning of the enterprise that performers were mere players in some secret theatre of his mind. Marshall now imagined Entertainment State was some vast script being written by him in an attempt by him to contact the world again. In this vision of a performance super-technology, he supposed that Fields thought that the transformation techniques of an Acting and Advertising culture would lead him to the secrets of the elusive alchemy of Time and Change.

But like many a man on a mountain-top, he suspected that Fields was still vainly waiting for something that appeared to have missed a long-crest schedule. If this elusive something did not arrive, the Bunter knew that he would have to come down from the mountain without any message, and he would then have to move on, become an intellectual gypsy until the end of his days.

He sensed disappointment in the man. But wasn't angry, he was getting bored. Something hadn't quite come off the way he had wanted it to. What had finally emerged was a successful but rather rational plan, which could have been thought up by a thousand or more reasonably clever folk. Though original enough, Entertainment State had finally emerged as being no more than another super-plan for getting people back to work, reforming an economy on a radically different basis, and forming a possibly quite unique new society. Already coming out of the wings were the first generation of people who would take over from Fields, manage, direct, control, and improve the Great New Performance Society. His object had been that Entertainment State should not degenerate into yet another technological superproduct; but industrial society had quickly struck back. Entertainment, it seemed was only to be yet another industrial and corporate game ready to breed the next generation of political controls.

Indeed, some Fieldsian egg had been laid, but the super-stuff of the small-print hadn't hatched. Soon, Marshall guessed that Fields would be no longer interested in Entertainment State; he would move to some new system of possible cosmic realisations. Already the man was back at the cream-horns. His trousers and shirt were splitting again, and soon Marshall guessed, he would become fit for a wonderful era-photograph, a last prime-time interview, and a good story or too, but little else. This was the moment of greatest danger for him. He was in several troughs between several different kinds of expectancies. He was also playing a public role for which he was hardly suited amidst people with whom he had almost nothing in common.

Marshall had to assume that the Apache would of course, know all this. When she was ready, she would strike along the seam of these many vulnerabilities. She usually met violence with violence, but regarding Fields, the Intelligence consensus was that she would rough him up a bit as a preliminary. She would want to show him that she was more clever than he was before finally uncoiling. The psychological analysis was that somehow she would try and break him up by reversing his game, by making his own advertisements turn inwards and savage him. To do that, she would have to meet him. Though how and when she would manage to do this, Fields' protecting team of coast-watchers did not yet know.

Whenever he wanted to be by himself, which was quite often these days, the quiet *Hanover* coffee-shop in the narrow Macklin Street was Fields' favourite place of meditation. The horrendous expense of its items kept out the braying noise of the day from him for an hour or two. Here, in a large, cool, back room, with plain pine tables, the head of a stag, and shelves of steins, he could eat his diet-banned *kuchen* and *apfelstrudel* to his heart's content, and the broken fragments of a extended self could take refuge in a history which was his, and yet not his. The timber-walled *Hanover*, with its hung Westphalian *schinken* and Bavarian *aufschnitt*, gave something of a restful framework to his travelling to press-conferences, and broadcasting studios.

The experience of being an internationally famous figure was a new world to him. At first, immediately after he left Tower House, he felt like some astonished lunatic, pumped full of Largactil, suddenly freed by some enlightened decree, and left in a one-horse railway station with an apple, a bun, and a label around his neck with the address of the nearest Department of Social Security. But now, a part of him certainly enjoyed the constantly ringing telephones, first-name terms with public figures, banquets, dinner-parties, and his hotel reception desk packed with letters, messages, and flowers from admirers.

A camouflaged *Land Rover* reversed past the doorway, with the roof-mounting for its absent half-inch *Browning* now taped over with black plastic bin-liner, but Fields did not see a land of strife. He did not even see a specific Belfast. He saw an entrance to an enchanted land which was the world of his book, opening like a flower before him. The flower would consume all in its passion, healing, nurturing, forgiving, indeed, loving. Fields was not interested in the Troubles, past, present, or indeed probably to come. He simply could not understand why people were still interested in gangrenous cartoon-frames still feebly battling for some outdated frontier of Public Relations. To him, issues which festered long before Luther and Zwingli, debates which threaded through King Henry's murderous divorces, Cromwell's genocidal violence, to Casement's confusions, were mere discarded historical sales-lines. He also included in this category De Valera's condolences to the German Ambassador on hearing of the death of Adolf Hitler.

He bit deep into a piece of diet-forbidden *kuchen* and contemplated a city in which the two great advertising constructs of the Western World were still at raging war, though for the historical moment, bullets had ceased flying. He found it was difficult to think that in this land a large section of the population gathered each day come rain, come down-payments or no, to bear witness to a total breakdown in the laws of science, rationalism, a wilful breaking of every single law of the so-called Age of Enlightenment. In these sacred places they gathered to witness and experience a great Impossible; there they gathered to witness the completely preserved cultural body of Alchemy, that cursed pseudo-science of impostures thought to have been put long ago into the funny-farm of bottled absurdity on a dusty shelf with the pickled four-headed baby, a two-headed penis, and the claimed bones of mermaids and unicorns. That Rutherford had fulfilled Alchemy's every expectation and prophecy because he had a primitive source of radiation, high voltages, and better glassware, was hardly stated as such within the educational curriculum. Myth in action, thought Fields as he bit into a second portion of *kuchen,* was still heady and dangerous stuff.

But though he had not been in Belfast for long, here for once he felt the exhilaration of a whiff of the sulphur of battle-action, instead of the lonely promise of eventually becoming a bottled and shelved curiosity himself. Though he had started to gain weight again, The years had fled from his mind at least with these new excitements, and it was as if his vanished flesh had become a greater body which was the great Outside of *StarPower.* Two businessmen reading the book on the plane. A girl with it under her arm in the taxi queue. Advertisements for it glimpsed along the streets to the hotel. Two breathless teenagers requesting autographs at Reception. For the first time in a bunkered life, he had defeated his eating display by producing a world-dramatisation of it.

With a pang of guilt, he thrust aside further pastries. There was no need now for all that sugar to accumulate in his blood, piling up internal horrors for his old age. What need for such things, when he had liberated dancing chains of glistening sweetmeats from his brain to weave a super-body in the external world. Already tentacles and latticework of his vision were at work, undergoing endless cell-division in the reading minds which jostled through the traffic beyond the potbellied window of the *Hanover* in the brightest daylight anyone could recall.

Conspiracy theorists were already having a feast. For it was certainly true that on the very day Fields arrived, the weather changed. The dreadful summer of what had been a particularly hard and murderous year, vanished almost overnight, replaced by limitless blossoms of heat and light. The delicious shimmer of day had a constant quality, as if a great high dome of pleasure had been clamped over the entire province. Comments were that it was a theatrical light which seemed to have a manufactured dimension, as if the most ordinary situations were part of an emerging film or theatre set.

The city, with all its savage divides, and its maniacal religious hatreds, had turned its head and looked at Fields. The city had wondered. Its face was scarred with the assaults of centuries, and its face looking at him was as a dog expecting to be cruelly hit yet once again. The city saw a man who offered not a bomb, or a shot, not even a new Policy Conference, or even a 'new initiative' hot from those who were known in Belfast as SAC & B, meaning Squires And Clerks, and Business Bums. The city wanted to enjoy itself for once. And the very messiah of enjoyment himself had arrived on cue.

Forever writing notes, he was in the middle of one of those thoughts which had been the despair and amusement of his colleagues over the years, when Nora came in and sat at a table next to his, ordering coffee and cakes in a broken German accent. At the sight of her, his urgent pencil strokes, his phrases and thoughts, all came to an abrupt and swaying stop

Alice. To the life.

His beloved wife. RIP 1968.

Look? He hardly dare. He caught the radiance from the corner of a fluttering eye as he nervously tried to calmly sip his too-hot *kaffee*. Good God, a warm smile coming his way. And the wonder of the face! She was a vision from some long lost Eden his present form could not possibly have experienced. This smartly-dressed woman of late middle age was surely from a scene retained by some curious hereditary quirk, photographed before his birth, and carefully preserved in the great helix for this moment alone. His dead wife Alice, to the life. And good God, even a smile.

He gripped the table. The time and place of this almost complete hallucination could have been middle-class Vienna, or Berlin, in the 1890s. With a slightly pale oval face, her straight black hair in a tight bun, she might even have been Jewish, from one of the great eighteenth-century houses along the Unter den Linden, long razed by the RAF. His mouth dried in disbelief as even a duet from Kalman's *The Countess Maritza* came from the cassette above the counter as her coffee was served.

Alice. And any minute she was going to speak to him.

'Sag ja, mein leibe, sag ja....'

The melody of old Vienna cut through the shaking rattle of pneumatic drills two streets away and induced a dream produced by a reconnaissance system latent in the very depth of day around him. The thickset man reading *The Daily Express* at a far corner table did not even give either of them a glance. Fields' shadows were changed so often and with such subtle variety that for most of the time he thought he was quite alone. Nora knew that he was never alone. She had already noticed that the thickset man's jacket bulged to the left-hand side, and his stomach was as flat as a board.

She greeted the waiter in German. Concealing his excitement and palpitation, dabbing his mouth, brushing crumbs from his lap: dare he make even the most polite of approaches? His newly-acquired layers of fat ached as he urged on tribal muscles pulled from the deepest freeze. Resisting a temptation to straighten both his tie and his hair at once, he spoke in his very best accent. Almost slipping out of his century altogether, he very nearly rose from his seat and bowed. The complete hidden body-language of quite another century possessed his arms, legs, and neck, which he now held still stiff, like a Prussian of old. For a moment he was Balzac's Eugene Rastignac, about to take tea with a Duchess, conscious of a hole in his trousers, and feeling in his pocket for the fifty francs he had just borrowed. He heard a voice and was surprised it was his.

"May I recommend *die chokoladekuchen?*"

"Ja. Danke schön."

A good German accent. Another warm smile. Only a passing Belfast Corporation dustbin lorry interrupted his thoughts of a terrible fall from other lives, in which there were no dustbin lorries, and far fewer advertisements.

Praise the gods, she was *ein Berliner.* Though she said she had been away from her grandmother's city for some twenty years, they talked in good German of every avenue, for Berlin was Fields' favourite watering-place.

Behind Nora's rosebud smile, every grain of Fields' mental dust was being taken apart and put together again. Contemplative, heavily involved with his thoughts, and projecting great power and depth of concentration. Recent loss of weight. Suit still too big. Constantly jotting things down as if inspired. Sense of power and the isolations that went with it. Sense of vast inner exhilarations. But not the air of a leader or soldier. Sometimes muttered to himself, she noted. Grey Polish jowls. Somehow European, but nevertheless, a faint air of Bertie Wooster England about him.

She smiled to herself. She was astonished. An innocent. She hadn't see an innocent for years. And no apparent sense of danger. Possibly cuckoo. And pastry all down his shirt. And look at that suit again. They must have let this one out from somewhere. Scan again.

The murky analogues she detected were of psychological regions unfamiliar to her. She felt for edge, bite, point, cut, raised images of violence, landscapes of rage for bits of code-matching, the identity of the merest scrap of twinning correspondence. She searched for anything which might grudgingly yield a scrap of plain-text to unweave the make-up of the stout fellow now ordering more coffee. She noted that Fields would still occasionally take notes, not from events beyond the window, not from other customers, or from the place itself, but from some great landscape of intense inner developments with which he was vitally involved.

Another probe into the interior. Innocence again. A considerable body of it. Scan again. Glaring hypnotic intensity. A yielding mass of brilliantly lit texture. Pulsing bursts of possible analytic suggestions. Look for cell division. No? What about exponential? No. Exponential again, though. Then clowns. That's better. But clowns?

Fields and Nora talked on as coffee and cakes were served to a morose Irish couple, and a jolly family with three bouncing children. Immediately fascinated by Fields, the children listened to amusing stories, jangled their toys, and sat on his knee. Scan again. She got nothing from anyone else in the restaurant. Burnt-out faces of the moon, she thought, compared with the powerful broadcasting planet that was Fields. A couple of reps, a shiny business man. Perhaps ESP was no more than Round Britain Quiz, she thought. Irene Thomas on mental heat. Tease out Roman Conquest from tractors, Latin names of flowers, and W.G. Grace's score-sheet for summer, 1900. Switching, re-patching, trying new networks, spinning aerials, test and try. Run through the new programme. Don't force solutions. What does the system itself suggest? Fission. Try fission as metaphor. That's better. The man at the table by her side was rewriting every available head, installing his own script-circuits to create a massive interlinked story-animal which would eat the Impossible bit by bit. Fission. Fact. Fiction. Faction, that's better. An unstoppable runaway ball of bastard suggestions. Half and quarter-truths carefully juxtaposed. The grey-scale of the advertising chain-reaction. She gulped at her own phrase, almost as if he had fed it to her from the plate in front of him.

She looked him straight in the eye.

"What is your inspiration?"

"Happiness."

"Happiness?"

"I remember a picture. In the house of one of my uncles. The portrait of a famous Lutheran Pastor of the time. I forget his name. What most people would still call a fine specimen of mankind. An entire being built and designed for suffering. The face reflecting agonies of soul. Poor creature. The mind probably racked with guilt, a fact-paranoid brain within, crippled by a wide spectrum of bourgeois terrors. A bad design. A six-inch iron bar would have done the job infinitely better. The man had virtually killed himself. Tortured himself to death with the difficulties of trying to do some good. I cannot understand crucifixions. I prefer their alternative: well-planned success."

A natural and unselfconscious pause, as if both understood the need to allow antennae to unlock, re-focus. Though circuits were screaming warning, he was overwhelmed and exhilarated by a manner and a grace which though slightly old-fashioned, delighted him beyond all measure. The *nostalgia mysterieux* aroused by her face was become a focus in which she was quickly fitted into his own equations of destiny, time, and purpose. He was free to choose the restrictions of what most people would call real, namely an attractive face across a table, or to risk the thrilling and adventurous vertigo induced by the presence of what he could only call a warrior-guardian from first dream-time.

He was never the one for any mundane choice. Unlike his scientific enemies, he was not one to simplify the world in order to make it easier to analyse. In front of him was living proof that his original calculations had been correct. Here was the predicted particle. He had forecast that by activated by some radiating picture-alarm, such aboriginal soldiers would awake, climb out of their stored cartoons after the sleep of a thousand years. They would battle with a *forgetting*, perhaps not knowing who they were, or what they were doing. Their lives might be painfully confused, indeed quite pointless until at an exact and certain hour they were to go to a rendezvous.

Which might be soon. For he now knew of course that the beautiful woman by his side was not Alice, and was no more *ein Berliner* than Max Bygraves. Here was part of the evolving antidote to his Entertainment State. Before him was death. Before him was the Apache. And judging by her reputation, there was no chance his thickset guardian near the door could do anything in time. To his credit, he calmly continued his story of the picture.

"Not a single theologian seemed to have paid any attention at all to the possibility of Christ actually succeeding in his quest. The 'pain equals moral worth' process is the most evil and destructive thing I can think of. It had taken over this good man in the picture, set him up, eaten him alive, and probably giggled at his last breath."

He sighed.

"Poor Old Deadly Serious Analogue Man. Just think what the Beatles or *The Monkeys* could have done for that piece of pre-digital granite in the portrait. He could have been a Star. Prime Time would have melted all that twisted wire in his gut. He could have been a Gypsy Tango King or something, done a tap-dance with Dame Edna, or joined The Sex Pistols."

She seemed amused and most impressed. He scratched his nose and stifled a sigh as his discovery responded by talking rather naively about some out-of-date films she had liked. A nice act. Never mind. He could imagine the difficulties. He imagined her possessed by several

216

kinds of lopsided strengths for which the world now hardly had a use. His wonder knew no bounds. Perhaps she heard a call to arms from distant interiors to wake in the night to take up ageless arms from an ageless store. He looked at the smiling oval again and was terrified. He didn't believe a single word she said. Perfect. Now he could die.

But it appeared that he was going to live. The music had stopped, and the bulky man by the table near the door was restless, as he had been ever since he had heard German being spoken.

She was getting up and saying goodbye. Fields was beside himself as the curves of a close-costumed voluptuous figure rose up before him. What a specimen of intense advertising radiation. A land guardian, She'd just woken up. Long sleep. Deep cover of centuries. Ancient coast and hill sprite. Activated by intense picture field. He had actually found one. Must not lose her. Who was she? Good God, she was going. Dare he?

"Please take my card. Perhaps sometime, you might like tea?"

"Of course. Thank you. I'm at the Carlton Hotel. My name is Steadman. Laura Steadman. Do call."

"Thank you. I'd love to talk again."

"Auf Weidersehen."

He was quite unable to reply. The last words and the accent paralysed him. For a moment the veils of birth and history were so thin he almost went outside and called for a carriage for them both. Fragments of what sounded like an archaic Latvian and some strange old broken German resounded in his head. And yet other similar languages he heard on the very edge of consciousness. He tried to jot down the mix of strange, nonsensical words. With her going, he had completely left the century, and if someone had bumped into him, he thought, they would perhaps, have passed through nothing but clothed air.

Mortality twisted the knife. His face in the mirror opposite wasn't the face that Alice saw in 1968. It was a face now beginning to be unusually flushed with embarrassment at his stained suit, and his odd socks as if he were coming alive again after the dead years, coming out of a dream so deep he could hardly remember what he had been doing or who he had been. If everyone in the surrounding city was beginning to forget, Fields was beginning to remember. The woman who had just left had taken his life with her just as if she had shot him. All he could remembered was Marshall quoting a line from a film he had seen long ago. *'The Comanche go round the mountain, the Sioux go over the top, but the Apache, the Apache is an act of God...'*

Looking at the puzzling words on his notepad again, some were almost familiar. But getting up, he wiped his lips with his hands, and now conscious of his grease-stained carrier-bags for the first time in his life, he knew he would have to go back to his hotel room, where his weights and his cruel diet-sheets waited for him, his only companions of the night.

The waiter came, with a tray and a pot.

"Would you like some more coffee sir?"

Fields could hardly manage a stuttered reply.

Her face. And that music. That music was starting again as she vanished. Gazing down the long room at the stag's head as if galaxies of warring Explanations were balanced on its antler points, he was still several historical interiors away. The waiter, with a surprising grasp of the situation, filled Fields' cup with almost a smile on his face.

The thickset man, astonished, noticed that there were tears in Fields eyes. Thoroughly alarmed, he got up and spoke to the waiter.

"Have you seen her before?"

"Who, sir?"

"The woman who has just left."

"I've only just come to work, sir."

"But she was paying her bill when you came in."

"I can't say I noticed, sir."

"Who gave her the bill?"

"Mary's just gone home this minute, I'm afraid."

The plain van across the road outside the *Hanover* which was the stout man's radio backup was hemmed in by a hooting dustcart, and a lost petrol tanker. The second backup vehicle seemed to be always in the workshop. With all the recent Cuts, sometimes the stout man wondered what he was doing here in Belfast at all.

On one thing he was prepared to place a bet.

It was no use looking for a beautiful well-heeled continental matron in the whole of Belfast.

He turned from the door, and saw his charge holding his head in his hands, and shaking with great sobs fit to burst.

In the back of the bread-van, taking off her various layers of masks, she was pleased she had finally met Fields. His power was of such a dimension that she doubted if he was aware of a thousandth of it. She hadn't thought it would be so easy to locate the secrets of his strength. He was possibly an Adept of the highest order, imprisoned in a century which had almost no use for him. Alone, and reduced to science clerking and fag-end eccentricities, he was just discovering himself, flexing his muscles and larking about with tinsel dynamite. Possibly not to be blamed, like a child. She had found his weakness.

Fields didn't know who he was.

218

From figures of state to road-sweepers, she supposed many such cuckoo-children didn't know exactly who they were. Many merely disappeared with their creations and inventions and prophecies, unwittingly bending the Cartesian frame to escape like ejected cartoon heroes through ten smoke rings of astonishments to the land of monster sightings of fabulous dimension fit for the most demanding old salt. All they ever left behind were rounds of odd calibres, strange trajectories, sudden malfunctions, fractured frames of reference, and not a few mysterious deaths.

Fields was the standard stuff of prophets and visionaries. Given the slightest tremor of genetic dust, she supposed he would be in a shed somewhere making engines which ran on water, or anti-gravity devices for bicycles. Or else in the past, he would be just as he was today: high on a hill, performing mass brain-surgery on hundreds of thousands. Some of these creations and endeavours actually worked for a while, she supposed, but only when the prophet was present, or in a particular mood, but work they did, if only as Nature's rehearsals, pallid imitations of part-actions of part-actions, *deus* with only one foot intermittently in the *machina*.

She supposed that like their creations, such super-citizens rarely lived long. On those occasions when they were conformist enough to leave their bodies behind, it was as if their death had been *imagined*. As in spontaneous burnings, only part of Fields' death would probably occur within the common lattice of cognisance, which was never ever quite squared. Laughing, she saw him dying before her to the strains of *The Blue Danube* in the little German theatre of the *Hanover,* a collapsed and smoking heap beneath the stag's head, and the suspended hams, killed by a temperature difficult to attain within even a crematorium. She saw his odd socks and the stained lapels of his jacket left completely alone, only inches away from heat which had calcined his bones, but which hadn't touched his carrier-bags or the burst collar of his shirt. He was so unreal, a beam of powerful thought could possibly sweep him away, which was something other, more solid dimensions of power had difficulty in doing.

As Nora sped back into her web, Fields, still sitting hypnotised before coffee long gone cold, knew he had heard her voice before. He had heard it in the first high-arched railway stations full of steaming engines, gas-flares, and horse-breath. He had heard it in European alleys only a brewer's cart in width, and in thatched workshops of the even older century, when he was much thinner, his hair was longer, he was always hungry, and his name wasn't Hieronymus Fields. He had heard her voice preach the new creation myth of enlightenment with its utterly convincing announcements of the first miracles of piped water, simple disinfectants, crude injections, flush toilets, and the Worker's Educational Association. He heard her speaking before roaring crowds, beyond which were men with cudgels, ready to beat her into paste.

'Science would liberate, Science would enlighten; it would smash the old world to pieces of fortune-tellers and mystics, of gods, priests, and witch-doctors. Forward to enlightenment!'

He had heard her voice by great capstans, winches, gear-trains ten feet high, and flywheels big as circus roundabouts. He saw her pale, dedicated face trudging by mountains of glowing slag and sky-high flashes from mills, ironworks, and collieries. At her back, chimney-flames rose into the falling snow and steam blinding as sunlit polar ice shot from red and green engine cabs. He saw her with shabby coat and torn skirt with muddy hem, bent over with heavy bags and turning endless corners by the last doomed 18th century houses, avoiding lines of uniformed men on nervous horses, swords by their sides. Over many decades, they watched and waited all over Europe for whatever the many forms Laura Steadman were called once upon a time.

In Fields' head were now thoughts from a time before cities were lit; thoughts running as fast as the new machines assembled in huts, workhouses and attics of the old century. His soul became a thing unwound as it flew back and back, by flywheel, balance-weight, and coiled spring; by candle, rush and reed-light; by stone oil lamps as old as Jesus, and by flaring logs, paraffin, gas, and dangerous early Direct Current. He saw his own thoughts written on his own, eager 19th century face amidst such fantastic shadows as were gone from the tainted blandness of his own time. He heard the sound of a flight of migrating souls from under ditches, flagstones, concrete, cellars, and memorial-granite from all over Europe. And the voices of these hosts, he supposed, were still in the analogies within the black and grey boxes of the chips.

The thickset man's worried face was before Fields now, his mouth opened and closed, But Fields was not listening. Laura Steadman was speaking within some upturned box in the brain.

'There was at last something to do. The Great Work. Kill the kings, open the madhouses and the prisons, and tear down the castles. Slit the throats of the oppressors. Kill all the guards. Burn all the old laws, rules, smash all the idols. Calculation is here. We have found the solution, we have found the answer! We can free ourselves, demythologise nationalist impostures, destroy phony religions. March for Communism and the Scientific Cause!'

This was a level of comradeship whose intensity in recall annihilated him. As the thickset man took his arm, Fields looked at the strange incomprehensible words he had written on his notepad a few

220

minutes previous. What was this rubbish? Bastardised German, Russian, Polish? Colloquial, slang? Look again. And there, a film coming into swooning focus before his guard caught him as he looked yet again, and almost fell, as the unknown words cleared in his brain.

Romany and Yiddish.

The thickset man led a weeping and shaking Fields to his car.

The thickset man's name was Merrill, and he used a bracing language which Marshall understood more than most in his organisation.

"He's gone completely fucking crazy. I don't know, I'm sure."

"He's been ambushed. Somebody's pressed his trigger. Somehow."

"Who? We know everyone he meets, where he goes, what he does. Who could deliver something like that?"

"When is he by himself?"

"He's never by himself."

"Are you sure?"

"Except in the *Hanover*. Can't be there. He goes there to have a rest."

"What does he do there?"

"He has a rest."

"What does he do when he has a rest?"

"What d'you mean?"

"Does he lean back in his chair, does he look at his shoes, for God's sake?"

"He writes. Jots things down."

"You sure he doesn't talk to anybody? Not even kids, waiters?"

"Yes. Nothing. Nobody. Well, a few kids maybe. Sometimes."

A blush like his polished oxblood shoes crept round the back of Merrill's stout neck. Marshall tapped a single finger.

"Who was it, Merrill?"

"Well nobody. Really."

Merrill looked at the floor as Marshall tapped again.

"Who?"

"Well he did most of the talking."

Marshall closed his eyes.

"Jesus Christ."

His eyes flared open again.

"A woman?"

"Yes. But it was nothing."

"It was her."

"Could have been."

"How long?"

"Quarter of an hour."

"Do you know how long quarter of an hour is to her, Merrill? About ten times longer than we have been on this Earth."

"This was purely social. He must have fifty contacts a day like that."

Marshall leaned forward as if at a difficult point in a tutorial.

"What's the betting that the other forty-nine looked nothing like this one?"

Merrill squirmed.

"Well that's right."

"And you didn't have her followed?"

"The plain-van was blocked."

"What with?"

"Lorry, tanker, bread-van."

"What a lot of traffic. Did you search the bread-van?"

"You know we no longer have authority to do things like that."

"That's where she was."

Merrill was a beaten dog. The man was brave, and daily operated within seconds of death. Marshall felt for him. The opposition knew what they were doing. A complex of situations had got out of Merrill's single control. Marshall just didn't have enough resources. And with the coming of peace, and after the bollockings because of the bungled raid, they had no power to go rampaging as of old.

"I had to stay with *him.*"

"Description, please."

"A rare bird. Very well-heeled. Early middle age. Expensive outfit. Quite a picture. Broken German."

"That was the way to him."

"I know some German, but I couldn't hear it because the music started."

"What bloody music?"

"Oh, something they play on the system there."

"German music?"

"You know: waltzes, light stuff. Singing."

"Operetta?"

"That's right."

"There was a whole team around him, Merrill. She could have killed him there and then, you know that?"

"She wasn't going to kill him."

He looked at Marshall in triumph as if this was his round.

"Give me some credit. If I thought she was going to kill him, I'd have dropped her there and then."

Merrill liked the single throat movement this produced from Marshall, and he exploited the gap.

"She might have drugged him, on the other hand."

Merrill was very pleased that this looked like a new idea to Marshall.

"We'll have him checked out."

"She could have scratched him, pricked him, you know things like that."

"She's pricked him alright."

Marshall was angry. The Apache had come in by the bathroom window and pressed their buttons as easily as she could float up a chimney stark naked.

At first, like Marshall, Fields thought someone had slipped him one of the designer-drugs of which the well-heeled young were rather fond. But tests revealed not a trace. Meanwhile, Laura Steadman's face continued to open out into history. Murderous, shattering history which broke his strengths into pieces. He was become episodes both of slaughter and destruction, magic and love. She was become the nostalgia of all cathedrals, she was the smell of all seas, he tasted restored youth and inspirations within him beyond all tolerable compass, the elusive mystery of her being setting transcendental summer fire to his brain.

He was become a teenager even down to the whimpering, which had Elmon laughing for the first time in his life, as he listened: '...if only she would just talk a little to me... If only she would just give me a call, Elmon; leave a note...'

This, Elmon noted with glee, was all the bubble-gum pain, the first real bicycle, the café on the corner, long trousers, and the scornful toss of curls become the presence of magical writ. And still it went on: 'if only she would...If only'. And the last fragment was always the same: 'Elmon, I wonder if there is a light in her window? Where? Somewhere. Maybe this street. Maybe that one...'

Elmon listened wryly amused as Fields hallucinated the searing unbearable detail of the life of Laura Steadman which opened out within him. He heard about the moods of her infancy, her first hesitant (unbearable!) sexuality, tears, triumphs, jealousies, even her natural motions, as if he, Elmon, were sitting in the centre-circle of a full-feature. To Fields, the grain of a toenail clipping became the Elysian garden of women. Laura Steadman was a simulation rampant, destroying all his disciplines with a scouring pad of time-grains.

Apart from the now mocking city of Entertainment, Fields was wandering through several other cities: the cities of his youth, the cities of past lives, and Laura Steadman herself as a complete city, rising as an Atlantean vision from the vast oceans of his previous intense preoccupations.

Even as he walked, it seemed the very depth of day was listening for her name. Stead, steady, steadfast... from parts of number plates to scraps of street-shouts, to caught broadcasts, a flexing agony were these never-ending compilations of *steed, steal, steam...* Each array, each statistical cluster contained part-echoes of the name of Laura Steadman. Some were near, some far. There were very tempting runs of three, a couple of runs of four, and (what second of ecstasy!) discovered over a Chinese takeaway, a complete L. Steadman. But the tarnished sign was all that there was left of a crippled saddle-maker, long gone to Canada with his wife and twelve children.

She was spread like a lexicon over the whole of Belfast. Bits and pieces of her haunted certain streets and times of day. Elmon, getting an appetite for the sheer cruelty of the chase, even located two Steadmans who did not have a telephone. One was ex-directory (A fellow-travelling *Telecom* friend soon obliged for that one), and the other had the installation pending. None fitted the description. These broken alphabetic portents were once, Fields guessed, part of a whole vessel. He was sure their part-codes were her shouts across a cavern, but he couldn't interpret the direction analogues of the synchronous groupings. Like his world of Entertainment, this world of pure Her was a seamless texture. Anyway, which way, was everywhere.

He would sleep all day, eat nothing, listen to his beloved Lehar, Strauss, or soaring Puccini, then wander all night, those around him fearing for his safety and sanity. He spent a small fortune on hiring researches and private detectives to try and find her. Laura Steadman. German. Middle-class. Well-educated. Well dressed. The professionals took his money gratefully, and shrugged their shoulders, knowing that such in Belfast could be counted on the fingers of half a hand, or just about.

In his agony, he imagined her as involved in an equally intense search for himself, but somehow they kept missing one another. It was a horror without any blood or guts, just limitless vacancy of the almost-near. At times, outside a supermarket or a newspaper shop, he would sense her near, or an advertisement hoarding with a woman's face would become her. At times, a distant vehicle's shape would become the possible shape of her possible car, though he had never seen such a thing. Such was his obsession he was being bypassed by his own Entertainment creation; he was become an embarrassing eccentric on the very fringe of the centre of activities.

He now lived almost completely in the *Hanover.* He would wait for her there, oblivious of the smirks of the waiters and the impatience of Merrill. In his visions of Laura Steadman becoming once more framed in the doorway, he seemed to travel back along the spider-lines of some scattered super-body of his to come across an endless procession of the Century's persecuted faces. The daydreams took him back and back, then burst to all points of the political compass. He saw imprisoned Communists; he saw piles of dead, naked Jews; he saw gypsies being hunted and shot like squirrels; he saw a river running with dead Russians, Poles, and Slavs. And he saw lists. Endless lists of the dead and the hunted, lists of those running and hiding, lists of the imprisoned and the lost. Names and words and atmospheres, some older than he could recall, ringing long lost bells, fathoms, deep. There, in his brain were 1930s records of the Russian CHEKA, OGPU, and NKVD; there were Fascist and Gestapo files, 1960s Klan records, 1970s GUARDA lists, and even old Tsarist catalogues of names familiar to Dostoevesky and Gorky. Back and back, and to and fro, went the long lines of the dead; he saw the wanted of the Inquisition, and the French Revolution; he saw hunted Chartists, Communards, and Bonapartists. Some of the arrays of names became blood-trails in snow and mud which led to a shed, a ditch, a shell-hole, or a wretched piece of cover in the forest where the trail ended, and he died, bits of him exploding into other orbits.

He looked towards the door. She wasn't there. He'd left her somewhere in history, probably standing on a corner in the rain in Petrograd, Berlin, or Madrid. What year? It was as useless as trying to enter a scrap of accidentally-caught dream. If he couldn't get back, keep the meeting, he would rather be dead. Her pathetic sodden half-form in the doorway was now annihilated with more names stretching back to the limitless ant-hills of the Austro-Hungarian Empire; in his head were broken lines of almost-annihilated East-European families stretching back from the time of young Solzhenitsyn to the time of Chopin, Turgenev, and the infinity beyond Peter the Great; there were anarchist back-rooms and bomb-making hovels which ran back through the Special Branch through Peelers to the Bow Street Runners, and back and back still, to the first crude handwritten records of the New York Police Department.

Where was she? Where had he left her? He could feel her waiting. Would she think he had betrayed her? Would she think he had been killed? He could hear her breathing, even in the nineteenth Century, even in the centuries before that. In fear and trembling, she was waiting for him

A young man carrying a guitar-case passed the door and looked in briefly, his eyes meeting his. It was the young Paddington bricklayer he had been so offhand with at the Paris Conference, months back. Now, the only thing in the world Fields wanted to do was speak with him. His family, dog-leads, the state of his garage, his new kitchen sink he had fixed himself, anything would do to start a healing process. His mouth opened, the man looked, recognised, but disappeared without speaking. Now, in addition to unrequited love, for the first time in his life, he was deeply ashamed of himself. But he was learning. It was savage, slow, and agonising, but he was learning. Somewhere, in the deep of him, there were new ships, and summers other than this.

Two weeks later, across the road from where a demolished Fields sat in the *Hanover*, in the darkness of an old warehouse window, the sight of a *Steyr* sniper-rifle focused steadily on the doorway of the cafe. The subject of his transcendental speculations had come to finish him off.

A shadow in the doorway. he looked up, expectant. Only an old man with a stick, accompanied by a young boy. Fields looked down at his coffee, and saw shots of the early 1920s now. He saw Rosa Luxembourg being beaten to death. Erhardt's armoured cars coming out of the bloodstained snow along by the Postdammerplatz. Now someone he had strangled in 1934; a face going blue, thick-lensed spectacles falling onto the stout serge of the jackets worn at the time. German. Chemicals. Wipe him out. He almost got the name, but it was dissolved by the terror of missions unfilled, of comrades calling for help through many centuries, on land, sea, and air. Damn her. She'd opened him up, filled him with history, and left him for dead. And he knew that any time now she would come for the last time.

The boy now left the old man, and came to him, holding out an open autograph-book for him to sign. The page began to blur. The child was the new century. The blank page was time itself. He did not know which name to put. When he finally wrote, neither boy nor himself could recognise the language or even the name. Elmon appeared, looking irritatingly at his watch, he stood up to go. But torn apart by past and future, he touched the boy's head for a moment, and broke into such a flood of unstoppable tears, he fell prostrate to the floor before an astonished Elmon and a white-faced Merrill, who whispered urgently into his mobile.

She tensed. Now. He was here.

The trigger, carefully adjusted to the slightest of pressures, was

226

already halfway through its travel. But was it him?

The door opened.

What? The bastard was horizontal!

Fields was being carried out to a car by several helpers. She recognised Elmon, and Merrill. But having no expected vertical aim-off destroyed one second of her expectations, and with the third second collapsing, she pulled the trigger.

Click

What?

Eject the bad round.

Now even the horizontal plane swayed into vanishing as Fields was rapidly put into the ambulance and the doors slammed shut. But even now, perhaps she could still do it.

Fire!

Click.

Eject.

Click. Round stuck.

Jamming procedure.

Click.

Reload. Click.

No good.

Now move out.

No good at all.

She had never come across a power like this one before.

III

Entertainment State is Born

The Official Inauguration of Entertainment State took place in the last week of August in Tent City, which was five-hundred acres of hastily-erected canvas, at night a great permanent mushroom-cloud of multicoloured light on the Belfast horizon. With his special pass, in his usual cover-role as Managing Director of *Seelex*, Marshall entered by lines of limousines guarded by squads of RUC. He made his way to the temporary main road, a rubbish-strewn strip of ungraded ash and cobbles, flanked by the great tents of the Famous Faces, striped and flagged as if for a mediaeval tournament.

There had been an official ceremony in the town, with a glowing speech by the Princess. The sky had quickly swallowed her up like a ministering deity, and 150,000 Entertainment inhabitants of the circles of the advertising inferno had wound its way to the EuroDump and Tent City. This area had risen in five breathless months. Desperate for electrical supply, one of the scores of Belfast firms involved had bought a couple of dozen ancient ex-army *Matador* generator trucks from a bankrupt circus. These bulky vehicles with their battered World War 2 outlines, still had gaudy red-and-gold circus names painted on their dented sides. Tent City was alive night and day with the shimmer and scream of these phlegm-chested old generators, which, as he walked to the reception tent, gave the smell and presence of beasts and sawdust and sweat and burnt oil of long ago as the machines strained to keep up with the ever-increasing demand for current. Current was also needed for the expanding light-engineering complex and test-sheds of *The Most Unusual Aeroplane Company,* who this evening, were to roll out the *Black Mountain Bird* as a fitting climax to the celebrations. The aircraft would hover, and make complete triumphant circuits of the EuroDump.

Intense flashbulb salvos by the glaring mouth of the main reception tent mixed with the tones and glows of all kinds of hastily improvised lighting. An air of fried onions, hot diesel, cannabis, and extremely expensive perfumes joined mixed planes of reflection to throw into circus relief the faces of the Rich and Famous. The first rank of walking fairytales were flanked by their smart official blue and khaki protectors, but the as-yet-unedited walking-stories had to make do with beer-bellied privateers, and their snarling pit-bulls.

Leering clowns jumped out ahead of Marshall, painted Apprentice Boy midgets passed by in columns, fire-eaters practised, and wine drinkers cursed and rolled over in the dark gaps between the tents of luxury. The occasional Famous Face glided by like a potentate, complete with glittering entourage, to disappear into one of the ballooning marquees, whose interiors had all the pageantry of a first class hotel, complete with bar, swimming pool, weatherproof exterior, and a parking-canopy big enough for several limousines.

In the central marquee, as big as a large ballroom, scores of TV cameras surveyed a mass of World Dignitaries and the Famous and Influential as they shuffled respectfully to the surprisingly moderate tones of saxophones and violins. Marshall wished he could paint, somehow capture on canvas the pure Third Republic iconography. An androgynous English novelist, with politically-correct views, wearing old-fashioned National Health spectacles and sporting a ponytail, gazed deep into the blue eyes of an athletic blond male security guard. A senior CIA man chatted by the bar, and two SAS officers desperately tried to look invisible; he also noted a round dozen of his own men, trying to avoid congregating at the bar all at the same time. And yes, over there chatting to a group of Faces, were the now-famous Fields' twins, Alison and Mavis, but looking a little lost without the man himself. Young Barsby was also here, eyeing the spectacular cleavage, and Annie, probably on her last roundup before her sunset cottage, nibbled a sandwich and tried hard not to look superior.

Trying not to notice, he caught the Mayor attempting resolute waltz steps with his youngest daughter, who held a tight smile as Da's ex-brick-laying foreman's feet descended on her hammertoes. By the TV cameras, a starched-linen flurry of stout Protestant Daughters of the City, were out on the straight town with glistening cheeks; they were determined to outdo their token Catholic equivalents, who had lower tops.

Apart from Famous Faces, he noted that he might as well have been surrounded by dramatisations of his own files. Having not having had a lot of social experience of this sort, he was intrigued to see what Entertainment State had thrown up. Here, hanging on to the coat-tails of the Faces, was yet another typical EuroMix, a veritable swirl of collaborators, informers, stool-pigeons, suspect businessmen, and myriad shades of Police and Intelligence interest. A few score famous rockers stood hesitant to one side, greying hair over wrinkled faces which suffered in the full lighting; they nibbled uninspiring sandwiches, sipped warm near-beer, and with their girlfriends of just legal age folded over their varicose arms, they looked as if they were about to die on this night of enforced good behaviour. He had the idea that it might be possible to collect such late twentieth century scenes as the one before him as other people collected Turners. These authentic Vichy characters came complete with genuine UDR armoured trucks just over the horizon, and even a full string orchestra playing the Führer's favourite selections from Lehar.

He heard many enquiries about Fields' state of health, and he had the impression that many of the power-brokers gathered here saw the Bunter as purely harmless and amusing curiosity value. He was to them an eccentric, a good old-fashioned upper-class Englishman, the joke being that he was the kind the middle-class never understand: he might compose a symphony of vacuum cleaners and hair-driers, keep coal in the bath, and have two fine mares eating in the dining room with the family. It struck him that as yet, most present here didn't understand the unique nature of Entertainment State. Most gave the impression that they thought it was just another flashy money-jamboree, rather large and energetic, yes, but really just another media ice-cream parlour with trimmings. Few, he thought, realised that Entertainment State was now a muscular and questing animal, thirsty for depth-propaganda, desperately anxious that its liberally scattered first spores fell on fertile ground. Passing by him now was a gaggle of shifty pink-rinse lecturers in the now approved Pop Culture courses at colleges and universities; most talked to a carefully chosen selection of media power-brokers in carefully cultivated working-class accents which he reckoned in quite a few cases must have cost a lot of money to acquire. The left-wingers of yesteryear were also here, plus many of the aging ear-ringed bangle-wrists who were still the vital power-brokers between several vital intellectual and artistic sanctions. But from what he could judge from the conversations around him, he was somewhat glad to know that if Jimmy James and Tommy Trinder and Bo Diddly and Sharon Stone were to be seriously studied to the same depth as Einstein and Shakespeare, then a hell of a lot of resistance had still to be broken before the worn-down middle ground was captured and secured.

Fighting his way to the bar, he noticed that John Carlton had arrived in state, and was rapidly circulating, complete with entourage, though copies of his compromising photos now adorned every club, workplace, and even many households. Though he was loth to admit it, he had acquired several himself, Barsby had one he could not understand, and Elmon had paid good money for a box of originals. It was rumoured that he had sold some choice scenes to Fields, who complained incessantly about the price. There were even rumours that even the Directrix had got hold of a few. As for Carlton himself, he had faced the business out with a typical combination of denials and charm, blackmail and bribery, threats, mocking laughter, and even a blushing admission or two. Many wished he would occasionally divert such skills for the benefit of the nation.

The Carlton business made Marshall wonder whether at times he was now looking at people who were less human beings than bits of Fields' 'advertising-process' on legs. It was a reconnaissance in force, was this powerful assembly, a queasy betting-shop of sorts. Most here were looking for the way several cookies were going to crumble before they joined other bits of walking advertisements in a new molecular game called Entertainment. As well as Carlton, there were many present who had been at the Joint Security Conference some months ago. Some ailing Banks were here, also the ever-hungry Corporations, and as Managing Director of *Seelex,* he was given the impression throughout several introductions that if he ever considered a career outside his job as a 'business consultant', then himself and his admired skills (in 'management') would be gladly received. With the sighting of a good half-dozen European faces straight from his files, of a sudden he knew that there were energies here far beyond those demanded by any media ice-cream parlour. As far as he was concerned, a pleasant hour-off for a drink was gradually turning into a fascinating technical briefing.

In the midst of this forming chaos, he felt the need for thought. Such a thing being almost inconceivable in the company he was in, he felt glad that he still had such a capability, which pressed upon him with the urgency of a natural function. Thankful for being still inexplicably alive, despite having soaked his head in Entertainment for over six months, he left the marquee, and wandered over to one of those baffling physical contrasts unique even to a Belfast at relative peace. A quarter of a mile from the glowing and rowdy Tent City, the EuroDump was flanked by the perimeter fence of the Ulster Defence Regiment's 16 REME Workshop. Leaving the high dome full of laser light, he made his way past the airstrip and hangars to the harsh glow of the tall floods of the camp perimeter by the UDR vehicle park.

Marshall drew deeply on his cigarette, and wondered how Fields was progressing in hospital. A cheeky consultant had the nerve to suggest to Fields that he take counselling sessions with a psychiatric social worker. One of the few joys of his present life was imagining Fields being interrogated by some one A-level feminist-Marxist polytech-person with the face of an evening-class wrestler, and being asked about ethnic roots, masturbation, social 'adjustment', racist 'attitudes', and whether he ever fancied men or not.

The man he was thinking of lay on his bed five miles away, thinking of killing himself. Getting Fields into hospital for a week's observation had been difficult. He had threatened Marshall with everything he could throw at him: lawyers, civil liberties, the tabloids. Fields hated being in the hands of any kind of bourgeois professional: scientists, doctors, whatever. To him they represented everything he was accused of himself: pseudo-scientific quackery. He screamed. He wept and wailed. This was war. He had been captured by the analogue-priests. He was in the hands of the timeservers, little stick-folk with their ludicrous tests, probes, facts, and drugs.

Fields' worst expectations had been fulfilled. A worn-out thick-lensed twenty-five-year-old doctor, who looked as if he had been willingly crucified on any of several phony dedications each beginning with the word 'social' or 'democratic' had led him reluctantly to an expensive private suite, which the exhausted practitioner obviously despised. Marshall, not without something of an inner smile, reflected it couldn't have been worse. Vaguely left-wing, and resenting Fields' accent and permanent bodyguard, the white-coat, crucified by as many plausible dedications as had a name, muttered in nasal tone of tests of bodily fluids on the morrow. A much more sympathetic nurse, who asked in all reason if the uncrowned king of Entertainment State would like a television in his room, was sent packing with an irritated reply, much to her surprise.

At his bedside, seeing a case of books being brought in by a grumbling Elmon, Marshall had envied the complete rest Fields was going to have.

"Hello, Hieronymus. Congratulations. The Indian has fucked you. Have a grape."

A scowl. Here was the man at bay. Marshall had never seen him annoyed and resentful before. He had certainly never been able to make him such himself, though he had tried many a time. The Indian packed quite a punch. He could tell the nasty Elmon was well pleased at that. The patient now lurched from his bed, his voluminous pyjama-sleeves flapping.

"What was that, Marshall?"

"I said the Indian has toasted you one side. She might want to put you on her fork and turn you over. That's why there's two men with tommy-guns at the door. You poor thing."

"I must find her."

"Stay where you are, for God's sake. You've been sold a pup."

"Rubbish. You have no idea what this woman means to me."

"It could be chemical."

"Chemical? You don't understand."

"Save me the brilliant strivings for a few days. If she's slipped you a mickey, we'll find it and scrape it out."

232

"Scrape it out?"

"That's what I said."

"I have news for you."

"Save it, for once."

"I have news for you, Marshall. I shall beat you, all of you."

"That's the boy I know. Congratulations. You're back on Earth."

"I shall beat the whole bloody lot of you."

"You probably will."

"Including her."

"Now that would be nice."

Meantime, the rejected television had nevertheless arrived on a trolley pushed by two slaves. Fields, Marshall, and dumb-show alike looked down their combined noses at it. It seemed TV was universal and obligatory, even inevitable, like a toothache, rancid milk, or a twenty-four-hour disturbance of the lower intestine.

Marshall switched on the set. Fields winced. Others giggled.

"There. Just up your street. *Come Dancing.* Have a letch at the *Lycra.* Toodlepip."

As he thought of what further problems Fields was giving, not only to the doctors and nurses, but to the furiously jubilant Elmon, now camping-out in an adjoining room in the hospital, a half-mile away due North of the EuroDump, high on Floor 20 of the long-abandoned *Fermanagh House* tower block, the intensity control of a 3-inch starlight target-scope was turned up. It brought into sharp relief Marshall's solitary figure as he carefully rolled a cigarette, laughing privately to himself over the Fields business. The sight was mounted on the identical *Steyr* sniper-rifle, which not long ago had stared down at the doorway of the *Hanover.* The weapon now rested on its tripod in front of a prostrate Nora. Target-watching was a true calling. For as many reasons as the century had crimes, she had spent a full five hours by the tiny window of a shattered bathroom, watching the REME base to the southeast and the landing strip to the southwest, clearly visible a few hundred yards from the entrance to the great marquee due south of her.

She lay with blackened face, her stomach flat on a pad of blankets on top of a crude wooden platform built up to the level of the bathroom windowsill. Although the night was warm, the inside of *Fermanagh House* had the chill of nearly three generations of unhappiness which had exploded in vengeful disruptive abandonment. Below where she lay, planner's bones rattled in the doom of a once-hopeful civic rationale. The sounds of forsaken bunker-life filled the last glum spaces of the massive high block, as it stood waiting for eventual demolition. Dripping pipes and banging doors accompanied the groan and creak of loose stanchions and torn handrails. Sudden upward shifts of fetid air brought to Nora the scrape and rattle of long-lost domestic objects pushed by drafts across a hundred floors behind broken doors, as if the place were a rolling ship in a moaning swell of post-industrial emptiness.

Marshall enjoying his roll-up with the wire at his back, struck her as a Rudolf Hess figure in a brief exercise hour, his isolated shape against the very last light of evening looking sad to the brim with mighty imponderable questions. Whoever he was, he looked exhausted, as if he had spent many hours desperately trying to remember something. She pulled the blankets tight around her as if a shield against emanations of both the man and the 1965 sarcophagus she was obliged to risk her life in.

Not knowing that but for a gap in Nora's intelligence information, he would probably have been annihilated there and then, the weary Marshall's thoughts were with Fields' ideas, whose overwhelming realisation he had just seen in the marquee. Entertainment State now occupied the larger part of the Intelligence spectrum in Northern Ireland. The mighty computers, now in full surveillance of the new State, had been particularly good at building whole crystal-like structures of the changing speculative patterns of major corporations and investment companies, whose financial fortunes often interfaced with Intelligence operations. The patterns of the many lines of such investigations had first shown Entertainment State as rushing, touching, children-in-a-playground cells, forming coral-like molecular bubbles and clusters, then linking antennae to form larger groups. The picture brought to mind the Von Neumann self-replicating robots he had heard Benson talk about just before his death.

As he thought of the unprecedented rate of positive-decision traffic which had impressed him, the calm air carried door bangs and laughter to Nora from the surrounding barracks. A guard-dog whimpered, clattering weapons and boots and mixed curses rose up to her as perimeter sentries changed duty. In the vehicle park, she could just see the big olive-green nose of one of the last 20-ton *Scammell* recovery lorries in UDR service, its vintage *Rolls Royce* engine wailing like a last lament from a vanishing world.

She wiped the clammy rifle-grip with a tissue, and sipped potent coffee from a small flask. The man deep in thought at the wire pressed upon her thoughts. He certainly wasn't a half-drunk who had wandered from the celebrations to sober up. He was history and personality, barbed wire and memories that were not hers, yet the shape of his thoughts were an almost perceptible pressure in her head as if they were magnetically induced. She had an idea that human beings were forever nattering to one another in such a manner which ignored life and death, even one head from another. This was a cellular chat that could sometimes be tuned, refined, communicated with, and messages and greetings left and only received generations later, perhaps even before some were even born. She felt the psychic pressure of a lot of minds working on a single problem. Thoughts became to her swarming bees dedicated to unceasing creation of cartoon-processing, video-frame refining, editing, selecting; they were forever engaged in test-runs, rehearsals, and developments.

Who was this man with such concentration in his brow?

The cross-hairs of the sight met his face. The man turned, touched the rusted security-fence wire like a mournful prisoner, and looked down to where hastily-laid concrete strips met the fresh earth of the EuroDump.

He was nobody.

Nora's inner chat had decided.

And Marshall was covered more effectively than either himself or assassin would ever know.

She switched her view to the barrack-square. Two *Foden* 3-tonners lurched unsteadily through the main gate with a returning squad of new recruits in training. The men were so exhausted they could hardly release the tailboard and jump out holding their weapons. The first truck had acquired a cracked sump, and with a seized gearbox, it crawled to a stop, bleeding thick transmission oil over an irate sergeant-major's swept paving in front of the white-rope fence and red fire-buckets of the Battalion Orderly Office. The second 3-tonner towed a burnt-out green-and-black *Land Rover*, whose scorched windscreen was a opaque web of shattered Triplex. A team of UDR medics rushed two stretcher-cases, one screaming like a torched demon, to the temporary buildings of the Field Hospital. She didn't know what had happened, but if this was peace, it didn't look or sound like it.

Must have been a riot, or demonstration somewhere, she thought, as she switched her electronic eyes to the southwest, and the nose of the 8-inch-long original *WerBell* helical silencer attached to the barrel moved with her steady gaze. The greenish-orange glow of the scope showed a noisy cavalcade moving to and fro through Tent City, and crowds starting to line the airstrip. But Fields was as yet nowhere in sight. She knew there was a possibility that he would leave hospital for this occasion, but judging by the exotic U.S. Special Forces ammunition she had chosen,

Nora was after the *Black Mountain Bird.* If Fields was in it, then all well and good.

To most minds, the *Steyr's* superb accuracy would be the tactical key to the situation. But given ammunition development since the beginning of the 1990s, the accuracy of such weapons and the range-skill of the user were not nearly so important as semiautomatic action (rarely available, if at all, on previous sniper rifles), and also silenced rounds, each with the punch of five grenades. The tips of her 9 mm high-explosive M19 rounds were made of depleted uranium which could crack and penetrate an inch of 45-degree sloped conventional (pre-Chobam) armour-plate at 800 metres. If a fusillade of just two or three of these merely whispering flashless missiles hit anything within 10 to 15 feet of any target, then anything less than light tank armour in the immediate vicinity, would be torn apart by a terrible something which would appear to have come from nowhere.

As if with such thoughts in mind, the stopped 3-tonner inside the wire gave an irate screech from a locked back-axle as the *Scammell* roared into life and towed it off in the direction of the Base Workshop. A *Land Rover* swung from beneath a noisy *Wessex,* which rose unsteadily off the helicopter pad by the UDR Base Hospital. As he looked to and from the glowing EuroDump to the base, Marshall felt that the familiar world he knew and worked in, the world of Intelligence management and complex investigation, the daily workload of military and police and government liaison, that potent experience called *reality* was gradually being replaced. As a primary universe, eventually *reality* would wear thin, like the *Scammell* truck, the *Matador* generators, and the *Wessex,* shot through with malfunctions of time, and be eventually confined to some cosmic potting-shed like a pair of old shoes, to be used for gardening on fine days only.

He shuddered, and intent on a stiff nightcap, walked straight back into the circle of laser light.

She also shook her head. For the first time in her life she found concentration difficult. She knew she had been infected. A colonising virus was now within her. Though she could detect it like a tumour of the mind, the growth felt quite benign, even friendly. By its very nature, Entertainment colonisation could never have anything to do with the vicious threats, the torture and violence and sadistic coercing of old analogue politics. Like reported UFO experiences, all the influence asked a contactee to do was look at the light. All an Entertainment State citizen had to do was to gaze for several hours at a screen or a stage which showed countless half-forms posing as authentic inspirations.

236

She imagined the Entertainment-virus was an ever-opening series of computerlike simulations of mental journeys which induced a steadily increasing anaesthetizing of individual will. The thought of something entirely alien working and developing within her mental processes was chilling. She thought such things would come with bug-eyes, and green tentacles. This was certainly different. Soon, she could well become a piece of an n-dimensional Shopping Channel, harnessed to some great switching network of Stars which would reduce all her responses to mental *muzak*.

The power of the appeal was the slippery slope of its pleasure. She was used to resisting pain and fear. She could only stop by an exhausting effort of will what was an enjoyable hypnosis whilst the virus ate up the assumption-chains of the world like a cabbage-caterpillar, making even the cherished concept of the *concrete* yielding. Already the world around her seemed more uncertain by the day, as if she could almost put a fist through a wall. Entertainment replaced whole constellations of questions: why did anything work? Because Di did it. Or Elvis thought it. Or Elton wanted it. What was a malfunction? Not due to weights and measures, or friction or wear, but some Star didn't like it. This was Entertainment Causation. But perhaps all systems of the world worked like that in the first place. Was this Fields right? Were the Primordial Bubble, the Big Bang, and the Cosmic BioSoup really intellectual Marx Brothers *shows* in different cultural disguise? And with that thought, for a brief moment in advertising-time, Nora didn't know whether she was an anarchist, a Catholic, or even a Fieldsian.

She bent to her target-watching, hoping that at least her weapon had not become affected by such questions.

After Marshall had left him in hospital, only partly conscious of the passage of several days, Fields had stayed prostrate, staring at the ceiling, with hardly a thought in his head. In his dreams, Belfast became the days and nights of an alchemical city in which he lay wounded, ready to be finished off by a face which still would not let him go. He supposed that he was having what the stick-folk would call a breakdown. But over the days of rest, his only real friends, his thoughts, crept back, a stream of mental activity which had never failed him, and was completely allied to his nature. Today, though his mind was with the Inauguration, he could not attend. He felt he was near a pyramid-region of almost-death. He was now so vulnerable even a toy gun would blow him away. From Oswald's humble mail-order rifle down the scale of piss-poor rifles to a complete pantomime rifle, anything would be sufficient. She had so cut him up, even a thought could blow him away.

To Fields' mind, only when a man was completely convinced that he had almost ceased to exist, was he justified in switching on the television.

His hand moved towards the remote-control in that ultimate twentieth-century consumer-moment called switching on.

Click.

A satellite channel was continuously running the Inauguration. He livened up a little when he saw many voodoo-masks of EuroTime gathered in the marquee. He decided that the Famous Faces, the business men, the soldiers, and especially the big-time criminals and 'grey-area' priests; to him, they all were unlicensed traders of different specialities. They were buyers and sellers of different levels of both shadow and substance; their business, as always, thought Fields, was really about just how stable the world was *allowed* to be.

The solidity quota, he supposed, looking at the throng, was a semi-intellectualised trade agreement, like internationally agreed restrictions of diamond mining, 'solidity' being merely an artificial market commodity, like silver or gold. He supposed that there were varying amounts of 'solidity' about in every Age; its mining, production, licensing, distribution and sanction were matters for endless and delicate negotiations, as a Papuan grandmother would guide the young in an ancient art of communication without radio, drum, smoke, or flag. Watching the coming and going on the screen, the questions became almost tangible to him: where were the limits of Mind and Matter to be set against this background of sulphurous cultural fault-lines which spread way back through Europe and Time and the Sea?

He was coming out of shock. The imp-thoughts were back, pouring unstoppable into the empty vault of his brain. Hot coffee was served by Elmon, somewhat downcast once more on seeing his master's new-found energy. Glad to be getting back his mental strengths again, Fields watched the television show a beaming John Carlton twisting a model of the *Black Mountain Bird* in the air before a trio of American men with whom he had previously had dinner, and who looked as if they were straight out of *Godfather III*.

"What is with this aeroplane, Carlton? It looks like Coney Island on a bad day."

"It's one of the most amazing things ever built."

"Will it fly?"

238

"Will it make money?"

"Will it make next week?" (laughter)

"Looks like Chinese lanterns and chopsticks to me."

"Are you sure this is the revolution?"

"It don't look like no goddam revolution I ever seen."

"The only revolution you ever seen is when they wallpapered that whorehouse on Marla Street." (louder laughter)

"Well at least those girls knew what they were doing. And where's the fucking wings, for Christ's sake?"

Carlton beamed again.

"She'll fly."

"No shit, John?"

Watching the changing weave of faces and interviews on the screen, Fields supposed any respectable weeping Virgin living in rocks in Cróg Patrick had to have her own protections against such people, and indeed his good self. She was perfectly entitled to mount a reality carve-up whose confusions and blindness were an essential part of her diversionary camouflage, a thought-cover as natural as the zebra's stripes. Before she could weep again (for whatever private reason of her own), there would have to be a reality shareholders' meeting, just like the one he was watching on the screen. The families and guardians and rationalist-magi and priests and scientists would have to decide on the territorial divisions of different degrees of allowability, rather like mafiosi in a spaghetti-house, or dogs at a barbecue, scenting their particular domains of allowability.

Watching a beautiful female Face interviewing a top NASA scientist, he supposed *mind* had its own equivalent to the massage-parlour, whorehouse, or string of Chinese restaurants and late-night grocery stores; and woe to those who did not pay the right amount of protection-money in terms of prayers, wishes, desires, or even part of their soul signed in blood. Tariffs and barriers regarding the sale and distribution of belief-stuff operated in as basic and vicious a market place as that for cabbages, sex, weapons, or even perhaps love.

Love? He blushed, and was thankful that no-one was in the room.

He turned off the TV, turned its face to the wall, and commenced reading his beloved *Tristram Shandy*.

As Fields buried himself in the doings of Uncle Toby, back in the marquee, Marshall glimpsed the rheumy eyes of Father O'Connor as he listened to yet another glamorous female Face spouting half-digested

239

bits of Fieldsian theory for all she was worth

"Christianity is locked you know, static you know. It does not have a developing mythology. It has lost its theological mobility."

Father O'Connor was a head-cocked listener, somewhat tired these days of worldly illustrations. He felt half-dead with compromise, and bored off his arse with the world's excuses, the world's great tree alive with infinite twittering vanities, and of late, he was fed up to the back teeth with Entertainments.

"I beg your pardon?"

"Why on earth did you get rid of the fairies?"

"Why on Earth did I get rid of what?"

"They kept Heaven and Earth mobile."

"They kept Heaven and Earth what?"

"Like the Greek pantheon. They were an intermediate control, a third grid to control the flow of imagination into substance and back again."

"Good lord. Too clever by a half. Do you play tennis?"

"Do you have the higher disturbance?"

"Good Lord. What's that?"

Marshall smiled. The famous *third grid* and the *higher disturbance* were still good value.

Fields, now shaving in the bathroom mirror, decided that the launch of Entertainment State was the launch of a stock-exchange of Belief in which a decision would be taken not only as to whether such things as the *Black Mountain Bird* would be allowed to fly or not to fly, but by *how much*. To him, the very principles behind designs, engines, and electronics were part-functions of this fuzzy black market in which weeping virgins were closer than was ever thought to the laws of thermodynamics. The working out of this solidity-quota was not only the connection between the two warring religious communities, it was the connection to the outer shell of world: housing, prices, wages, all stuff sold on the top of the counter whilst the hearts always yearned for the forbidden food at the back of the store.

And just when the solidity-quotas had been allotted, and all was calm in the reality marketplace once again, a child would twist a one-inch metal bar under impossibly severe laboratory conditions, and the whole damn market-trading carve-up would have to begin again. Virgins would weep, and Joyce and Ben, and Mr. Mellow would appear again with new messages, and again disappear like the figures of a cuckoo-clock. Reality-control was forever like trying to keep a dozen well-fed healthy young chimpanzees under a blanket in good quiet order, reading

240

the score of Verdi's *Requiem Mass*. Try it, and you finished up with more than egg on your face.

Buxom starlets beamed at the cameras as Fields shaved, Faces gave interviews, and the world looked and listened, Marshall circulated, hearing new metaphors being minted like Christmas fairy-lights on a Taiwanese production line: *architechtonics* of Entertainment Concept; *Subliminal* Entertainment Design; *Virtual*, and *Total* Entertainment. This latter included the wrapping of mountain-sides with silver foil, and the taking into outer space of 100-mile long squares of reflecting polythene, to make images from the very heavens themselves, with Famous Face's heads (and other bits) as big as the moon in the night sky. The new sky-gods could possibly appear courtesy of Rupert Murdoch, the desperate corporations, and the redundant robot-toys left over from the Strategic Defence Initiative and the Mirror Fusion project.

But apart from such media-madness, Marshall noted that to most here, Entertainment State was still not much more than a mere set of Pavlovian consumer-salivation equations which were amusing to play with, but meant little else. Such simple ideas as a little luxury, money, excitement, glamour, interesting work provided by the technical support base: why hadn't anyone thought of it before? As was the way with men and power, Marshall could detect that around him there was now some puny attempt at rescaling Fields' ideas. Everybody it seemed, had now thought of Entertainment State. It was a perfectly simple and rational sociopolitical move for the contemporary world to make. Fields' concepts, stripped of the dodgy metaphysics, were of such a simple dimension that even civil-servants and academics from provincial universities thought they could have produced them at a pinch. If experience was a language, then it was now obvious to even the most dimwitted, that earth, sea, and ozone layer were pregnant with the warnings and disasters of five decades of Rationalised benefits to Mankind. Entertainment, on the other hand, was still a comparatively innocent activity. Here was an intact, most modern, and very Green New Creation Myth ready and waiting for action. For troubled and fading Church, Technology, Science, Marshall supposed, read now The Myth of the Successful Entertainer.

As the once-more miserable Elmon laid out Fields' clothes, his master now switched on again (he was getting the TV bug, Elmon noted, with just a little glee), and watched once more the American trio, who were harassing Carlton again, or perhaps it was the other way around.

"Godammit, Carlton, what do you want?"

"Money." (loud laughter)

241

"You surprise me. We came here to ask YOU." (louder laughter)

"No good asking me. My interest rates are too high." (laughter declines)

"Wait till you see ours! (laughter up again) No, serious - who is the fat guy?"

"He makes money."

(voice from the back) "Maybe he should make a health farm now and then."

"We're trying to get him there."

"Because if he gets any bigger he's going to die before his next pizza-order."

"Where'd you get him from, boy?"

(voice from assembly) "Hell!"

"Well he's got plenty of blood to sign his cheques with."

"That's not blood, that's Jello!"

"Carlton, how much do you want, you bastard!"

"About two-hundred and fifty million." (total silence)

"Two hundred and fifty million? Shit, the fat boy'll eat that in two weeks! (loud laughter) You sure you don't want the Empire State full of corn-beef and crackers?"

But Marshall, listening to all this, knew that like all men only a decade or so away from their last street fight, they had already made their quick decisions; from this moment he guessed, oil, chemicals, minerals, gold and silver all began to move towards Entertainment State. There was no democracy, no staff, no meetings, no warnings, qualifications, no timid hesitancy, just the searing knowledge that the Chiefs knew that Carlton knew what would happen if he cocked it all up. The sheer speed of their decision was their very invisibility. Any culture or political philosophy which could not match this decision speed did not stand a Darwinian chance. Carlton's stylized image and presence were mere elements in a purchased day. He was obviously thought of as pure quality shopping, and was being nicely roasted with a loving skill, flavoured and slowly cooked, prime meat for the next smasheroo, and nobody could make smasheroos like the group of Chiefs now patting him on the back. And in the Chief's eyes, Entertainment State was going to be the biggest smasheroo of all time.

Marshall saw Father O'Connor look quizzically at the full-size scale model of the *Black Mountain Bird,* revolving on a plinth in the middle of the marquee, and surrounded by bikini lovelies as if it were in the annual Boat Show in Ulster Hall.

The Famous Faces had long christened her a 'Starchild', being a thing ready to rely not on mechanism, but on the levitating power of a witching glitterati, whose hands now stretched out as if in supplication to a deity. Over the previous weeks, twisting and turning on her stable pillar of thrust, the *Black Mountain Bird* did indeed seem to want to break free of any association of metal, petrochemicals, rubber, and plastic. She was a great preening dragonfly in the early cool of the day before seeking shelter from hot rocks and sand. Some saw a face in every stone and blade and leaf of green which watched her as if she were a thing breaking from a chrysalis and not part of any human endeavour. She wobbled, nodded, preened, shook as if to dry her wings, then bowed gently to the ground to be fussed over by uniformed acolytes to cheers from the ever-present Famous Faces. She was often splashed from the now ever-present bottles of *Evian* in what *New Balls Magazine* called 'an act of unpolluted blessing to a flying queen of new Entertainment Faith'.

But although the 150-strong work-force was carefully divided between Catholic and Protestant, the leaders of both sides of the religious divide had grown increasingly uncomfortable. Many claimed that what was rising up was not only Nature's Aeroplane, but Nature's State. Father O'Connor had already described the attachment of Entertainment State to this aeroplane as 'healthy but disturbing'. Other more radical clerics, both Catholic and Protestant, were more definite about what kind of sacrilegious fluids flowed through the veins of the *Black Mountain Bird*. Some went so far as to say that the cheeky little devilish nymph of an aircraft who danced in the dawn so unashamedly might have the nerve to forget what the rules were. And that, thought Marshall, was the most devastating religio-political challenge he could think of.

Fields changed channels as in the next room, the muttering Elmon furtively stowed away his copy of *Hebrew Babes*, and took orders to bring in the exercise weights. Fields lifted steadily for a quarter-hour before leaping to a bathroom mirror to flex his arm like a secretive sixteen-year-old to see if any possible new tee-shirt muscle might just show in the summer weather.

He looked hard at the mirror.

The summer was not yet over. Still time to find Laura Steadman. Haircut. New contact lenses. Hard gym early every morning. Where *was* Laura Steadman? New diets. Health farm. And no television. He could make it. Even have a cosmetic tuck in his threble-chin.

He must get advice. They could do miracles for the over-forties these days.

He put down his weights. The TV bug was getting to him.

Change channels.

The Inauguration again.

He was again delighted with the Entertainment Reactor he had
constructed. There were even some rare collector's items gathered in
the Marquee, men and women whose roots stretched way back to the
European Coal and Steel Community, the Berlin Airlift, and the Suez
Crisis. One or two stooped specimens of the rarest of the rare could
even remember chimneys belching human smoke and millions of corpses
with waists as thick as fingers being shovelled and sluiced from trucks
into quicklime pits, and they were the lucky ones. Whether these now
haggard men Fields saw had been inside or outside the wire, nobody had
ever been able to say with certainty. In any case, there existed now those
extraordinary creatures who said that none of that business ever really
happened. In front of him was a whole economy of just such belief-
adjustment, though fortunately in quite a different area.

Change channels.

The weather forecast. This was always one of his favourite pieces
of intellectual holocaust. There was the usual puff-sleeved gnome-woman
straight from a 1950s *Currys* boxed game. With a face a little like Laura
Steadman, she was pushing around absurd pieces of multicoloured
playpen counters to represent some lunatic scheme of sunshine and
showers. As a connoisseur of junk culture, Fields loved the weather
forecast. It was the very essence of the nonevent which used massive
and expensive technologies to mount its utter vacuity.
Change channels.
Now the Chief Clerk. Blinking behind his glasses. Another man-
robot high on Fields list of systems-jokes. Some of the best brains of the
century in electronic technology to mount the politjunk essence of the
wey-faced Chief Clerk. What was the garden-gnome saying tonight?
Something had gone up. Something else had come down. There had been
a meeting. Everything would be alright when it all bottomed-out. Fields
remembered the Green Shoots, the Feel-Good Factor, and the traffic
cones; he also remembered the worst mind in British politics since Neville
Chamberlain.

Change channels.

What? Now flames, upturned cars on a some woebegone British
housing estate long descended to the level of a rubbish dump outside

244

Rio. What? Could this be? Some wonderful holy magical beings back in the old curiosity shop had the cheek to go on a riot to try and set fire (said a girl who looked like a twelve-year-old Laura Steadman) to the 'entire fucking whoredom.' He held his sides as the tribal manikins were wheeled on. Even Elmon laughed as he came in to clear the empty cups and plates. It was too much affluence, said an Assistant to the Chief Clerk; it was too much poverty, said a socialist; it was too much sin, said a Bishop; it was too much white male hetero-bonding, said a black feminist academic from a polytechnic which had just had the cheek to call itself a university.

Great entertainment, thought Fields. The world as Joke City. Such cultural candyfloss was become the entire end-product of the culture. The only thing that could be said for a society which could not even make a decent cheap car, was that its products were more amusing than ships, steel mills, and even great steaming engines which would run unfailingly for scores of years to the ends of the universe and back. To Fields, hard goods and hard experiences were fading analogue forms, as if a vicious mental weather had descended upon the roots of consciousness itself, scraping and tearing away any solidity until the only thing that was left was pure software of image-decay. Software folk. Image ideas. Media intellects. Trash-chatter as universal building stuff. Like the almost fleshless Chief Clerk and the doll's-house weather forecast, here at the Inauguration were ghost-folk, systems-doodles you could almost put a fist through, cell-culture rehearsals for God-only-knew what final forms of genetically accelerated super-trash Nature herself had in mind for the next series of games. A Greater Dodo twenty feet high with eyesight problems perhaps; or an original fly, with twenty sets of wings, fourteen sets of bulging eyes and no mouth; to disintegrate in agony before midnight because of the lapse of celestial memory. Great holographic TV were the Roman games of God, he thought; like the Creator, humanity had discovered trash-systems with a vengeance.

Such good cursing always raises the spirit. But getting up, he tipped over a glass of water on his small bedside table, and Elmon threw a temper. Sometimes Fields thought that he himself was not meant for this world. Perhaps he should just wear a dressing gown and stand quietly tranquillised all day somewhere so as not to be a danger to himself and others.

Change channels again.

Now he gazed upon a 'presenter' who looked as if he were about to open a caseful of brushes before the door of a semidetached.

'Tonight's programme will consider the question of just how these dozens of newly independent states will handle the thousands of nuclear weapons of various types virtually abandoned on their territory by a Moscow administration which is incapable of extracting such weaponry.'

Now, a little more weight training before having rest before dinner.

Ten, push, breathe. Eight, push, breathe.

What?

The face of Laura Steadman. On the screen. In some film. Driving a car. What? Flicker, flicker. She was gone. Where? He must phone the TV station. What TV station? She was lost in a hundred channels! Only just realising that he had no telephone anyway, to the everlasting memory of a maternity ward directly below him, he dropped his weights onto the floor from a height directly above his head.

Heart beating. Rest. Sip of water. This was extraordinary. The entire information system was now contaminated with her. Just like Troilus, all shapes on the horizon were now become Cressida. Rest. Sip.

Change channels. Change channels again. And again.

An African Party Political Broadcast from the potty BBC. Must have had fewer viewers than the small print of a Matrix Churchill contract. Still, the feathers and the drums were a change from the Bath by-election.

Oh, look at that! He could get two channels at once. One big, one small. And times, dates, programmes, in further small squares on the main picture.

Now a motorway protest. Some ringed-nosed ones were being hauled down from a makeshift dwelling at the top of a great oak by the Falstaffs in blue. His patriotic sense was touched by wagging beards, floppy sandals, designer-torn jeans, and even designer-accents. Great Entertainment. He would never live anywhere else but England, and in such moments as these, he could forgive the worst food in the world, and even the donkey Leaders. These middle-England tree-games were modern wonders of the world, as was the quaint pre-electric arts culture, *Any Questions?* and taking a thousand years to put café-tables on the pavements. At that rate, he thought, *bidets* and intellectuals were a long way off. He marvelled again as he saw countless pre-steam cultural casualties firmly pulled down, assisted back on their feet, and even politely handed back their fallen guitars by the bored Falstaffs. Fields marvelled. Only the English could think of launching a revolution from a Wendy-house up in a tree, bless their boiled turnips. And just look now: lots of pony-tailed snappers underneath to record faithfully the designer-suffering for the Supplements. Apparently, even suburban guerilas were still worth at least a coffee-table illustration or two, or even a Hampstead chintz-novel. He fancied even the violated oak was laughing, and he was sad he was not up there with the *didgeridoo* folk; he wanted to climb the tree and shake a teddy-bear at the Falstaffs below, to show the world that England was alive and well, and mercifully as daft as ever it was. But he feared for the nation he was prepared to die for. It couldn't pick at its Edwardian gut forever.

Flick, flicker, flick!

But try as he could, he still could not get those gorgeous Channel 4 black lesbians Elmon raved on about. Now where were they...

He was working up quite an enthusiasm for channel surfing. He felt nostalgia for a large box of *MarziPig SnackPaks* he saw being thrown out the back of an ancient truck in Croatia and being fought for by a crowd of at least two hundred who looked as if they had just stepped out of a Breughel landscape. Cameras panned to three rusty Russian T55 tanks parked nearby. They had M48 *Patton* muzzle-brakes, odd Czech tracks, French aerial-mounts, Italian smoke-dischargers, and even a couple of ancient *Panther* road-wheels, Fields noted, which some heroic village workshop must have strained mind and muscle to fit. In one of these grey-scale vehicles, he gazed at over *fifty* years of semi-illegal exports, and that was only on the outside of the vehicles. The tanks were draped with giggling pantomime soldiery, one with a Chinese pistol, and another whose equipment was South African, Israeli, and British. One soldier played a few bars on a gleaming piano-accordion which sounded vaguely familiar before the scene was cut to a frying-pan full of a popular brand of pork sausages sizzling before a slavering three-TV two-car British family.

Flick.

No.

A concert orchestra in full cry. No. Please. Not *The Countess Maritza*.

And Laura Steadman to the life, in a long white dress at the side of the conductor.

'sag ja, mein liebe, sag ja...'

Fields feared for his sanity. Was Laura Steadman a BUAC? This idea was still there, buried under the a toad-in-the-rock impossibility made almost-inconceivable by a morass of social rationalisations structured for the quarter-brilliant by the half-dead. There were no such things as BUACs. But that was what the Chief Clerk would say. A great sadness flooded Fields, sapping his will and last strengths. Death was near again. But he must not let the Chief Clerk win. Despair flooded his weakened mind and body. It was too late. The ground-flies had probably won, their odious chemicals coursed through his mind and body, the billion cries of a billion tested animals sapping his strength and vision. They had beaten him. Not only had he failed to find Laura Steadman, but his great structure of Entertainment Impossibilities had failed, buried under measureless dead advertisement-rubble of the century. The stick-folk had won, and somewhere in his luggage Fields remembered he had his father's .45 *Smith & Wesson*, which dated from an age when on certain rare and proper occasions, gentlemen had to do what gentlemen were expected to do.

But not yet.

Flicker, flicker, flicker, flick!

IV

Entertainment Fission

It is time! Blazing fireworks cracked and burst over the heads of the hundreds who poured out from the marquee to see a great lanterned river of Entertainment knights, ladies, and their retainers, all now moving in procession towards the hangars of *The Most Unusual Aeroplane Company*. Firework moons and suns burst in the early twilight, and flanked by back-flipping clowns, men on stilts, animal-costumes, and great nodding papier-mache heads of cartoon animals, came a snaking column of the cartoon characters of the Entertainment world. They came down through the main avenue through Tent City towards the flying area, only a single strand of rope barrier separating the Famous Faces from adoring faceless thousands held back in the anonymous murk beyond the glistening spheres of the *Black Mountain Bird*.

Here was a stream pouring from some great Child's Book of Wonders. Famous cowboys, flyers, lovers, enchantresses, spacemen, waved to the crowd. Here were faces so deeply embedded in the flickering mind of nearly one hundred years, they had long ago gone quite beyond the great white bearded God in the sky of childhood. But something struck a deep professional chord without Marshall. For a moment, like a drowning man, he fought off the smiling rainbow-octopus that was strangling his brain, and realised that he had not seen Barsby and Annie for nearly half an hour.

He punched codes into his mobile.

It was not working.

But he could do nothing. He had been silly enough to get trapped by an immovable mass of excitement and expectancy, and now it was as if he were set in concrete. Arc-lights now illuminated the nonstop activity around *The Most Unusual Aeroplane Company's* test-sheds. The prototype *Black Mountain Bird* hummed with electrical and mechanical life as her circuits were tested and engines warmed-up on the apron outside the air-conditioned hangar. The strange-looking aeroplane was now ringed by legends which were the focus of intense loving attentions of far-flung ranks stretching to the outer rim of the centre of intense light.

Entertainment Enterprises Unlimited had been very busy. Susan Macintosh, a Very Famous Face Indeed, had just arrived in state from America, and as a finale to this Inauguration of Entertainment State, a kind of mini-coronation had been organised. It had been planned that Fields and Susan would be passengers in the *Black Mountain Bird;* whilst the machine was hovering on her sixteen computer-managed jets before the eyes of practically the entire planet, the pair would open the hatches of the two passenger-spheres. Illuminated by spectacular lasers, then would then put out their heads and shoulders, and wave to the assembled Entertainment tribes. With Fields in hospital, his place had been taken by David Stein, a planetary Film Face.

At 1934 hours Greenwich Mean Time, Susan and David climbed into the aircraft. Seconds later, as hundreds of multicoloured lasers were switched on, the machine roared straight up into the damp early evening air as if hoisted by the circular roar of thousands.

Marshall desperately checked his mobile again.

It was not working.

Twenty miles away, Fields was still clicking his remote as Susan and David waved to applauding thousands. Fields had certainly caught the bug. Flick. Muslims. Flick again. The channels became indistinguishable from his thoughts. Radiation. Laura Steadman. What? Breughel's *The Beggars*. Des O'Connor. Now he knew what a true Entertainment Citizen felt like. What programme? Flicker, flick. *GazzaMugs* being advertised again. Cézanne's *Self Portrait* (which looked curiously like himself). Flick, flicker again. What frequency? Now he could not tell whether he was watching his mind, or the screen. What channel? A 15th century Flemish miniature depicting Charlemagne and his Court. Now the woebegone Chief Clerk again. There had been another meeting. The Junk Nirvana. What station? *Station?* What *frequency?* They had all long disappeared. He realised he might as well have been thinking about the Jitterbug, the Festival of Britain, The Concordat of Worms, or even the Magna Carta. Click. Where was the fabled pornography? Beautifully rampant tits would demolish the traffic-cone man. Which channel? He must ask Elmon. But there were now hardly such things as channels, programmes, even less *broadcasts*. There was just a great everything become a *MarziPig SnackPak*.

And he hadn't even tried the smart-card, the coin-option, and the possibilities of the two illegal decoders; but what was this? Flick, and *this* TV became a computer with a modem. Fields sat down and sipped a little water. He now had the world's libraries on-line through *Internet.* He stared down at his QWERTY pad. He could now call up a commentary on the bad text of *Hamlet* simultaneously with (according to Elmon), a half-hour film of four young nymphs in bed together with a large and very happy Alsatian dog. God only knew what the coming *interactive* channels would do further for his sense of Literature and History.

Red light.

Information-burn.

Laura Steadman a Body of Unadulterated Advertising Concentrate?

Advertising overload.

Shut down all primary systems!

He sprang from the bed, picked up the television, and was about to fling it straight through the plate-glass window to give the maternity ward below yet another eternal memory, when Elmon rushed in, grabbed the remote, and pointed at the screen.

"Mr. Fields, she's up!"

Fields could not believe his eyes and ears. If Elmon was *running,* and *shouting,* somebody had either stolen his choice porn collection, or a world war had been declared.

But there was Elmon, with the snatched remote shaking in his hand like Fields supposed his penis did before the centre-spread of *Hebrew Babes.*

The *Black Mountain Bird* appeared. In the air. What was Elmon screaming about?

There was no sound of the aircraft's motors.

Elmon screamed. Fields sat heavily on the bed.

The Entertainment Pile had gone critical.

The miracle had occurred at precisely 1937 hours, GMT, 55-year-old Stan Rotman was at the controls, with his copilot James Ferris, a relative youngster at the age of 39. An ex-BOAC Flight Captain, Rotman could just remember the days of war-surplus canvas bucket-seats, draughty unpressurised cockpits, and a last generation of aeroplanes such as the *Bristol Britannia, Avro York,* or *Short Sunderland;* these were stately-slow and friendly beasts from a grass-runway and Empire-seaway Age as lost as Arthur's Merlin. This evening, for some reason, names equally gone with a Guinevere-England of just-yesterday sang in Stan Rotman's head: *Handley Page Hastings, Vickers Viscount;* these were almost steam-age craft which could very possibly be crash-glided onto pastures green with thirty quaking passengers shaken but alive, the only real loss perhaps a good vintage spread alas on real- silk laps and creased trousers with wide turn-ups. And hardly any high-tech instabilities in them. And no suspicious loans or tricky equipment deals with continental conglomerates whose Head Office in Marseille could never be located. And certainly no pressures, temperatures, and strains reaching into what Fields would probably call advertising regions; these being areas where the white-faced experts crossed their fingers and changed their jobs before any scapegoats were hunted, or excuses were made.

Both Stan Rotman and James Ferris had been close to miracles. No man who handles tons of metal moving at high velocities at great heights under the moon and stars above the weathered turbulence of Earth has not heard of things only muttered about amongst pilots whose sharp eyes look into infinity and change the subject as smoothly as any perfectly controlled landing. As Fields might have said, a mind has to stop somewhere, stake out its territory, live out its limitations and hope for no trouble from the neighbours who may inhabit some of the many mansions. Neither do they want bother from those who were rumoured to live on other islands just beyond the mental horizon.

Some pilots stop, draw a magic circle around themselves and their machine, and decide on what level of a theory of descriptions they wish to perch in order to get some sleep at night. They decide that when they go through all their cockpit checks, that they are not going to fly many surreal slices of a history of ideas which was in itself a flying mess of highly respectable technological risks. They do not like to think that their craft is a cat's tail trailing tin-cans full of a history of cock-ups, lucky breakthroughs, and rigged assumptions, some of which made Fields idea of advertising concentrate look positively honest. They like to think they are flying a MK IV (lengthened) version as stated by textbook and manual, with recently reconditioned engines, new American fuel-pumps, and a *Fortran* radio compass linked to a *Marsden* MK XVI integrating accelerometer with improved data-transmission links.

The largely unrecorded history of battery-development and electrical generators throughout the Century would be too much to bear as a flight crew headed for New York with 450 children, women, and men on board. Full of contradictions, half-guesses long ago, it would not settle down easily in the cool pilot brain, would this history of frustrated men and dark alleys, grease and smells and first small loans and investments in and for mysteries which left glazed the eyes of the first technological entrepreneurs. Neither cool pilots nor even good modern graduates of electrical engineering know much of the first guessed-windings of equally guessed crude drawn-wire densities, strengths, and diameters. Every man and every vehicle and every journey has to take care of a deception-allowance, an unreality quota without which, like a Fields BUAC, all would split and shatter as would a high building so rigid it could not sway.

Camouflage. Things made to look difficult and complex, things made to look intellectually formidable, or even things made to look as daft as a brush, the miracle moves through the seams between flickering cultural cartoon-frames. The miraculous crawls through the camouflage gaps left by what has been swept under the carpets, cushions, test-sheds and laboratories and observatories of whatever advertising emporium or religious poodle-parlour happens to prevail at a particular time in the cartoon history of human kind. Men and women, of course, would have themselves attached to something far more dignified than a cartoon, a banana-skin, or the accidents and poverties of thought behind scintillating achievements, advances, progressions, or whatever claims for physical dominance have managed to fight their way forward with blooded brow from hissing snake-pits of thought. Miracles whisper on the night-winds to inspired madmen everywhere. In 1948, Shockley had to reintroduce impurities to make the first transistor work. In the circle around the *Black Mountain Bird* there were now impurities enough to make the wishes work, those little impulse hunter-gatherers who lived on the night-side of the ecology of belief.

Twenty-five seconds. Twenty-five seconds of an aeroplane staying up by itself, quiet silent, with all its power cut, was an impurity not all that easy to confirm, but it is still more than long enough to bring the anomaly into the respectable courts of proper debate. And too long, far too long to avoid technological notice of this little interrupting sprite of a event which just managed to get on stage before running off into wings as if it had got into the wrong play in the wrong theatre at the wrong time.

When Stan Rotman throttled back the vertical thrust stabilisers, thinking at was later presumed, to make a circuit, all sixteen cut out simultaneously. This left the *Black Mountain Bird* hanging in the early evening glow, a slightly puzzled looking insect, 500 feet above total astonishment and not a little spreading fear. Some later wrote of seeing an air of astonishment about the face of the machine, as if it were a bird which had stayed for ten well-photographed fantastic seconds too long in the late summer, and was anxious for the warmer air above the blue and white oceans of some equally fantastic southern compass. Twenty-five well-filmed seconds of silence in which all noise of the raging motors was gone, and there was nothing but the feel of a stiff damp breeze from the Black Mountain itself, which pulled at Marshall's jacket as he marvelled.

Here was Entertainment fission. Bang on time and target.

Fieldsian laws had entered the universe and nudged aside the whole and entire and proper field of causation. And though in the days of violent controversy that followed, there would be accusations of fraud, mendacity, and mass-deception of many a kidney, for the scores of thousands watchers it was the seeming sheer playfulness of the curious event that was the most shocking. The Universe was supposed to be a very serious affair whose truths were only available to those of serious and proper mien. The truths apparently, were only to be given to those who had gone through such perversities of torture and suffering they were almost all permanently deranged.

But the hour of the Fool had come. Here was the Universe showering such a profusion of miraculous goods free of charge, and goods moreover just about as daft as The European Song Contest. It was downright insulting, was this lack of the Profound that millions had died for. It was like some art critic finding somebody pissing against a wall in a carefully restored Rembrandt. Up in the evening sky before an astonished moon was a joke aeroplane worked by joke-forces of Entertainment State so powerful and so undeniable that the thing stayed up when its engines failed. Quite static up there at 500 feet she was, reflecting a last weak sunlight towards the city, over which rain-clouds were now gathering strength. And hundreds of Very Famous Faces Indeed below the unbelievable, upturned faces known to all the very planet, desperately trying to take in the utter absurdity of that thing religions proper call witness. And not single bill as yet in way of friction, losses, or guilt. And not even a single pennyworth of work-ethic. Mr. Toad had won more than a round. He had beaten the stick-folk, the Chief Clerk, and a whole lot of other traffic-cone and weather-forecast folk who would keep the world as a most unexceptional place, locked up by the tyranny of the mundane.

As many were to say later, the universe was not supposed to do this. The universe was supposed to play fair, and present its bills on time. There must always be someone or something to pay, if only the Devil. That alone made sense. In the days to follow, the serious philosophers of Courts, Enquiries, and Commissions would have grave difficulty with the idea of Nature being playful, a Nature being as wicked and childish in deception as human beings could be themselves, a Nature which listened, was alive, and put out its tongue at human beings not only behind their backs, but now it seemed, in front of them as well.

A fear aroused by sheer playfulness was not a common fear. Not a foul outer-space monster or a hypodermic-wielding Bosche psychopath, or even a humourless peasant-messiah dedicated to putting the world to rights, but a bouncing bunch-of-cherries of an aeroplane, suspended in clear sunlight, a bowl of post-technological fruit which did not come down for just twenty-five Entertainment seconds.

Upon the fifteenth second, as Fields and Elmon and over a hundred thousand others watched, the laser-lit Susan put her fair head out of the hatch on the roof of the starboard sphere, and David's broad shoulders appeared likewise to port. They both waved to the crowd.

Two miles away to the east, on the twentieth second, seeing a completely stationary floodlit target, Nora squeezed her trigger.

Upon the 22nd second, a sharp explosive report was heard from the North by many of the now thoroughly disturbed crowd. A windblown forest of Irish heads, quite familiar with the sound, turned. The heads turned back, and upon the 25th second, a great sighing breath welled from the Earth as Susan, David, and the *Black Mountain Bird* became a spreading arterial-red stain against the last western light reflecting laser, moon, and first starshine. The scarlet ball now expanded to a thing of billowing yellow and rolling jet-black streaks, sending metal, plastic, bone and searing streaks of fuel into the first heavy drops of rain.

As Fields said later, of a sudden, Jesus Christ and Isaac Newton, with their everlasting moral and gravitational bills (which Fields thought were a unity anyway) were back. What was left of the carcass of the *Black Mountain Bird* came down in six seconds from 500 feet, hitting the tarmac at 178 feet per second, translating calculation and miracle both to pillars of Old Testament flame. The crowd were now, like Fields himself, within seconds of reaching advertising overload. The sight of old Brian Murray approaching the flames and throwing away his crutches of twenty years into the conflagration did not improve matters, as did not the many distant sirens soon heard echoing from all inner and outer

255

horizons of Irish Time.

Fields fainted, but his hated stick-folk had been ready and waiting. An arm was bared and rubbed, and the leprous stuff from a billion animal-screams coursed through his veins as he gulped oxygen from a mask. As was pointed out later, he was perhaps the only king in History to have reigned for exactly twenty-five seconds.

By the now flaming airfield, as leg-irons, artificial limbs, wigs, spectacles, and even sets of false teeth and a stretcher or two cascaded into the flames, the crowd took to their heels over ruined projects, collapsed tents, panicking Faces, and many fires. But the situation could possibly have been contained if to the north, a tall building had not appeared to begin to walk completely by itself. It was not difficult after that, for an older form of advertising to reassert itself. The preacher's hour was come.

Entertainment State was a satanic contrivance.

It took two days and two nights to burn it all down.

Though at the time, it was thought Final Judgment had come, the walking building was no miracle. Nora, for once, had missed a microscopic shadow within the microscopic framework in which she moved. She might have born in mind that the Gestapo had only two hundred operatives throughout France; they let the indigenous mass, and pieces of silver do almost all else that was required. Nora had been betrayed by her own kind, and for similar temptations. The man who had given her the video of Fields had cracked. This meant that soon before the *Black Mountain Bird* had left the ground, pulling like a tightening but invisible noose about Fermanagh House was a killing-team. It was the spearhead of many covert agencies, whose names would make a modern European demonological list, and with approximately the same function as in 1300 AD.

Barsby and Annie had been summoned, but had been quite unable to raise Marshall. They stood back and watched as a plain-clothes SAS team calmly assembled two *Milan* rocket-launchers behind a wall in a nearby local builder's yard. Barsby sounded nervous as he spoke to the SAS commander.

"Aren't we going wait until she comes out?"

"Wait until she what?"

"Wouldn't she be at the top?"

"Yes. That's why we're blowing out the bottom."

Annie supposed they were right. If she was at the top, it would take them days to clear out every cupboard of 200 wrecked flats. When they finally cornered her, there would of course be a fire-fight, and it wouldn't take long for the world's cameras at the Inauguration, only three miles away, to be over here for another world-satellite grenade-throwing jamboree to end all jamborees.

This way it was over very quickly.

Barsby was nervous as he looked at the towering structure and its menacing tilt.

"But won't the-the b-building f-fall down?"

"Yes. It will. When it does, crawl into there."

He pointed to an upturned skip under which it was just possible to crawl.

"It's leaning already. It will fall in that wasteland to the north, or so we are told. So don't worry."

"But what about people who live around here?"

"There aren't many. And most of them are at the airfield. So it doesn't really matter."

Barsby and Annie, impressed by the immaculate logic, approached the skip.

A few minutes later, not seeing Nora's silent and flashless round, and ignoring the thumping crash of the *Black Mountain Bird* as if it were a local traffic accident, the *Milan* crews pressed their buttons, and two optically-guided wire-command HEAT missiles streaked towards the entrance of *Fermanagh House*. The first buried itself in the ground-floor lift-shaft, where its detonation sent blazing debris almost to the 20th floor, setting light to the entire structure. The second round ruptured the main structural spine, lifting the reinforced concrete like a toy. Four more rounds followed quickly, and within a minute, the entire building started to waltz like a drunk before collapsing. When a dirt-blackened Barsby and Annie emerged from their skip, Fermanagh House, like the *Black Mountain Bird,* was gone.

V

Accounts Of Creation

The *Criminal Investigation Sessions of the Air Crash Enquiry,* and the rapidly formed *Ecumenical Council Hearing Concerning Claimed Miraculous Events Within Entertainment State* were held in late September. They occupied identical rooms in the Crumlin Court, only separated by inches of Victorian lathe and plaster. Both sessions vied for Prime Time, and both managed to move major TV soaps down the listings ladder. Entertainment State may have suffered a blow in Belfast, but in most other places on the planet, it was thriving, with many upturned faces expected such a gypsy-event as had occurred at the EuroDump. Fields (now called the Miracle Man, and more adored than ever, especially with stage-props of hospital blanket, walking-stick and two lovely girls) took a triumphant world-tour with the twins, only returning to Belfast for the various Enquiries.

The world tuned in with sub-titles, instantaneous translations, and even deaf-and dumb fingers. Outside the Crumlin Court, amidst claims for more safeguards for the Right to Suffer, there were seething placard-chants and yet more claims and counterclaims for God, Fieldsian Forces, Entertainment, and some even for the Devil, who had rapidly been conjured up from that historical obscurity sophisticates had tried to vanish him to.

A famous magician appeared, noted for his psychic debunking shows. After trying to assure everyone that he knew how the twenty-five seconds were 'done' he went back to the mainland rather depressed, complete with his girl assistants in spangled tights, and a large van full of scaffold-poles, balloons, mirrors, and drapes. Famous scientists followed him with their equivalents to spangled tights and balloons sealed inside intimidating black boxes; they made frantic efforts to counter-ritualise the twenty-five seconds back into mundane time. But the scientists disappeared as rapidly as the magicians, muttering under their breath about ball-lightening, planetary warming, and things called sun-dogs. Those who were neither scientists nor magicians rained down countless accusations of bribery, fraud, and corruption on all and sundry. Given a month off by a strangely pleased Directrix, and aching for a roll-up at the back of the public seating at the *Air Crash Enquiry,* Marshall

258

noted that there was no explanation offered as to how an aeroplane could be held silently aloft without power for twenty-five seconds by sun dogs or ball-lightening, still less bribery and corruption.

Between massed ranks of television cameras and hot floods, the two investigations were phrenological maps of Western *sapiens*. Within their interweaving modulations of one another's advertising, analysis of the extraordinary twenty-five-seconds occurred within the split *cerebellum* of a modern techno-demonology. The deviant event was scanned through many overlapping metaphors: espionage, theology, biology, and advertising. Legal, journalistic, and scientific x-rays of mighty concentrations were expensively involved.

As with many historical miracles, there were those who missed out completely by being drunk, adjusting their loincloth, or wondering whether they had enough spare change to get some cat food without having to seek out a cash-dispenser. A few said they saw nothing at all. But there had been a miracle, according to many thousands of witnesses and the forms of the world's recording apparatus. Taken apart in many laboratories were film, video, and still-camera frames, some being split into hundredth-second sections, computer-analysed, and digitally mapped out fragme nt-by-fragme nt by some of the world's most advanced equipment.

Marshall was glad that conditions had now changed such that he could meet his friend again. He bought Fields dinner at the *Hanover*, and was glad to see that Mr. Toad was now his usual self again. They both laughingly agreed that Entertainment State was anything but dead, for the effort to prove and disprove involved almost the same level of organi sation, hum an ene rgy and techn ol ogy used to scan Sarah Ferguson's holiday arrangements, Mark Thatcher's business-deals, or Princess Diana's digital telephone frequencies.

Within a few weeks, what was termed locally as the M&M (miracle and murder) industry had nurtured complete subcultures. Lavishly produced coffee-table books and videos appeared, and throughout the world, the hovering perspex spheres of the doomed *Black Mountain Bird* vied with lush books on the mysterious corn-circles. The image of the spheres also appeared on flags, knickers, enamelled mugs, and engraved cigarette-lighters. The fabled twenty-five seconds even competed in attention with the almost-thoughts of porn-stars, the British upper classes, lisping thespians, media folk, and international prostitutes. But what else to do with it? As Fields said to his many admirers, you could do things with a Royal Family, you could even do things with a weeping Virgin, if only run a profitable café and garage near her grotto, but there isn't much you can do with a cosmic joke. Except laugh. And that would never do. The fickle and disturbing light-and-shadow claims for grainy truths would be put on the historical shelves as quickly as was decently possible, said the man himself. There they would be alongside other famous curiosities of advertising antiquity, such as pickled elves, the certificate verifying the senile dementia of Earnest Saunders, unicorn horns, pirate Di recordings, fragments of the True Cross, and that past king of the continuous-tone grotto of wonders, the Zapruda film of events once upon a time near the Dealey Plaza

Whilst to Fields it was a replay of 1300, to Marshall, with a few changes of dress, some anglicizations of surname, and updating of saloon-car model, both the *Air Crash Enquiry* and the *Ecumenical Hearing* reminded him of any post-1945 American Top Mob show-trial. A Famous Face listened earnestly to a Catholic priest, a tanned gangster courted a piece of faded showbiz, and a British stockbroker with illegal arms-dealing connections talked earnestly to a Police Commissioner. Given this setting, Neither Fields nor Marshall were surprised when they heard that Minister John Carlton had been chosen to head the *Air Crash Enquiry*. Carlton was smarting for revenge on the Security Services, almost accusing them of throwing poor Benson off the roof themselves to spite him. Although hundreds of compromising photographs were still circulating, a system working as a complete and alert unity had chosen wisely. John Carlton was the perfect filter. He would become a superbly functioning part of the implicit masking of the event. Not that he would do anything so crude as conceal anything. He would simply not see anything worth concealing. The whole complex of anomalous intention would be quite invisible to him. He would never wonder why in his life he had been over-promoted and over-praised but to meet this moment squarely, and form a road block whose brute strength was in inverse proportion to his intelligence. After he had properly activated the required schedules of denials, Marshall knew that Carlton would finally be cast aside, a quickly stiffening doll, quite empty of its last few drops of specific identity. Function of birth, destiny and character would have been fulfilled. As an appropriate piece of perfectly designed Fieldsian counter-process, any miraculous event that happened to come John Carlton's way would be almost annihilated by a formula programmed perhaps even before the man himself was born.

To Fields, this choice of man and purpose raised disturbing questions of the independence and uniqueness of personality, as to whether a person was something unique called Mr. Pickwick, or more a highly specialised sliver of digitised tissue; or perhaps a human being was a piece of systemised two-legged track-switching scheme, within which life and death were a mere shimmering and flexing of a windblown curtain to cover moves which went over the rainbow or under the hill.

The debate raged on. Was the whole thing an hallucination, could perhaps the precious twenty-five-seconds have been the trial of a new secret weaponry? Perhaps the whole thing was some kind of holographic experiment by the Ministry of Defence, or even (Fields remained grim-faced), the Security Services. As for the miracle cures, these could have been 'accidental', though as Fields (now the toast of Conspiracy Village), told the world, the combination of accident, mixed with technological apparatus, mixed with anomaly, was surely ßthe height of a philosophic comedy not seen for some time.

Throughout the world's laudatory media, Fields could be seen and heard summing up what had happened by saying that a man who walked on water was setting up a stall on the wrong side of town; a man who made a engine that ran on water would be asked for protection coinage. Both, he added, like himself one day, would probably disappear. Their deaths (or disappearances, call it what you will, said he) could only be avoided for a time by them saying there was a hidden plank below the water beneath their feet, or that the engine ran on petrol. In any case, such a man and machine would not last for long. Both would be eaten alive; denied, vanished, kicked out of court without a single word as rotten and dangerous and illegal food, not fit for fertiliser, or even grunting porker's fare. If such things escaped into what was now called the Fieldsian Allowance Spectrum, similar such commodities would also shame the market, write its tawdry sins on walls, cut prices at a stroke, and profit empires based purely on Commerce of Fact would collapse overnight.

For a few weeks, it looked as if Fields, riding the crest of a wave, was going to perform another miracle by saving Entertainment State from the wreck.

It took some time to clear the rubble of Fermanagh House, and even SAS nerves were somewhat shaken to know that no corpse had been found. But a large skip with no less than eight foam mattresses piled in it, showed that in this case there had been no miracle; Nora's jump from the twentieth floor caused even hard-cases to whistle. There were more whistles as it was revealed that the mattresses were soaked with no less than two pints of fresh female blood, mixed with a small amount of splintered bone and some muscle-tissue. Reports also came in that hours after the attack, a plain van crossed the border and disappeared somewhere along the mountain roads. This van was found some weeks later, partially burnt-out, with another pint of blood of the same group congealed on the steel floor at the back.

Marshall knew as well as Fields that an authentic twentieth-century litany was bound to follow

John Carlton soon decided that it was best to stick to those peculiarities which were artifacts. And in the wreckage of the *Black Mountain Bird* there were found enough of those. Lodged in the port undercarriage was a *wooden* round, of all things. It was explained to a grateful Enquiry anxious for the mundane to come on stage, that this was not so peculiar as it might sound. In order to save many thousands of lives, wooden rounds in unfilled metal jackets had been used for years by the Armed Forces, Police, and indeed other organisations to demonstrate handling and loading of weapons and magazines to school cadets and recruits.

Many relished the ensuing debates in the politics of the pseudo-real. The timber round (Exhibit Number One) had far less peculiarity than another round (Exhibit Number Two), which had far greater claims for being called a round proper. This round was an old honest-to-goodness .303 *Lee-Enfield.*, found lodged in the main cockpit instrument-panel. But it wasn't the round that killed Susan. That round (Exhibit Number Three) was found in her skull, and came from an American .38 *Police Special.* This item, which would seem to have at least accomplished some kind of mission, was soon relegated in importance to all the other joke-rounds, which, as imitations of approximations of part-intentions, had all appeared to try and get through one bottle neck of a small event-stage at the same time. The circus was made complete by the finding of a 7.62mm SA 80 cartridge *case* (Exhibit Number Four), underneath what had been Susan's seat. This cartridge case had no firing-pin indentation in the base, the case had not even been filled, and a minute examination of its machining showed that it was of a batch of Detroit Arsenal cases which could not have been made more than two days prior to the day of the twenty-five-second event.

John Carlton himself was obviously most impressed by a smart-suited crew-cut young American, who revealed that Susan was a member of an American Rifle Club. Now here indeed was what Fields called a designer-reassurance in embryo. The additional information that Susan was only a provisional member of the Miami Rifle Association for one day in order to allow her to attend the clubhouse birthday party of a friend of the family, was quickly relegated to background noise. A similar fate awaited the American's opinion that he thought it was hardly likely that the technical function of the Association had so affected Susan within such a short space that she carried strange rounds and even stranger cartridge cases upon her person.

Whilst Marshall preferred the sober mysteries of the Air Accident Enquiry, Fields himself was more fond of the sessions of the Ecumenical Council. He liked nothing better than listening to good stories. As the

262

sessions proceeded, he was back on his father's knee, and the only thing missing to accompany these delicious tales of the realm of chaos and old night was a roaring fire and hot-buttered toast. With the very best class of stories here encountered, he thought he could possibly use the proceedings of the Ecumenical Council to rebuild his health, sanity, and inocence in one. Watching even highly intelligent women and men try to assemble outrageous rationalisations about what happened, he told all that he had now formulated the Third Fieldsian Law of Conspiracies, which stated: 'Since all structures of consciousness are built of pure advertising texture, any single piece of experience is as fraudulent as any other'.

This fluttered the hawkish lids of a tall Cardinal, and even made bright the rheumy eyes of an arthritic Anglican Archbishop. Flanked by robed acolytes, to Fields this decorative crew were much more amusing and interesting than the Marshall's Cartesians, next door. They, with a far more crude system of advertising, were left with nothing much but a bundle of burnt wires and no colour code, as distinct from the far more interesting characteristics of that 'infernal region' which the priests of the Ecumenical Council now called the EuroDump. According to them, the EuroDump had become, because of Entertainment State, a cursed partial-geography, suspended between an absolute *yes* and an absolute *no*. Within it, there had occurred a witching re-emergence of the half-forms of those banished pagan 'kingdoms' which were the source of all evil and dread in the world.

In these proceedings, the twenty-five-seconds were a mediaeval All; here, rifle-rounds, video cameras, had not even been invented, and film-stars not even spawned. Only what Fields called the funny hats and the men in long skirts were the same. In any case, in these deliberations the finite which shattered Susan's skull was irrelevant; rather someone had Sinned. And Sin excluded all Cartesian considerations; someone (or *something*) had *thought* the deaths; but that someone (or something) might have also thought the thousands of cures was a question which was not raised.

There was a possibility, said one Jesuit, of thoughts being inserted in the skull with as much deliberation and *quota of actuality* (Fields, delighted, noted his own term again) as any rifle round. Annoyed and disturbed by the blatant cosmic cheek of the cures which paraded before them, the main aim of the Ecumenical Council was to try and stop such things immediately. Their second aim appeared not to find out who-done-it, but who *imagined* it. It was generally felt something peculiar must have happened to inspire those previously supposed to be joyously content with carefully and properly administered rationalisations of their suffering. Now it seemed that a Something had actually had the nerve to throw off a supposedly seamless devotional cloak of industrial and theological tasking, and make a run for the barbed wire perimeter. Now here was a big problem. There was no telling how many more such disguises and subterranean intentions there were.

Fields, called to give evidence, did not help matters. The eyes of the earnest cleric who asked him questions were wide.

"Shall we at least try and get rid of some of the many contradictions in this matter, Dr. Fields?"

"No use trying to get rid of contradictions. The mind could not possibly work without them. They help miracle-control. Good performers call that staying sane. You can cancel out your best expectancies that way. "

"Do you have any explanations for what happened?"

"Plenty. But none of them are any good. Mind you, explanations should be on the National Health. They're the only painkillers that really count. But no-one really wants solidity. It is much more expensive than Christmas, and what you really want never comes down the chimney."

"How would you define a miracle?"

"It's easy. *Marks and Spencer* call it stocktaking."

"What do you mean by that?"

"It is extremely simple. You are never alone with an intention. It brings in its flocks of camp-followers, and hangers-on. Part-families of rounds and their supporting relatives tried to get to Susan and the *Black Mountain Bird*. The intention bringing in the complex of shapes and forces in this case was intercontinental. Some missiles and would-be missiles had limped, some had lost their way, some didn't know who or what they were, and some were even newly born, clinging to bits and pieces of their origins as their only comfort. It appeared that there had been a specialised call for what I myself call counter-performances to Entertainment State, and an entire spectrum of possible rounds had tried to respond as best they could. Even bits and pieces of bullets, pseudo-forms of rounds and approximations of rounds had gathered, as resistance to what was being constructed. This was an emergency, and under-rehearsed, they threw their premature and imitative bodies into action on the somewhat less than metaphysical thought that certain targets can be hit and perhaps destroyed by flung frying-pans as by high-velocity bullets. Miracles, like people in a temper, work with what is handy at the time."

As is to stifle what some called such monstrous conceits, these thoughts of Fields were followed by a three-hour speech from a Cardinal which could have come direct from the Latin deliberations of any of the great mediaeval trials. The invading demons were an armed host, said he, whose weapons were an intellectual pornography consisting of numberless invisible suggestions. But where did the rare information-genes for this cuckoo-event come from? How did they achieve such concentration? Were they part of a much more devious complex of intention? Had those who had been cured of their physical and mental afflictions heard any kind of inner voice, did they feel that now they had some kind of mission? Were the cures *authentic?* Or were the twenty-five seconds merely a trick of the suggestive light? Had the Devil been running much more of the *advertising operation* (again, Fields noted his own term, now passed into theological realms) than was known or guessed at? The Council noted that previously within the sphere of 'intense influence' Doubles and Presences had already been noted by trusted observers. Elvis Presley had been seen at a local football match, and according to 'a trusted and sober observer', a W.C. Fields and even a Sid Fields had both been seen in a bar In Cookstown.

There were Fields all over the place.

The air was run riot not only with anagrams and half-forms of the famous living and dead, but by the formation of an inquisitorial milieu not heard of since the days of Torquemada. By what means could the cures be doubted? Could the agents be double-turned? Could some bastard-seed devilry be still within those folk who had cast away their afflictions? Where was the source of the leakage of information which the cultural guards had not detected? Father O'Connor, the only cleric present with a twinkle in his eye and a line of wisdom in his brow claimed that the only question the Devil ever asked was: what is your desire?

In what both Father O'Connor and Fields thought was a deliciously inspired move, the Ecumenical Council proposed that any equipment which recorded the event be gathered up and destroyed. In the words of the Council's first Provisional Paper, *A Preliminary Report on Claimed Miraculous Cures and Events within Entertainment State,* such equipment had become *contaminated.*

Contamination. The metaphor spanned the Century, from the first tragic marks on the Curie's hands through all the laboratories to Sellafield via Hiroshima. The root of the word contamination was *transmutation.* Experience, like the flesh, had changed itself by asking questions as fundamental as the particles. The *Preliminary Report* claimed that the equipment recording the event had become *question-infected.* It claimed that such equipment would never be the same. Its transducers and sensors and interfaces and lenses and recording heads and aerials would henceforth lie, being possessed instrumentation. Its analogues of operation were therefore suspect, and if these particular items of

265

equipment were not quickly located and ritually destroyed, then the plague would spread to other ancillary items. If this happened, the world's artificial eyes and robot sensors would be destroyed by a kind of technological AIDS. No ruler would be able to measure another ruler. No clock synchronise with another clock. There would be a virtual Babel of seeing and measurement, of counting and calculation, of orbit and circumnavigation. There would be flat Earths and cone-shaped Earths, there would be stirrings at the bottoms of gardens, lights in the midnight forest, and serpents back in the seas. There would be a million-channel Entertainment Inferno which would make the banks of the Amazon look like breakfast TV.

The shouts and screams outside the rooms of Sittings, Sessions, and Enquiries increased; Profundity, Seriousness, and particularly Suffering must fight their way back to the High Frontier of Metaphor. More magicians appeared, hired by skeptical magazines. They soon departed, their laser-holographs, fireworks, smoke-trailing parachutists, and dry-ice-dropping light aircraft being accused of being a public nuisance. More scientists appeared, with sea-serpent stories about quantum-holes in the biosphere, and things called Dense Pollution Nodes, though, as Fields said, no-one had ever seen one of these hold up so much as a psychiatric social worker, never mind a ton of aeroplane.

Back at what Marshall called the left-lobe sessions of the Air Accident Enquiry, he listened to a ground-crew member who had a spotless record of religious violence.

"But for Christ's sake, you couldn't have a messiah who messed about! What? It would be a denial of everything that a Christian God stood for. What? No laws to learn, no hard and terrifying experiences to go through, no moral destiny, no sacrifice, no proper earning of worth?"

The *Telegraph* thundered. What had happened out there in the EuroDump was the most wicked piece of Popery that ever there was. If they weren't all careful, they might get something for nothing, as in the Catholic Mass, or the Satanic rite, or the Vatican Bank, and everyone knew to where those things led. To make things worse, the blackened ruins of the crash were still alive. In the sight of the world's cameras, an unceasing stream of invalids headed on up to the ashes of the EuroDump on crutches, were carried on beds, helped out of the back of trucks and cars, the lame, feeble, mentally afflicted, the blind. Leaving their charity-sponsored vehicles behind, many left seeing, walking, and even running. This of course, could not go on; if it did, human beings might commit the grave sin of thinking that they were in control of their own destiny.

As Fields pointed out, it might have been wonderful for the afflicted, but for the healthy it was terrifying. As in Knock (that Republican parish dedicated to the resurrected Saviour of a previous anthropological sales campaign), there were already plans for a ring-road, an airport, and an hotel near the EuroDump site. Here, thundered *The Sun,* the world's first 'Entertainment Techno-Miracle' had occurred. Pushing up through the devastation were a thriving crop of fresh symbols. Transfers and designs of the four spheres of the *Black Mountain Bird* were almost ready for tail-fin, road-sign and smart red Entertainment Hostess blazer, just below the *Entertainment Breakfast TV* station badge. Things were not improved by Fields giving a lecture entitled 'Theological Advertising as Anthropological Entertainment.' According to Fields, Trash Culture had gone through its first Death and Resurrection. To complete his analogy, there was also evidence of a Fall. His mortal enemies, the Clerks and Priests, if they had not won outright, had caused some considerable failure of nerve. A haemorrhage of spirit began: the Famous Faces, now extremely baffled and uneasy, began a great trek back to the outer world of a more familiar order of substance. Frightened, defensive, even for once puzzled and reticent, the Faces began to be seen less and less in the days that followed.

If Fields himself thought he could forever remain as uncrowned king of Entertainment State and try and rescue something from the wreck, he was about to be disappointed. The dead Susan's father, a major American conglomerate magnate for many years, and an ex-USAF General on the Pentagon Staff, took fast action. Secretly aided by John Carlton, he promptly unloaded well over twenty years of personal papers onto *The Washington Post.* The depth of the implications of these thousands of neatly-written meticulous notes of nearly three decades stood world-weary hair on the back of equally world-weary necks. Fields' name was everywhere. His presence at secret conferences, in covert scientific studies, and on combined military-industrial policy boards. His presence and influence threaded practically through all the significant interfaces of Propaganda, Intelligence, Technology, and Media, from the Nixon years and onwards. The papers revealed an unpredicted and total Anglo-American unity whose power and influence practically constituted a hidden government which made national democratic political structures irrelevant and ineffectual games. The Official Reality exploded, just like the *Black Mountain Bird.*

As torchlight processions now appeared in the streets looking for Fields with cudgels, and he prepared to flee, there were now frenzied claims that the dead woman wasn't Susan after all, but a stand-in burnt alas, to an unrecognisable crisp. There were also accusations that Susan was deliberately killed by revenging enemies of her father; or indeed that she was killed by the British Security Services, who indeed had probably killed Benson; or that she wasn't dead at all, or indeed that she had come back from the dead. Susan had already been seen in a Belfast supermarket, but then both Little Richard and Louis Armstrong had been seen together in a pub in Derry, and statues of Bette Davis, Ginger Rogers, and Janis Joplin were effecting miraculous cures all over the province.

Fields, once more squealing with protest, was shot with enough tranquilliser to put a small bullock to sleep, and manhandled by four SAS into a VC10. He awoke on his camp-bed in Tower House six hours later, to be greeted by the protesting voice of Nellie Goby in the far distance, and a familiar aroma; the psychedelic curtains parted, and a scowling Elmon brought into the Dansette Den a *Bumper Jumbo Wombat Sausage,* and a styrofoam beaker of steaming *ersatz.*

Mr. Toad was back home.

Marshall and Mary lay on a beach which curled at the edges of vision into an horizon which was a furnace of white and blue. The bleached roots and sodden driftwood either side of them were the shocked spines and wrecks of their previous perspectives. As Marshall said to his wife, the trouble with miracles is that it is difficult to go back down the mountain path to the land where all the bullets fitted the right gun at the right time. With gaming moves pushed right over the horizon, he felt himself to be now in a loincloth by the side of a road watching trucks and planes roar past his mud hut. A blink, a quick rub of wondering eyes, and the magical chariots and their miraculous cargoes were gone. A woman walking by became to him a smiling girl on the faded label of an empty peach tin stuck in a patch of oil-soaked sand, and wondered at by a native. His wife's blouse was half a scrap of coloured cartoon from some kid's pull-out from another universe.

Entertainment Fission. Damn. Fields was still in his head as Mary spoke

"You're his father. He'd made a toy. He wanted to show it to you."
"To prove what?"
"That toys work as well as anything else."
"I like seriousness."
"All serious things were toys once."

Marshall looked at the sea. Toys. Daubs. Partial events. BUACs. Rehearsals. He was a half-form himself, now. Damn Fields. He induced a kind of self-hypnosis which was quite infectious. It was a feeling that all possible worlds were again as they were at some Beginning: utterly

268

fantastic places. The Bunter had a gift. He aroused a kind of feeling of the deepest pleasure, not rooted in any sense of sexual or other kind of physical wellbeing, but much, deeper. The ultimate weapon was this. There was absolutely no defence. In any case, Fields the salesman was quickly on his way. The housewife, could ask what 'myth' was forever more, if she asked at all, but the salesman would not stay for an answer. All she knew was that now she had a vacuum-cleaner that looked like a spaceship instead of a Victorian diver's suit. Perhaps, he thought, that was the function of all legendary salesmen; the best of them laid a cuckoo's egg of a possible dream, and motored quickly back to town, before the banks closed. In the housewife's hand would be an address for spare-parts, which in turn were the seeds of yet other dreams in other towns, where they made dreams to order.

Marshall gazed in alarm at the line of rubbish-marks glinting offshore like signals from an abandoned castoff fairyland.

Perhaps all possible worlds started that way.

He took his wife's hand, she stood up, and he put his arm around her shoulder. Making their way back to the hotel for dinner, Sir Harry Marshall now knew for the first time what the Bunter had not been telling them.

Fields was back in the land he both loved and hated, where cabbages were boiled in vats, and garlic, sex, and metaphysics were considered plots against all that was sane, white, and rational. But like the storybook character he was named after, he was undaunted. He had a piece of half-melted perspex sphere from the *Black Mountain Bird* mounted on an oak plinth, and this he proudly exhibited by the side of his *Dansette,* just below the photograph of Jane Mansfield. The piece, though cracked and charred, still looked as if it was ready to pose for the ark of any new covenant that might be constructed and worshipped.

Fully recovered, Fields was very pleased with himself. Enthusiastically writing his report in Tower House to the music of Eddie Cochrane and Earl Bostic, this first attempt at creating an Advertising Theology had been a success, in his opinion. He had up-dated the mysteries of Saviours to the modern mystery-cycle of the consumer-product, and twenty-five-seconds of Advertising Fission had been achieved. The pile had been crude, like the first nuclear pile, but nevertheless an Entertainment Bomb had been constructed, and it had worked. Now for a much more advanced model. He looked forward to

269

future summers, tracking BUACs perhaps, or investigating UFOs, something he had always been interested in; perhaps he might even try using the resources of Tower House to find Laura Steadman. Or he could resume work on his already notorious *Skunk Cloud Explanation Test* within his General Theory of Conspiracies. Although a final form of words had not yet been settled, he had formed some conclusions. Brushing apple-cores and onion-fritters from his notepad, he read his notes from the day previous: 'Explanations had one common characteristic: they were dull, and they were dead. They made a mind go away from them as if from a skunk on heat. *Therefore something was being protected...*'

After making a few notes, he tore off the sheet, and attached it to the manuscript of his new book, *An American Coronation.* In this, he had traced the Merovingian dynasty (and hence the House of David), to America, through one of the original Pilgrim Fathers. He was now absorbed in communicating with mystical Royalist cults throughout Europe, and he could not wait to tell Marshall of the structural Advertising possibilities. Perhaps this time, there could be more than twenty-five-seconds.

He supposed that with the idea of American Royalty, as with Entertainment, there would be the beginning of a process-war. There would be libel suits, fraud cases, and not a few plain disappearances of those who had not managed to stay completely factual, or pay their reality-dues when some very strange boys indeed called round on a Friday night. As with many an almost-assassin's not-quite-a-bullet, there would be pseudo-investigations, resulting in partial assumptions of pseudo-claims, and certainly there would be righteous voices. Like Mr. Mellow and Mr. Gold, Fields now supposed that there would be shadow-men and shadow-projects *nearly* appear which mimicked higher levels of solidity. Men in nightshirts and funny-hats would come, waving authentic claims for reality. There would be urgent counterclaims for Truth, and the grocers would cover up the embarrassing thefts of factual peaches, replacing them quickly with a hundred weight of non-quite factual pears, and hope the customers and the supervisors from the retail reality scheme supervision service would not notice. As with intelligence tests, the periodic table, radiation, and exactly who finances Bugs Bunny, there would be denials of qualities, and quantities, who bought and believed what, and where.

7.30 am. Fields looked up from his *Dansette*, on which he had just put on a rare old Ted Heath record. As his favourite saxophone section commenced *Begin The Beguine*, he sniffed the air.

The first breakfasts of the morning were being served in Tower House canteen.

He tucked his manuscript under his arm.

Yes, he could not wait to show it to Marshall.

He might well be interested in something like this.

He moved to the window and looked out on a grey morning where a Council truck was gritting a light covering of the first snow of December. Startled, he adjusted his *pince-nez*. Two slight female figures, apparently shivering with cold, were drinking coffee at the stand by the Black Taxi Hut, where again he was wont to fill his famous carrier-bags full of *KebabKobz* with curried onion.

He looked again.

The girls crossed the road and looked up mournfully at Tower House. Alison and Mavis! He hadn't seen them for nearly three months.

Looking desperately back into the interior of the Main Computer Hall, and back at the girls on the dismal winter pavement again, he had a familiar thought. Find the way. Don't tell. Just whisper.

Whisper what?

That it might be possible to escape.

He jumped at the ringing of his red telephone. It had not rung since the Gulf War. Either it was the Second Coming, or a nuclear attack.

It was far more serious.

It was the smiling voice of the *Entertainment Defensor*.

"Hi, Hieronymus, I hear you've written another book..."

VI

The gods go Home

On a lowering late-afternoon in mid-December, amidst first snowflakes, a limping figure, with one arm in a sling appeared along one of the partly-finished tarmac strip-roads of the EuroDump, now cracked and holed by nettles and bracken. Nora wandered through an abandoned fairground, with its garish gods vanished. As if in final salutation, high beyond the Black Mountain over Laughan, there was a great flash and rumble in the earth as if the old war had started again. By the deserted airstrip joyriders and packs of wild dogs raced one another between bushes and wrecks. Like casualties from some armoured battle, overturned cars poured thick greasy smoke, their torn intestines trailing the scorched earth.

Without so much as a snap, crackle or pop, all the doll-gods of this *infernal region* as the Pope now called it, had now disappeared. In a collective tribal decision quicker than by any birds on any wire, hundreds of private jets had flown from Belfast faster than gulls from gunshot. They left only these fires, flickering as if from some flesh-sacrifice, licking the air by half-dug drainage ditches and lighting up the wrecked hangars and test-sheds of *The Most Unusual Aeroplane Company,* now with collapsed roofs and growth of graffiti.

She gazed into these damp and echoing halls where once men and women, machines, ideas and systems, had all dreamed of one another, and had embraced briefly, only to flee into the night. Her steps echoed across the oil-flecked floor of what had been, a million De Laurean cave-mouths ago, the main assembly shed designed to produce ten *Black Mountain Birds* a month. Now the dream was nothing but a few trolleys, steel tables, metal scraps, wooden frames and chocks, and a sign which said Rehearsal Room. Funny stuff for industrial man, rehearsals. Yet here, she supposed, for a brief moment in dream-time, many different systems of human reference and perception had lain together to exchange spores.

A great gap in the roof showed flights of executive jets high above the wreckage. The last fairy folk were going under the sky-hill with no goodbyes, leaving their canvas and cocktail domain, their momentary dance of summer, to the mercy of the rain, the coming winter, and the first wave of vandals. Kids in the drawing office urinated on dream-sketches; drunks decorated the almost-possible shapes on A2 drafting sheets with the first evening servings of instant *sweet and sour*; there were burnt patches dotted between heaps of wrecked stereo and video, piles of charred canvas, blackened furniture, and sodden carpets littered with the thousand-four-colour names of postcard escapes. The EuroDump was a smashed and burnt world of departed peacocks, strewn with the glass of a million toasts and congratulations and tinkling hopes half-buried under a shifting sand of headed papers, and a thousand champagne-sealed contracts for bulbs, generators, gas cylinders, cables, batteries, computers, engines, airframes, and fuel. In the middle of this catastrophe of vanity and technology, a torn photograph of a group of Faces gave her a momentary nostalgia for pure sugar, made her eager for even a candyfloss *shaman,* one of those 'lollipop gods on a stick' as that blasphemous old clown, Fields, had once described them.

She wandered to the site of Tent City. Here amongst shattered canopy beds, were broken bottles of perfume and spirits, empty boxes of cigars, ruined clothes, and shoes, all of which would now be replaced within the few seconds of a non-thought in Hollywood, Paris, or Rome. Time would sink these down upon layers of other tomb-stuff: boxes of obsolete spare-parts, sealed and buried in original rust-protective paper and grease. What she was looking at were the jewels of some great meccano-set Queen of Leviathans, to be entombed with her in the elemental dust of the EuroDump, accompanying her on her last journey across the darkest of waters.

The snow, heavier now, covered the skeletal bits and pieces of the first and last real *Black Mountain Bird,* pushed for a lark by kids against a bare tree; it was the stage machinery of a joke, with all its dancing puppet sweethearts become but a trick of the western industrial light. In the last blue above the rubbish fires, *Turbofan* and *Learjet, Snowgoose,* and even an *Apache,* left brief radar traces before the gods were gone into the western sky. The last millionaires were shooting down the runway of the far airport, heading for rumours of some new joke-hunt, becoming high silver by the moon coming over the EuroDump through gathering snow clouds. Amidst spiralling black smoke and flame, she found a 6-inch model of the *Black Mountain Bird,* which she threw high into the air, and for a moment the shining spheres of the dream-craft glided, reflecting the snowflakes, merging with the real aeroplanes above. The shape twisted down into the wrecks and fires below, making a three-point landing on a sodden and torn portrait of the Princess, who defiantly looked up and laughed at her, still proud of her twenty-five-second shot-down domain.

Nora pulled up her collar with her free hand.

Time to go.

Like the Princess, she had a lot of dressing-up and rehearsing to do the next day.